Mischief and Menace

A Year and a Day: Part Two

Lisa Courtney

Cover design by Sally A. Sloley of daisyprincess.com

First published in 2015
ISBN 978-0-9971968-1-8

Table of Contents

one

THOMAS SAT SILENTLY on his couch, holding a glass of whisky that he hadn't asked for, hadn't noticed, and hadn't touched. He was staring at nothing, thinking nothing, and feeling nothing. Although he had had Callie's permission to speak to anyone, anywhere, until sundown, and he was in his own rooms at present, he had nothing to say. The hand that held the drink trembled, but he was oblivious to it.

He hadn't said a word, or so much as acknowledged Zodiac's presence. The Lord High Chamberlain of Elvenhome had stripped off Thomas' bloody clothing. In silence, he had cleaned him up and redressed him. Thomas had wept, eyes filling and blinding him, tears rolling down his cheeks, but there had been no sound at all. Perhaps the Court Singer's voice had died with the High Queen.

While Zodiac had worked on Thomas, Guardian had gone to his own rooms and washed the dirt and the blood off of himself, and changed his clothes as carefully as he could so that he would not jar his injured shoulder and broken arm.

When Guardian finally arrived at Thomas' apartments, the Elf and the Water Faerie exchanged worried glances over the Court Singer's head.

A few minutes later, Zodiac and Guardian stood alone together in Thomas' bedroom, looking out at the garden.

"How much damage was there today?" Guardian asked with a sigh.

Zodiac's face darkened. "Seventy-six wounded, some fatally. Currently fifteen dead, including both young Pixie pipers, Scribe, Boston and Atlanta."

Guardian turned, faced Zodiac, and winced. "Boston is dead, too?"

Gravely, Zodiac nodded. "Both generals fell this day. But as Her Grace was the last of the Green-Ribbon army to fall, the day goes to the White Ribbons, with eight survivors standing."

Guardian tightened his shoulders, wincing at the sharp pain the movement cost him. "She does hate to lose."

The High Chamberlain raised an inquisitive eyebrow at Guardian. "Do you need something for the pain, My Lord?"

Shaking his head, Guardian turned and looked into the living room at the couch, where Thomas sat staring. "A drink will do. I can manage well enough until the morning," he sighed, and nodded his head toward Thomas. "He's a bit too immersed in the game, don't you think?"

Walking over to Thomas, and sitting down, Guardian leaned over and took the untouched drink from Thomas' shaking hand. Sniffing it and recognizing the smell of quality Highland single-malt whisky, Guardian took a long drink from the glass, held it in his mouth for a moment, and then swallowed, letting the smooth warmth ease into his cramped stomach.

Thomas hadn't moved; neither had his silent tears or his trembling stopped. He was deathly pale. Guardian finished the whisky in the glass, set it down on the table beside the couch, and tried to comfort his friend.

"Thomas," he began, "Is something else wrong that I don't know about?"

It took Thomas some time to realize that Guardian was speaking to him. When it finally registered, he shook his head and continued to stare dully at nothing.

"Thomas," Guardian tried again, "do you truly understand what happened today?"

"Yes," Thomas whispered so softly that Guardian could not be certain for a moment that he had spoken at all. "Yes. Callie is dead. Callie is dead." Thomas forced the words out past his shock and grief. "Callie is dead. She is dead."

Zodiac stood in the doorway between the bedroom and the living room, watching this exchange with growing alarm. Suddenly, the two Fey gaped at each other with a dawning realization, one far more upsetting to them than Callie's death had been. Zodiac moved to the chair nearest the couch and pulled it close to Thomas and Guardian.

"Thomas, you don't *know*???" Zodiac sputtered, dumbfounded and horrified at the same time.

Guardian groaned, and rubbed his left hand over his chin, exhaustion and disbelief mingling in his eyes. "Thomas...you didn't know, and she did say that she'd failed to tell you something..."

Wide-eyed, Zodiac looked at Guardian. "She 'failed' to tell him? She *failed* to tell him???" he all but shouted.

Guardian nodded his head. "As she lay dying, she said she'd forgotten to tell him something. She remembered what it was at the last, but then she...died."

"By the Stars," muttered Zodiac with uncharacteristic hostility, "he doesn't know!"

3

Seated between them, Thomas had no idea what they were talking about, but he didn't care. He noticed that he was breathing, and that seemed to be enough for the moment.

Guardian put his hand on Thomas' arm, pressing hard until Thomas finally moved his head and met Guardian's eyes, glazed-over brown ones peering hollowly into sad, determined blue ones. "Thomas, she never would have wanted you to you suffer such anguish. What she failed to tell you was that she couldn't really die in the battle. This was a game to entertain the Fey! She is not dead!"

Thomas' expression didn't change. He stared at Guardian.

"Thomas, hear me! This was a Faerie battle, and the Green Ribbons lost the day, and the generals fell, yes, but all will be well when the sun rises tomorrow. That's the way of it, I swear to you." Guardian tried to push the information into Thomas with his mind; the Water Faerie was worried by the bleak and soulless emptiness he saw on the Court Singer's face. He looked to Zodiac for assistance.

"It is true, Thomas. Everyone who fell and died today will be present tomorrow for the feast. It is always so. I swear it!"

Guardian found another inroad, and used it. "Thomas, do you remember that you are performing at the victory feast tomorrow evening?"

Thomas did remember, but it didn't matter.

"The reason the victory feast is the day *after* the battle is because that's when everyone will be alive and whole again. Everyone who is dead or injured from the battle will be well—and very hungry—at sunrise tomorrow."

Thomas' eyes narrowed as he tried to take this in. Guardian pointed to his own broken arm. "At sunrise tomorrow, this arm will be healed. I'm faerie, Thomas, so I could participate in the game and would be well no

4

matter how it played out. Callie will be alive tomorrow, I promise you. This is why you were not permitted to participate—any wounds you sustained might have killed you, and as a mortal you would *not* have come back tomorrow at sunrise. Are you listening? Do you understand?"

Zodiac nodded encouragement when Thomas looked at him for verification.

The Court Singer exhaled, thinking about this. "If that's true, and everyone knows that Callie will be alive tomorrow, why is everyone weeping and grieving and...if she was going to be alive tomorrow, you wouldn't look now like you've lost your best friend," he said doubtfully to Guardian.

"Do you not remember me telling you that we love to play the theatrics?" Thomas eyed Guardian, but said nothing, so Guardian continued. "We were all surprised that Callie was killed this time. It was unexpected, since she usually is the champion. We are a bit stunned, and saddened, for the Folk dislike not having her among us, even for so short a time. But the theatrics are part of the game. We grieve, and plan funerals, and attend them before the feast, despite the fact that the processions and mourning are, by that time, for Folk who are very much alive." A smile was more than Guardian could manage under the circumstances, but relief crept across his face as he watched Thomas slowly begin to grasp the words and understand.

Zodiac sighed. "We did not know that *you* did not know, Thomas. We Fey do not die easily in Faerie unless, for reasons of our own, we choose to end. Upworld, we are as vulnerable as mortals, but here, we are protected by the magic in our land. Sometimes," and here he looked at Guardian sadly, "there is random illness and death that we do not understand and cannot explain but, barring the occasional UnSeelie uprising where weapons are truly

5

engaged and damage done, our battle games are harmless to us. They are only for fun. That you were unaware of this is shocking, and unforgiveable."

"Callie will be furious when she learns of it," Guardian added.

Will be furious. When she learns of it. Future tense, Thomas thought, feeling dizzy now. *That's future tense...* He felt the whole truth of Guardian's statement in a frenzied rush and, finally understanding, covered his face with his hands, his body shaking. "Oh my God," he choked.

Zodiac got up out of his chair at once and poured three very generous glasses of whisky.

The day was over at last; the sun eventually faded from the sky, and with it went what little was left of Thomas' energy. At Guardian's insistence, he finally lay down on the couch, and fell asleep at once. His body jerked fitfully, fingers grasping the air, and he mumbled as he moved through restless dreams. Guardian and Zodiac watched over him with a shared sense of protective sympathy.

"It is well that he is finally sleeping. He has had a very trying day," observed Zodiac as he lit candles on the dining table, in the wall sconces, and on the tables on either side of the couch, as if the presence of additional, softer light could better banish the darkness of Thomas' nightmares.

"The double shots of whisky didn't hurt, either," Guardian grinned, finishing his own glass with a heavy sigh.

"It never does," replied Zodiac, smiling. "How is your arm, My Lord?"

"Well enough," Guardian replied, running his left hand over the broken right arm and wincing. "I don't have too long to wait for it to heal. Don't concern yourself with it, my friend."

6

There was a soft tapping at the door. Zodiac moved at once to open it so that Thomas would not be awakened. Orchid stepped through the doorway, bowed to both Zodiac and Guardian, and then she noticed the sleeping Thomas.

"Oh," she breathed. "He does not look at all well."

"This has not been one of his better days," Zodiac told her in a whisper. "But he will be all right once Her Grace awakens."

Guardian, sitting in the chair beside the couch, nodded in agreement. "Where is Her Grace...now? Has she been returned to her apartments for..." Although he was calm, his voice shook at the thought of Callie even only temporarily dead.

Orchid's head bobbed sadly in the affirmative. "Yes, My Lord," she replied, her voice low. "Master Ocelot finished attending Her Grace, and then he himself escorted the guard carrying the bod—the Queen to her apartments. The Ladies are preparing her now for the Lying in State and tomorrow's funeral. I am here because Lady Iris wishes to be able to assure Her Grace straightaway that all is well with Thomas."

An uneasy thought occurred to Zodiac. "He will want to be there when she awakens," he pointed out in some distress.

"I know," Guardian admitted in a hushed voice. "But he will not be able to speak in her rooms without her prior leave, which of course she has not given."

"And he *will* speak," Zodiac added. "Without a doubt, he will speak to her. He will be unable—or unwilling—to stop himself."

The two tired Elves looked at each other with some anxiety, pondering the situation and its repercussions. Only a moment later, each smiled as the solution came to them both in a flash.

"We'll bring her here," they said simultaneously, voices still low enough to avoid disturbing Thomas.

Now Orchid looked distressed. "You cannot," she frowned, her gaze traveling back and forth between them. "Or, rather, you ought not. The Ladies are expecting to watch over Her Grace until sunrise, stand the vigil, weep and mourn. Lady Iris has already arranged for the Lying in State in the Queen's Presence Chamber. Preparations have begun. There are traditions to honor, and as it has been so long since the Queen has fallen in battle, everyone should get as much play out of it as possible."

The Heir Apparent and the Queen's High Chamberlain exchanged a decisive look; Zodiac tilted his head in unspoken question, and was answered with a fractional dip of Guardian's head.

"I will return with you to Her Grace's apartments, and will speak with Lady Iris about a small change in her most excellent plans," Zodiac told Orchid. "A change that would most certainly be in Her Grace's best interests, and thus be appropriate for all concerned."

With a last glance at Thomas, who, agitated by his dreams, had rolled onto his side in his sleep, Zodiac led Orchid out, and closed the door behind them.

When Thomas woke from a heavy sleep several hours later, he was surprised to see Guardian dozing in the chair beside the couch. Sitting up, he groaned when a sore back muscle bit into him. The sound woke Guardian.

"Sorry about that. What time is it?" Thomas asked.

"It's two hours past midnight," Guardian replied, stretching.

"I fell asleep," Thomas said, confused and groggy.

"It's all right," Guardian offered. "You had help."

Thomas stood, and started to walk toward his bedroom. Guardian shot up, swiftly moving to a position immediately ahead of him. "Where are you going?"

"Privy."

Guardian stopped, which forced Thomas to stop moving as well. Thomas eyed Guardian.

"Before you go in there, you need to know...Zodiac and I decided...oh, Thomas, Callie's not awakened yet, of course, but we knew you'd want to be with her, and talk with her, so we had her brought here so you wouldn't jeopardize your obligation to silence."

Thomas stood still, trying to take in the new information. "She's *where*?"

"In your bedroom. On a sort of a bier."

"You put her on the bed?" Thomas asked, stunned and feeling slightly sick.

"No. Well, we were going to, but Orchid said something about that perhaps being too upsetting for you, so the bier is beside the bed." Guardian put his hand on Thomas' arm. "I didn't want you to walk in not knowing that she is there."

Shaking his head to clear it, Thomas forced himself to smile at his friend. "Thanks. Seeing her that way might have...never mind," he finished. He pointed at the closed bedroom door. "Can I...?"

Stepping aside, Guardian nodded. Thomas moved into the room.

"You should probably use the privy first. Don't look at the bed," Guardian advised from behind him.

"Yeah," Thomas said, sweating a little. He locked his eyes on the garderobe, sped toward it and dashed in, closing the door behind him.

A full five minutes later, the door opened and he emerged, his anxiety giving him uncontrollable shivers. Guardian was sitting on the bed beside the bier; he looked up as Thomas edged toward the form lying there.

There were four large, thick candles positioned on five-foot iron poles at each corner of the bier, shedding soft, kind light on the beautiful features of the dead woman who lay upon it. As Thomas made his way to her, he marveled at how very peaceful she seemed to be. There was no obvious evidence of the day's battle.

Thomas looked down at Guardian, who had been watching Callie but now met his friend's gaze.

"I have never watched her like this, Thomas," Guardian whispered, as though he didn't want to wake her. "Ah, it is hard, seeing her so still." Even in the muted candlelight, Thomas could see tears trickle unheeded down Guardian's face. "There is something mysterious, enchanting, and entirely beautiful about the lithesome movements of women. A bewitching, endless dance that, if we but know how to see it, we are fortunate to observe and sometimes share. Until—"

The dark and pain-filled faraway look in Guardian's eyes told Thomas that his friend was speaking about more than Callie. He knew that Guardian was also thinking about the mortal woman he cherished, his private wretchedness over their separation bleeding over into his present grief over the loss, however temporary, of Callie. Someday, when Guardian's lover was finally still, as Callie was now, that stillness would be permanent. The thought of it was tearing at Guardian's broken heart.

Not knowing what else to do, Thomas sat down on the bed and shared the silent burden of Guardian's private, tormented suffering.

After a time, Guardian took a deep breath and centered himself. "Thank you, Thomas."

Thomas nodded. The depth of the silence between them had steadied him, too. He looked at Guardian with a faint but wry smile. "I would have, you know. Talked to Callie, I mean. I wouldn't have been able to help it."

"I know," Guardian murmured. "Zodiac and I felt we owed it to both of you to prevent the breaking of your obligation. The circumstances as they are would not have mattered in terms of the consequences of the breach.

10

There would have been unhappy repercussions." He rose slowly. "I must go. I have some things to take care of before sunrise. And at sunrise, I sleep." Thomas darted a look of alarm at him, and he smiled back wanly. "Once my shoulder and arm heal at sunrise, I'll sleep until breakfast, Thomas. Do not worry. All is, or will be, well. I gave you my word." Guardian looked at Callie. "She will wake at sunrise. Although she may well recognize her surroundings, ease her by telling her where she is. She will wake slowly, but she will wake. Do not rush her." He moved to the door, and turned to face Thomas. "And tell her I shall see her at the Feast." With a slight wave of his left hand, Guardian, exhausted, turned again and walked out of Thomas' rooms.

Alone with Callie, Thomas slid along the side of the bed to be closer to her face. She almost looked as though she were sleeping, except there was an added layer of something he could not define which seemed to lie all around her, a fabric he could not touch but which entirely covered her and separated her from him.

In defiance of that separation, he reached out and touched her hand.

She was cold; solid and cold. She could have been a marble sculpture. This unbidden thought unnerved him. He had expected that she would be cold, but what startled him was just how cold *cold* actually was.

Of all of the words I could use to describe you, he whispered to Callie with his mind, *"cold" is one I could never choose. It doesn't fit you at all.*

Thomas touched her hair, which had been washed, dried, brushed and braided into one long woven plait and laid along the left side of her body. It reached almost to her waist. He lifted the braid, brought it to his lips and kissed it, all the while breathing in the fragrance of her, catching the earthy scent he had come to love, as well as the sharp, pungent perfume of sunlit rosemary that had been added to her hair. The delicious, familiar smell of her made his throat ache and his eyes fill again.

He tried not to dwell on the fact that she was not breathing. He couldn't help himself; from the corner of his eye, he sneaked stray looks at the lifeless markings on her face and her unmoving chest, as if to catch her cheating at this hideous game, perhaps taking surreptitious deep breaths and then holding them when he looked at her.

But of course she wasn't breathing.

He had to work hard to make himself breathe.

The full moon had risen in the night sky, spilling its glowing, protective light into the room through the windows.

"This is ridiculous, Callie," he muttered aloud. He rose from the bed and lit more candles. Her face was still beautiful in the delicate illumination. Moonbeams and candlelight are always kind and comforting, and Thomas very much needed the comfort their equable glow offered him tonight.

He sat down on the bed beside the bier again, and breathed deeply as he watched her, as though he breathed for both of them. His face pinched into a tight parody of a smile when he realized what he was doing.

After a time, he found himself wondering about the wound that had taken her life. It had been painful for her; he tried not to remember how she'd looked when he'd reached the field after she'd been stabbed, despite the images that tore through his brain. There had been so much blood, and she had died so fast. Too fast for him to tell her...to tell her what?

Thomas shook his head to dislodge and erase all the words and feelings that surged into the forefront of his mind. He did not want to think.

Carefully, so as not to disturb her—although he was certain now that she was not breathing and could not feel his touch—he opened the front of the bodice of the royal purple gown the Ladies had chosen for her, and felt with his eyes and saw with his fingers the wound the dagger had left in her flesh.

The exit wound, a raw, red gash below her sternum and between her voluptuous breasts, was a little more than two evil inches long. He did not want to turn her over and look at the long entrance wound in her back. He did not think he could stand it.

Studying the exit wound, transfixed by it, he ran a tentative finger over its roughness. The wound had not been sutured. There had been no point by the time she had been taken to Master Ocelot's tent.

"Oh, Callie," he said, sadness washing over him again. "I'm so sorry it had to hurt..."

Bending down, he kissed the frozen, torn skin, wishing that he had been able to take the actual pain away at the time. Then he caressed and kissed each of her breasts, remembering with a sharp twinge of longing how often they were warm and yielding to his touch. He loved the sounds she made when he touched her; the deafening silence she offered him now was almost unbearable.

Tears welled in his eyes as he redressed her, and kissed her face, her eyes, and her mouth.

To comfort her, or, perhaps, to comfort himself, he took her ice-cold hand into his own, and held it. He sat there for a long time, his numbing pain cloaking him as surely as death cloaked her.

Much later, as the serene candlelight shone through the darkest hours of the night, he talked to her, knowing that she could not hear him but speaking his heart and mind anyway.

"How could you have forgotten to tell me you really couldn't die today?" he began, his voice tight and bitter. "I heard about nothing but the damned battle for a week—the rules, the courtesy, the weaponry, the strategy, the history, who was wearing what—and no one remembered to tell me that it was a game that really couldn't hurt you. I never considered that the weapons would be real. Or that the blood would be real…"

He remembered the confusion on Zodiac's and Guardian's faces when he'd reacted to Callie's death. "They must have thought I was as much out of my mind as I thought they were," he told her. "What will you say when you remember you didn't tell me? Do you think an apology, an 'oops, Thomas, I was busy and forgot to tell you' will make this all right? You scared the life out of me, Callie. And you've scared hard thoughts into me, too, damn you."

His grip on her hand tightened. "What goes on behind those eyes of yours? What is it like inside your head? How does someone who's all but immortal get from one day to the next without giving in to sheer boredom? Is that why you play games like this? To keep the madness away? You all live by a very different set of rules than we do. So it doesn't matter if something awful happens to you, because even if it does, the consequences don't last long, and no matter how anyone feels about it, it's all better the next day?

"How arrogant is that, Callie?" he hissed at her, realizing with a start just how angry he was.

"Given that you need continuous entertainment, how in the world can any one man be enough for you?" He glared at her. "It's not possible, is it? That's why you need an unending series of us, every so often, just to break up the monotony. My God, it's like what I've spent the last ten years doing, only on a far grander, possibly less romantic scale." He stopped, surprised at the revelation. He took a deep breath, and thought about it, not liking what he was thinking.

"One man could never satisfy you for the whole of your life—we don't live that long, we can't help it, we're mortal, dammit…and I shouldn't be bothered by this, since you've

14

been truthful about the hows and whys since the night we met. But still...

"Is it that I want one man to be enough for you, and that I want to be that man?" He closed his eyes in an attempt to test this idea against his heart. "God, what have you done to me, Callie? And what the hell am I doing to myself? This could be more dangerous for me than the drugs. Maybe *you're* more dangerous for me than the drugs!"

He shivered, more from strain and emotion than from cold. "I have been happy here, happier than I could ever have imagined. It's unreal. You are unreal, this place is unreal. Maybe even I'm unreal now. I'm losing it, Callie, I'm losing my grip. I thought, before this, that maybe I was finding myself. But I'm not. I'm not! What is this place doing to me? What are *you* doing to me?" he demanded, his voice shrill, closer to panic than he realized. He released her hand, and it dropped with a heavy thud back onto the bier with a cold and bitter finality that shook him to the core.

UNDER THE BRIGHT full moon, outside the windows of Thomas' bedroom, a moonshadow shimmered in the sad darkness. His usual sparkle was subdued this night as he let himself stream through the garden doors and across the still form on the bier beside the bed.

The moonshadow's shining glow flickered, as if he were trembling; he had never seen her so pale and cold. He realized with a jolt that he had never seen her dead before. Despite the fact that he knew that she would be alive and well with the coming of morning, seeing her now, like this, sent a sudden razor-sharp ache into his chest, a deep, burning pain that he had not allowed himself to feel for longer than he could remember. He closed his bright eyes, denying to himself that they were welling with tears that he would not shed.

The Court Singer was sitting on the edge of the bed, his hands resting on the bier beside the High Queen's body, his head bowed in private anguish mingled with the blurred vagueness that comes with the dizzying need for sleep. He was not touching her, which surprised the moonshadow. He did not stop to consider why this might be so.

It was not immediately discernible to the moonshadow that Thomas was actually watching the High Queen, although he saw that the Court Singer was looking at her; he seemed to be staring inward.

Thomas' bedroom was growing dim as the night's candles burned themselves out. In any event, Thomas certainly had not noticed the moonshadow bathing the High Queen in his glittering light.

Sighing, the moonshadow allowed himself one soft touch of the High Queen's cheek, and a final look at her, and then eased his light across her lifeless face as he began to move at last away from her. Before he departed, he brushed a shining beam across Thomas' bowed head in what might have been an acknowledgement of Thomas' pain and sadness.

The moonshadow chose not to admit that as he saw Thomas' misery and torment, he felt and fully recognized the depths of his own.

Carrying his denials and his aching heart, the moonshadow flowed back out through the garden doors and vanished, unnoticed, into the night.

THE HEALING SUN rose jubilantly in the sky, its fingers of rose-colored light caressing Elvenhome and its inhabitants with a celebratory warmth. The new day's air was somehow sweeter, its colors more vivid, its sounds more vibrant and alive than perhaps was usual.

Half-sitting on his bed, Thomas was asleep, head on the bier, pressed against Callie's hip. He held her hand; he had found it while he was dreaming, and had not let go.

Callie took a long, deep breath, and let it out. And then she took another, and another.

Thomas' eyes flew open. He raised his head and looked at her. Her eyes were closed, but she was breathing. He squeezed her left hand, the one he was holding, and was rewarded with a small squeeze back: a squeeze with a familiar, warm touch.

Remembering Guardian's words about letting her awaken slowly, Thomas sat still and watched her. Her right hand flexed, and with a gradual, deliberate movement she inched it toward the front of her gown, up to the space between her breasts, and touched her fingers to the spot where the dagger had torn through her skin. After a moment, she seemed satisfied, and slid her hand and arm back to her side.

Her face was coming alive. Healthy color was tinting her body, and he could see small twitches of life reanimate her lovely features. Her royal Fey markings moved slightly, as though they, too, were stretching themselves awake.

It was not until she had cleared her throat and fully opened her eyes and looked at him that he trusted himself to speak. "Welcome back," he said as casually as he could manage. Without moving her head, her eyes darted around. "You're safe, Callie," he assured her. "You're in my bedroom. You've been here all night."

She nodded then, understanding. She was calm, much calmer than he was, and she began to sit up. With some apprehension, he stood and helped her, and in a moment she was standing beside him.

And then she remembered. Her hands flew to her mouth. "Oh, Thomas! I didn't get a chance to tell you I couldn't be killed...oh, my dear, you must have been so very frightened. Can you forgive me?" She sat down on the bed and looked up at him.

He had several biting retorts ready for her; he had had the long night to consider and savor them. He was going to tell her that he was tired of the games, and that the childish arrogance of a Queen was more than he could stomach despite their growing friendship and their wonderful romps in bed. He was prepared to let her know in very specific terms that he had had more than enough of the dream-like euphoria of Elvenhome, which was too much like the recreational drug experience he was accustomed to, and that he'd rather be the master of his own hallucinations, thank you very much, Your Grace. He would tell her that while he loved being her bedmate, he was fundamentally used to a wider variety of women, and that he hoped she'd been serious when she said he could enjoy sex with anyone at Court he chose, because that's what he was going to do, effective immediately, to get himself back in control.

He dropped onto the bed beside her and, meeting her eyes, glowered.

She met the angry heat of his gaze with characteristic calm, and did not turn away. "I never meant for you to be hurt by this, Thomas, I swear it," she said, and he knew by the look in her eyes that she was, as always, telling him the truth.

He opened his mouth, ready to hurl his bitterness at her but, to his surprise, nothing came out. As he searched the warm cinnamon depths of her eyes, he saw the kindness and the open affection written there, and all of his anger and fear and frustration and resistance dissolved in a conflicted wave of misery and relief, vulnerability and hope.

In a strangled voice, Thomas managed to say the words, "Oh, God, Callie..." before his strained and thoroughly overtaxed emotions choked him. Fighting desperately for inner control, he touched her face with his hand. They both felt him trembling.

"Thomas," Callie said, her tone soothing and low, "it's all right now."

Her words and the sad kindness in her voice were too much for him. He took a jagged breath, and finally he wept, sobbing hard and brokenly. Callie put her arms around him, held him safely against her beating heart, and just let him cry.

two

SOME HOURS LATER, in the late mid-morning, they woke in each other's arms. Most of their clothing was piled in a heap on the floor, with the notable exception of Callie's purple gown, which she had taken the time to fling over the top of the closet door so it would not wrinkle too much, in deference to the loving work her Ladies had put into dressing her.

In the earlier hours of the newly-lit morning, they had given themselves and taken each other. There had been no need for talk; enough words had already been said, enough pain had already been shared, and enough tears had been shed. They found solace in the now-familiar comfort of each other's bodies, and that reassuring pleasure had been sufficient to move them together safely past the strain of the previous day and night.

Callie's hair was unbraided and wild; she had to tug on it a little to get it out from under Thomas' shoulder as she started to get out of the bed.

"Where are you going?" Thomas whispered as he watched her.

"I need to get moving," Callie answered. "I need to dress and give the Ladies time to get me ready for the Lying in State and the royal funeral this afternoon."

He looked half-asleep and serene, but his voice held a firm edge that got her attention at once. "No," he said.

She turned at looked at him. "No?"

The fierce, still-wounded look in his eyes left little room for debate. "No."

She bit her lip. "No Lying in State, or no funeral?"

He didn't answer. She touched his chest. "Thomas?"

Thomas' hand moved to the small, smooth discolored place on her skin between her breasts, and stroked it with a finger. He couldn't see the larger one on her back at the moment, but he had seen it earlier this morning. It had almost physically pained him to touch it, although it was fully healed, and Callie assured him that even the discoloration would be gone in a matter of hours. Now he could not take his eyes from the mark between her breasts, and he would never forget how it looked when the tip of the dagger had pressed through it...

"Thomas?" she repeated, bringing him back to the conversation. "It's been such a long time since I had a funeral, and I was looking forward to it. And it's such fun to Lie in State and have everyone file past me and—"

He sighed, his face showing her how determined he was to have the game over and done with. "No Lying in State. No funeral." He stared hard at her now, his eyes more demanding than pleading. "No," he said again. "No, Callie."

She opened her mouth to say something, but closed it again as she watched him. She thought for a minute, and then told him, "Very well. I will forgo the Lying in State and my rightful place in the funeral, because it is important to you—for reasons that I do in fact understand. It is a fair price to pay for the hurt you suffered, and I will bear the cost of your pain by honoring your wishes in the matter. But I must at least attend the funeral for the sake of the others, and for my part in the playing of this game. I will not command you to attend with me, Thomas, but I will ask you to do so, as a favor, in honor of the Fair Folk who died in the battle. This is their right, and their pleasure, and for the entertainment of all. Will you honor me by attending?"

His eyes narrowed. Before he could reply, however, there was a sharp rapping on the front door. "That will be our friend Zodiac," Callie said, leaping up from the bed and hurrying out to answer the knock.

Thomas could hear their voices in the living room. It was indeed Zodiac. She always seemed to know when he would appear. He wondered if Callie had called him somehow. He decided he didn't want to think about that. Instead, he half-listened, half-drifted as they talked.

He heard Callie give Zodiac a few crisp instructions, Zodiac responded as blandly as ever, and the High Chamberlain was gone in a literal flash. Callie returned to the bedroom, and slipped back into Thomas' arms.

"You could have put something on before you went to the door," Thomas observed drily.

Callie looked at him with amusement. "Why?"

"Never mind," he said, shaking his head. "I keep forgetting about faeries and clothing."

She smiled and kissed him around a small laugh. "Breakfast is coming. And then I must go. Would you please attend the funeral with me?"

"Callie, I hate funerals. I avoid them at all costs Upworld, even when not going to them makes me look bad." He said it as if this sufficiently answered her question. When it was clear that she felt it had not, he approached the issue from a different angle. "What will happen at this funeral?"

"You will see when you attend." She had him there.

He waited for her to say something. She didn't, of course; she kept her eyes locked on his, that exasperating and very-Callie expression playing openly on her face,

22

indicating that she had all the time in the world to wait him out.

He'd won the point, but not the overall encounter, and they both knew it.

"As Your Grace pleases, but with serious reservations," Thomas muttered, giving up, and wondering, with some irritation, what he was supposed to wear to a faerie funeral.

THOMAS HAD TO admit later that he'd actually had a good time mourning the Not-Truly-Dead.

Dressed in a black tunic, black hose and boots, and sporting a small black cap with a down-turned black feather, Thomas stood silent just beyond the castle gates beside Callie, who was wearing her royal purple gown with black trim, a black cloak, and a large purple hat with a thin black veil hanging fetchingly in front of it, partially obscuring her face. Thomas saw Zodiac standing on the opposite side of the stone-paved walkway; he flashed his friend a sober but grateful smile, which Zodiac acknowledged with a subtle nod. Guardian, on Callie's other side, was also wearing somber black. Thomas had noticed right away that Guardian's arm was no longer in the protective sling he'd seen last night, nor did it seem to be giving him any trouble. As promised, the morning had seen to Guardian's healing as well.

The Queen's Ladies, each in the black of deepest mourning, were gathered beside Thomas and Guardian and behind Callie. Iris was sobbing loudly into a large black handkerchief, oblivious to the comfort that Violet and Dahlia were trying to offer her. Iris simply adored funerals.

The entire Court, dressed to kill, was lined up on either side of the castle's main gate, weeping and murmuring in hushed whispers as the biers carrying the Not-Truly-Dead prepared to make the journey from the castle yard to the hill above Loch Elvenhome.

A total of twenty-eight of the Fair Folk had perished during yesterday's battle, including young Scribe and Callie's favorite Council advisor, the Naiad known as Boston. Nine Dwarfs, eight Brownies, six Elves and three HobGoblins had also lost their lives, however temporarily.

Four sharp blasts on horns somewhere above their heads heralded the commencement of the ceremony; the faerie funeral began.

The court musicians led the procession, playing a mournful tune on pipes, lute and drums. Thomas thought the tune seemed vaguely familiar, but couldn't quite place it. When he saw that the High Queen was attentively watching the advancing Folk with tears brimming in her eyes, he took her hand and gave it a small, comforting squeeze, which she acknowledged with a squeeze in return.

As the musicians reached the point where Callie stood, they continued playing their tune but stopped and bowed to her, never missing a beat. Callie in turn nodded her head at them, and then they continued on, playing for the mourners standing along the funeral route.

Next came the families of the Fallen, who marched together and handed flowers to the crowd as they passed.

An ancient, tiny Sprite reached high above his bald head and handed Thomas a bright blue flower on a long stem. "I'm great-great-grandsire to 'Scribe', sir. He's a good boy." Thomas nodded his head in agreement, and the Sprite smiled up at him before moving to stand in front of the still-sobbing Iris. He handed her a flower, and she cried harder.

The castle guard followed, sixty strong in full formal livery, their swords and spears lifted high in honor of the Fallen. More horn blasts sounded in the air from the castle gatehouse above Thomas' head as the Queen's Colors were raised and carried in the center of the honor guard. The banner was a large oak tree in a green field, with a huge white-gray horse and a shining golden harp in its center. As the colors passed through the throng, the Court applauded and shouted "Long Life and Blessings to the High Queen of Faerie!" Callie smiled sweetly, accepting the loving homage of her people.

And, at last came the cheerful remains of the much-mourned Fallen.

Those carried on biers lay peacefully under the day's glittering sunlight, not moving much, simply enjoying the ride in the open air. Those carrying the biers walked somberly in procession, humming tunes that sounded to Thomas less like dirges and more like faerie drinking songs, slowed down somewhat to match the alleged sobriety of the occasion.

Thomas could not help but notice that the pallbearers and their burdens alike waved surreptitiously at Callie and the rest of the Court as they passed by. Despite her tears, the Queen's dignity slipped once or twice when she covertly returned their waves and even blew a loud, exaggerated kiss at Boston when his bier moved past them.

Guardian caught Thomas' eye and winked. Thomas couldn't help it; he had to smile. The Faerie Court really did love its funerals. Thomas chuckled to himself when he considered just how badly this moment would play Upworld.

When the last of the twenty-eight biers had passed with as much decorum as possible, the Queen and her Court swelled into the flow of the procession, which stopped at the knoll above the loch. Once the biers of the Not-Truly-Dead were carefully placed on the ground in the shade, the non-funeral rites began. There was only one mishap: a fat Not-Dead Dwarf was accidentally dropped from his bier unceremoniously to the grass, and landed on an elderly, crusty Spriggan, who bit him, and also bit pallbearers who'd dropped the Dwarf on him in the first place. It took several minutes for order and decorum to be restored.

Callie, Thomas, Guardian, Zodiac, and the Queen's Ladies stood at the front of the assembled company, nearest the cheerful Fallen. There was a growing hum of quiet conversation as the Folk prepared for the finale of the non-funeral, speaking in hushed voices to their neighbors and, in some cases, to some of the Not-Truly-Dead, who were lounging comfortably on their biers in the shade.

Out of nowhere, a very short Pixie—whom Thomas had never seen before—wearing nothing but a very tall black hat hung with long streamers of black crepe, suddenly stood before them all, and raised his delicate hand over his head for silence before he spoke to the crowd.

"Your Grace, Honored Fallen, Lords and Ladies, Musicians, Court Notables, and all other Folk here gathered, I welcome you to the non-interment of our friends and family members." The Pixie scanned the large group with his tiny dark eyes, and then smiled as he indicated the Fallen on their biers. "These Folk fought bravely, with skill and merriment, and played the game through to the end, for which we give them our heartfelt thanks and only a small measure of censure for their lack of care, thus getting themselves somewhat messily killed in the first place."

There were small murmurs of agreement buzzing in the group. One of the Not-Truly-Dead sat up on his bier and scowled at the Pixie. Another Formerly Dead faerie, a female Brownie, sat up and made a rude gesture at the Pixie, and stuck out her alarmingly long tongue in playful contempt.

"We are grateful for the sacrifices these brave Folk made for the sake of the battle. We shall not see their like again...until the next battle." The Pixie sought the Queen's eye, and found it. "Your Grace, do you have words for us before we do not bury our friends?"

Callie took a solemn step forward, and in as stately a tone as Thomas had ever heard her use, said, "As I look at our Honored Fallen, and at this distinguished company all around me, I am most pleased as I say this: Friends, this has been a lovely funeral, and soon it will be time for the Victory Feast, honoring General Boston and all his White-Ribbon army for their battle prowess, as well as consoling the Green-Ribbon army, who fought with great vigor but, sadly, lost the day. Food will be served in the Great Hall within the hour, and wine is already flowing, as many of you are doubtless aware." She rolled her eyes in mock exasperation, and was wildly applauded by several dozen of the Fair Folk who had very recently and liberally helped themselves to the wine meant for the feast. "Feast, sing, dance and revel, by command of your Queen," Callie laughed, her eyes sparkling with merriment.

The Fair Folk went wild with delight, and pandemonium ensued.

Grinning at Thomas, Callie leaned against him and whispered something in his ear. He nodded at her, beaming, and headed back toward the castle, his smile broadening as he passed Folk he knew. Callie chatted with Folk as she too strolled in the direction of the castle, her mind on a more private, intimate victory celebration.

Food and wine, war stories, wild dancing and laughter reigned in the Great Hall that evening (and well into the next day) as the Fair Folk celebrated the White-Ribbon Army's victory at the recent Battle of Bannockburn. The festivities were all the more enthusiastic as nearly everyone eventually forgot which side of the battle they had actually played on.

Thomas Lear, Court Singer, found himself sitting on top of the High Table, facing the dozens of trestle tables and benches occupied by beautifully- and daringly-dressed Sprites, Elves, Pixies, Dwarves, Goblins, Banshees, Water Folk, Trolls and Giants. Wings were jeweled, skin was decorated in colors worthy of the festivities, fantastic shoes and hats were everywhere. The Folk were in high spirits.

The Court Singer's spirits were high, too; he'd had more than a fair share of excellent French wine with his dinner, and after that had enjoyed his favorite single-malt whisky. He was not entirely certain how he happened to be sitting on the table, but here he was, and it seemed to be all right with everyone around him, so he shrugged contentedly.

A glance from Callie, who sat on the table beside him, told him it was time to play for the Folk. He smiled at his High Queen, then looked at Zodiac, seated behind him several feet away. Zodiac nodded, and immediately an eager HobGoblin brought the Faerie Mahogany guitar to Thomas, who thanked the Hob and waited for quiet.

The quiet came, filled with anticipation. All eyes were on Thomas Lear. The Folk loved it when their Court Singer played and sang his songs.

After a long moment, Thomas ran his fingers over the strings, took a breath, and added his own magic to the feast.

DAYS LATER, GUARDIAN sat with Master Ocelot in one of the small rooms in the castle's Library.

"What do you think?" Guardian asked.

Master Ocelot scratched his beard and considered the Water Faerie beside him. "It is hard to say. If it has been done before, and successfully, there is no documentation that I know of, no anecdotal evidence to support the notion, either, and therefore no proof."

Guardian frowned. "I was afraid of that. I have been looking for some time. But that does not mean it cannot be done. It only means that we have no information. True?"

The Master nodded. "True, to a point. You must be wise. Your experiments have shown you the danger, and you cannot ignore the possible consequences that an ill-advised—and forgive me, a reckless—plan may cause Her Grace, and Elvenhome, and indeed all of Faerie."

Sighing, Guardian met Master Ocelot's eyes. "In my place, would you abandon the search?"

"Were I in your place, Young Lord, I would search all the more diligently. And I, too, would ask for help to resolve this most challenging problem." He grinned at Guardian, eyes sparkling; Master Ocelot loved discovering new things and finding the answers to riddles and puzzles. "The Library, the gardens—and their humble servant, too—are at your service."

As Guardian talked with Master Ocelot in the Library, the Lady Lavender moved with deliberation through the castle. *The Faerie Queen's Mirror*, the book written by Guardian's mortal lady, seemed to dance in the deep pocket of her rose-colored gown.

Happiness made Lavender nearly breathless as she made her way down the corridor toward Thomas' apartments. It was so easy, and she knew she was doing the right thing. She would show him the truth, and explain it with care so he would understand all. He would forgive Her Grace for her deception, and he would look at Lavender with new eyes.

Thomas would be grateful.

And then she would offer him her heart.

three

Once upon a time, in a magical land known by some as Faerie, there lived a handsome and powerful King and his beautiful Queen. The King and Queen were very much in love, and they ruled their kingdom and its people from a large castle set on a hollow hill above a vast and lovely forest of oak and white thorn trees.

They were seldom apart. It was said of them: If you seek the King, find the Queen. They were happiest in each other's company. They seemed to have always been together and in love, and they always would be together and in love.

The Fair Folk, sometimes called faeries, were a happy people. They spent much of their time attending court, dancing, feasting, making music and love, playing chess, hunting and hawking, farming, and parading. They loved to be in the company of their beloved Lord and Lady, to *whom they gave their allegiance, their obedience, and their affection.*

The King's strength and courage, and the Queen's beauty and wit, were legend. Thus was the kingdom one of safety, laughter and merriment.

And all was right in the world.

One summer's day, the Queen gave birth to a much-wished-for and long-awaited son, and there was rejoicing in the kingdom.

Then, without warning, the unthinkable happened. The newborn princeling died suddenly when he was but seven days old, in the arms of his father the King. The King had been singing a song to his son while the Queen sat nearby with her needlework. In a terrible instant, the baby shuddered and ceased to breathe, present one moment and gone the next.

The Queen, her wit lost and her great beauty broken, locked herself in her Tower Room alone with the depths of her grief, and wept. The King, stunned to the core of his handsome strength, took himself to his own Tower Room at the opposite end of the castle. There he drank alone with his bitterness and rage until he could no longer think or feel.

Thus the King and his Queen each stayed alone, apart for three days, longer than they had ever been separated since the beginning of their time.

He could not go to her to help ease her pain.

She could not go to him to comfort him in his despair.

On the fourth day, the sound of strangled, maddened screaming came from the King's Tower; the King's Men were alarmed. They tried to break down the door to the King's Tower, but it had been sealed by a magic strange to them, and they could not pass through it. The screaming went on for another hour before the now-frightened Men went to the door of the Queen's Tower and, along with the Queen's Ladies, begged the Queen to come at once to the aid of her husband.

The door to the Queen's Tower Room opened slowly, and the Queen, drawn and pale and sad and silent, went with the King's Men and the Queen's Ladies toward the King's Tower Room.

They could hear his desolate cries from the Great Hall, which was at the heart of the castle. The Queen's eyes widened in fear, but she pulled herself up sharply, and ran to her husband's Tower Room, bidding the others to wait in the Great Hall until she summoned them.

When she arrived at the door to the King's Tower Room, she knocked, but he ignored her. She called to him, but he only howled in bitter rage and loss. He would not allow her to witness his madness. He wanted her to leave him to his grief.

But the Queen did not leave. She stood alone outside the King's Tower Room, and waited.

She waited for what seemed to be a very long time.

The King's cries turned finally into agonized, inconsolable weeping. Then the Queen raised her hand in the air, and made a small flicking gesture with her fingers against her thumb. A cool green light flashed, and the door to the King's Tower Room opened to her.

She moved into the darkened chamber and found her King, drunk with wine and sadness, sitting woodenly in a chair, sobbing. Her heart melted at the sight of him so lost and broken. She knelt beside him, put her arms around him, and tried to comfort him.

He would not be comforted. And he offered her no comfort in return.

She held on to him anyway, and poured into him what strength and courage she could find within herself, because his was gone.

After long moments had passed and the King's sobbing had frozen him into a deadly silence, the Queen got up, and moved across the Tower Room to a table, upon which sat a pitcher of cool water. She poured water from the pitcher into a crystal goblet, and this she gave to the King, encouraging him to drink.

He drained the goblet only because she asked him to; in his drunkenness and pain and unreachable sadness, he seemed to have no will of his own. He gave her the now-empty goblet and she returned to the table to refill it with more water.

As she refilled the King's goblet, the Queen felt a sudden raw and angry energy flowing from and around the King. She turned from the table and faced her husband, her eyes wide with the awareness of what he might do.

"My love!" she cried, frightened when she saw the ravaged but determined look in his eyes, "My love! Do not!"

At the sound of the fear in her voice, he forced himself to look at her. He saw that she was still very beautiful despite her grieving, and that she had kept her wits about her despite the pain of her loss.

He knew then that she would heal, as surely as he knew that he would not.

And so it was that the King raised his hands high above his head, commanding the raging, fire-bright golden energy swirling around him. As he bent the energy to his will, he spoke the words that would seal his fate, the fate of his Queen, and the fate of their kingdom and its people forever:

> By Moon and Stars
> By Sun and Sky
> I curse the Fates
> That allowed my son to die!
>
> By Wind and Rain
> By Sea and Earth
> As my son is lost,
> No Faerie child shall come to birth!
>
> By Flower and Tree
> By Night and Morn
> Until I have a son,
> No child in my kingdom shall be born!

The Queen watched the King in growing horror. She understood his agony and his rage, but she saw that because he had shared his grieving over their child with no one but his bitterness and a good deal of wine, he had not *thought clearly enough to manage the magic he was working with his words.*

For the very first time in their life together, she was afraid. She saw that the powerful King was about to achieve a purpose he would never have contemplated but for his drunken, grief-induced madness. She knew that he could, in his incapacity, create something wrong and damaging that would curse the kingdom forever. The King had already contradicted himself in the spell-working, and that would bring certain disaster on them all.

She had to stop him before the spell was further distorted, before he made things even worse.

As he took a deep breath for the next words of his working, the Queen raised the heavy, water-filled crystal goblet from the table, and with a fast and forceful burst of green light, sent it speeding at the King.

At that very instant, it occurred to the King that he had indeed misspoken, and that there was a dangerous contradiction in his spell which he needed to rectify at once, before the working was finished. That staggering thought made him falter; his intention was less clear than it had seemed only moments before. In confusion and doubt, he turned to look at his Queen for help...

...and the crystal goblet slammed into his handsome face, and shattered, cutting a deep and painful slash across his mouth, leaving a jagged wound that bled like wine pouring from a dozen casks.

The Queen's action had ceased the words of the ill-cast spell in mid-making.

The King collapsed on the floor in pain, and the Queen stood unmoving by the table, weeping in wretched misery at the King's words, and at the violent and bloody results of what she had done to stop them. Tortured, she watched the King's tainted golden energy blow out of one of the Tower Room's open windows. Irretrievable now, it moved through Elvenhome to obey the King's misspoken, unrevoked command.

The Queen's heart broke then, her great love for her husband turning cold and bitter as death as she felt in her own body the jarring consequences of the King's word-working.

No one heard what had happened in the King's Tower Room that day. The King's Men and the Queen's Ladies had remained obediently in the castle's Great Hall.

With tears streaming down her face, she left him in his Tower Room and did not look back.

With tears streaming down his face, he let her go.

When all was said and done, life was forever changed. There was a flicker of sadness that lived in Elvenhome and its people for many, many years. The nine women in the castle and out in the village beyond its walls who were expecting new babes at the time of the King's spell lost them. The once-handsome King had a terrible wound across his face that in time healed into a painful, tight, ugly scar.

No one ever again heard the King and Queen speak to each other with gentle kindness, when they spoke at all. The deep love they had carried until that fateful day moved, over the years, from an angry, bleak silence to a quiet antipathy.

And there were no children born at Elvenhome in Faerie from that day to this.

SLOWLY, THOMAS CLOSED the paperback book and placed it on the table in front of him. His brain was on overload. He looked at Lavender, who sat beside him at the table, watching him with something in her eyes that he didn't have the energy to read.

"Why?" he asked, his voice slow and dull. "Why did you show me this?"

Calm, Lavender met his gaze. "Because it is good to know what went before."

"She should have told me." Thomas' whisper was hoarse and tight, more to himself than to Lavender.

"But she did not, Thomas."

"No, she didn't," he murmured, looking away.

He was not reacting the way she'd anticipated that he would. He did not seem jealous or hurt by the tale, and this confused her. Still, she reached over, took his hand and waited until he lifted his head and met her eyes. "Would you like me to stay with you? I was here at the castle at the time, of course, and I can tell you more of it, if you wish..."

He shook his head. "No." He couldn't decide which of his emotions was strongest; he was going numb. "No, I don't need to know more than this, at least not right now."

She was beginning to think she might have made a mistake. This was not going according to plan, so she did not know what to do now. He was not looking at the information in the right way. The tale and its revelations were somehow not bringing him closer to her. "What are you going to do, Thomas?"

His answer was spoken with such softness that she didn't hear it. "I don't know."

IN A BUOYANT mood after an exhilarating ride with Cassane, Callie went to see Thomas that afternoon. Zodiac followed her in through the doorway and toward the dining table, carrying a tray of bread and honey and wine and water.

As she entered, Callie sensed at once that something was wrong. She dismissed Zodiac, who evaporated on command. The heavy tray fluttered to the tabletop on its own.

"Thomas?" Wary now, Callie moved through the room. "Thomas, where are you?" She crossed the living area and stopped at his dining table.

Beside an upside-down, empty wineglass sat the castle's copy of *The Faerie Queen's Mirror.* She understood at once.

Callie went out into the garden. She found Thomas sitting on the bench, examining the rowan, hazel, and birch trees around him as though he'd never seen them before. He did not watch her approach. He kept his eyes focused on the garden. Undaunted, she walked over and sat down beside him.

He did not look at her.

After a few minutes of agitated silence, he nodded in the direction of a bed of wild thyme, pansies, and cowslips to his left. "The thyme is taking over the garden. Those pansies won't have a chance unless…" His voice trailed off.

"Thomas, my dear, what has happened to make you unhappy?" Her steady scrutiny, coupled with the gentleness in her voice, was almost too much for him to handle. He pulled away from her, as if she had touched—and burned—him.

She waited.

He released a heavy sigh. "Why didn't you tell me that ScarF is the High King of Faerie, and that he's your husband?" he asked, searching her face for answers he didn't think she would give him. "I had no idea that he...that you...oh, hell, Callie...why didn't you just tell me?" He looked down at the paving stones at his feet, unwilling to let her see the chaos written on his face.

To Thomas' utter surprise, Callie began to chuckle.

He jerked his head up and watched in disbelief as the chuckle grew into rich, full laughter. "What the fuck are you laughing about?" he demanded, confused now and thus getting angry.

His startled reaction only served to make her laugh more merrily. "Oh, Thomas, I thought something was truly wrong! I thought you were ill or..."

"Something *is* wrong, Callie!" he glared at her, appalled. "You're *married* to ScarF! It's not a secret that we are lovers, but you have a husband right here, and he's the King, the High King, and he really doesn't like me very much, and—"

"And what, Dear One?" she asked. "Where is there a wrong?"

What was wrong with her? Obviously she doesn't understand, he thought. But looking at her, how unaffected and calm she was, how she was genuinely relieved that only *this* was the problem, made him wonder if somehow there was something going on here that he didn't understand. This thought frustrated him, and he did not especially like it.

He shook his head, as if to clear it, and told the truth. "I don't understand, Callie."

"Very well," she said. "Let me try to help you. But come, there is food and drink inside. You look as though you need a little refreshment."

"I need more than that," he muttered under his breath. "I need a little goddamned sanity..."

If she heard him, she did not respond.

39

With muted hostility, he followed her back through the garden doors, into the bedroom and through to the living room.

"Food," she said, moving through the now-familiar ritual. "Water from Faerie wells, for me, and for you, a sweet wine from Spain. The bread was baked by faeries but with all Upworld ingredients, and the honey is from Upworld, too. Eat and drink free from care, Thomas." She touched his shoulder, and then caressed his arm with unmasked affection.

He loved her touch, he couldn't help it. So he found himself giving her a tentative smile, despite his confused frustration. He took some bread and honey, and poured himself some wine, and sat down in one of the chairs beside the couch. Callie sat down on the floor in front of him, her chin resting on his knee. She spoke, watching him as he ate and drank.

"I'm sorry you're unhappy. What started this? Tell me what happened. Then I'll tell you anything you'd like to know."

He didn't think he wanted to tell her. He felt as if he had to, though, since she had asked him directly. *Was his enchantment changing his normally secretive behavior?* he wondered. He had never been this honest in his life, and he wasn't sure he was in favor of it in the long run. Before he could decide for sure whether or not to tell her the whole truth about it all, he found himself telling her everything.

"I mentioned to Lavender yesterday that I wanted to read something new, and she brought me a book...it's—"

"The one on the table. Yes, I saw it. The book of tales Guardian's Lady wrote."

"Lavender wanted me to read one of the stories. And it's more than a 'faerie tale,' it's kind of a history, isn't it?"

Callie sighed a little. "After a fashion, yes, it is." She waited while he swallowed some more bread and honey.

"Do you know why Lavender wished for you to read that particular tale?"

"She said I should know some things you hadn't told me."

Callie's face was unreadable, although there was a trace of something in her eyes that Thomas had never seen there before. "Callie?"

She shrugged, and the unspoken sense of threat—if indeed it had been a threat at all—vanished. "I suppose I haven't been paying as much attention to Lavender, and what she believes she needs, as I ought to. She's usually forthright about what she wants." She gave Thomas a tiny smile. "I've been distracted, thanks to you. Still, I'll speak with her."

"Are you angry that she gave me the story?"

"Not really," she told him. "Although I didn't consider that she would bring it to your attention on purpose."

"Is the story a secret? Did you command that no one should tell me?"

She grinned then. "No, Thomas. History is rarely a secret, no matter whose history it is. This one belongs to us all. I never demanded silence around this tale—or any other, for that matter. I admit I'm surprised that she shared this with you, but I suppose I shouldn't be."

"So she's not in trouble, then?"

Callie took his hand. "No, she's not 'in trouble'. At least, not in the sense you mean it. I will have a talk with her, however, to discover what I can do to help her to be happier."

If this puzzled him, he let it go for the moment to deal with more pressing matters. "Callie, is the tale true?"

"In its way," she admitted, with a small nod of her head.

"Tell me. I need to understand."

"Very well, Thomas." She turned around then, and leaned her back against his legs as he settled into the chair

41

and waited. She nestled against him and made a contented sound as he ran his fingers along the top of her shoulder.

"The facts of the tale itself are true enough," she began.

Opening his mouth to say something, Thomas closed it again, and listened.

"The man you named 'ScarF' is the High King of Faerie, overlord of all the other Faerie kings. And yes, the High King is indeed my husband. Granted, he's my husband in name only, has been so since the day you read about in the tale."

Thomas' curiosity was still a bit tentative. "How long ago did it happen?"

She was still facing away from him, leaning against his legs, and he felt rather than heard her chuckle. "A lot longer ago than you'd like to imagine, a very long time ago. You see us as all but immortal. Time here has little meaning in the ways that it matters to mortals."

"I'd still like to know."

"All right," she said, in almost a whisper. "But remember, you insisted."

"Tell me."

"Just over seven hundred years ago." She waited, and then laughed at his shocked silence as he struggled to take it in. "Time is different for us, Thomas," she repeated, and turned around to face him, laying her arm across his knees.

Her face was serious. "The events in the tale are close enough to the actual events. There was a child, a boy. He did die suddenly, and in his father's arms. ScarF never got over it, never learned how to fight the fear and the sense of helplessness and loss. He has lived with his fears and his anger and self-defeat every day since then." Her eyes met Thomas' own with matter-of-fact honesty. "Since that day, we have not touched each other. We are not often alone in the same room. He has gone his own way, and, of course, I have gone mine. He does his duty, however. It is his birthright responsibility, and he honors it. It is he who protects Elvenhome in particular, and answers for Faerie at large. The lesser kings in the land still seek his counsel, still owe him vassalage, and he sits Court with them annually as is his right. He is very good at it; he is fair, and just. I sit Court here in Elvenhome, as you have seen. It is a rare thing for us both to be in attendance at feasts and the like." She looked at him, her face sincere. "I am sorry I did not tell you the full truth when you first asked me about him. I did not think you needed to know the whole of it, so chose not to burden you with what I presumed would cause distress, despite its irrelevance."

Irrelevance? He thought. How could she believe ScarF and her history with him were irrelevant? ScarF was dangerous, ScarF was the King of Faerie, and ScarF couldn't like the fact that Thomas was fornicating with his wife and making friends all over Elvenhome.

Thomas wanted to press Callie for some sign of reassurance about his position with her, but when he met her deep brown eyes showing him patience and kindness, his focus shifted. His own unhappy sense of inadequacy changed to a somber curiosity about her feelings about the tale, and the realities of her own life hidden somewhere in the shadows beneath it.

Thomas took Callie's hand and squeezed it. "Did you love him very much?"

Her nod was solemn, but without a trace of the sadness he expected to see. "Yes, I did, once. There was a time when I loved him beyond measure; he was wonderful and loving and strong and good, and he made me laugh. He sang to me, songs that warmed my heart. I loved him with every breath in my body, every glimmer of life in my soul." She squeezed Thomas' hand in return. "But that was long ago, a time well out of memory. We acknowledge each other's presence, and we tend to quarrel when we are forced to speak to each other, but that is all. Our love is dead, Thomas. We will never be to each other again what we were, and neither of us pretends otherwise. But we do our duty to our people, and to our land. That is sufficient."

He had to ask the question. "And the reason that there are no children in Elvenhome...is it because of what the tale says happened?"

There was no apparent hint of pain in her voice or in her eyes. The wound was so old that even her internal scars, if she carried them still, were immune to any genuine hurt. "In a way. The true working, as he spoke it, was not retold accurately in the tale, of course, but it was the right idea."

"And if he hadn't been so unhappy, and hadn't been drinking...?"

She sighed, without bitterness. "He was, at the time, very powerful. He could have done several things to correct the mistakes he'd made in the words. But he hesitated, and I stopped him with that damned goblet. There was no saving it, after that."

"How does the spell work?" Suddenly Thomas wanted to know.

"How does it work?" At first she didn't understand what he meant. She thought for a moment. "Oh. I see. It is only the Folk of Elvenhome who are affected with childlessness. Children have been born all over Faerie, of course, in all the other kingdoms beyond Elvenhome, for the past seven hundred years. The Fair Folk who live under flowers and in trees and under water, in castles and villages and beneath hills, all of them can have and have had children. There are fewer faerie children born every year, but that has little to do with ScarF's long-ago spellwork that deprives Elvenhome of new life."

"So it's a location problem?"

"Not exactly. Everyone who was in Elvenhome at the time of the spell work was and is affected. Even if those Folk leave Elvenhome and live elsewhere, they cannot make children. Those who leave tend to come back; they're happiest here. Folk who visit from other Kingdoms are not affected. They come, stay as long as they stay, and return home, but they do not, cannot, make children when they are in residence here. Out of a long-standing courtesy, they leave their very young ones behind when they come to us, until those children are grown; if the Folk from Elvenhome wish to spend time with young Fey babies, they visit other kingdoms. It has been ever thus. And fortunately, ScarF did not start in on the young of the animals in the forests and farms, the trees and the fields, or we would have had more difficult problems. At least we can eat, and grow food and flowers."

His voice was sympathetic. "And so you've never had another child, all these years."

"No."

"Is that why you haven't forgiven him?"

She considered this for a moment, and then shrugged. "Perhaps, in the beginning. But it is not my forgiveness that he needs." There was a distinct note of compassion in her voice, but it was a queen's benevolence, a generosity about a wayward, suffering subject, rather than a kind accommodation for her once-beloved husband's disastrous actions. "He needs his own forgiveness, and that is something he is not willing to grant himself. Instead, he lives with his anger and self-loathing and bitterness, and his drinking. He finds his comfort when and where he chooses. I do the same, of course, but—I trust—for different reasons." She kissed Thomas' hand, her affection for him evident in her eyes as she looked up at him. "Does it trouble you that ScarF is my husband, now that you know the truth of it?"

He shook his head. "No. Or, not as much as I thought it did."

"Were you afraid you were not safe from him?"

"That had occurred to me. After all, I am his wife's lover."

She smiled at that. "He will never—no one can ever—do you harm, while you are with me and while you are faithful to your obligations. I swear it."

Believing her, he nodded, and finally smiled at her.

Without warning, her voice took on a somber, almost oracular sound, despite the forced lightness of her tone. "And let the moral of the tale be a lesson to you, my dear Court Singer..."

The look in her eyes made him uneasy, even though she was trying to smile. "Moral of the tale?" he asked carefully.

"Wine and words mix well only for a brief time; after that moment has passed, with wine and words blended with anger or fear, there is only pain and destruction."

It was difficult to tell which of them was more stung by the truth of this, the poet/musician who too often had not been able to write or sing, or the lonely, childless queen whose world had been forever changed by her husband's rage and grief. They studied each other's eyes for a long moment and then looked away, neither able to speak in the presence of the raw suffering they read in the other. The hurt, openly revealed, was too much to bear. She rested her forehead against his knee. He closed his eyes and stroked her hair.

After a time, she lifted her head and met his gaze again. "Thomas, will you take me to bed, please?" she asked, in a quiet, half-hearted voice. "A small part of me is suddenly very sad, and I would heal it with the gladness of your touch."

"At your service, My Queen," he whispered back, offering her his hand and helping her rise from the floor as he stood up. She moved into his arms, her kisses at first light and sweet, then restless and hungry. With tenderness, he lifted her, held her against his aching chest, and carried her into the bedroom.

four

HE HAD NEVER been much of a runner, but over time Thomas Lear was becoming a decent jogger. The notion amused him. If Jack Grandberg or Stan Williams could see him now, the shock of seeing the usually-sedentary Lear jogging would probably kill them. The guys in the band would think they were hallucinating. Thomas laughed out loud as he sprinted through the trees and up over the small hill that led to the loch.

He didn't really spend too much time thinking about the people and things he'd left behind in Los Angeles. He didn't have to think too hard about his career, either. He'd begun to look at his time in Elvenhome as the next step in his professional (and personal) life, and he had the added benefit of knowing he would get back to Los Angeles later on, and pick up where he'd left off. The Butlers would take care of his home. The songs he had written since he'd been with Callie would jump-start everything when he was ready.

The songs he hadn't written yet made him smile as he jogged across the long field where the 1975 version of the Battle of Bannockburn had been fought. He noticed that the grass was healthy and smelled wonderful as he moved across it. It seemed only natural to avoid stepping on bluebells and buttercups.

When was the last time he noticed grass, and stray flowers that would be considered weeds in gardens at home?

He marveled at the stuff in his head, and how it had gotten there in the first place, considering he'd spent too many years either drunk or high, or both. He wasn't that guy anymore; it had been five months since he'd had drugs of any kind, and he often stopped drinking these days well before he was intoxicated.

He was a jogger, now, by the look of things. He had changed, in half a dozen ways. He wondered if the changes were part of the enchantment, and would fall away when he went back to his other life. God, he hoped not.

Turning back toward the castle, more than a bit smug that he wasn't totally winded, he saw three Gnomes, wearing bright red caps and carrying walking sticks, headed in his direction. He hoped they would remember that he could not speak to them. Gnomes are fun-loving and hard-working, but a large portion of their population is not terribly bright.

Thomas knew he didn't have to worry about any kind of encounter. About twenty feet above him in the air, one of Callie's guards, a reed-thin, handsome Sprite (who now answered to the name "Hemingway") flew at a discreet distance behind him, giving Thomas the illusion that he was jogging in solitude. Hemingway was on Jogging Detail, and had been since the day Thomas had mentioned to Zodiac that he'd planned to start jogging to get, and stay, healthy.

As Thomas jogged, Hemingway darted through the air toward the approaching Gnomes, then hovered above them and spoke, pointing at Thomas, who was within thirty feet of them.

The three Gnomes stopped walking and, with Hemingway hovering, waved at Thomas and greeted him in their earthy, gruff voices as he raised his hand in salutation and jogged past them.

In the interest of meeting people and spending time with "the guys," Thomas instituted a weekly poker game in his rooms. This event became known as "The Friday Afternoon Poker Game." Every Friday, at around three, five or six of the Fair Folk showed up with snack food and ale, both Fey and mortal.

In truth, Thomas never knew for sure exactly when it was Friday. He had never seen a calendar, or anything that might reasonably pass for one, anywhere in Elvenhome. He was fairly sure that if anyone at the castle had a calendar, or knew what day it was, it would be Master Ocelot. Thomas decided he'd feel strangely embarrassed about asking the very busy Master what day or month it was, so he opted to let it go, and somehow The Friday Afternoon Poker Game took on a consistent cadence of its own. It might have been a weekly event, and it might not have been. Thomas didn't know, and didn't much care. He was having fun.

The stakes were random, subjective, and sometimes funny: coins, stones, anything shiny (especially when there were Dwarves or Pixies at the table), bottles of wine, books, IOUs scribbled on big pieces of brown paper, and (only once) a litter of kittens. Anything considered valuable to any of the players was fair game, and only added to the merriment. Thomas had never laughed so much during serious poker in his life.

Zodiac and Boston were immediate and enthusiastic regulars. In time, Buick, a cheerful if not overly-intelligent Elf who was the son of one of the King's Men, became a regular as well. Two Dwarfs, guards from the end of Thomas' corridor renamed Harvard and Yale, came to the first poker game, and once they bragged to their fellow guards about the fun—and profit—they'd had, Thomas met, and sometimes had to name, a new guard every "Friday" for cards. The Royal Guard Poker Rotation became a standard at Elvenhome Castle that continued through Thomas' year and well beyond it.

When possible, Guardian joined the game, too. Adept at most everything he did, the blond Water Faerie enjoyed the game, understood the nuances and the odds, and added to the camaraderie of the Folk who came to play.

It did not take Thomas long to realize, however, that Guardian could not manage a bluff to save his life. The blue eyes of the heir-apparent spoke volumes about the cards in his hand, and what he intended to do with them. Thomas, along with Boston and Zodiac, tacitly chose to ignore Guardian's face when they played any of the variations of the game Thomas introduced.

"It almost pains me to take your money, Gentlemen." With a dramatic sigh, Thomas pulled a pile of loch stones, a cup filled with Elf-shot, a small and, surprisingly, *unopened* bottle of peach Schnapps, twenty Scottish pennies, a palm-sized chunk of raw silver, and a small turtle toward him. "But I'll do it anyway."

SHE WAS SEARCHING for him, running hard toward a lonely stand of trees some fifty yards in front of her. The razor-sharp sense of fear, something she had never truly tasted before, was bitter in her mouth. Her heart pounded with exertion and the tears she would not shed. She had to find him, but she could not be certain of where she was in this moment. Nothing around her looked at all familiar. How was she to find him in the coming darkness?

Desperation mingled with rage strangled her and she heard a choked sob tear out of her throat, but she ignored her deepening sense of hopelessness by the sheer force of her will as she raced into the woodland.

She flew through the trees, scanning for any movement as she ran. In the middle of the greenwood she stopped, gasping, her trembling hand resting against a tall oak for support.

"Where are you?" she called, the terror in her ragged voice leaving her breathless. "Where are you?"

Spinning to get a look at everything around her, she filled her lungs with the chilly air. "I'm here, and I'm going to find you. Where are you?"

An eerie silence answered her.

Angry now, she slammed her hand against the trunk of the oak tree and swore vehemently.

A small red fox, frightened by her noise, darted past her and fled deeper into the wood.

It occurred to her to follow it, but in the same instant, it made more sense to her to dash in the opposite direction, the way from which the fox had come. Turning, she ran hard and fast for half a minute, then froze in her tracks, her heart all but stopping when she found what she was looking for.

Glancing around to see if anyone or anything else was near, and satisfied that he was alone, she moved quickly toward him, and tried very hard not to cry.

SLUMPED FORWARD, SITTING on the ground, he was secured to the tree trunk by cords of heavy, ragged rope. Blood and dirt were matted together in his long blond hair, which hid his face. His clothes were torn, some of the blood on them still wet.

She knelt beside him and settled him back against the tree, moving his hair away from his face with great care. He was unconscious, and she felt a sick stab of gratitude for this. He'd been badly beaten. His skin was pale, far too pale, beneath the blue and purple bruises that covered much of his face.

"Oh, Arrendel," she whispered, "What have they done to you?" She couldn't help it; she was so relieved to have found him and so frightened at his condition that she began to weep. Her sobbing shook her body so roughly that it seemed as though the very ground beneath her knees and the tree to which Arrendel was tied were shaking with her. She began to cry harder, tears blinding her to everything but her misery. "Arrendel, forgive me. Arrendel..."

Her shoulder began to move then, gently at first, and its force increasing. What was happening to her?

"Callie? Callie, you're dreaming. Callie, wake up, come on, wake up..." The voice she heard beside her cheek was soothing, calm, and strong. Familiar, too, she realized. "Callie, it's all right, you're safe, you can wake up..."

She opened her eyes, and found herself in her own bed, with Thomas curled around her, brushing her tears away with his fingertips and studying her with his sleepy brown eyes. She took a couple of deep breaths and steadied herself.

He kissed her lightly on the cheek. "Are you all right? You were thrashing around by the time I woke up enough to understand what was happening," he frowned. He saw the lost, faraway look in her eyes change and calm as the dream receded behind them, to a place he knew he could not go. "Callie?"

She gave him a half-hearted smile. "That was not a good dream. I must have frightened you. I'm sorry." She settled her body against his, her heartbeat slowing as she took another deep breath and forced herself to relax.

"Do you want to talk about it?"

She shook her head. "All is well, Thomas. A dream is but a small journey, and that one is over now." Stretching and leaning over, she blew out the flame of the solitary candle that still burned beside the bed, then snuggled against him once more with a heavy, relieved sigh.

They were silent in the dark for some minutes.

"Callie?"

"Hmmmm?"

53

"What's 'arrendel'?"

"What?"

"You said something that sounded like 'arrendel' when you were dreaming. What's an 'arrendel'? I've never heard the word before."

There was a pause, and then she said: "Let it be, Thomas. It is nothing for you to be concerned about."

"As my Queen commands," Thomas returned in a whisper, pulling her tighter against him and, without another word, began banishing the effects of her nightmare with the warm certainty of his body.

Callie spent a busy afternoon in her apartments working her way through a large pile of documents that Boston had brought her earlier in the day. Seated at the ornate rosewood table that stood in the middle of her private study, she read document after document and made decisions. Royal petitions from all corners of Faerie, requests for the Queen's presence or assistance in various matters, the announcements of all recent faerie births, deaths, and transitions, plus an in-depth series of carefully-recorded Fair Folk movement around Faerie lands and Upworld, covered the table and had the full force of Callie's attention.

The Queen did not look up when Iris came into the room carrying a tray that held a small decanter, a goblet, and two generous slices of goldenfruit.

"Your Grace?" Iris interrupted in a whisper as she lowered the tray to the table and poured wine from the decanter into the goblet.

Callie's mind pulled away slowly from the petition in front of her. The smile she gave to the elegant, trusted Banshee who had served her longer than any other of her Ladies, was a little tired. Iris passed the goblet to Callie, who nodded her thanks and took a long sip.

"You have been in here for too many hours," Iris said, with faint disapproval. "You look exhausted."

"There is much to be done. The Folk are very active these days, and all need the attention of their Queen."

"The Folk need to learn to look after themselves, and let their Queen attend to her own needs for a while," Iris sniffed protectively.

Callie laughed. "I don't think there's any more work to do than usual. It only seems as though there is more work because Thomas is here. He is a welcome distraction."

"One that you have needed, and one that you deserve, Your Grace," Iris replied. "Few know how hard you work. You make ruling the land and protecting the Folk appear effortless, but I know otherwise."

Shrugging, Callie drank the wine and handed the empty goblet back to Iris. "What has been happening in the world today since I closeted myself with 'Queen Stuff'?" She chuckled at Thomas' now-famous reference to her royal duties. "Where are the Ladies?"

Iris placed everyone's location in her mind as she offered Callie a slice of the goldenfruit. "Juniper is spending the day with one of her lovers—or perhaps two or three of them. Lavender and Rose went to speak with the Master Cobbler about new shoes. Orchid is reading in the Library, as usual. Daisy is repairing your yellow gown—which reminds me, you really should ask Thomas to be more careful with your clothing, Your Grace. Rose is supervising the cleaning of your bed chamber, and Dahlia is mooning, rather pathetically, I'd imagine, over the charming young Dwarf who arrived last week from her father's kingdom. Violet," Iris pointed at the study's open window, "is in the garden, picking honeysuckle flowers for the bedchamber. And I," she concluded with crisp dignity, "am doing what Thomas calls 'holding down the fort'."

"Whatever would I do without you, my friend?" Callie grinned. She rubbed the back of her neck to ease the strain in her weary muscles. "Thomas will join me here for dinner, so I'll have no need of the company of my Ladies until tomorrow morning. He prefers privacy over Queen's Attendance, and it pleases me to make him feel comfortable. Oh—and in the event that you spend any time with the Lord High Chamberlain this evening," and here Callie winked at Iris, "do give him my kindest *personal* regards for a...*restful* night."

"As Your Grace commands," said Iris with a strangely Zodiac-like air of resignation which was contradicted by the sudden twinkle in her eyes.

There was a knock on the main door of Callie's apartments. With a slight bow to Callie, Iris left the study to answer it.

Focusing again on her work, Callie absently licked the goldenfruit nectar from her fingers and reached for another document from the pile.

She ignored the voices in the other room, knowing that Iris would handle anything that needed the Queen's attention until she was finished with the day's business. Callie sighed and began to read another petition, this one from one of the northern Faerie kings, formally requesting the Queen's official permission to summon a gathering of The Host of the full Seelie Court. He did not provide details, she noticed. "Whatever do you want *that* for, Therion?" Callie wondered aloud.

A few moments later, Iris tapped on the open door of the study.

"Your Grace, a messenger has arrived from Elvenwood, and is waiting in the Queen's Presence Chamber."

Looking up, Callie laughed and clapped her hands together in delight. "Iris! The Wheel turns!"

Moments later, a happy and excited Callie, attended by Iris, Carnation, Dahlia, and Violet, hurried through her Castle to receive the messenger, the "Queen Stuff" and the

56

documents still piled on the rosewood table all but forgotten.

IN THE ROYAL stables, in dazzling sunshine, The King of Faerie stood brushing his handsome stallion, WindRunner, the strokes long and affectionate. He looked over at three of his Men, who were also grooming their horses after an invigorating ride across the shire. Nearby, the watchful eyes of the Master of Horse ensured that His Grace and the King's Men had everything they needed to settle the horses down for the day.

"Emmel," ScarF said as he worked, "you understand which items I wish to have retrieved from Glasgow?"

Beside him, Emmel nodded, his long gray hair sweeping his face as he gave his own horse an apple and an affectionate pat. "I do, Your Majesty. And I thank you again for the opportunity that will allow my son to serve you well."

The King nodded confirmation as he fed WindRunner a carrot. He considered the list of things he had asked Emmel to collect for him, knowing that it was potentially dangerous emotional territory. There was no way around it, so he trudged straight through it.

There was a fair amount of Elfshot, collected over the years by mortals, much of it from the small but enthusiastic Unseelie battles that ratcheted up every hundred years or so. There was also an oak-handled amethyst dagger that the King particularly liked, and had done without for long enough. But the most important thing, by far, was the Greencrystal Pendant, which, at that very moment, was on display in a glass case in the museum at the Glasgow School of Art.

The Greencrystal Pendant was the gift he'd fashioned for his Queen once upon a time, to celebrate the coming birth of their child. He had carefully mingled the green, earthy magic of his cherished wife with his own radiant, golden power, and placed it in a beautiful piece of sheer earthstone roughly half the size of his palm. The Stone, a lightweight yet strong piece of timeless crystal, rested on a long silver chain. His Queen had worn it for less than a week, long ago, but he remembered the long silver chain from which the Stone had hung, and that, while standing, the Greencrystal had sparkled with verdant pride on the same line as the Queen's luscious hips.

A powerful, beautiful Stone it was. Dangerous, too, in the wrong hands, but since it was only Upworld in Glasgow—in a small museum, of all things—he had not been concerned about getting it back. It was safe enough where it was.

It had taken more than a decade to discover that it had been stolen in the first place. After the death of his son, the Queen put the Greencrystal away in a casket she kept in her Tower Room. She had offered the Pendant back to him, but he had not wanted to see it, either. They both ignored its existence and the memories it could awaken.

He cringed at the notion that one of the Queen's Court Singers had come across it, and had likely pocketed it when his time in Faerie was over. In any case, at some point his Queen informed him of the loss of the Greencrystal Pendant. He remembered now that her eyes had brimmed with unshed tears, but neither of them acknowledged that. It had taken very little time afterward to locate it.

Had the Greencrystal been comprised solely of his own energy, or if it had been given considerably more of his energy than that of his Queen's, the Stone would have called to him directly, and there would have been no need to have the Folk looking for it.

When it was eventually found in the private art collection of a Highland laird, the King decided to leave it in the laird's care indefinitely.

Through the centuries, the Pendant was handed down as part of the natural inheritance from father to son. Because the King knew where it was, he stopped thinking about it, and got on with his life. That life had been lived more or less in Elvenstone Castle, in the far west of Faerie. As a rule, the King only showed up in Elvenhome when duty or circumstance required him to do so.

He had received word several months ago that the laird's family had lost their vast estate over death duties, and thus had moved their land and most of their more significant possessions to the Scottish National Trust. The Trust had passed some "interesting ancient artifacts" to several national museums and art galleries, mostly in Edinburgh and Glasgow.

It had not been until he'd seen the way his Queen had looked at Thomas Lear at her door that night that he'd decided that he wanted the Greencrystal Pendant—and anything else that was truly Fey and belonged to the Folk—back where it belonged.

"Sire?"

The King pulled his mind out of the past, and pushed it into the present. He looked up to see Fiall, a King's Man who was a slender but muscular Gnome originally from Elvenmere, watching him. He followed Fiall's nod in the direction of one of the stable grooms, who stood a respectful fifteen feet away from the King and his Men, waiting to speak.

"What is it?"

"Your Majesty, there is word from Elvenwood. A messenger from King Drowwardin awaits you and Her Majesty in the Queen's Presence Chamber."

The King and his Men exchanged a happy look and a laugh, and left their contented stallions in the care of the Master of Horse and his stewards.

IN THE QUEEN'S Presence Chamber, Callie sat in one of two cushioned, tall-backed chairs on the dais, and talked with her Ladies as she waited for the King to arrive.

He strode in with his Men behind him. The Ladies' conversations silenced at once.

As the King approached the Queen, she signaled her Ladies with a subtle nod. They moved to resituate themselves in the sunny corner of the chamber closest to the dais, and waited.

The King gestured. His Men stopped, remaining still as he walked alone toward the dais to address his wife.

"Your Majesty," said Callie.

"Your Grace." He bowed his head slightly.

"We have news."

"So I understand."

The corners of Callie's mouth twitched a little, and slid into a small, teasing smile. "Given the circumstances, can we—for a little while—suspend our normal fashion of dealing with each other, do you think?"

The King appeared to consider this, but his gray eyes sparkled with mirth. "Are you suggesting that we entertain a small truce, Madam?"

"I am." Callie tapped the arm of the chair beside her own.

"I accept," the King replied as he mounted the three steps to the dais and sat in the empty chair beside her.

With practiced stealth, the Queen's Ladies watched Their Majesties.

"Violet, flutter over there and find out what they're talking about," Iris whispered, only half in jest.

The tiny winged faerie hovered above Dahlia's head, frowning. "People always expect more from you when you can fly."

"You do make an excellent spy," Dahlia reminded her. "Remember when I asked you to find out if—"

60

"Shush!" Violet shrieked, darting to a spot in front of the Dwarf's face. "You know I would never break a confidence—"

"Quiet, all," Iris chided. "Else you'll hear me wail like my great-grandmother in a nasty mood." She stole peeks at the Queen and the King as they talked. "Look...do you see them? It has been an age since they have been that close together, or had a wee conversation that has not come to bad temper or sparks.

"Carnation," Iris continued, "What they are saying? Now would be a perfect opportunity to take advantage of your pretty ears, would it not?"

The shy Goblin listened for a moment, her long ears twitching. "They are speaking too softly. I cannot hear them."

"I would imagine they are discussing the coming of the royal child," the ever-helpful Rose piped up.

"Of course they are talking about the royal child, Poppet," Iris sighed. "I want to know *what* they are saying to each other, and how they are saying it. I do not want the King's Grace to anger our Queen."

"Her Grace will tell us later," Orchid observed.

Iris chuckled, and patted the kind-hearted Selkie on the arm. "Yes, she will. But she will likely omit a thing or two."

"Only the things that a wanton Banshee would want to hear," Dahlia laughed. "Violet, perhaps you should sail over there and—" (Violet made a very large and explicit gesture with her very small hand) "—oh, never mind."

As it happened, the quiet, quarter-hour conversation between the Queen and the King did not appear to anger either of them. Most surprising of all, they were smiling as they spoke. The King's Men were as intrigued by at this as were the Queen's Ladies.

When the discussion was over, the Ladies and the Men all had their instructions: preparations were to be made for the first official Royal Progress, a true Faerie Rade with both King and Queen, in more than seven hundred years.

The King would be attended by four of his Men, the Queen by four of her Ladies, and these would be joined by an estimated one hundred of the Fair Folk. They would Progress northeast from Elvenhome toward the Eastern Kingdoms, and arrive at Elvenwood, the castle of King Drowwardin and Queen Alyria, in time for the birth. Afterward, they would take a leisurely route north, and then far to the west, to spend a day and a night on the west coast, at the King's other home, Elvenmere Castle. Finally, their Majesties would travel south for their return to Elvenhome.

The sight of the King and his Queen standing together on the dais before they announced their plans for the Rade was mesmerizing for their attendants. It was, for a moment, as if the long tragedy of their collective past had evaporated.

That moment faded as everyone focused on their appointed tasks, and scurried into action, leaving the King and Queen alone together in the Presence Chamber.

"I have much to do before the journey," the King murmured.

"I, too," replied the Queen.

He walked down the steps of the dais, and then turned to face her. "This was good."

"Yes. It was."

"And you do not need me for...Arrendel?"

She shook her head, but kindly. "No. I can do it alone."

"Very well." He turned and began to walk toward the door.

"I thank you for asking," she whispered, more to herself than to him.

As he moved through the door, his words danced in the air around her:

"You are most welcome."

THOMAS MADE BEST efforts not to be annoyed with Callie for not telling him herself that she would not be joining him for dinner later that evening. He had been writing all day, working in a happy but feverish passion, and wanted nothing more than to hold her, share the new song, and then relax with her in the afterglow of his spent creative energy.

The person standing in front of him in his living room was not Callie. It was Lavender, and she carried a basket that contained his dinner.

Thomas struggled to keep his frustration and his disappointment to himself.

"Her Grace is very sorry she cannot be here, Thomas," Lavender was saying. "I thought it would be well if I brought you something to eat, so I stopped at the kitchens on the way." The pretty blonde Elf moved to the dining table and began laying a place setting and some covered dishes on it. "Here is a Highland meal: lamb stew, fresh beans steamed with mushrooms, and applesauce. All Scottish. And ale, and water, too. *Eat and drink, free from care.* Chrysler made everything herself tonight, and she hopes you will enjoy it very much."

Thomas's eyes roamed over the food. It looked and smelled marvelous; he hadn't realized how hungry he was. "I'll be sure to tell her the next time I see her and have permission to speak, Lavender—but in the meanwhile, would you thank her for me?"

Lavender nodded. "You should eat while everything's warm."

He tried not to complain. "You're certain she's not coming?"

She nodded again. "Yes. Do eat, Thomas."

With a shrug and a sigh, Thomas sat down on one of the chairs and filled his plate. After a moment, Lavender sat down in another of the chairs at the table, and watched approvingly as he ate.

"Her Grace regrets not being able to dine with you. She instructed me to tell you that she will come to you sometime before dawn. She knows you have been working hard, and she was eager to hear the pieces of the new song." Lavender's eyes sparkled with a glimmer of sudden excitement. "Have you *finished* it?"

The look of satisfaction in Thomas' eyes was unmistakable.

She clapped her hands in delight. "You have! You finished the new song! How wonderful!"

Thomas couldn't help it; he was grinning now, glad to be able to tell someone that the song was finally ready, even if that someone wasn't Callie. "Yeah, I finished it about an hour ago. I think I got it right."

"This is excellent news, Thomas!" she beamed at him. "I know you must play it first for Her Grace, but may I be the one to tell both Her Grace and the Queen's Ladies that you have completed the song?" She looked at him imploringly, with such shining wistfulness that he had to force himself not to laugh as he took a long drink of ale.

"Yes, Lavender, you can tell them it's finished, and that I am waiting on the Queen's good pleasure."

"That is as it should be, I think," Lavender pointed out. "But it does not mean that there are not those of us who are aching to hear it as well. Those of us who would give much for—"

The look of complete seriousness on her face was as charming as it was soothing, and it gently satisfied most of his bruised disappointment over not spending this evening with Callie.

Suddenly feeling playful, Thomas sighed dramatically and murmured, "I hope I still remember the song by the time the Queen gets here. If I forget it..." His voice trailed off tragically and he gave Lavender a sad, forlorn look before he began to chuckle.

Lavender arched a blonde eyebrow at him, humor and something else lighting her face as the first colors of sunset were visible from Thomas' windows. "I think you like to tease, Court Singer. It is an attractive quality in a man, provided he doesn't take too great a pleasure in it and over-use the practice." She smiled, catlike and mysterious. "But it seems that you like to be teased in return, and that is well. Teasing keeps the wit sharpened, does it not?"

"I suppose it does, at that," Thomas conceded. "And the best part of teasing—"

He was interrupted by a knock on the door. He smiled at Lavender, rose from the chair, and moved to open the door. Orchid and Carnation stood in the doorway, each carrying an ornate box: a backgammon board and pieces, and a chess board and pieces. The Selkie and the shy Goblin looked up at him, and blessed him with huge smiles as he greeted them with a bow of welcome.

Thomas moved aside and the Ladies entered. "Her Grace," Carnation announced in a breathless whisper, "asked us to keep you company in her absence, Thomas. We bring backgammon and chess—unless you prefer to be alone..."

Orchid nodded at Lavender, who was still sitting at the dining table. "Oh, thank you, Lavender, you brought Thomas' dinner. Her Majesty said that you would think of it without having to be asked."

If Lavender was annoyed by the arrival of her friends, she did not show it as Carnation walked toward the dining table with her box. Instead, Lavender looked at Thomas, her question obvious in the glow of her bright-blue eyes.

He seemed to consider for a long moment, scratching his chin and looking for an answer on the ceiling. It took her another moment to realize that he was, in fact, teasing her again. Once she knew it, and gave him a saucy pout, he laughed and told her: "Go ahead, you can tell them."

"Tell us what?" asked Orchid.

Lavender glanced at Thomas again to make sure she truly had his permission, and when he winked at her, she stood and proclaimed "Thomas has finished the new song! He finished it today! And as soon as he's played it for Her Grace, he will play it for us!"

The Ladies' collective uproar was gratifying. He groaned to himself as he mentally admitted how much he had needed external recognition of some sort for the amount of effort he'd put into the new song. But he couldn't help it, dammit; he wanted to see Callie's face as he sang it to her.

He wanted her to hear it right now.

What was more annoying, he forced himself to confess, was that he still needed the applause, some sense that the parts of his heart he'd woven into the music and the lyric were acceptable, were—and he felt his stomach clench as he recognized the truth of this—*worthy*. Worthy of her, yes, but also worthy of Thomas Lear.

The Thomas Lear he wanted to be.

He knew he should have come far enough down the road by this time to be able to do without the kind of approval he felt compelled to look for in this moment, but somehow he wasn't able to keep himself from sliding into the dark, insecure waters he worked hard to avoid. He still needed reassurance from some unnamed thing that stood apart in a place outside of himself, something to make him feel better about the new song, even though he was aware that the song was as pure a thing as he'd ever created. It was perfect, he was sure of it. He didn't need Callie or anyone else to tell him so; still, the ugly truth was that he needed the attention, the praise, and the applause. He needed it badly.

Hello, Thomas, you pathetic fraud. Who are you trying to fool this time? The Monster In His Head was instantly alive and awake, and it was hungry.

It began feeding on him. He would never be free of it.

Thomas shuddered as a familiar, sharp stab of disgust and self-loathing knifed him in the same loving and aching heart from which the music had come not all that long ago.

He was startled to notice that Orchid was at his side. "Thomas, are you unwell?" she asked, concern evident in her dark eyes.

"I'm fine, fine," he mumbled, taking a breath and noticing that Lavender and Carnation were still chirping somewhere behind him about the new song. "It's okay." He took a deep breath and put on a standard smile. "It is."

The small Selkie did not look convinced.

Thomas gestured at the box still in her hands. "Is that backgammon?" he asked, his voice shaking only a little.

She nodded. "Would you like to play?"

"Sure."

Orchid inclined her head toward the dining table, where Carnation had placed the box that held the chess set. "Unless you would rather play chess?"

"Hell no!" replied Thomas in a haste that would have made Guardian roar with laughter. His bleak mood was dissipating as quickly as it had appeared. Relieved, Thomas felt himself slide into a sardonic smile as he felt himself start to relax again. "According to *some* people, I should not be allowed to play chess. Let's play backgammon. At least I'll have a chance of winning."

"Perhaps," Orchid said with a bow. "Although it is only fair to tell you that I am considered an excellent opponent."

"Oh, great," Thomas gave her a mock frown. "Want to spot me a couple of points?

"No," Orchid snickered, less delicately than he expected.

"Uh-oh..."

It was late. The stars had danced in the night sky while the Court Singer and his Queen had danced in his bed. Now the night and the lovers were serene.

"I still don't understand why you have to leave," Thomas said.

Her Grace propped herself up on her elbows, and smiled at him. "I still don't understand why you don't understand."

"Stop playing with my brain." He tried for a growl, but it came out as a chuckle. "Just explain it again, please, Callie." Reaching for her, he gathered her in his arms and settled in for the rest of the conversation.

"It's simple. My niece, who is the daughter of...ScarF's...elder sister and who is queen by her marriage to the king of Elvenwood in the Eastern Kingdom, is soon to have a child. It is possible that the child will be next in line for the throne—after Guardian, of course.

"It is the duty of the King and Queen to be present at all royal births that have a direct impact on the line of succession...or as soon as can be after the event." Her brown eyes sparkled as she looked into his. "It will also be a merry pleasure. It has been a long time since there has been a royal child...and even longer since I have held one in my arms."

He studied her eyes. "Is this painful for you?"

"No. It is a source of joy and delight. All that went before has very little power to wound me, or any of us, except perhaps the King." She shrugged against him. "The mother-to-be is dear to me, and her child will be precious to all of us. We will greet the child on her first day –- the child is a girl –- and we will give her gifts worthy of her place among us."

Thomas was thinking about this. "So when do you leave?

"By moonrise tomorrow night."

"How long will you be gone?"

"No more than a fortnight." She crinkled her face at him. "That's *two weeks*, Thomas."

"I know how long a fortnight is, Your Sarcastic Grace. You and the *King* are going together?" He was not at all comfortable at the thought of this, but he couldn't have said exactly why. He knew she had been truthful about her relationship—or *non-relationship*—with her husband, and he understood that they did not deal with each other often or well. Something bothered him somewhere about it all, but because he couldn't frame the issue, he set it aside and listened as Callie explained.

"We have spoken, and have decided that this is an appropriate occasion for a Rade. We will Progress across the land, and greet the Folk as we go. It has been many long years since the Folk have seen their King and Queen ride among them. I am not unaware that I have been lax in my duty in this way. So we will accomplish several important tasks at the same time, which is often a good thing."

With affection, he rubbed her shoulder. "A Faerie Rade, though...that would be something to see."

She swatted his hand. "Not something for mortals to see, and especially not something for *you* to see."

"I've seen a Faerie Rade," Thomas countered. "Well...I've seen the painting by Paton, anyway."

"Good for you," she replied with a snicker.

"The painting...is that what a Rade looks like?"

Callie thought about this for a long moment. "Actually, no."

Thomas grimaced, and Callie started to laugh. "Don't look like that. He did get the trees, the sky, the ground and the standing stones right."

"You're enjoying this," he accused.

"I am!" She rolled over and kissed him. "Now that that's settled, Thomas, why don't you play that lovely new song for me again?"

five

THE MERRY RESIDENTS of Elvenhome Castle lived in an uninterrupted rush of excitement over the next twenty-four hours. The Folk chosen to accompany the King and Queen hurried to make their personal preparations, aided in no small measure by the Folk who were not participating in the Royal Progress this time. It would be a relatively small Rade, with one hundred of the Fair Folk riding, walking, running, dancing or flying in the company of Their Majesties.

Food was prepared and packed, casks of wine, water and ale were loaded into carts, and horses were pampered.

In their respective Tower Rooms, Callie and the King each considered what it meant to have new royal magic into the world, and planned the work they each would do to welcome it.

The four King's Men who would remain behind were commanded to guard and protect the Lord Arrendel, to purposefully stay away from Thomas Lear, and to ensure that His Grace's orders regarding the mission Upworld to collect the so-called "Museum Faerie Artifacts" were obeyed. The King expected to see the Greencrystal safely in Elvenhome by the time he returned from Elvenwood.

Callie chose to take Dahlia, Carnation, Rose and Lavender to attend her. Dahlia, Carnation and Lavender loved riding horses, and Callie was pleased to have something to offer Lavender for pleasure. Rose would ride in the first carriage behind the group on horseback, which would be led by Boston.

Those staying behind at the castle had much to do in Her Grace's absence. Iris would supervise any minor but pressing matters of State that Guardian might refer to her. Juniper would track the Queen's Progress by speaking with the Water Sprites that visited the castle's loch. Violet was responsible for managing any messenger errands that Lord Guardian might require. Orchid was given the task of acting as Thomas' companion, in any way that suited the Court Singer and the sweet, dark-haired Selkie.

"He does not like backgammon, Your Grace," Orchid confided to Callie with a tiny grin. "Well, he does like to play. But I do not think he likes to lose."

The Queen grinned, too, and pointed to one of the two gowns that Lavender carried to her. "That one, please."

Approving, Lavender handed the gold-colored gown to Iris for packing, and took the silver one back to the Queen's Dressing Chamber.

Orchid had a serious question. "Your Majesty, about Thomas and the backgammon. To cheer him, should I let him win?"

Callie smiled. "Do what you think would be the most fun in the circumstances." The Selkie bowed her head in acknowledgement. "But if it were up to me, I'd let him lose the game until he learned how to best me!"

The moon rose as the Folk eagerly prepared to leave on their Rade.

Zodiac stood beside the King, receiving final instructions with a nod of his head. Boston was nearby, issuing directions to the guards and information about the journey to the King's Men. The Queen's Ladies were checking and rechecking the Royal Wardrobe, the large chests that held gifts for the newborn princess and her parents, and bidding their friends and lovers farewell.

Inside the castle, Iris, Violet, Juniper and Orchid waited outside the tall, heavy oak main doors of the Throne Room. Two small side doors were, at that moment, guarded carefully by two of the King's Men.

Above and below the closed doors came a shimmering of green light. This was followed by a deep blue glow that joined and seemed to dance with the sparkling green. Words were being spoken at the far end of the Throne Room, in front of the double thrones. Neither the Ladies nor the Men could hear exactly what was said by the Queen or her Heir, but all knew that it was a sacred binding ritual that would empower Lord Guardian to fully rule in the High Queen's place during the temporary royal absence.

Iris observed Orchid. The pretty Selkie stood watching wide-eyed while the flashes of green and blue moved around the closed doors. "I had forgotten that this is your first time," Iris said.

Enchanted, Orchid nodded, taking it all in.

"Orchid, watch! Here it comes..."

The green light shimmered on the other side of the door, then faded away as the blue light gave an unmistakable, audible snap, then sparked and glimmered into a still deeper, crisper shade of blue.

The Selkie gasped. "That was beautiful!"

"It is, to be sure. That's that, then. All's well with the world, and Her Grace is off to the Eastern Kingdom."

"Thomas would have liked the bright lights, I think," Orchid said.

The older Lady put an arm around the younger, and gave her a quick squeeze as the voices of Queen and Guardian approached the door, rapidly discussing last-minute details. "Her Majesty and the Court Singer have said their farewells. He is in his rooms, with a very large pile of books and a healthy supply of wine. Between you and me, I believe he is more in favor of having bright lights shine for—and on—him." She winked at Orchid as the doors to the Throne Room opened. "And here's Her Grace, all ready to Progress through her kingdoms."

SITTING ON HIS couch, he sipped a nice, heady zinfandel and turned the page. He'd never heard of this story, but it was well-written, engaging, and it met his exacting, private standard for literary escapism: it took up about ninety-seven percent of his attention.

As he read on, that last three percent of his mind considered tonight's parting from Callie, which had occurred where he was sitting now. She'd been even more beautiful than ever, if such a thing were possible. She was happy and excited, eager to travel her kingdom and then see and hold the new royal child. He had seen the now-familiar Fey decorations on her skin move slowly across her cheekbones and cheeks when she laughed.

"Don't look so surly, my dear," Callie had giggled as she chucked him on the chin to get him to smile. "Taking you with me was never a possibility. You know that."

"I know. But it sounds like a great trip anyway. And—"

Callie had nodded and interrupted him. "Pay attention, please. Zodiac will be here, and will always have time to spend with you. And of course Guardian will remain here to ward Elvenhome while I am gone, which is no small task. He will manage things well." She took his face in her hands, and sighed. "Ah, Thomas, much as I wish to go to Elvenwood, I also wish that I did not have to leave you." She kissed him with a possessiveness that made his heart skip a beat. He held her tightly in his arms.

Just then, there was a tentative knock on Thomas' front door. Orchid, on the other side of it, spoke to someone in the hallway. "They are ready, Your Grace," she announced.

"Very well," Callie replied, just loud enough to be heard. "Tell them I'm coming." She kissed Thomas once more, and added in a whisper, "Write songs and sing them to the Folk, to keep all hearts merry and light. Sing any song that pleases you, and teach it, so that we will always have it.

"And be of comfort to Guardian if you can, Thomas. He values your friendship. Your presence will lighten the burden my absence places on him."

Thomas had nodded and squeezed her hand. With a last kiss, followed by a dazzling smile, Callie turned away and left without a backward glance.

THE NEXT EVENING, in Thomas' living room, the two men studied the chessboard on the dining table between them.

"Did you truly mean to put your knight there, Thomas?"

"Yes, I did," Thomas replied, eyeing his opponent with exactly the right air of indifference.

Guardian moved a castle, and removed a piece from the board. "So you didn't want to keep this bishop?"

Thomas scowled at Guardian, and then laughed in spite of himself as he finished up the whisky in the glass beside him. "I've either had too much whisky tonight, or not enough. I'm beginning to think I'm never going to beat you."

Guardian took a drink from his own glass and smiled. "Your game has much improved since our first one. You have to remember, too, that I've been playing chess longer than you have."

"Yeah," Thomas quipped, "That's a serious understatement." He grinned wickedly at his friend. "Did they even *have* chess when you were born?" he teased.

A sudden look of remembered delight blended with unspeakable sadness crossed Guardian's face, and he was silent.

Thomas was startled by the immediate change in the air. "What did I say?"

The strained look disappeared as quickly as it had come. Now Guardian smiled a sad, crooked smile, and shrugged at Thomas, as though it didn't matter. "That's something Maggie would say. And often *has* said, when she's trying to distract me from something she doesn't want to talk about." The look in Guardian's eyes told Thomas that his friend still took the separation from his lady rather hard.

"I'm sorry, Guardian."

"All is well enough, Thomas. It is as it is. I'll continue to go to her as often as I can, and stay as long as I dare."

"You miss her," Thomas offered.

Guardian nodded. "It's impossible not to. I have been looking for a way to—" He stopped speaking, and downed the last of his drink instead. "It doesn't matter." He poured himself another, and then reached over and poured one for Thomas, and motioned for him to drink.

"To women," Guardian toasted, but Thomas couldn't tell for certain if his friend was happy or sad about it.

"Women," Thomas said, drinking. He looked down at the chessboard and groaned. "At least we're not drinking to this game."

"No," Guardian retorted, "we are drinking our way *through* it."

"Which is the best thing I can say about it," Thomas complained.

Guardian snorted. "It's your move."

Thomas closed his eyes and shook his head. "Good. Can we stop?"

Guardian nodded, looking at Thomas. "We can. Are you bored, or drunk, or only not in the mood to lose again?"

Thomas opened his eyes and shot Guardian a mock glower. "Very funny. No, I wanted to ask you something. I don't know if I should, but I figure either you will talk or you won't."

An eyebrow lifted in interest, Guardian said nothing as Thomas pushed the chessboard away and laid his hands on the table in front of him.

"I haven't mentioned this to anyone, not even Callie," Thomas began. "It's driving me crazy." He met Guardian's gaze. "I understand if it's not something I'm supposed to know about, but—who's Terena?"

If Guardian had been anticipating any particular topic of discussion, this was not it. He made no effort to conceal his astonishment. "Terena?"

"Yeah. Terena," Thomas repeated. "Can you tell me about her?"

Guardian eyed Thomas for a long moment, considering. "Why," he asked, his voice sounding careful, "have you not talked with Callie?"

Thomas ran a hand through his brown curls. "I've been asking myself the same question. At one point, Terena asked me not to say anything to anyone, so I haven't. I'm sure she's not here. Before you arrived I made a point of talking to her. If she's here, she answers me. She didn't, so..." he wound down, looking at Guardian for help.

The Water Faerie drew in a heavy breath, and took his time releasing it. He watched Thomas for a long moment, and then said, with resignation, "Tell me what you know, and I'll fill in the rest."

So Thomas told Guardian about his small and sometimes confusing encounters with Terena, the first here in his rooms, the second in the garden outside, and about their regular weekly afternoon discussions about poetry and music. "She's told me some things, but I don't understand a lot of it. I don't get who she is, how she fits in around here, and why she's invisible." Unable to help himself, Thomas burst into a self-conscious ironic grin at what he'd just said in all seriousness. "You know, there was a time that I would only have been able to say that out loud if I was stoned out of my mind."

Guardian laughed. "It seems to me that you've acclimated rather well to life with the Fey."

"Uh-huh. Druggies, drunks and delusional liars seem to have a happy predisposition for functioning well in Faerie, Guardian," Thomas said, sarcasm running rampant for a moment.

"Poets and musicians, too," Guardian added with a chuckle.

"Isn't that what I just said?" Thomas retorted with only a touch of his old habit of self-loathing, which he decided to save for later. "So, tell me about Terena."

Guardian pushed his chair back, reached for his glass, and stood up. He moved with unselfconscious grace to the couch, and beckoned Thomas to follow. When Guardian was settled, and Thomas was comfortable in the easy chair across from him, they both took another drink, and Guardian spoke:

"The first thing: the Lady Terena is not a secret. You can ask Callie about her. It's something of a courtesy to not discuss Terena, and not just because she might overhear it. She was once a delicate subject with Callie, and with a lot of us, for reasons that will become evident." Guardian paused, trying to decide where to start. He shrugged. "I suppose it's best to begin at the beginning.

"The long and short of it is that Terena mortal. Mortal. She's lived in Faerie all of her life."

"She told me she is mortal, but I don't know if I believed her." Thomas interjected. "How did she get here?"

Guardian's eyes hardened but his voice remained cool and objective. "She was brought here from Upworld when she was a newborn."

"Brought?" Thomas considered this, his mind working around the alcohol. "You mean stolen?"

Guardian nodded. "That depends on which story you believe, but that's the foundation of the tale."

"Who stole her?"

The Water Faerie groaned; Thomas almost didn't hear it. "It brings me no joy to say this: it was the King."

"ScarF stole an infant from Upworld? And got away with it?" Thomas was appalled. "I'm beginning to really hate that fucking bastard. He did that?"

Frowning, Guardian nodded again. "He is the High King. And he seemed to have...his reasons. The Folk were horrified. Such behavior is legend about Faerie, of course, but we have never really done much of that sort of thing. In any event, he arranged to have the child cared for. He was an attentive and doting 'uncle,' for lack of a better term. He adored the child. She was a remarkable beauty, and smart, and she grew up adoring him in return.

"The Folk were amazed at how much happier the King was in those days, how much more focused he was on his royal duties, how much more approachable he was, how he interacted more with the Folk at Court—"

Thomas couldn't help it; he had to ask. "Were things easier between him and Callie, then?"

"Not easier with Callie, no." Guardian admitted. "Nothing was soothed between them. She was upset by his abduction of the child, and perhaps by his attachment to her. But since he was in a gladder frame of mind, he was less of a trial for her in other areas, and I suppose that counted for something. The harsh flashes between them didn't surface over Terena.

"She grew into a beautiful woman. She is sweet, clever, endearing, and funny, too. She'd been raised as one of the

Folk, knew our traditions, lived our life. She was as Fey as any of the rest of us. Everyone loved her. Especially the King."

Something alarming was occurring to Thomas as he remembered Terena's talk about her beloved.

"Guardian, when Terena spoke of her lover, she was talking about ScarF?"

Guardian nodded. "When she grew up, she made it known that she was in love with him, and that was that. She was not quite twenty years old. They lived together quietly in Elvenmere Castle. They were happy. They used to come to Elvenhome several times a year, and each year she seemed to have grown lovelier. An enchanting face, and an even more beautiful heart. He loved her deeply."

Struggling to get his head around the pieces of the story, Thomas grasped for the threads to put it together. "Wait...you've seen her?"

"Of course I've seen her." Guardian's careful words seemed doubly measured before he spoke them. He knew where this was going.

"She wasn't always invisible?"

"No."

"Oh. Okay. Well, how long ago did ScarF first bring her here?"

"About one hundred fifty years ago, give or take." Guardian's answer was passive.

"She's mortal? And she's a hundred and fifty years old?" Thomas sputtered in confusion and a little fear.

"She is," reassured Guardian. "Remember, she's lived in Faerie her whole life, and has eaten nothing but Faerie food. She's one of us, except she's still physically mortal. So she has, of course, aged. More slowly, certainly, than a normal mortal living Upworld would, but she has aged. And she seems to be losing her..." He paused. "Mentally, I mean."

Thomas frowned, but with compassion. "There's something kind of *off* when she talks sometimes. Confusion, but not exactly."

He braced himself for the hard question and realized, when he looked over at his friend, that Guardian was braced as well, waiting. Face cringing, Thomas asked it as if he were not quite ready to know the answer, but he wanted to know anyway. "Why is Terena invisible, Guardian?"

It took a long time for Guardian to respond. When he did, he met Thomas' gaze, and told the truth. "Eventually Terena grew older...old to the degree that the King found that he could no longer bear to look at her. He couldn't stand to see Terena's fantastic beauty so withered and lost in the folds of old age. In what must have been a difficult moment, he cast an invisibility on her, so the sight of his lover's fading would not wound him so." The sadness in Guardian's voice all but choked him.

"She got old, so he made her invisible so he wouldn't have to *look* at her?" Thomas gasped in disbelief.

Guardian's voice was calm and quiet, and he studied the diminished contents of his whisky glass rather than meeting Thomas' glare. "That is perhaps a harsher way of expressing it."

"That bastard!" Thomas shouted. "She loved him her entire life, she still loves him now, and this is what she gets?"

Guardian said nothing.

"How long has the poor woman been invisible?" Thomas shouted.

Guardian looked as though he'd been struck, but he looked at his friend and answered the question. "Not quite fifteen years," he said.

"Fifteen years!" Thomas bellowed. "That bastard! Someone ought to—"

"Ought to *what*?" interrupted Guardian, his brows furrowed in a blend of misery and irritation. "Tell the King that he was wrong to steal the child? That's been done, for a century and a half. Tell the King that he's a selfish bastard for putting his own feelings above the feelings of another? I believe that he is fully aware of the wrong that he has done, and has carried the weight of it from that first day to this one.

"Thomas, we do not age as mortals do. He had to watch his beloved fade for a long while, and it broke his heart. I know he suffered and grieved over the natural, mortal changes that life brought to his precious Terena; I was there. Should we blame the King, or blame Terena, for the unkind turning of the seasons of love?"

Fighting to control himself, Guardian shuddered and took a deep breath. After a moment he refocused on Thomas, and tried to smile. "No, Thomas, no. We cannot peer into the struggles of anyone else's life and presume to determine what makes sense, what is most right, and what is the best good for them and for the situations they create for themselves. We cannot justly point to this moment or that event and say how it should be, or how it should not have been. That belongs to the lovers, and to them alone. Regardless of our feelings on the matter, it is not for us to judge."

He sighed then, and got up to get more whisky. "You are a troubador. You know, far better than almost anyone, a basic truth: all we can really do is hear a tale, and then smile—or weep—as the tale reveals itself to the yearning places in our own hearts."

Thomas was moved to a sad stillness as he finished his drink. "I think your friend ScarF is a miserable, selfish goddamned bastard," he said with a barren finality.

Guardian's mouth quirked; it was not quite a smile, but a faint touch of irony lightened his face. "I know you do. But the only significant issue in the matter is that Terena does not share your opinion."

"You said it yourself. She's losing it. Her mind is going."

"Not the point, Thomas."

"Dammit," Thomas snarled.

"Precisely," Guardian conceded.

"CALL THAT. AND I raise you...something *shiny*," Thomas said to Zodiac at the Friday Afternoon Poker Game. He had a full house in his hand and was feeling lucky. He tossed a sparkling button from one of Callie's gowns into the pot and gave the Lord High Chamberlain a smug look.

"I'm out," Zodiac sighed, and folded.

Thomas watched as Guardian studied his cards. His friend had taken time away from his duties as the Regent to play cards, even though he was still terrible at it.

"How many cards would you like, My Lord?" asked the dealer, a Wood Sprite bearing the Lear-given name of "Rome." Rome was one of the castle guards generally responsible for overseeing the Queen's privacy when she was alone in her Tower Room. Part of the Royal Guard Poker Rotation roster, he took his momentary role as the dealer with far more gravity that necessary. Somehow Thomas found this almost endearing, and laughed to himself. He'd been around Callie too long, he mused with a grin.

"Hmmmm...four, I think."

Thomas and Zodiac exchanged a knowing look and waited as Guardian looked at the four new cards Rome dealt him. "Good!" Guardian exclaimed, then realized he'd spoken aloud. "Oh...damn..."

Everyone folded, laughing.

"I am hopeless at this," Guardian laughed.

"You are," agreed Thomas, all courtesy. "But I won't mention that too often, or you'll remind everyone about how well I play chess."

"Wise man." Guardian smiled as he added: "I had a royal straight flush, Gentlemen."

"We know," everyone at the table replied in unison.

There was a new player today, and Thomas was fascinated by him. He was a Spriggan; Guardian had introduced him to Thomas as "Menace," a name he'd earned Upworld, although neither had given much of an explanation about that. It was clear that there was a bond between Guardian and Menace. Thomas presumed, based on the way Menace reacted to Guardian, that they had a long history. The Spriggan appeared to be both deeply respectful to and personally familiar with Guardian, to whom he only referred as "My Lord," even when playing cards.

Thomas was grateful he didn't have to come up with a new name for the Spriggan. He also figured he'd eventually come to understand Menace's connection with Guardian.

Menace had never played poker before, but he was a fast learner. His calculating, dark eyes moved over the table, and at the cards in his hands. Thomas couldn't help but watch the constant twitch of Menace's long fingers, which were mesmerizing rather than alarming. In the first few hands, once the rules had been explained to him, Menace had done more watching than active playing, and he listened when given suggestions by the others. By the fourth hand, Menace was taking his share of the pot. His shrill voice belied the sharp and powerful mind behind his eyes, which took up most of the real estate on his hairy face.

"Dealer takes one," Menace said, as he looked around the table. He also took the hand, queens full of tens.

Buick gathered up the cards and shuffled. He loved card games and had become one of the weekly regulars. He was a handsome, athletic Elf that sometimes jogged with Thomas in silence unless they were in Thomas' own garden. He was not brilliant, but he was friendly and had a ready smile. He usually had a clever comeback when the men bantered and bullshitted during their poker games. Thomas liked that Buick was uncomplicated and easy to get along with. They shared an interest in music, and Thomas learned a bit about falconry from Buick, who had two gyrfalcons that he was proud and fond of. There was locker-room inference that Buick and the Lady Lavender were an item, although Thomas didn't think he had seen them together.

Today, though, Thomas thought Buick seemed a little distracted. He wondered what was on Buick's mind that could pull him so far out of the poker game. His curiosity was such that he almost asked Buick what was going on. Then Buick dealt him a straight flush, and Thomas' friendly question about the Elf's mindset evaporated.

Buick looked at his own hand, smiled about the four Jacks that looked back at him, and wondered why his father had sent word that he wanted to see him tonight. He hadn't seen his father in several weeks, which, in light of his father's position, was not unnatural. The message he had received had been written in his father's own strong hand, so Buick had no reason to think that his father—who was, in truth, quite old—was ailing. Buick was certain that he had done nothing in particular to inspire irritation, either, so that was all right. What could be on his father's mind?

Zodiac's ale-tinged voice brought him back to the card game: "Buick? Buick! Do you think that if you stare at them long and hard enough, those cards will transform themselves into aces?"

LORD EMMEL, WHO had long held the honor of being the High King's Chief Man, sat in a basket chair in the center of his private gardens as he spoke to his son.

"This is the King's charge, Borril, and after only a little persuasion, he has granted me leave to give the responsibility for its success to you. When you present to His Majesty the items you will have retrieved from Upworld, he will be greatly pleased. It is at that time that I shall ask His Majesty to allow me to relinquish a great many of my duties."

Borril looked startled. "Father? Are you unwell?"

Chuckling, Emmel shook his head. "I am only beginning to feel the tiredness that comes with old age, Boy. I shall be far less tired when you have completed the King's business, and found favor with him. At that very moment I will suggest to him that you be considered to take my place as one of the King's Men."

Borril's eyes brightened. "You would step away from your office so that I might step up?"

Emmel nodded. "It is one of the privileges of office, and, I dare say, one of the duties of family. Now stop looking like you are about to fly into a daydream, and pay close attention. There must not be a single mistake, or even a thread of mischief. Do I make myself understood?"

"Yes, Father. No mistakes, no mischief."

six

LEADING THE RADE in the coming twilight, the Wood Sprites sang multiple layers of ancient Fey harmony to announce the coming of the King and Queen as they Progressed through the forest. The trees and their residents woke and nodded in respect as Their Graces rode among them, their open hands held out in blessing.

Thomas would love listening to this, Callie thought. *It would inch him close to madness, but he would love it anyway.* She smiled, considering how the wonder and pleasure of the moment would slide across his face and shine from his eyes. *And, after he'd tasted the magic of it, oh, the song he would write...*

Cassane interrupted her reverie with a contemptuous snort.

"Yes, I know," she allowed with a whisper of a sigh, and returned her attention to her duty.

Behind the Queen rode Lavender, wrapped in a happy reverie of her own. She could imagine Thomas sky-clad, walking toward her in the gardens behind his apartments, a guitar in one hand and a harp in the other. *Which shall I play for you, Sonorielle?* he would ask her, for one day soon he would know her True Name. She liked being called "Lavender," because it was the name he had chosen for her. Still, having him speak her True Name would be a large step toward holding on to him forever. It would certainly prove to Her Grace and the rest of the Court that she loved him beyond question. In return, Thomas' love for her would keep him happy, too, through the long years he would live with her in Faerie. He would write songs for her, and sing them to her when they were alone...

"Lavender?" Carnation's low, gravelly voice pulled her focus. The shy Goblin's horse walked next to Lavender's, behind the Queen. "Lavender, we are nearly at Elvenreach. Dahlia says Her Grace has chosen the blue gown for the feast."

"Yes, the blue one," Lavender confirmed.

"We cannot find it in the wagon. Rose has looked everywhere. Are you certain you packed it for the journey?"

The blonde Elf sighed, and her tail twitched in quiet frustration. She turned her horse around and rode back with Carnation toward the wagon that carried Rose and the Queen's traveling wardrobe. Her gentle thoughts of Thomas Lear faded into the air.

ELVENREACH'S CASTLE GATES and doors were open in welcome to the High King and Queen. The Court and most of the villagers attended the feast in the Great Hall. King Lorim and Queen Dashya, rulers of the small but beautiful county bordered by Elvenhome and the vast Eastern Kingdom, had planned a wonderful night for the royal party. Imaginative food filled the tables, and there was music and dancing, followed by a drunken sing-along led by a Troll from the mountains in the northwest. When the Troll finally passed out under one of the tables, a pretty young Merrow sang hopeful songs about the wild oceans and finding a lost lover.

Callie, looking regal and beautiful in the blue gown, sat beside her husband. According to custom, she was sharing a plate and large golden goblet with him. "Someone might want to kick that Troll," the King said, biting into an apple.

"To make sure he hasn't drunk himself to death?" Callie asked.

"No..."

"Then why?"

"Because he sings rather badly. Isn't there a law about that somewhere? And that damned song about the Fachan and the Fern is going to give me nightmares."

Husband and wife eyed each other for a moment, and then burst into laughter.

Callie lowered her voice. "You know, despite all, you have not changed. You still have a wicked sense of fun. It is good to see it."

The King lowered his voice as well; they were both aware that they were being observed, however covertly, by all the Folk gathered in the Hall. "Madam, I have changed, then changed back, and changed again, many times, for such is my nature. But if my behavior of late pleases you, well, then, that is a good thing."

She studied him for a moment, and her smile grew a shade broader. "They are all watching us, as they did when we first met. As if they cannot believe we can sit together and enjoy a feast. I do not know whether I should be happy in their pleasure, or wary of their wishes."

"Let us confound them. It will do them good, and it is usually entertaining."

"You only tease to distract all listeners from the truth: you have great love and care for each and all of the Folk."

"Which is helpful if one is their King, don't you agree?"

Callie laughed. "You can be a delight."

"And you, My Lady, can be delightfully confusing."

She did not understand. "What do you mean?"

His answer was soft, and without challenge or judgment. "I am of course aware of the name your Court Singer has given me. I know that it is used, albeit sparingly, among the Folk. But I have not heard you use that name, nor is it one you have been heard to speak."

She met his eyes calmly. "It is right that he named you, for that is the way this game is played in order to protect True Names."

"Just so," he replied, his voice quiet.

"In his defense, Thomas did not know who you were when he first encountered you. And perhaps because he found you somewhat intimidating, he was more reactionary than elegant and creative when you approached him."

"I cannot disagree with your premise."

"What, then?"

His smile grew slowly across his no-longer-handsome face. "The name does not offend me. That it offends you is a small gift I did not anticipate."

She may have blushed; if she did, neither of them acknowledged it. "I have indeed referred to you as 'ScarF,' My Lord. But," and here a slow smile inched across Callie's face, "only with Thomas, and only when discussing something relevant to you...so as not to have you, in conversation, confused with Cassane or Guardian or a chair or..."

She was laughing now, and he began to laugh with her. For a moment, it was as though time and pain and sorrow had never stepped into the spaces between them.

"My Lord...look..." Callie indicated Boston with a subtle nod of her head. "It would seem that our dear friend has a secret mission in mind."

Boston, who had been seated toward the end of the long trestle table that sat above the salt, was making a subtle exit.

"Watch, My Lady," the King whispered. "Let us see what he is up to."

As he moved through the Folk in the Hall, Boston seemed to be aiming for a side door at the far end. Just before he reached it, a tall, beautiful, black-haired lady happened to meet up with him. After casually glancing around to see that no one was paying any attention, Boston opened the door, and the lady hurried through it. One last look around, and Boston followed her.

"Well done!" the King approved with a laugh.

"Yes," agreed the Queen. She shot the King a smirk. "You, I hear, have never called me 'Callie," Your Grace."

"Of course I haven't, Your Grace." He ticked off items on his fingers. "First, I don't have to play your game, as we agreed many long years ago, provided I stay out of the way. Which I generally have done.

"Second, it's a damned silly name, unimaginative, and doesn't suit you at all."

Callie shrugged amiably as he continued. "Third, even if it did suit you, I doubt I could force myself to refer to you in that way, even to distinguish you from Cassane, or "Guardian" or a chair..."

She couldn't help herself. She laughed in delight, unconcerned that the eyes of their immediate world were on the two of them. The Folk were thrilled that Their Graces were enjoying each other's company in public.

"And finally, My Lady...it's a damned silly name."

"You already said that."

"So I did."

The Queen crinkled her nose, and dropped the gauntlet. "Oh, don't be such an old *ScarF*..."

The surprise that registered on the King's face was considerable.

Everyone who heard the Queen's taunting held their breath for a fraction of an instant. What had she done? What would he do?

It was later whispered in private among the Queen's Ladies and the King's Men—and most of the Folk present in the Hall that night—that it had been difficult to decide whether it was the King or the Queen who had laughed more merrily, and longest.

BORRIL PACED HIS father's study as he spoke. "This is going to be both easy and hard. But we will please His Majesty; that is the most important thing."

"Yes," Emmel allowed. "The King would also appreciate the return of as much Elf-shot as you find, as well as his amethyst dagger, and any of the Queen's jewelry that has found its way to that art gallery. Remember that you are to take nothing else from the place, only that which rightly belongs to the King. But your focus is the Greencrystal Pendant. Bring that back, and all else, as we say, is good wine in the cellar. The King will be pleased, and his gratitude will honor our house." Emmel poured himself a goblet of water, and studied his son. "Tell me of your revised plan for the mission."

Emmel listened as Borril explained how he was going to collect the King's belongings from Upworld, in Glasgow. When Borril finished detailing his planned course of action, he sat down and waited for his father's opinions.

"I do not think that having only Bogles to do the work is your best choice overall," Emmel advised. "Perhaps take two, and fill the rest of the party with members of other races."

"I've spent a day and a half considering every possible combination. The Goblin race has always made the best thieves in Faerie."

"Spriggans are better," the old man pointed out.

"All right, that is a fact. But Spriggans are almost impossible to manage; that is also a fact. Pixies will never do, they talk too much. Dwarfs will get distracted by shiny things, sorry to say, Father, and there will be many shiny things where we are going. Goblins—even the more placid HobGoblins—grouped together are too argumentative, and that gets in the way of the work. Sprites always think they know best, and will not take orders. Trolls and Giants are out entirely, of course."

"What about Elven Folk? You could lead our own kind Upworld and—"

Borril frowned. "I thought of that, too, Father. Our race does not often participate in this type of stealth work, although it is true that—if asked for help with the King's business—some would certainly come to my aid." He eyed his father, trying to find a way to say what his pride would not allow him to admit easily. "I fear I could not command other Elven Folk. I lack...something. But I can command Bogles in this task."

Emmel sighed. "It is unworthy to speak it aloud, yet it is a true thing. Unmonitored, unguided, Bogles added to any recipe too easily equals mischief. Bless them, when they are not busy and focused, they get themselves into trouble."

"The issue is already resolved. I have spoken with a Goblin, one Mazzin of Elvenglen. He and five of his company, who are all Bogles, will accompany me Upworld. We have agreed: Mazzin will keep the company in line, and will defer to me in all things. Thus I will succeed with the retrieval, and all will be well."

Emmel thought for a moment. "I do not know this Mazzin of Elvenglen. Who is his family? Why is he in Elvenhome? How do you know him?"

Borril smiled; fathers always worried about their sons. "Mazzin made his presence known to me only two days ago. He is a trustworthy soul, and will take direction from me," he reassured Emmel. "We have talked, and shared wine. He is intelligent, resourceful, he has been Upworld many times. His Bogles will obey him without question. As a matter of fact, Father, just this evening, Mazzin sent his company Upworld to gather information, to confirm the timing, methods and details of the venture so that all will go according to plan. There will be no mischief."

"Excellent. That will please the King." Emmel ticked one more thing off his mental list. "You will be prepared to go in three days' time?"

"Yes, Father."

"And you sent word to Sheila at the Queensgate that you will be using her stables for the horses."

Borril hesitated, but for only a moment; Fair Folk do not lie. Remembering his conversation with Mazzin earlier that same afternoon, Borril told a version of the truth. "I sent the messenger when you told me to."

"Well done," said Emmel.

As he listened to his son's plan, Emmel found himself wondering why Goblins and Bogles from Elvenglen (the province located at the northernmost tip of Faerie, most of whose residents have always had strong ties to the Unseelie Court), would happen to find themselves here in Elvenhome at a time when both the King and the Queen were not in residence, and would be away for a full fortnight.

Still, Borril's was a sound, well-considered plan, and only good would come of it—so long as he kept a solid, firm hold on the Bogles and their leader, this Mazzin fellow. Emmel settled back in his chair and imagined His Majesty's face when the Greencrystal Pendant was neatly returned to him by Emmel's only son.

The old man smiled.

ALTHOUGH HE MISSED Callie, especially at bedtime, the solitary side of Thomas Lear's nature contentedly asserted itself as he spent a good deal of time alone in his apartments reading, writing poetry, thinking, playing his guitars, and composing music. He felt clearer of mind and genuinely lighter of heart these days than perhaps at any other time in his life. He was in touch with his creative gifts; music and words flowed from depths he thought were closed to him. Not for the first time, he

94

marveled at how far he'd come back to regain his balance. Callie had opened the doors for him, and he had at last remembered how to find his way through them.

It shocked him, now, how stupid and carelessly self-destructive he'd been before coming to Scotland. He thought about the road he'd been on, considered its beginnings, and marveled that he had been damned lucky to not have killed himself one way or another, or—what seemed even worse, in light of the good work he'd done since he'd come to Elvenhome—utterly destroyed his ability to write songs and sing them.

He had always known he could create a little magic with his music, and he'd liked the thought of that. He'd traded nicely on it as he'd made a name for himself in the recording industry. He was so good at it that most people thought that the man who'd written the songs *was* the man in the songs. While not necessarily true, or rarely so, it had created and maintained the famous romantic troubadour image of Thomas Lear, Rock Star. He'd held audiences in his hands, and still held on to the music; he'd always told himself that the Lear magic that audiences paid for belonged to him alone.

Now he recognized it for what it was. He readily accepted that the personal angst-to-poetry (both Callie and Terena had simply called it "energy") he translated from his heart to his guitar was as essential for his own balance and happiness as it was for whoever listened to it. It no longer mattered to him that what he sang and played belonged both to him and to his audience; he could continue to sing his songs, and be glad about it. Anyone who enjoyed the music could and would take it with them, and make it their own.

Creative transactions, he thought. Yeah, he was learning a lot these days. Especially about stuff he thought he'd already completely understood.

Sprawled on his couch, he lifted a book from the big pile stacked on the table beside him. He smiled, and wondered where the magic would take him next.

"I CONFESS, FATHER, that I am concerned about the Greencrystal Pendant," Borril told Emmel as they sat at their dinner in Emmel's rooms the following evening.

"Why?"

"The tales about it do not inspire one to be willing to touch it without some sort of protection. Your stories were somewhat frightening, as I recall."

"What, Borril, the tales I told you when you were a *wean*?"

Embarrassed, Borril nodded.

Emmel laughed. "Borril, those were tales to make a small young Elf mind his elders. The Greencrystal is not a danger, for all its wild beauty. It was made by our King and Queen, and it is powerful to be sure—but you cannot awaken its magic, so do not fear collecting it for His Majesty."

"I cannot be harmed by its power?"

"No." Emmel seemed clear on this point, Borril noticed.

"Why not?"

"Because you do not know the Word that must awaken it."

"What if I could guess it?"

"Do not be such an ass, Borril. First, you would never discover the Word. Second, even if you did carry the secret of the Word, you would not wish to awaken the Greencrystal without permission. Third, by its very nature, the Greencrystal's power would require a great deal of energy from anyone who dared to wield it, including Their Majesties. As you do not naturally possess that kind of power, you would likely harm yourself—or

96

others—with the effort. You would not wish to be answerable to His Majesty for such a thing, would you?"

"No, Father," Borril said, telling the truth.

Another thought occurred to Borril as he handed his father a basket of bread. "Do *you* know the Word that can awaken the Greencrystal?"

Emmel broke a piece of off the end of the loaf, dipped it in the last of his stew, and popped it to his mouth. It took Borril a moment to realize that his father had not responded to his question.

"You do! You know the Word to awaken it!"

Emmel continued chewing his bread.

"Father! You know!"

"When the Greencrystal Pendant was created, all of the Men serving His Majesty knew the Word. There. Be impressed and amazed, dance merrily on the supper table to prove it, and then pour me some more ale."

"You will not tell me the Word."

"Of course not. You have no need of the information in order to do the King's business."

"Are you certain of that?"

"I am."

THE RADE PROGRESSED through the Eastern Kingdom, under a sunny sky. The only member of the merry traveling party who was not enjoying the day was Cassane, who had awakened in a foul mood and scowled at Callie one time too many since breakfast. Since they could not come to terms about whatever or whoever was annoying the stallion, Callie had opted to walk this morning instead of ride.

The King walked beside her, followed by her Ladies and his Men as they strolled through another fragrant forest.

"The country seems larger than I recall," he confided to her, feigning surprise as he looked around.

97

Callie's apparent nonchalance was given the lie by the giggle in her voice. "Your Grace, I believe it has always been this large. I find it quite shocking that you do not realize the size of your own kingdom."

He turned to her, and would have said something playful in return, but stopped himself when his eyes met the gentle laughter in hers. He didn't want to ruin the moment.

He said nothing.

They walked in silence for several minutes, taking in the sights, sounds and scents of the beautiful woodland.

A tiny, winged faerie flew up to them, carrying a buttercup. She bowed, and handed the yellow flower to the King. Then she moved to Callie's face, and kissed her on the cheek before she bowed again and fluttered away.

"It is good to be King," the King murmured, appreciating the perfection of the buttercup and the affection with which it had been proffered.

"And Queen," Callie replied. "Which brings up, again, a conversation that we should have. We have avoided it, but it should not be set aside now, should it?"

He shook his head.

Callie opened the discussion directly: "Arrendel should be released from his obligation as Heir Apparent."

"He does love the mortal, then? Enough to step away from his birthright and duty?"

"He loves her; that is obvious. But I do not think it fair or true that he would step away from his role as heir with little care for the land and its Folk."

She stopped walking, and he stopped too. They nodded to their attendant Ladies and Men to continue past them, then moved out of the way of the parade. Standing together under a grizzled old hawthorn tree, they looked at each other, wrapped in a seriousness they had skirted since calling the truce.

"We must give him the opportunity to choose his path," whispered Callie. "He would never choose to leave us, and he would not choose to turn his back on his lady." She searched the king's eyes, and frowned. "It is uncharacteristic of him to turn his back in any direction; he has always felt things far too keenly. I rely on his goodness, but that is not the only quality a King must have to rule all the kingdoms steadily. His kindness keeps him from making difficult decisions quickly. He cannot bear the thought of causing harm. He sees all sides of a question, and his vision all too often keeps him from moving in one direction over another."

"You are right, My Lady. We must give him the freedom to consider ways to release himself from the line of ascendency of Faerie, if that is what his heart requires him to do."

Satisfied, Callie nodded. "I am pleased—and relieved— that you agree. So it is of great importance that we are about to meet the new Princess. We may find in her the solution to our situation."

"She does have the right lineage, and once we see her, and..." The King's voice trailed off as memories of another child, long gone, filled his mind unbidden. He cast the memory aside with an effort, and, when he looked over at his wife, saw that in her own way, she had shared the same sad memory. They gazed at each other for a moment, and resumed their walk in silence, each occupied by their own thoughts.

"On the other hand..." The King began.

"Yes?"

"We could cause quite a stir, don't you think, if we elect not to get to the point where we must fade and die." He winked at her, a soft touch of humor replacing the remembered sadness that had threatened to bruise his heart. "Your Grace, we could rule forever. What do you say to that?"

Callie's eyebrows shot up. "Oh great gods! You are impossible!"

"Don't you think," he chuckled, "it would be great fun to try?"

"IT WILL WORK."

"It will not."

"It will. All you have to do is what I told you."

"He said we do not need to know, and I believe him."

"I understand, My Good Lord. I am certain that you are right. However, I am afraid that my friends will not feel safe enough near the thing."

"That is ridiculous," Borril sniffed, but he was beginning to have his own doubts about that.

"We cannot know what not to say unless you discover the Word."

"My father said—"

"I know what he said. Nevertheless, we will not participate unless—"

"Oh, all right, damn you." He considered this again. "And you think it will work?"

Mazzin's unattractive black eyes glittered. "It worked on you just now, did it not?"

THE NIGHT WAS inching carelessly toward sunrise when Borril finally poured enough of Mazzin's North Kingdom ale into his father to make his move.

"This has been fun, Boy. I am quite merry and drunk," Emmel laughed from the warmth of his favorite chair. "More than likely, I am also a disgrace."

"You are indeed drunk, Father, but you are never a disgrace," Borril reassured him.

Emmel patted his son's face. "You are my only son. And you are going to please His Majesty. You will bring great honor to our family."

"I will," Borril agreed. "Except..."

Emmel tilted his head. "Except what?"

"Except I am not going to be able to retrieve the items for the King. I cannot do this work, Father. Someone else will have to lead the mission Upworld."

Even through the warm, welcoming blur of drunkenness, Emmel understood the situation. "What has happened? You are prepared to leave on the morrow! Why will you not perform this service for our King?"

Borril stood up, stretched, and looked at his feet so he could avoid his father's scrutiny. "The Bogles are fearful that they might say the Word in casual conversation, so they will not accompany me. I need them." He looked harder at his feet. "I, too, am still afraid of the power of the Greencrystal, although I have tried to be courageous for your sake, Father, and for the honor of our family."

There was a heavy silence for what seemed to be a long while. Borril held on to as much of the truth as he could find, while Emmel thought as quickly as his ale-muddled brain allowed about how best to resolve this new twist.

Neither father nor son was happy now. Borril sat down beside his father, and waited in uneasy silence. In a haze, Emmel considered several options, discarding the one that shouted the loudest in his mind; the obvious and most natural choice was a bad idea.

He struggled to think of something—anything—else that would salvage the mission, and thus secure the family's standing in the eyes of the King. Nothing was more important than that, was it?

No other option asserted itself in his mind, which, unfortunately, was too foggy for clearer consideration.

With a twinge of regret, the King's Man made his decision. Everything could now proceed as planned, and all was well. No one need ever know...

With an unhappy sigh, Emmel sagged against Borril, and whispered in his ear.

Then, because of the excessive quantity of ale his son had poured into him through the long night, he finally passed out, and subsequently slept through his son's departure the following morning to retrieve the King's possessions from Glasgow.

Unfortunately for all concerned, however, Emmel's sweet oblivion came about five seconds too late.

seven

THE HANDSOME ELF and the not-so-handsome Goblin, both on horseback, neared the Oak Portal that would open their way to Queensgate. Behind them, two other horses carried two Bogles each.

Tugging at the empty bag that was strapped across his chest, Borril was frustrated, and not certain why. "I do not understand where your fifth companion is," he complained to Mazzin. "I did not send him ahead of the company. Am I not commanding this venture in the name of the King?"

"You are, My Good Lord, you are," the Goblin reassured him. "Yet did you not order me to ensure that all will move according to your most excellent plan?"

Doubtful, Borril nodded.

"And so it is, My Good Lord. Rierg, who is the son of my own cousin, is standing guard at the Portal, awaiting your good pleasure."

"Why? What is at the Portal besides the Portal?" Borril wanted to know.

"My Good Lord, in my view, we must slide in and out unobserved by all Folk, lest we must delay our mission to explain to the Folk why they cannot accompany us on our business for the King. As it is said, *Too many Pixies under the same tall hat is never in fashion.* We must remain a small company, do you not agree?"

Borril saw the logic of this, and nodded again.

Mazzin continued. "We must also move in silence so as not to disturb the trees overmuch. Rierg will get us to and through the Portal to Queensgate without incident."

Feeling petulant for no obvious reason, as petulance was not a natural response for the easy-going Elf, Borril frowned at Mazzin and ordered, "See that no one alarms the trees."

"Understood, My Good Lord," Mazzin said, bowing his head in respect.

There were no incidents at the Oak Portal. The trees were serene as they watched the group, now including a fifth Bogle who had spent several hours walking around the forest and mumbling to himself, move through the Portal.

"The King's business," murmured the ancient oaks to each other as the company and their horses shimmered out of sight. "Thus the King's permission. All is well."

Mazzin and Borril watched as the five Bogles attempted to settle the horses in the stables behind the main house at Queensgate. To Borril's surprise, there were four other horses already in residence here: Sheila owned eight horses, housed in two separate stables. Over the years, all of her horses had been ridden by mortals and Fair Folk alike. The four in this stable stayed in their stalls, unperturbed by the arrival of their Fey equine cousins and their riders.

The Bogles were pushing each other around, arguing in their own abrasive language about who should do which task.

"Why are they not speaking the common language of the Fey?" Borril asked Mazzin with some annoyance. "I would prefer to understand what they are saying."

"It is the Word, My Good Lord. The Word is likely part of the common Faerie tongue, and they are afraid to speak it, so they converse in their racial language instead."

Borril grinned with pride in his secret knowledge. "Even in the common language, Mazzin, they will not stumble upon the Word. It is quite specific, and has not been uttered by anyone at all in...well, in a very long time."

"Truly, My Good Lord?" Mazzin lowered his head. His eyes flashed as he processed the information.

"Yes." Borril loved that he knew the Word, and that Mazzin didn't. He was also enjoying the authority his informed position gave him. "What is more, even if someone said the Word right at this moment, since we are not in the presence of the Greencrystal, the Stone would not awaken anyway."

Mazzin raised his head, considering this. "Hmmmm. We do not have to fear for our lives after all."

"Of course not," Borril assured him.

"Excellent," said Mazzin. "But will we have to fear if the Word is, *accidentally,* of course, spoken when we are near the Greencrystal—or does its power awaken only if the Word is spoken by someone who is touching it?"

"The power wakes only when the King holds it tightly in his hand," Borril explained. This was probably true; Borril didn't know for sure, never having considered waking the Greencrystal under any circumstance. But it sounded good, and made Borril feel superior.

"Ahhhh. I understand. Thank you, My Good Lord, for..."

The barking and snarling of the Bogles had gotten louder.

"Quiet!" Borril hissed in alarm. "Someone will hear you!"

The Bogles were silent at once, and continued dealing with the horses.

Mazzin pulled a pipe out of his vest pocket, then frowned. "No tobacco. Oh bother...oh well." He put the pipe back in his pocket and sighed. "So you did not tell the woman of Queensgate that we are taking advantage of her hospitality," Mazzin said, wishing he were smoking. "Whatever would your father say?"

"I did not lie to my father," said Borril. "I told him I sent the messenger."

"And you were referring to me, My Good Lord?"

Nodding, Borril scowled. "I was. I did not tell my father that the messenger was wise and decided to keep our presence at Queensgate a secret."

"You are the one who is wise, My Good Lord."

Borril did not feel wise. He did feel, however, ready to command the mission.

When the Bogles at last finished with the horses, and then secured the stable doors and shuttered the windows, Borril gathered the company around him and gave his instructions a final time.

"We know the items we are looking for. We know where they are, thanks to the information provided by Rierg and...and—"

"Slole," Mazzin supplied the Bogle's name.

"Yes, Slole. Thanks to Slole and Rierg, we know, too, that the pieces we must collect reside in only two rooms. That will make our task much easier than the original plan." He tugged at the brown cloth bag strapped around him. "Remember this: when you have collected each of the items we seek, put them into my hands, and I will place them in this bag, to hold them safe and secure.

"Do not," he admonished the Bogles, "put them in your pockets, even for a moment. They must move at once from their cases and into this bag. Is this understood?"

The Bogles nodded, mumbling affirmations in quiet barks.

"We go to Glasgow, we collect the King's possessions, we return here, get on our horses and race back to the Portal and then home. Any questions?"

No one had any questions.

"Well then," ordered Borril, "Let us go. Now."

In a flash, Borril was gone, followed a second later by three of the Bogles.

Mazzin eyed Rierg and Slole. "You know what to do. And when to do it."

The Bogles nodded, and then disappeared, leaving Mazzin alone for a few more seconds for a last look around the stable before he, too, vanished into the air.

The modest Glasgow art gallery that held the King's missing property was located on Sauchiehall Street. It had variously been called The McClellan Galleries and the Corporation Halls, and had at one time housed the Glasgow School of Art.

When the seven Folk appeared from nowhere in front of the gallery, it was half-past six on a Sunday morning, and it was raining hard.

"Shall we, My Good Lord?" invited Mazzin, pointing to the locked front door.

"Indeed we shall, Mazzin."

The company spontaneously evaporated—and reappeared, safely out of the rain, on the other side of the locked door.

It must be said that, as heists go, this one was easy. There were no guards on the premises, there were no tourists or students or staff in the building. There were only seven of the Fair Folk, standing together in the larger of two exhibition rooms, surrounded by walls filled with paintings, and glass cases that held art treasures.

Mazzin pointed Borril to one of the smaller, side rooms. "You will find much of what we are looking for in there, My Good Lord. Rierg, follow and help our captain collect the King's treasure."

It took very little time to take the several large handfuls of Elfshot that lay decoratively strewn across the inside of a glass case. Slole and the Bogles called Vot and Treln lifted the heavy glass top from the case and held it as Borril piled the Elfshot and then scooped it into his brown bag.

A bark from Polg, the youngest of Mazzin's Bogles, announced the location of the amethyst dagger that had long been one of the King's favorite small weapons. Borril strode across the room and grinned as he looked into another display case; there was the King's dagger, laying on a sheet of heavy white satin, in the company of other dazzling jeweled knives and assorted blades that someone with a little imagination might believe were also Fey, but weren't. Slole and Vot lifted the elegant wood and glass top from this case, Rierg took the amethyst dagger from its place, tore off a bit of the white satin, and draped it around the King's dagger before handing it neatly to Borril. With a glow of pride, Borril slid the dagger into his bag.

When Borril turned to examine another display case, Rierg stealthily slipped three of the other daggers into his vest pockets before his fellow Bogles replaced the massive glass top.

They found two necklaces in the gallery's extensive jewelry collection that indeed belonged to the Queen: a silver chain that held a sleeping moonstone, and a long string of perfectly-shaped pearls and rich, round emeralds. Both necklaces woke at once, glimmering in the presence of the Folk. Faeries never mistake Fey stones for any others.

Having successfully retrieved these (Borril placed them in his bag with great care), the company moved to a huge glass case that was attached directly to the wall.

And there, resting among other beautiful and priceless jewels, was the Greencrystal Pendant, surrounded protectively by its long and sparkling silver chain.

Had the Folk bothered to read the card that detailed a description of the glorious, beautiful Stone, brought into being by raw, royal energy, they would have laughed. This stone was not a rare emerald, it had not been found at the bottom of Loch Ness some four hundred years before by a Highland bard, nor had it been forged by a great Highland laird for his lady on the occasion of their marriage. But it was, without question, the Greencrystal Pendant.

It seemed that Fate had truly granted Borril the privilege of taking the Stone back to Elvenhome where it belonged.

Borril would not allow them to break the wall display's glass case. He meant to keep his promise of No Mischief. So it took the Bogles half an hour to coax the glass casing away from the wall. Once that was done, they stepped away as Borril lifted the Greencrystal and its chain from its place in the display. Nervous, he kissed the Stone, and, with a sigh of victorious relief, slid it into his brown bag with the other objects they'd rescued. He tied it closed, then tucked the ties under his shirt. He patted the bag for luck.

When Borril looked up again, Rierg was stuffing some of the other jewelry from this case into his pockets.

"Put it back, Rierg!" Borril commanded.

Startled, Rierg looked at Mazzin rather than at Borril, who stood in front of the Goblin. Mazzin gave a subtle nod, and Rierg moved to return the jewelry to the display.

"Apologies, My Good Lord," Mazzin offered. "He will be punished."

"He doesn't need to be punished, Mazzin; he just needs to not steal anything, by command of the King. Have your men replace the glass case, and then we can leave."

"As you say, My Good Lord," Mazzin said.

Satisfied, Borril turned and left the room, patting the precious contents of his bag. He could feel the Greencrystal flickering against his chest; it was alive, and powerful. He was grateful that his father had been right about this, too: there had never been a reason to worry about accidentally speaking the Word that would bring the Greencrystal fully awake. Borril, Mazzin, and the Bogles were perfectly safe.

Mazzin watched Borril walk away. Then he looked over at his Bogle friends and smiled. "Stay here for a short while. I will keep him occupied. Take whatever pleases you, provided you can carry it without notice. We are finished here."

THE NEW PRINCESS was born the morning of the day before the King and Queen and their Rade party arrived at Elvenwood.

Less than an hour after their arrival, the Queen and her Ladies were in the nursery, make the requisite fuss over the child.

"Alyria, she is perfect!" Callie ran a finger through the baby's thatch of blonde hair, and then rested it on a tiny pointed ear. "What will you name her?"

Queen Alyria, looking radiant as Callie handed the child back to her, smiled. "Drowwardin wants to call her Lyrica."

"Lyrica," Callie repeated, feeling the sound of the name. Her eyes widened when a stray thought made her burst into saucy laughter. "Lyrica!"

It took a moment, but then Alyria was giggling wickedly, too. "My dear Aunt: you must tell all about your Court Singer. The Folk spread the most astonishing tales!"

THAT NIGHT, IN Drowwardin's private sitting room, the royal new parents and the High King and Queen of Faerie sat in comfortable chairs and discussed the child's future. All attendant Ladies and Men waited outside.

Callie, closest to a table holding a tray of refreshments, handed a goblet of wine to Alyria, Drowwardin and the High King. "To the health and happiness of Princess Lyrica," she raised her goblet in blessing.

"Princess Lyrica," they responded.

"Will the child pass the test?" Drowwardin asked.

"Truly, I do not know," the King answered. "One never knows until it is done."

"I have never witnessed it, Uncle," said Alyria. "Did you test me?"

The King nodded. "You were given the test soon after you were born."

"And found wanting, then," Alyria murmured, without rancor.

Callie shook her head. "No, my dear. You were found to be meant for other things than ruling Faerie as High Queen; that is all. You walk another path, one far more suited to your gifts and your passions."

Drowwardin took his queen's hand. "Are you disappointed about that?"

Alyria raised his hand to her lips, and kissed it. "No. Of course not."

The King winked at his niece. "Your mother was greatly disappointed, however. She swore that I had not done something right, or that I had done something wrong...I was never clear on which position she settled on."

Callie chuckled at the memory. "She demanded that you be tested a second time, and on the same day. She was still irritable about your Uncle crowned as High King; she believed she should rule the land. When her younger brother here was tested as an infant, and chosen over her, she was outraged. She believed she had been born to be High Queen. She's been a trifle prickly about that for ages." Her husband looked at her and rolled his eyes. "Oh, all right: she has never *not* been prickly about it. There," she made a face at the King, "are you happy now?"

"How *is* your mother, Alyria?" the King grinned. "I have not seen her for several hundred years—and I have enjoyed the quiet."

Alyria smiled. "She is well. Not happy, but well. She will be here to see the baby the next time she chooses to visit the Eastern Kingdoms."

The King nodded at Drowwardin in unfeigned sympathy. "For your sake, I hope that, if it must be, my sister's irritating wind blows in slowly, and blows away quickly."

Drowwardin nodded, lifting his goblet. "May it always be so."

They were laughing when there was a respectful tapping on the door.

"Enter," Drowwardin called.

The door opened, and Fiall stepped into the room. "Forgive the intrusion, Your Royal Majesties," he said with a bow and nodded at the High King. "The New Moon rises, Sire. It is time."

The night sky was filled with quiet stars. Serene moonlight flowed in through the window of the small chamber in the eastern turret of Elvenwood Castle.

The High King of Faerie finished preparing himself for the test, stealing looks at his wife. She was focused on the infant she held in her arms.

112

"It doesn't matter if you are chosen to rule all of Faerie someday or not, Little Lyrica," she crooned, cuddling the baby close to her heart. "Your tiny, sweet Royal Majesty will still hold the hearts of your people, all your days. Your father the king is already besotted with you—as he should be. Take all of your guidance from your mother, though; she is of the blood, and she is actually a little bit smarter than your father is...but don't tell them I said so."

Below them, distant sounds of a merry feast were coming from the Great Hall. "Can you hear that, Princess?" Callie continued. "There will a feast, regardless of the outcome...which is something you should remember for later: there is always a reason for a feast, even if you have to look very, very hard to find one."

Callie glanced at the King. She realized then that he'd been watching her, and winked at him as she gave him a wry smile.

The light from the New Moon began to shimmer and glow as it shone down on them. "Shall we?" he asked.

Callie nodded, and kissed Lyrica's blonde head.

Bathed in dancing moonlight, the High Queen of Faerie turned and stood in front of the King, and took his hand. With the child nestled securely between them, they looked into each other's eyes.

At the King's silent command, golden light flashed into the turret room and danced around him. Seconds later it was joined by earth-scented verdant light that surrounded Callie. Gold and green blended, tentatively at first; after a bright flash of coalescent greengold and goldengreen, the united colors welcomed the moon's gift of silver light.

Brilliant, sparkling flashes of warm, questing radiance surrounded them, as powerful it was silent.

"Will you rule the land and its Folk, Lyrica?" the King whispered his question to the child.

"Are you one born to stand in line to serve the land and all its Folk, Lyrica?" Callie asked the baby.

It was a gesture they had only performed once before; together, the King and Queen lifted the infant into the air above their heads, in the ancient rite of offering the newborn to the Light.

A faint yet irrefutable burst of shining amber made its presence known for an instant, and then went to sleep.

Green separated from the glistening gold around it, then each shining glow of color faded ever so slowly into the night sky, leaving the King, his Queen, and the newborn Elf Princess crowned with joyous, silver-laced moonlight.

The feast celebrating the birth of the Princess Lyrica and her position as a potential ascendant for the throne of the High Queen of Faerie went on for two full days. The Rade party danced, drank, played, sang and ate with typically-Fey wild abandon. At intervals they slept in comfortable beds, either solitarily or in interesting combinations.

Late on the second day of the feast, the King and Queen sat at the table in the Great Hall, watching a team of adolescent Giants attempt a variation of caber tossing with Pixies (in tall hats) sitting on stools. As another stool soared through the air in front of them, followed by a horrific crash (no one was injured) and then a roar of applause and approval, the King nudged Callie, who was lost in thought.

"What are you thinking?" he asked her.

"I was wondering about Lyrica's life, knowing she'll be raised to be prepared to rule, should the need arise. I understand what that is like, and I wondered how she would feel about it."

"She is less than a week old, My Lady. I suspect she will grow into it, as you surely did. Besides, she will not have to consider it for a very long time. After us, Arrendel may still take on the responsibility. Still, I'd say we have a couple of thousand years before we need to concern ourselves overmuch."

Callie turned and looked at her husband in feigned disbelief. "Now it's *two* thousand years, is it?"

He was having fun. "What was it that I heard said the last time I was Upworld? Oh yes – 'If you're going to dream, dream *big!*'"

"You," she chuckled, "are impossible."

"Untrue, Your Grace. I am merely unlikely."

ONLY THREE HOURS after they had left the horses and gone to Glasgow on the King's Business, Borril, Mazzin and the five Bogles popped into the back stable.

Rierg made a fast inspection of the stable doors and windows, and confirmed that nothing had been disturbed. It was unlikely that the company's presence had been noticed by any of the mortals who lived or worked at Queensgate Inn.

Without warning, a saddle fell from the stable's loft, and hit Slole squarely on the head. The Bogle hit the floor, face-first. At Mazzin's nod, Treln and Vot ran to Slole's aid, and half-carried, half-dragged the unconscious Bogle across the stable and dumped him on a big pile of hay near the stalls.

Mazzin ordered Polg to climb to the loft to investigate; the Bogle discovered nothing amiss. "Perhaps the saddle was too close to the edge, and fell on its own," Mazzin told Borril. "A strange occurrence, to be sure, but an accident nevertheless, My Good Lord."

The horses watched with interest at the activity around them.

Borril was startled by the falling saddle and the brusque activity. He looked to Mazzin for guidance. The Goblin walked over to the Bogles and barked some questions, which were answered with typical Bogle snarls and yelps. Mazzin then growled what was clearly an order in any language, and returned to where Borril stood waiting.

"My Good Lord, it seems that Slole has a nasty bump on his head. He will live" (and here the other Bogles yelped in something that might have been laughter) "—but we will need to wait until he comes fully to his senses. I would not imagine it will take too long; Slole has a very thick head, and there is not very much in it."

"But—" began Borril uneasily.

"I know, My Good Lord. I agree. But wait we must, for the good of all concerned. Yes?"

Frowning, Borril nodded. They should not split up the party; they needed to stay together and all go through the Oak Portal at the same time. If Slole fell off the horse while they were flying into Faerie...he did not want to think about that. "All right," he told Mazzin. "As soon as Slole recovers enough to ride through the Portal, we go."

"As you say, My Good Lord," said Mazzin meekly.

So they sat and waited for Slole to regain consciousness. The four other Bogles rested in the hay. They did not speak among themselves, nor did they look directly at Borril; still, he had the uncomfortable feeling that they were watching him.

After a while, Borril's tension made him restless. To calm himself, he tried to focus on the look he imagined on his father's face when he showed him the Greencrystal Pendant, the Elfshot, the King's dagger and the two necklaces that belonged to the Queen. There would be pride in his eyes. And then Borril would talk with his father about arranging for him to marry the beautiful Queen's Lady whom Thomas Lear had renamed "Lavender." A King's Man and a Queen's Lady was a good match indeed. It was true that Borril had not once thought of sweet Sonorielle since he'd agreed to retrieve the King's property, but he was thinking about her now: the light blue eyes, the soft, long blonde hair, her sweet mouth, her twitching tail…

A quiet hiss from one of the Bogles jerked him mentally back to the stable. Borril looked around, saw that nothing had changed. Still, he had a strong sense that the Bogles were studying him. He did not like it. He also did not know what to do about it, so he stood, stretched and, without a word to the Bogles, went looking for Mazzin.

The Goblin had climbed up the tall ladder to the loft some time ago, presumably to figure out how a horse's saddle could have fallen from there unaided, and how it could have hit Slole on the head.

Without a sound, Borril climbed the same ladder. When he reached the level of the loft, he gasped.

Mazzin was sitting on a bale of hay, staring down into the large wooden bowl he held in his hands. Even twenty feet away, where Borril stood frozen in confused shock, it was obvious that the bowl was filled with a large quantity of strong faerie wine.

At Borril's strangled intake of breath, Mazzin's concentration shattered, and he dropped the bowl. The wine sprayed in all directions.

The Goblin swore as Borril joined him in the loft.

"You were *scrying*, Mazzin," Borril accused in alarm, pointing at the wine stains on the loft floor. "Scrying!"

Unmoved, the Goblin wiped wine from his hands onto his trousers. For the first time since Borril had met him, Mazzin showed no deference, no meek tendency toward respectful obedience of his betters. "Of course I was scrying, you fool. How else would I have known where everything was in that art gallery?"

Borril struggled to put pieces together that did not yet quite fit. "You told me you'd sent the Bogles Upworld to scout."

Mazzin sighed, as if he were attempting to explain advanced astrophysics to a slightly mentally-challenged child. "I did not need to send them anywhere for the information. I simply had to look." He indicated the wooden bowl at his feet.

"Scrying is a serious undertaking, with consequences. Only royals should use this magic. We are taught that from the time we are small."

The last thing Borril could have expected in this moment was what happened next: Mazzin threw his head back and began to laugh. The sound was both merry and malicious. "It is understood, that is true. What else is true, Boy, is that I *am* royal." The Goblin enjoyed the Elf's discomfort as a few more pieces of the situation inserted themselves into his awareness. "I am the cousin of His Most Royal Majesty, King Horshog of the Northern Kingdom. I am *Duke* Mazzin, and I scry to serve my King and to entertain myself." Mazzin bent down and lifted the wooden bowl from the floor, then nodded toward the loft's ladder. "Let us go down, Borril. Time grows short and we must talk of serious things."

When Borril and Mazzin climbed down, Treln informed his duke that Slole was groggy, but coming to his senses.

"Good," said Mazzin. "We will be able to leave soon." He turned to Borril, who had gone pale and had shaky knees. The reality of his situation was beginning to dawn on him. "Sit, Borril, before you faint."

The worried Elf sat on a bale of hay, and held his bag tightly against his chest in an act of pitiful defiance. Mazzin nodded to Rierg, who moved to Borril, and held his hand out for the bag.

Borril shook his head.

Rierg raised his long arm, prepared to strike him, but was stopped by a low growl from Mazzin. "No. It is better that he gives us the Stone himself."

Eyes wide now, Borril shook his head again, this time more slowly. This was bad.

Rierg snarled, but a sharp bark from Mazzin silenced him. Cowering, Rierg moved away and joined the other Bogles, who were sitting on the stable floor ten feet from the horses.

Mazzin stood in front of Borril. "Give me the bag."

Borril shook his head and closed his eyes, trying to figure out what to do.

There was a sound at the stable door. Someone had discovered that it was bolted closed from the inside. "Hey! Is anybody in there?" called a male voice. "The door's bolted, and the windows are not supposed to be—"

Mazzin flicked his wrist, and the long bolt across the doors fell to the floor.

In a flash, Vot and Polg pushed one of the doors open, and grabbed the young man in mid-sentence. They dragged him before Mazzin.

He was about twenty years old, with short red hair. He was wearing denim jeans and a green tee shirt under a plaid flannel shirt. His brown eyes bulged with fear as he looked at the strange five-foot creatures that held him firmly by both of his forearms, their sharp fingernails digging into his skin. "Hey, what is this? Who are you? What do you—"

"Be silent, Mortal. I have no patience with pointless questions." Mazzin glanced across the stable at Rierg, who approached the group. He stopped in front of the frightened young man. "Now—Borril. Give me the bag."

"I cannot," Borril whispered. "I must not."

The Goblin sighed. "Very well. If you do not give me the bag, I will kill this mortal."

The young man struggled to get away from the two Bogles. They were much shorter than he was, but they were far stronger. His eyes flickered back and forth between Borril, Mazzin, the bag, and the Bogles. "Give him the bag, man. Just give him the bag."

Borril's hands shook. His mouth was dry, and despite the fact that he was too slowly beginning to understand what was happening, he had never been more confused and frightened in his life. Nothing unpleasant had ever happened to him before, and he had no idea what to do— except to try to protect the King's Greencrystal.

Borril looked at the young man. "He won't..." he began.

"The bag, Borril," Mazzin interrupted. "Now."

"No."

It happened fast. Rierg pulled one of the daggers he'd stolen from the art gallery out of his jacket. Without a sound, he reached his long arm high and wide, and sliced the young man's throat open.

In horror, Borril watched and listened to the young man die. He did not notice when one of the Bogles untied his bag, removed it from his shoulder, and handed it to Mazzin.

Slole, fully awake now, was grumbling as his companions walked him around the stable. Mazzin ordered Borril to move away from the dead mortal, away from the considerable amount of blood. The Elf staggered his way toward the horses, stumbled, and sat down hard on the floor.

The Goblin sat down beside him, and opened the bag that held the King's valuables. He sifted through the items until his hand rested on the Greencrystal Pendant; this he pulled from the bag.

The Greencrystal flickered a tentative greeting in Mazzin's hand. "Soon, my prize," he told it as he ran a long, heavy finger over the Stone. "Very soon."

With a satisfied laugh, Mazzin wrapped the long chain around it, gave it a proprietary squeeze, and replaced it in the bag. "Rierg!" he commanded. "Take this. Tie it securely to my saddle."

The blood-splattered Bogle took the bag from Mazzin, and obeyed without a word, leaving Mazzin and Borril alone.

"You are wondering if I will kill you," Mazzin told Borril as the Bogles prepared the horses for their departure. "Set your mind at ease. It does not serve me, or my royal cousin the King, to do you harm—so I will not. You are of no consequence, which provides you a certain degree of safety." He waited for a reaction, but was not surprised when he got none. "You do realize, however, that you are going to have to tell me the Word that will awaken the Stone."

Borril groaned. "I do not understand any of it. I do not understand why you wish to awaken the power of the Greencrystal. I do not understand how you knew where to find it here, Upworld. I do not know how you knew the King wanted it retrieved, or how you knew I had been chosen by my father to retrieve it in his stead. I see now that I was foolish to trust you to help me with the King's Business, but I did not see that you had a plan to steal the Stone for yourself." Bewildered, he met Mazzin's steely black eyes.

"The same way I knew the King and High Queen would be traveling across the land for the birth of another heir, Boy. Think, Borril, think! With Unseelie magic, of course. Scrying in Northern bloodwine. I am of the royal house of Horshog." He laughed almost giddily, patting the wooden bowl that sat in his lap. "I have the ancient gift of sight, aided by this scrying bowl, which has been in my family for seven generations."

Borril still didn't have all the pieces; Mazzin was dumbfounded, and getting annoyed. "You stupid, arrogant, pathetic boy. It was so easy to move you through the maze that I was almost mad with boredom.

"Long ago, when I saw in the bloodwine that the Greencrystal was no longer in Elvenhome, and was thus out of the King's possession, I began to look for it. This quest has been a slow and subtle game well worth the playing. I searched for many years, unaware that the King always knew where it was hiding. When recently the King decided to take the Stone back, I watched him talking to his Men about it, and I saw your father charging you with the task. With my cousin the king's blessing, I went to Elvenhome to assist you in retrieving it. It was not until the day I arrived in Elvenhome that I learned that the King, and, strangely, his Queen, too, were going on a Progress, and would be away from the castle and its Folk.

"My quest, as you can see, has been successful." Mazzin shrugged. "Tell me the Word."

In that moment, Borril would have done anything to take back his role in tricking his father to give him the Word. Mazzin knew he had it, and there was nothing he could do about it. He felt sick when he thought about what Emmel would say. He had to come up with any workable plan to get away from Mazzin and the Bogles, and reach the Portal before they did, and get to his father.

"There is no point in stalling, Boy. The horses are ready. It is nearly time to go. Speak up: tell me the Word."

Borril had a vague notion of distracting Mazzin and running out of the stable to find help. He was sure that Sheila would remember him and, since she knew the Queen very well, perhaps she could...? He sighed, trying unsuccessfully to jumpstart his mind.

"The Word, Borril. Let us keep this pleasant and painless."

There was nothing he could do. He did not know pain, but he knew enough to be afraid of it. He had no doubt that Mazzin and his Bogles would harm him.

Borril lowered his voice to something just below a whisper, and told the Goblin the Word.

Surprise, spontaneous disbelief, and then amusement registered on Mazzin's face. "Of course! How simple, how direct. It seems strange now that I did not puzzle it out for myself forever ago." He laughed. "No matter. Done is done, and I have what I need. Thank you, Borril, for your help. Well done!"

Laughing, he leaped up from the floor, and climbed up onto the horse that Slole was holding steady for him. Once in the saddle, he checked the brown bag that held the treasures, and smiled again when he saw the Greencrystal. After a moment he knotted the ties and tested them, reassured that the Stone was safe in his keeping.

Mazzin told Rierg to open the stable doors, and announced to the Bogles: "We are finished here. Slole, set the fire. Rierg, get the others to the Oak Portal quickly." And with that, Mazzin kicked his horse's flanks and galloped out of the stable.

Slole, set the fire? What fire? Borril thought hazily.

And there it was. Slole was pouring the yellow contents of a small glass vial onto the pile of hay that he had rested in, semi-conscious, only an hour before. Borril watched in horror as Slole struck a matchstick and dropped it unceremoniously into the hay.

Fire sprang to life.

Treln helped Vot and Polg get settled on their horse. He then smacked the horse's rump and sent it flying out the stable door. Rierg and Treln clambered up into the saddle of their horse, and they were off.

Slole fed the fire with more hay. He led the fire toward the dead young man, and then walked back to where Borril sat alone, helpless and miserable. "No stable, no evidence of mischief. Another of those random mysteries the mortals can never explain."

The Bogle's laugh was a wild bark as he struggled to get on his horse.

Sheila's four horses saw the fire growing as it moved toward them. They began to whinny in fear.

I have to get to the Oak Portal before they do. My legs are longer than theirs, Borril thought. He had been riding since he was a *wean*; he could sit a horse better, and ride faster, than they could. He would have to.

As Slole finally slid into his saddle and flew out of the barn to catch up with the others, the remaining horses were butting and kicking their enclosures hard with their heads and hooves to escape the flames.

With only the thought of getting to the Oak Portal before the others, Borril opened the gate on the pen of a wild-eyed mare. Ducking tendrils of burning hay, and despite the smoke, he threw a bridle on her, and climbed on, bareback, except for the blanket one of her keepers had buckled around her for warmth earlier in the day.

Without a backward glance, Borril sped out of the stable, ignoring the terrified screams of the doomed horses trapped in their stalls.

The oak portal was less than ten minutes away from Queensgate. Borril rode the frightened mare as if Mazzin were behind rather than in front of him.

He had to catch up with the Goblin and the Bogles, and then he had to pass them. He tried to focus his panicked attention on this hard fact, and he pushed the horse harder. But as he rode, he could imagine his father's face when it was revealed to the entire Court that Borril had failed to retrieve the Greencrystal for the King. Worse, he had tricked his father into telling him the Word. Worse than even that, he had told Mazzin the Word, and now Mazzin had the Greencrystal.

He could not think how his situation could be more desperate and terrible.

Borril rode harder through the trees.

He did not know, as he ran the frightened mare through the greenwood toward the Portal, that her blanket, upon which he was sitting, had begun to smolder.

eight

IT IS DONE then. Now perhaps Arrendel can choose to be free, Callie mused as she watched a group of HobGoblins walk ceremoniously through the forest clearing toward her. She elected not to think about Arrendel going Upworld. She always missed him terribly when he was away. Now was not the time to fret about things over which she had no control. There would be time for fretting and missing him soon enough, she supposed.

At present, she was seated on a huge tree stump. The High King sat comfortably beside her with about eighteen inches of space between them. Together they were receiving the Folk who had come to pay their respects to—and lay their petitions before—their Lord and Lady, for such were the pleasure and duty of royals on Progress through the land.

Yes, it is done, thought the High King, half-listening to the conclusion of the statement being made by an incongruously official-looking old Dwarf about the importance of reopening some long-forgotten silver mine in the area. *We have another rightful heir to the kingdoms. It is not as it might have been, or as it should have been; but it is done, for the good of all.* As the Dwarf droned on, the King realized that he and the Queen might be sitting here all afternoon; there were many Folk waiting to greet them.

She smelled wonderful, her familiar scent tempting him with bittersweet memories of a past he rarely visited, except in dreams. Right now she was saying something to the old Dwarf about the wisdom of allowing the silver mine to rest for another decade or so. She had carried the royal conversation when his attention had flickered away from the matter at hand. He shot her a furtive look, and was rewarded with a familiar, knowing smile.

Callie maintained her regal bearing as she spoke, never missing a beat, but laughed to herself when she saw the King's shy embarrassment at getting caught not listening to the Dwarf's petition.

Bowing deeply, the Dwarf promised to protect the sleeping mine as Her Majesty had so wisely requested. As he moved away from the royal presence, the group of HobGoblins came forward, pushing one of their fellows out in front to address the King.

The King nodded at the Queen, then focused his attention on the Hobs' spokesman, who bowed before launching a rambling petition to acquire Shetland ponies from Upworld so Hobs would be able to ride horses as well as Elves, mortals, and other taller races, since Shetland ponies were closer to the ground, like the HobGoblin race itself...

The King listened carefully to the HobGoblin, nodding and making well-timed *hmmmm* noises as the spokesman presented his case.

Callie watched her husband. *He's trying not to smile,* she thought.

The King was gracious and patient with the petitioner. Although he made it clear that the Hobs were expressly prohibited from going Upworld and appropriating Shetland ponies, he committed to talking with his vassal kings, and also to meeting with representatives from each of the eight kingdoms, to examine practical ways to address the issue.

The HobGoblins were thrilled. As a group, they bowed deeply and stepped respectfully away from the royal presence.

Fiall, attending the King, and Lavender, attending the Queen, moved to positions beside them and offered each a goblet of wine before the next petitioners approached.

Callie wondered what the King had been thinking about when he'd stopped listening to the Dwarf talk about the silver mine. She wondered, too, what he was thinking about right now, and reminded herself quickly that she had long ago moved away from the privilege of asking him what was on his mind.

She accepted that she was enjoying his company, although much of their public presence was for show. She had heard several reports that—all across Faerie—the Folk were very pleased that their High King and High Queen were spending time together again, ruling together, talking...

Her eyes rested their gaze on his hand as he returned the now-empty goblet to Fiall, and quietly asked his Man to see to something. She found herself studying that hand, as if it were something that had once belonged to her (which it had), as though it were something she had not seen for quite a long time (in a way, it was). She remembered touching that hand, holding it, and being touched by it. His hand was beautiful.

It had been in another life, lived far too long ago, and Callie knew it well. But his hand looked so familiar, so comforting too. It had been part of that other life, and for a breathless moment, Callie could almost see a way back to it.

There it is, she thought wryly. *You might as well own it.* She wanted to touch her husband's hand, to slide her own hand into the warmth she knew was still there. She suddenly ached to be touched by that strong, once-familiar hand—

"Your Grace, you haven't touched your wine," Lavender's quiet voice prompted, inadvertently pulling Callie hard away from her private reverie. "Are you well? Would you like some other refreshment?"

The Queen's blank expression was replaced with a genuine smile. She shook her head, drank deeply from the goblet, and prepared herself for the next petitioner.

IT WAS LATER determined that perhaps it was the burning blanket, more than anything else, that startled the trees into awareness of the coming disaster. Trees, of course, are very concerned about uncontained fire.

Many things happened both quickly and simultaneously. Mazzin, badly riding a staggering, bleeding horse—the Goblin had kicked and beaten him to make him run faster—charged into the copse where the Oak Portal stood. Seconds later, three other horses carrying the five Bogles flew in behind him. The Bogles were snarling and barking as Mazzin shouted the order to hurry through the Portal. Some Folk believe it was the loud, ragged and unpleasant noise that awakened the trees.

From a different direction, Borril came barreling into the scene on another horse. He was shouting for help, crying the words "murder," "mischief," and "thieves" at the top of his lungs.

As Borril pushed his mare after the Goblin and the Bogles, her blanket smoldered and sparked, trailing small burning embers. The embers dropped into the dry leaves on the forest floor.

Then the horse's blanket ignited.

The sudden bright yellow and orange burst of flame burned the horse's rump and flanks. She bucked and leaped sideways in a futile attempt to toss her rider and escape from what was left of the burning blanket.

Borril screamed too, both frightened and singed by the blaze behind and beneath him.

As all five horses were sent dashing through the space between the two ancient oak trees that warded the Portal, the Dryads and other Fey residents of the greenwood called desperately to their Sprite cousins in the trees on the Faerie side of the Portal: "Find Lord Arrendel! Tell him of pain and blood and fire! *Fire!*"

"We have fire," noted the trees sadly to each other.

And fire jumped around the Oak Portal, burning trees and creatures in its path as it danced wildly through the forest.

The fire also danced unrestrained in the space between the worlds, crackling around the horses, the Goblin, the Bogles, and the Elf. In its defense, the air called for a strong wind to push the now-unwelcome company speedily out of the space and through to the Faerie side of the Portal.

When horses and riders arrived in the forest that stood before Elvenhome Castle, the fire arrived with them, strengthened by the wind.

In a flash, too many more things happened at the same time.

The first out, Mazzin's badly-injured horse cleared the Portal, but only just. Foaming and shaking, blood pouring from his flanks, the horse shuddered and fell, and was dead before Mazzin hit the ground.

Rierg's horse reared, hurling his two riders to the ground. Rierg fell hard, and lay unconscious in the grass behind. Unhurt, Treln crawled to Rierg, shook him, then drew a dagger out of each of Rierg's two tunic pockets. He jumped to his feet, ready to strike anyone who came near.

The horse carrying Polg and Vot cleared the Portal. Angrily, the stallion shook his riders off with an angry snort, and galloped toward the castle, leaving Polg sprawled flat in the grass and Vot scanning for the dagger he had dropped in the fall. Slole's horse dumped him against a thick-trunked tree, kicked him, and ran after her brother.

Gasping for air, Borril hurled himself from his horse as soon as he was out of the Portal. Borril's horse, one of Sheila's favorite mares, crumpled helplessly to the ground. The spray of sparks that flew off the dying mare and what was left of her blanket landed in the grass.

Sprites were flying frantically in the air above the Portal, some crying and others darting around the Portal to give aid where they could. Other winged Folk hovered above the fracas. A visibly uneasy Zodiac spontaneously appeared next to a tree that was about to ignite. Master Ocelot and three of his Elven assistants popped in behind Zodiac, carrying blankets, and water in buckets, with which they began to rescue the trees.

Borril, still panting, scanned the growing crowd and found Mazzin, who was barking orders to his Bogles: "The fresh horses...get the horses! We must get back to..." Treln ran toward the small thicket where Rierg had left two horses waiting that morning. He stabbed two brave Wood Sprites who tried to stop him, and hurried on his way.

"Murderer! Thief!" Borril ran toward Mazzin. "He has stolen the King's Greencrystal Pendant!" he called to the gathering Folk. "He forced me to tell him the Word..."

Suddenly, Vot ran at Borril with a big, thick, sharp stick. Nearly berserk with horror, Borril struggled with the Bogle for ten seconds, then took control of the weapon and ran Vot through with it. Vot sank to the ground and did not get up.

Slole ran up beside Borril and raised a dagger. Borril turned at the last second and the dagger sliced his shoulder and arm open, rather than his neck and chest. His blood ran hot and wet into the grass as Borril stumbled. Pain, exhaustion, fear and despair finally knocked him down. He watched as Slole ran toward Mazzin and Treln, each now on a fresh horse.

"Stop them! Stop them!" cried the Sprites.

Despite the efforts of some of the faster-moving Folk, Slole reached Mazzin and the fresh horses. Treln grabbed at Slole's arm, and pulled him up and into the saddle behind him. Then Mazzin, Treln, and Slole fled into the woods away from Elvenhome, away from the Portal, and away from the fire.

Many trees were smoldering on the Faerie side of the Portal. Five or six had begun to burn.

Folk were pouring out of the castle, down the path toward the Portal. HobGoblins and Elves, Dwarfs and Pixies and Water Faeries, Spriggans and Trolls and Goblins arrived at the scene to see what was going on, and to give aid. Water Faeries put out the fires and worked with the Sprites to soothe and calm the trees. Pixies moved into the forest and comforted the wildlife. Wood Sprites dashed into the Portal to help the trees on the other side, taking Iris and Juniper with them. The Goblins in the Queen's Guard cared for the live horses, and two visiting Trolls—brothers who, as it happened, shared their solitary lives with wild horses—gently and tearfully dealt with the two dead ones. The Dwarfs surrounded the three Bogles that Mazzin had left behind. Master Ocelot tended Borril's rather serious wounds.

And in the middle of all the confusion, the terrible events and the shocking aftermath of Mazzin's escape, Thomas Lear's friend Guardian stood silent, watching and listening.

Beside his left shoulder, a miserable Violet fluttered, waiting for him to tell her—and the rest of the Folk—what he was going to do.

If Guardian swore furiously under his breath, or prayed for strength from the gods, or if he barely fought back bitter, heartbroken tears, only Violet knew.

NEARLY FOUR HOURS later, the Heir Apparent sat at the head of the long table in the Council Chamber with the members of the Queen's Council who had not gone on the Royal Progress. Guardian regretted that Boston was not here with them. His wisdom, experience, and perspective would have been welcomed.

Guardian rubbed his eyes, looked over at young Scribe, who was taking notes at a small table by the window. He voiced his thanks, then focused on the Council, acknowledging each individual with a nod or a grim smile. Everyone looked tired and sad, and even a bit frightened. *And well we should be frightened*, Guardian thought.

With more effort than he showed, he forced himself to look and sound like the strong leader the Folk needed him to be. "All right. You have had time to begin to do the things I have asked. Tell me where we are now."

The Council reported all that had been learned and done.

Two of the three Bogles captured had provided a good deal of information, in the interest of making an arrangement to spare their lives. From Polg and Vot, it was learned that Mazzin, who was a cousin of the Unseelie King Horshog of the Northern Lands, had long been obsessed with the Greencrystal, and had made it his life's work to track it down and ultimately to possess it.

The Bogles had even told them what they believed Mazzin wanted to do with it.

When further questioned, the two Bogles had no firm intelligence about where Mazzin, Slole and Treln had gone, nor did they know who—or how many others— might be involved.

"I do not know King Horshog," Guardian frowned. "But I know that he has long been a subtle if small thorn in both the High King's and the High Queen's work. Is it possible that he is ultimately behind this evil?"

"We cannot know for certain, yet there are suggestions that he could be," Atlanta said. "We learned from our two talkative Bogles that the third Bogle, who will not speak, is Prince Rierg, only son of King Horshog."

Guardian cringed. "That will complicate things further, in any event." He looked around the table at the Councilors, each of whom was watching him. "What can Mazzin do with the Greencrystal? He seems to have gone to a great deal of trouble if he is merely a collector of fine—and powerful—jewelry. Could there be more to it?"

No one knew the answer to that. The Council gave Guardian the rest of the information they'd gathered.

Borril, when questioned, told the full truth about everything that he had said, done, and planned. He understood too late that he had been used as a pawn by Mazzin to fulfill the Goblin's plan to steal the Greencrystal. He took responsibility for the layers of mischief that had caused the disaster. He was deeply sorry for his role in the events that had transpired. More than anything else, he was miserable about the anguish his father was suffering over all of it.

From Borril's information, Guardian knew that Mazzin had a royal talent for scrying, and that he used his talent to further his own ends.

"Thus it will be nearly impossible to sneak up on the creature," groaned an ancient green-haired Pixie now called "Denver," whose pretty, pale orange hat did not make her feel any better today.

"And the latest word on the damage?" Guardian moved the discussion toward a topic he could do something about.

The news, coming from three members of the Council, was not good. Upworld, at the Queensgate Inn, both barns had burned down, killing four of Sheila's horses and injuring three more. A friend of Sheila's sons, who worked at Queensgate, had been murdered by Rierg in one of the barns. Behind the Inn, the forest that led to the Oak Portal had caught fire, and many trees and their Wood Sprites had died in the flames. An as yet uncounted number of deer, rabbits, foxes, birds, and other woodland residents had been injured or killed as well. Many homes had been destroyed.

The Inn itself, where Sheila, her husband, and her sons lived, had suffered a small amount of fire-related damage, but the family was physically unharmed. Guardian was told that Sheila was badly shaken and bewildered by the day's events. She had been unaware of the presence of the Elf, the Goblin, the Bogles and the extra horses. Despite specific directions from his father, Borril had never spoken with her about the King's retrieval assignment.

In Elvenhome, the damage was devastating. The fire from the barns at Queensgate had followed the company through the Oak Portal, burning and killing trees and their Sprites as it roared into the forest on the Portal's Fair side. Two of the horses that came through the Portal had died horribly.

Worse than that, Faerie blood had been spilled on Faerie soil. The ultimate punishment for this crime had not altered since the beginning of days.

The Council had done a thorough job. There was nothing else to investigate, nothing else to report.

Overwhelmed with grief and sadness, Guardian shook his head, then bowed it. "When did the messengers leave to inform Their Majesties of this insanity?" he asked.

"Immediately at your command, My Lord," Atlanta said. "Three hours ago. We sent four Water Faeries and three Glaistigs into the loch. They will spread out across the waters Upworld to find the Progress. We know approximately where Their Majesties should be as they come Homeward. They will get your report, My Lord."

Guardian raised his head, and spoke to the empty space by his right shoulder. "Zodiac."

The Lord High Chamberlain appeared beside Guardian. "My Lord?"

Any other time, Guardian would have smiled. "I wish the King and Queen could return as quickly as you arrive."

Zodiac carried his grief behind a matter-of-fact façade. "If they were in Elvenhome, they could, and you know it well. But at the moment, they are outside the bounds of their strongest magic, and unfortunately must make their way in the more traditional fashion." He bowed his head respectfully. "What may I do for you, My Lord?"

"Please have the messengers prepared. Scribe has been documenting our conversation so we have all of the details. Give each messenger the latest intelligence, and send him or her after one of the first messengers. Whoever reaches Their Majesties will have this second report only a few hours behind the first one."

"An excellent plan, My Lord."

"And Zodiac...how much does Thomas Lear know about this calamity?"

"He is aware of some of it, but certainly not all. He has heard conversations, and from his garden he saw the fire in the forest. I have asked the Ladies Orchid and Iris to keep him occupied when he wants company. The Lady Juniper, as you know, was the first of the Glaistigs to volunteer to run a message to the Queen. The Ladies will not give him any specific information unless you instruct otherwise."

Guardian sighed, wondering what his friend would make of all of this. "If he asks, tell him what he needs to know, as long as what he needs to know has already happened. There is no need to discuss what is not yet done."

"Understood, my Lord." Zodiac bowed again, and walked across the room to the small, sun-lit table where Scribe sat waiting, the written report already in his hand.

THE FOLK ON Royal Progress took care of the last details for their departure from the greenwood in which they'd made camp last night. Everyone was involved in the clean-up effort, so that there would be no trace of the Rade party to detract from the natural beauty of the land.

Trees dislike unprovoked disturbance; the Sprites who live in and with the trees cherish the perceived silence, but still like a bit of fun every once in a while.

So it was that a large group of merry Sprites worked along with the Elves, the Dwarfs, the Pixies, the Goblins and HobGoblins, and the Water Folk to collect every piece of evidence of the Rade's presence in and through the forest. It was respectful work, and the Folk did it with cheerful diligence.

The Queen's pavilion tent was always the first thing assembled and prepared, and the last thing removed, on the Progress. At the moment, Callie was inside the white, flagged tent, seated on a short bench as Lavender brushed the Queen's waist-length hair. Rose paced nearby, moving almost steadily under a huge yellow pointed hat.

"Why are you so restless, Rose?" Lavender asked. The Pixie did not look happy.

Callie had noticed, too, a little belatedly. She had a headache, which was a rare thing. "What is it, Dear One?"

Rose tried to stand still to answer her Queen; her foot tapped anxiously. "I cannot say, Your Grace. I only know that something does not feel right." Callie silently agreed, but did not comment.

"Are you ill?" Lavender wanted to know.

"No, but I thank you for your concern," Rose replied. "Your Grace, something is wrong, only I do not know what it is."

Neither do I, thought Callie, as she wondered now if the anxious pounding in her head was really only a headache.

Lavender finished brushing Callie's hair, and slid her golden circlet crown into it. "There, Your Grace."

"Thank you, Lavender."

"We must leave the tent. It is time to go."

Callie nodded, her eyes on Rose. "Rose, come with me. Lavender, please find Boston and ask him to attend me— and The King's Grace?" Lavender bowed and left the tent in search of Boston. "Come, Rose. We must speak with the King."

Five minutes later, the King, Callie, Boston, several of his men, Rose, Lavender, Carnation, Dahlia, and all four of the King's Men stood in the clearing that had only an hour before had been the site of the King's tented pavilion. The area was surrounded by a dense forest populated by dignified birch trees. There was a very small, spring-fed pond fifty yards from where the King's tent had stood.

Rose was attempting to explain her unnamable concerns, and was getting frustrated by her inability to tap into the source of her uneasiness. Her voice slid higher and higher as her anxiety increased.

The King was patient with her. "Do you have any sense of where the wrong or harm is coming from?" he asked.

Rose shook her head. "No, Your Majesty. I know only that something *is* wrong."

Boston happened to be facing the pond at the moment the surface at its center started to ripple, at first gently, then violently. "Look!" he said, pointing.

She was very beautiful. She was also very familiar.

The Queen's Lady, the Glaistig that Thomas Lear had renamed "Juniper," rose out of the small pond with a natural grace. She was tall, elegant, sensual, and as natural and fluid as the sea. She was naked; pond water trickled down her lovely body as she looked around and got her bearings. She moved toward the dry land.

Callie and the King exchanged a look of grave concern.

Juniper hurried toward the group, the water nearly evaporated from her hair and body. She reached the others, and addressed Callie at once, forgetting to bow first. "Your Grace, there has been mischief, and great wrong."

That explains why my head has been trying to explode, the King groaned to himself.

It took Juniper very little time to tell them what had happened, and to deliver Guardian's message to Their Majesties. She told them that there were in fact several groups of Water Folk looking for them along the planned route of the Progress, and that another messenger would be several hours behind her.

"We cannot wait for another messenger," said the King.

Boston turned to Juniper. "If we leave now, we could meet up with the next messenger three or four hours closer to Elvenhome, correct?"

Juniper nodded. "Yes. Every messenger will wait for six hours before returning to the water and then back to Elvenhome. Lord Guardian was certain that a messenger would find you, although he did not know where on the journey you might be."

Boston caught the King's eye; they exchanged a long look, then Boston nodded. He turned and ran back toward the open area where the rest of the Rade party was preparing to continue on the Progress.

The King's Men received fast orders from His Majesty, and they, too, rushed off behind Boston. Callie thanked

Juniper for bringing Guardian's message. Juniper bowed now, with tears in her eyes.

Callie instructed her Ladies to be certain that no one was within thirty feet of her still-assembled tented pavilion. In five minutes she was going to disassemble it herself, and it was understood that this would be potentially dangerous for anyone inside or too close to it. The Queen's Ladies scurried away.

Alone now, the King and Queen looked at each other, horror and sadness and fear of the unknown shining unhappily in their eyes.

"Bloodshed? On Faerie land? By Folk?" The King could not grasp how such a thing was possible. He rubbed his temples, knowing it wouldn't help him feel better.

"He will do his duty, and be the source of justice," Callie choked on the words. "This will destroy Arrendel. He will uphold the law, but—"

"We are three days from Elvenhome," the King replied. "It will be done before we can take the burden from him." He searched her eyes. "We cannot get there in time, My Lady."

"Could we not have Cassane and WindRunner race us back ahead of the Progress so we can..."

He knew how hard she was trying. He hated to have to say it, but he said it anyway: "My Dear, we must remember that the Folk with us now are our people, too, and they need us. We have ended the Progress, and must move as quickly as we can, but we are constrained by circumstance and fate, to say nothing of duty. I regret this more than I can express."

Callie was shaken but struggled for control of her voice. "I know," she told him miserably as she looked up at him.

He saw the regal markings on her face pale as her natural happiness moved toward despair. The sight of it was nearly heartbreaking. He wished her strength and courage. He wished it for himself as well.

"We have much work ahead of us, and an anxious journey," she added. "We must go."

He nodded, and they moved to join the others.

The second messenger met up with them less than four hours later. He was a young, lean Water Sprite with pale blue eyes, and he looked at his King and Queen with a determined trust in their ability to make things right.

Boston had ordered a brief rest stop. Everyone was worried and unhappy; this was a no longer a merry Rade through the land of Faerie. The Folk trudged homeward. They would be traveling all night. There was no singing, there was no music, and there would be few opportunities to slow down and rest.

After the messenger delivered Guardian's report, the King's Men left the party on horseback, each riding in a different direction, to the kingdoms closest to the Progress route. They were to tell the neighboring kings what had happened, and to gain what intelligence they could.

Callie sat silent and still, her back rigid against a tree. Her head ached, but she knew there was no hope for it. It would just have to hurt until it didn't any longer. Lavender and Dahlia talked in anxious whispers some distance away. They quieted when the King, unattended, walked past them and over to his Queen.

Bending down to talk with her, he noticed a moment too late that her eyes held a flash of danger.

"What is it?" he asked, but he already knew.

Her voice was brittle and cold. "The more I think about it, the angrier I get.

"The Greencrystal was asleep, My Lord, asleep for age upon age. There is only one Word that will awaken it. *One.* And in all this time, over the years and the centuries, I have never spoken that Word to anyone. Not to anyone!"

Her eyes narrowed as she stood up. He rose too, knowing what was coming, aware that there was nothing he could do to stop it, soothe it, or change it.

"Only you and I knew that Word," she hissed at him. "Or so I believed."

"The King's Men all have the Word," he explained, without apology. "After its making, and...the unhappy events that followed it...I told them the Word. It was a stupid thing to do. Yet I knew they would never use it. There was never a need."

Callie glared at him. "There was a need, else Emmel would not have told Borril, who was forced to tell this Mazzin creature. Why did you not save us all the trouble and simply announce the Word in the Great Hall at GoldenFeast?"

There was nothing he could say, so he said nothing.

"Undoubtedly, you shared the Word with your Men when you were engaged in one of your many drinking sprees."

"Undoubtedly," he conceded softly.

"You wanted the Greencrystal back from Upworld, and instead of going yourself, sent an inexperienced, sweet and childlike fool of an Elf to retrieve it, and all but handed the power to..." She shook her head, disbelief and anger building in her voice. "Of all the absurd, irresponsible, stupid, misguided notions. Were you insane?"

He could not listen to her any longer; he had already roared these things at himself more than once today. Her bitter rage made his own self-loathing that much more difficult to bear.

With regret, recognizing that they were about to lose the fragile connection they had begun to rebuild, he silenced her with the only weapon in his arsenal. It was sufficient for the task, and it hit its mark: "Madam, the Greencrystal Pendant would never had left Elvenhome in the first place if one of your self-serving Court Singers had not stolen it, taken it with him after your playtime was finished. I own the responsibility for unwisely telling the Word to my Men, but you, Madam, own the responsibility for anyone else touching a powerful thing we created together, let alone using it. The fact that blood has been shed, mortals have been harmed, Folk are dead and wounded, forests burned and horses injured and dead, is far more attributable to the work of your hand than it is to mine. There is blood on Faerie soil. You might choose to remember that when you are casting blame."

They fumed at each other, their breathing coming out in ragged gasps filled with dangerous fury, sorrow, and guilt. In that moment, they might have found a way to forgive each other, and thus forgive themselves. Had they stood together glowering at each other for a few seconds more, they might have taken the single step that would have unified them and made them stronger.

The King called "ScarF" turned away from Callie, and did not look back.

Callie opened her mouth to call to him, but at the last instant, realized that she had nothing more to say.

The deep, age-old chasm between them—which had, over the past two weeks, astonishingly slimmed down to a manageable, friendly crack—widened back into a bottomless, borderless rift.

nine

IN THE THRONE Room, Guardian sat on Callie's side of the elevated oaken and jeweled double throne of Elvenhome Castle. He stared out at the large, hushed gathering of the Folk, and wished that he were sitting down with them on one of the dozens of benches and watching, rather than sitting up here alone, preparing to pass royal judgment.

He had been raised to think like a king, and he took his role and its responsibilities seriously. He understood his duty, and he recognized his obligation to carry it out.

It would be at least another two days before Callie and the King would return. He knew they were coming, but the law was the law, and he was as bound to it as were the Folk who had broken it.

He had spent the entire night trying to think of a way to hold off this moment until his cousin returned. She would not like this any more than he did, but she was better than he was: stronger, more powerful, more commanding by her very nature. She was decisive, and would not have doubts or reservations about what was right and just. She would do what needed to be done.

He had never been more miserable in his life.

The Throne Room was frozen in silence as the guards brought Borril, Rierg, Polg and Vot before him.

Zodiac walked Emmel and Sheila of Queensgate to a position beside the dais steps, where they stood and waited.

Taking a long, deep breath, Guardian surveyed the crowded room, and then spoke to the four Folk surrounded by the Queen's Guard.

"Have any of you anything to say now?"

Borril looked at his hands. The two Bogles nattered to themselves. Rierg glared imperiously at Guardian, but never opened his mouth.

"Borril?" Guardian prodded. "Is there nothing?"

Borril shook his head. "I have spoken with my father, My Lord. There is nothing else."

"Very well." Guardian's voice took on the strength of command as a crisp blue light flickered in the air around him. The Folk bowed, acknowledging Guardian's right to rule and pass judgment.

First, he turned to his left, and spoke to Sheila. "Sheila, you have ever been a good and beloved friend to the Fey. You have been wronged. Today we begin to right that wrong. We, the Folk, are grievously sorry for causing damage to your home, your family, your friend, your horses, and your lifelong fellowship with us. We ask your forgiveness as a people, and we swear that we shall not allow the evils of this Mischief to touch you and yours again."

His eyes met hers. He saw in them her personal affection for him, her remembrance of their long friendship, even her sympathetic support for the painful duties he had to perform in this moment. He could read her sorrow for her private losses. She did not smile at him, but he felt her forgiveness nevertheless.

He moved on. "Emmel."

The old Elf, pale and broken-hearted, took a single step forward, and faced Guardian.

"Emmel, you have betrayed the High King by betraying the Word entrusted to you by His Grace. In so doing, you have contributed to the Mischief that has wounded everything it has touched."

Emmel bowed, then raised his eyes to Guardian's, waiting for his sentence.

Guardian's declaration was heard clearly by everyone. "Your betrayal of the King and the Word was not of your design. The damage that has been caused—and that I fear shall yet be caused—was not of your making. You are Chief of the King's Men. By right and privilege of that title, I command that you wait upon the King's return, and, at his good pleasure, address this issue with His Grace in private."

The Folk whispered their approval, and were silent again.

"Borril, son of Emmel, you have betrayed the High King by betraying the Word you tricked from your father, a trusted King's Man. While I believe it is true that you were manipulated by another in the making of this Mischief, you made choices of your own that caused harm. You chose to go after Mazzin rather than save the Queensgate horses from certain death by fire. By your inattentions and actions, you are responsible for death of the horse you rode from Queensgate to the Oak Portal, although you did not choose to do her harm. You used Queensgate without warning or permission, and left our mortal friends vulnerable and unaware of the danger. The resulting deaths of woodland and wildlife and the Folk who live in and with them are indirectly your responsibility.

"The shedding of Fey blood has sealed your fate."

Guardian waited until Borril nodded his head.

"Prince Rierg." The Bogle did not look up. "Prince Rierg of the Northern Country, son of King Horshog, you have participated in theft of items belonging to His Royal

146

Majesty the High King of Faerie, including the Greencrystal Pendant. You have murdered a mortal in Queensgate, set fire to property, resulting in the death of horses, woodland and wildlife and the Folk who live in and with them. You are, to some degree, involved in Mazzin's plan to do harm to the land Upworld, to build a separate kingdom for Folk whose sense of mischief is not harmless."

There was a shocked gasp from the gathered Folk. Guardian waited for the room to quiet before he continued:

"You are personally responsible for great harm, and you have shed Fey blood. Though it may cause additional complications for Their Majesties, I declare that your royal blood will not save you. Your actions have sealed your fate."

The Folk listened as Guardian passed similar judgments on Polg and Vot. When he had finished with the Bogles, all the Folk assembled in the Throne Room to witness the proceedings rose to their feet as one.

Guardian made his final pronouncement. "As is our way, even in justice, we do not spill Faerie blood lightly, nor do we do so on our land. In one hour, the Queen's Guard will escort their charges from Elvenhome to a place of execution Upworld. We shall require the presence of Sheila of Queensgate, who was harmed by the actions of these individuals. We shall also require the presence of Emmel, out of respect for his position as father to Borril, and as beloved friend of the High King. In accordance with tradition, I personally also ask for the attendance of Master Snick and of Carraherne.

"Done is done," called Guardian, bright blue light flashing around him.

"Done is done," replied the Folk somberly, concluding the ritual.

FROM THE JOURNAL of Master Snick:

The execution of Borril and the three Bogles from the North Country was carried out in the deep forest behind the Queensgate Inn, in the Highlands.

For a time, the area was surrounded by members of the Queen's Guard, to keep forest residents (both animal and Fey) and any mortals from happening upon the event. No interaction occurred.

As in all Faerie executions (although these are rare indeed), not a single word was spoken by anyone. It was right that the only sounds that could be heard in that place on that day and time were the natural sounds of the woodland.

It is true that four Fair Folk died there, and that their blood spilled onto the forest floor. Not even under orders can the Fey shed Fey blood on Faerie soil or in Faerie waters without punishment. The punishment had to take place Upworld.

And so it did.

Present were Lord Arrendel, Heir Apparent of Faerie; Carraherne, Lord High Chamberlain of Elvenhome, also known then as Zodiac; Borril; the three forever unnamed Bogles who served Lord Mazzin; Sheila of Queensgate, the much-beloved friend of the Queen, the King, and the Court; ten members of the Royal Guard; Emmel, father of Borril; Master Snick (known then as Ocelot); and the four executioners selected for the task.

Among the sunlit trees, the guilty Elf and Bogles met their ends in silence.

Done was done.

The record indicates that Sheila, whose life and home had been clouded and then much damaged by the Mischief, remained silent during the somber proceedings, but that when it was over, she wept openly as she was escorted away. It was further noted that a substantial number of the Folk later assisted in the necessary repairs to the Queensgate Inn, the building of two new stables, and the acquisition of a dozen new horses to live in them.

Records also specify that Emmel, father of Borril, remained silent but staggered to his knees when his son died. He was aided by the worthy Carraherne and Master Snick, who together guided him back to Elvenhome.

By virtue of his sacred duty to act in place of the High King and High Queen, Lord Arrendel was the first to arrive at the place of execution. In accordance with Faerie law, he was the last to leave.

DESPITE THE UNEASY urgency that rippled through them, the Fair Folk Progressed through the Great Woodland toward home. Unlike the beginning of the adventure, there was no laughter or much talking among from the groups that rode horses, walked together, or flew above the Rade. Everyone was thinking about what Their Majesties had told them about the Mischief. They kept their voices low if they spoke of it as they moved; Elves and Dwarves, Pixies and Goblins, Banshees and Sprites alike were trying to understand, either in their own minds, or as they talked to their companions, what this unspeakable horror might mean.

In the middle of the parade, riding their horses, the King and the Queen of Faerie stared at each other, as if trying to find a way to erase their harsh words. She saw in his eyes the irritation and accusation she'd heard in his voice when they'd last spoken, as if the dire circumstances that they would face upon their return to Elvenhome were somehow due to her own selfish whims, her poor choice of a Court Singer she had chosen to toy with once upon a time, and her irresponsibility for not telling the King for a decade that the Greencrystal had in fact been stolen from her Tower Room.

As the King looked into his wife's eyes, he saw her anger and hurt at the knowledge that he had shared the private and most precious Word. He felt, rather than truly read, her sense of betrayal of that level of intimacy; it shamed him now that she had kept silent hrough all the long centuries, and he had roared the secret during a drunken evening with his Men less than a year after its making. She had not truly blamed him for laying the groundwork that had initiated the Mischief, but he saw her anguished rage and knew that he was responsible for it all.

Forever ago, they had spent contented hours gazing into each other's eyes, and had seen the mirrored reflection of happiness, laughter, strength and love shining between them.

Now they studied each other's eyes, and felt the shades of their individual failures and distrust flicker there, to be read only as recrimination by the other.

After a time, they each looked away and focused on the journey, both aware that it was unlikely that they would be talking and laughing together the way they had for the past fortnight.

The King mumbled something to WindRunner, and the stallion slid out of the parade and galloped to the head of the procession.

The Queen watched him go, and murmured reassurance to Cassane. She cloaked herself in a sad and heavy silence as she distanced herself from her feelings— and her husband. She did not let her worry show as she considered the Mischief once again, and wondered what unknown thing might be required of her to attempt to make things right.

THE LORD HIGH Chamberlain of Elvenhome Castle had just finished a lengthy conversation with the Master of Kitchens, and was scurrying down the wide, busy main corridor of the ground level of the castle when he felt the pull on the sleeve of his tunic.

He stopped, turned around, and saw Lady Orchid, a little out of breath and still holding on to his sleeve, her dark eyes wide.

He knew why she had come looking for him. "Thomas?"

The Selkie nodded.

"How much does he know?" Zodiac frowned.

Orchid's eyes were filled with misery. "He has heard about Borril...I mean "Buick," she told him. "He does not understand, and he is angry."

"This is madness!" Thomas roared at Zodiac in Thomas' apartments a little while later. "Complete madness!"

Zodiac nodded. "I agree. Only I am uncertain about which parts of this 'complete madness' you are presently yelling about."

As he had walked around the castle and its environs in silence, since Callie had not given him permission to speak freely among the Folk, the Court Singer had naturally overheard stray bits and pieces about the Mischief. Thomas had tried to make sense of the situation, which had been impossible based on the scant information available to him. All he was sure of was that his new friend Buick had been executed by the Folk for some botched Upworld business somehow instigated by ScarF. He'd overheard, too, that Guardian had sat in judgment and found Buick guilty of betrayal, death, fire, and a few other things that didn't make any sense.

Thomas had been unable to speak outside his own rooms. His frustrated attempts to drag in anyone he heard talking about the ghastly events seemed to have been purposely thwarted; not a single one of the Folk he'd come to know appeared to understand what he wanted from

151

them. He'd given up after a couple of hours, and gone back to his apartments in helpless confusion.

He had hoped to talk about it all with Guardian, but he had been informed by both Orchid and Iris that his friend the Heir Apparent was closeted with a great deal of work on Callie's behalf and, regrettably, could not make time to meet up with him for a while. Zodiac, too, had been busier than usual, Thomas noted.

The Queen's Ladies still in residence at the castle were of little help, although they all tried to make him feel better, even if he couldn't understand what was going on. They answered his direct questions, or deferred them to Guardian or Zodiac—neither of whom, of course, could be located. Both of them had passed on the weekly poker game, too, which was a sure sign that things were not good.

Thomas wished that Callie had not gone on Royal Progress. He wanted answers, and he knew she would tell him the truth about everything, if he asked the right questions. He glowered at Zodiac from them moment the Lord High Chamberlain had entered Thomas' rooms.

"So are you going to tell me about this?" Thomas growled.

Zodiac studied him. "I will tell you everything that I can. Are you prepared to listen?"

Nodding, Thomas dropped himself on his couch, and indicated one of the large easy chairs across the coffee table from him.

Zodiac took a moment to settle and get comfortable before he spoke. He then took a long, slow breath, and decided where he could start. "You have a well-rounded background in the literature. Do you know anything about the Unseelie Court?" he began.

Two hours later, Thomas thought he almost understood about the Mischief—the facts of the situation, anyway.

Zodiac had explained that while the vast majority of the Folk lived by certain natural and generally reasonable precepts, a small and somewhat feisty percentage of Folk chose a different way of approaching the world. They tended to live in the northernmost reaches of the Northern Kingdom under the loose leadership of one King Horshog, who was technically a vassal king to the High King.

Thomas now knew that King Horshog's cousin, the HobGoblin called Mazzin, had been at the center of the Mischief. The issue had not been that ScarF had wanted his property returned so much as that Mazzin, and possibly his cousin the king, had plotted and planned the theft of a powerful piece of Callie's jewelry called the Greencrystal Pendant for his own nefarious ends.

"Mazzin has not yet surfaced, although Lord Guardian is working to have him found. We are all a bit concerned about negative repercussions. Since King Horshog's son and heir was judged guilty and has been executed, there is likely to be a problem. There often are, with Unseelie HobGoblins."

Putting the pieces together, Thomas felt badly about his initial harsh thoughts about Guardian. "Poor guy...Callie leaves, all hell breaks loose, and he's the only one in a position to figure it all out, and then make the hard decisions." He looked apologetically at Zodiac, who had not lost his usual composure throughout the entire discussion. "And Buick truly had to be put to death?"

Zodiac sighed. "By Faerie Law, yes. Without question. And whether he had considered it at the time of the Mischief, Thomas, before he was tried he owned up to his responsibilities under the Law. He was a good Elf. Meant well, but was always easily swayed by Folk with stronger minds than his own."

"How is Guardian?" Thomas wanted to know.

"Not well. He is managing the 'Queen Stuff,' as you call it, and doing a noble and thorough job of it. But he is unhappy, and grieving for all we lost because of Mazzin and the Mischief.

"We are all of us—Guardian included, I daresay—eager for the return of Their Majesties."

"I'll drink to that," Thomas muttered.

"An excellent idea," observed Zodiac.

"There are still a few things I don't get about all this," Thomas confessed as he and Zodiac drank Highland whisky.

"You are not alone in that, Thomas."

"So...I'm not sure I see a big difference between the Mischief and your wild-ass Battle of Bannockburn a while back."

Thomas was rewarded with a look of genuine surprise on the face of the usually-sedate Lord High Chamberlain. "Are you joking?" Zodiac was shocked.

Thomas shook his head. "I'm not."

Zodiac took a long drink of whisky, took a moment to appreciate it, then set his empty glass down and leaned into the conversation. "The Battle of Bannockburn was a *game*. It was meant to be playful and exciting. No one playing could be harmed, not a horse or a Fair One. Only a mortal might be injured—or worse, yes, I concede the point, although we all took great precaution where you were concerned. Not a single Child of the Fey would seriously have been hurt, let alone killed. I thought that by the time Her Grace awakened the morning after her sorrowful demise, all was clear to you."

It had been explained to Thomas, and he had believed his friends. He had had no reason not to, even when he had believed what he'd seen on the battlefield, and seen Callie 'die.' He'd experienced the full horror of the event, and had suffered the grief and loss along with the others that day and night. He'd even forgiven Callie and his friends for not realizing that he had thought that what he'd witnessed during the battle was real, and permanent.

"True," Thomas conceded the point. "But this "Mischief" thing—"

Zodiac's eyes filled with formidable rage, but his voice remained calm and even. "This evil was planned. It was carried out without a care for faerie or mortal life. The forest, and many of its inhabitants, both animal and Fey, were not only put at risk, but harmed. With *intent*, Thomas. That is the key: the deeds were done with *intent*. I do not understand the layers of motivation behind the Mischief yet. But I am certain that there are many pieces to this puzzle: Buick's need to prove his worth to his father, and to bring honor to the family name; greed, although beyond Mazzin's I cannot see all clearly enough; the desire for great power, in the form of the Greencrystal. I will leave Her Grace to discuss this further with you if that is her wish.

"Still, all of that aside, you must understand that the shedding of faerie blood on Faerie soil, or in Faerie waters, is punishable by death. It was ever thus, and will always remain the Law. And though it happens rarely, the purposeful taking of a mortal life is also punishable by death. Thomas, based on our very long history, we have learned that the only way to keep our world at peace is to agree that bloodshed must be dealt with immediately, and with the appropriate amount of royal rage, so that in truth it does not lightly happen again.

"For that reason, Faerie justice is traditionally swift, which is why Lord Guardian had to move at once to get the facts, consider them, weigh the consequences, and act at once."

Thomas had been listening closely, and thinking. "Which explains why he did not wait for Callie and ScarF to return to Elvenhome and deal with this."

Zodiac nodded. "Intentional faerie destruction Upworld is forbidden. Even if the destruction is blamed on a 'natural disaster' or a misadventure that is not related to the Folk in any way, it is still considered a wrong. And wrongs need to be righted, balance restored, for the good of all."

"So like everything in my world, it's as much about intention as it is about outcome," said Thomas. "Buick didn't have bad intentions, but a lot of the things that happened did so because of the choices he made, even though he was a good guy and his own blood was shed by the Bogles." He sighed. "It sucks, Zodiac."

"Yes, my friend, it does. We do not fully understand what Mazzin intends to do; all we know is that it is unlikely that he is finished."

"Zodiac, could it be bad?"

Zodiac's face was now as grim as his voice had become. "Yes. He has the Greencrystal. He has the Word. He requires a great deal of power to accomplish his desires. I would suppose that whatever he is planning, it is going to be very bad."

GUARDIAN WORKED IN Callie's study, reading and making notes, organizing and putting petitions and other paperwork into piles on her rosewood desk. *Some things can wait*, he thought. *She will want to see these documents first, then she will want to read those...*

He was exhausted, but he had been unable to sleep much, so he kept working. When sleep did come, it brought vivid, bloody dreams. He wondered if he would ever sleep peacefully again. He worried that the memories of all he had seen, and heard, and had done would not easily fade...

He forced his mind toward practical matters. The Royal Progress would be in Elvenhome by nightfall; word had come from a group of Merrows that their Majesties and the Rade party were less than five miles away.

One brief, necessary ceremony, and he would at last be relieved of his duty to rule in Callie's place. He needed it to be over soon; he was spent. He had nothing left to give.

The deep and empty place in his heart ached for Maggie. He imagined her face when he knocked on her front door, and he almost smiled. He needed to see her soon, before the searing pain in his chest convinced him that what he had done in Callie's name had marked him, and made him unworthy of love, laughter and life. He did not want to be unworthy of Maggie.

For a second, he couldn't breathe. And for a few seconds after that, he thought his tired heart would break from sorrow and despair. He had never wanted to be with Maggie—his crazy, wonderful, passionate, funny Maggie—more than he did in this moment. He needed to swim away from Faerie for good this time, and offer himself completely to the woman whose love meant everything to him.

Abruptly, he rose from Callie's desk, hoping that the physical break from the royal duty would clear his mind. Seeing no one as he walked through the door that led out of her study and into her large living area, he decided to head back to his own rooms and put what was left of his energy into finding the answer to the puzzle he'd been forced to set aside since the Mischief: he had to uncover the secret of staying safely Upworld with Maggie—forever.

The Lady Iris hurried into Her Grace's study several minutes later. She was surprised, and perhaps a bit pleased, when Lord Guardian was not still sitting there working. She had promised Her Grace that she would keep a subtle, motherly eye on Lord Guardian, and all had gone well until the Mischief. Now he was working too hard, far too much of the time, although Iris understood why. She hoped that he had gone to his chamber to rest.

"Violet!" Iris called out into the royal apartments.

The small winged Lady, long purple hair flying around her fluttering purple wings, zoomed into the study. "Yes, Iris?"

"Would you mind calling on Lord Guardian, and informing him that the Queen's Grace is expected in the next short while? They will want to see each other at once. Please ask him to be ready to join Her Royal Highness in the Throne Room upon her return."

"I shall go at once, Iris!" Violet called, turning in mid-flutter to change direction.

"Oh, and Violet...?"

Violet hovered in the air. "Yes?"

"Make no mention of the fact that His Majesty is not with the returning Rade party."

"Whyever not? What if Lord Guardian should ask?"

"He will not ask. He is too tired and distracted for it to occur to him just now."

Swooping toward Iris, Violet asked, "Why is the King not traveling with Her Grace? Did something else happen?"

Iris groaned at the idea. "I would imagine so, Poppet. Go now, and speak to Lord Guardian. Whatever else may or may not have happened, we will know soon enough."

THE HIGH KING of Faerie returned to Elvenhome Castle the following afternoon. By the time he entered his private apartments, the royal power had been transferred back to the Queen and, by all superficial appearances, things were back to normal.

Except, thought the King darkly, *it was unlikely that the world would be "normal" again anytime soon.*

Three of his Men rose and bowed the instant he strode into his living area.

"Sire," said Dwindor, tension making his voice crackle, "what is your will?"

The King looked at the Dwarf, a duke in his own right who had served the King for three hundred years. "Where is Emmel?"

"He has not had the will to leave his bed, Your Grace."

"Go to him, and tell him I have need of him, and must talk with him before the close of this day."

Dwindor bowed and left the apartments.

"Where is Lord Arrendel?" the King asked his Master of the Chamber, a burly and worthy Goblin by the name of Roydd.

"Lord Arrendel is in his rooms. He has spoken only with Master Snick and Carraherne since the judgment. He has not spent time with the Queen, either, not since passing the power."

That was unlike Arrendel, but also was understandable. Still, the King did not like the sound of it. He took another tack: "What? Has he not been playing at cards with The Court Singer?"

"No, Sire. He has kept to himself, and to his studies."

"What 'studies'?"

"That I do not know. He spends his time with books and manuscripts from Master Snick."

The King considered this. "Very well, Roydd. Inform Lord Arrendel, or his friend the Spriggan, that I would speak with him sometime tomorrow."

"At once, Sire."

His Grace looked at the last of his Men standing before him, a handsome Wood Sprite. "Guille, have we heard back from the Men from the Progress? Have they sent word about intelligence gathered?"

"Not yet, Your Grace."

His Grace frowned, pondering his next move and his open options. "May I assume Her Majesty arrived safely yesterday, with no incident?"

"That is my understanding. Your Grace is aware that we do not have the communicative relationship with the Queen's Ladies that we had once upon a time. They no longer share information as readily as they once did. And to be fair, Sire, neither do we."

The King nodded. He was thinking about his Queen and how he would have to approach her so that together they could deal with the disaster that awaited the Folk and possibly the entire Upworld. What if the speculation about what Mazzin meant to do with the Greencrystal was true? "Guille, do you think—never mind. Find me something to eat."

"At once, Sire," Guille replied, and evaporated into the air.

SITTING HALF-SPRAWLED on the oak bench in the walled garden beyond his rooms, Thomas slept, dreaming in the afternoon sunshine.

He dreamt he was in San Francisco, walking with Callie. They were both wearing jeans and sweaters and leather jackets, and he put his arm comfortably around her as they walked along California Street, then up the steps leading to one of Thomas' favorite places in The City. Thomas dreamt himself showing Callie the labyrinth in the sanctuary of Grace Cathedral. They were the only people in the beautiful place, as the afternoon sun shimmered through the amazing stained-glass windows.

Standing beside the labyrinth, he bent down and touched it. "There's magic here," he told her, "and it feels a lot like the magic of Elvenhome. Callie...feel it."

Callie smiled down at him, her cinnamon brown eyes flashing mysteriously. As she stepped on to the path of the labyrinth, her jeans, sweater and jacket sparked, and transformed into her own Faerie clothing, the long moss-colored skirts flowing around her as if blown by strong, benevolent breezes.

"Yes, that's earth magic. It is wild and pure here, and it runs deep. I'd imagine most people who come to this place can feel it, and they take some of the energy with them when they leave." She met his eyes and smiled wider, evidence of her pleasure in his awareness. "You are getting a better sense of the magic in your own nature, Thomas," she grinned as he stood up again and saw that he was not fazed at all by her change of clothing. "Perhaps there is hope for you yet."

She reached for him, pulled him against herself and kissed him. His body responded with a delicious ache as the kiss deepened and he felt her hand rest possessively on his backside.

And then...he woke.

His body was still straining furiously for Callie's mouth and her touch. He tried to think about something else as he came fully awake.

His hunger shifted from the sexual to the physical; he remembered that he'd missed lunch. He considered looking for Zodiac and scaring up something to eat and drink with his friend, and then stopped as a familiar glimmer of internal light pulled his focus. The notes of an elusive melody danced seductively across his mind.

Zodiac and Callie were forgotten in the moment. Thomas Lear, Poet Musician, strolled out of the garden to get his guitar.

He had been working on the song, back on his bench in the garden, for an hour or more when he heard her whisper "Oh, Thomas, your music is so lovely."

He looked toward the sound of Terena's voice. He was used to not seeing her, but he wanted her to see that he acknowledged her presence.

"I'm hoping it will be, Terena. Right now it's...it's a bunch of nice notes that are almost but not quite strung together." He made a face filled with mock dismay, and she laughed, a little weakly, he thought. "Are you all right? You sound...different."

There was silence for a moment as she considered this. At last she admitted "I think I am more tired today than I have been before. Have you noticed that the days seem shorter? I would not have thought so, but..." Her voice trailed off.

Thomas was trying to suppress the faint sense of growing alarm that was hitting the pit of his stomach. "Terena? What's wrong?" He looked around for her, despite the fact that he knew he could not see her. "Can you sit down here, beside me, and rest? Do you need something? A glass of water? Should I call for Zodiac?"

Her voice smiled at him, and he felt her sit down beside him on the bench. He put the guitar down, and blindly reached for her hand, realizing as he did so that he had never actually touched her before.

Expecting to touch human skin, he recoiled only a little when he touched smooth silk instead. "What the—???"

She giggled. It took him a moment to understand that she was wearing gloves. "My hands were cold, Thomas."

"Oh," he said, relieved somehow, although he couldn't have said why.

"They were also feeling older, drier than usual. Not lovely at all. I think the cold does that."

He did not remind her that Elvenhome could be, even in February, as warm and sunny as Midsummer's Day. *The Fair Folk would not have it any other way*, he smiled to himself. "Are your hands warmer now in the gloves?" he asked.

"They're much better," she answered. "I used to have such lovely hands," she added, something pensive creeping into her voice.

Thomas didn't know what to say, so he said nothing at all as he took her gloved hand in his own, and held it.

ten

THE KING, EXHAUSTED, sat on the throne in his Presence Chamber, and stared at his friend Emmel, who knelt on the floor before the dais upon which the throne stood. Emmel's head was bowed in heavy, unspeakable grief.

"Emmel," the King said. "Emmel, done is done."

The Chief King's Man was silent and still.

"Emmel, I grieve too. I remember when he was born."

It was the kind of silence that spoke volumes, layered with too many emotions to navigate. The King waited as long as he could stand it. "Emmel, rise, and speak. I command it."

Lifting his pale face, the old man forced himself to stand as he solemnly met the King's gray eyes. There was no rage; there was only painful sadness wrapped in desolation. "Your Majesty."

They looked at each other for a long time. The King sighed, then stood, walked down the steps of the dais, and sat down on the bottom step, looking up at Emmel with tears in his eyes.

"My oldest friend...what would you have me do? Done is done, and it was just. I wish with my whole heart that it had not happened."

The King's Man's eyes grew wide with slow realization: the King was taking a full measure of responsibility for Borril's death. "Sire! This evil was not of your making!"

"I initiated it. I commanded the Greencrystal to be returned to me."

"You allowed me to send my son in my place. I know, although you did not say it, that you did not like the notion. I should have seen to the retrieval myself. We both know it. You are not to blame, My King."

"Neither are you to blame, Emmel." The King's eyes flashed, the smoldering rage in them balanced by the depths of his despair. "I swear to you that Mazzin and his accomplices will be found, and punished. I will deal with them *personally.*"

The King watched a subtle change move across Emmel's grief-stricken face. He was not certain how to read it.

"Your Majesty," Emmel began, "You called for No Mischief. There was Mischief. There was incompetence and incapacity, despite my son's willingness to do the work I asked of him. There were other forces at hand, things we did not see. There was death and bloodshed. Sacred trees and their Sprites, Folk who tried to offer aid suffered. Horses were brutally abused and killed. Our dearest mortal friend suffered destruction and loss, with no warning of the potential for danger. My son...willing or not, my son had a heavy hand in all of this inconcievable madness, this Mischief. And he has paid for it, in accordance with our laws, in the light of what we know to be right and true."

The King recognized that something was about to happen. He stood, and raised a hand to interrupt Emmel. Emmel kept speaking, meeting his king's eyes.

"And now this Mazzin has the Greencrystal, and has secreted himself away to do some greater Mischief. Until he surfaces, you cannot stop him.

"We would not have put the world at risk if I had not given my son the Word. My son has paid with his life. I stand before you and agree that this had to be. Done is done."

"Emmel—" the King tried to cut him off, suddenly aware of what was coming.

"My King, drunken or purposeful, it is all the same in the end. I carried the Word for seven hundred years without speaking it. I betrayed Your Gracious Majesty, and that betrayal has cost me the life of my only son. My life must also be forfeited to pay for this evil."

"No," the King said. "Your death will not change anything. It will not serve any purpose."

"It is my choice, and my right," Emmel reminded him with respect.

"I will not sanction your death. You do not have my leave to sacrifice your life."

"I know it well, My King. And, as ever, I love you for it, and for so much else. I thank you for the privilege of serving you these many years." Emmel bowed again. When he looked up and faced his beloved king, both he and the king had tears in their eyes.

Emmel took three steps backward, putting a bit of distance between them.

And then, Emmel slowly began to fade.

"Do not do this."

"It is done, Your Grace. Find this Mazzin, and destroy him, for the sake of the Folk, and for the sake of my son. Consider it," Emmel suddenly grinned playfully, "a personal request from an old, loyal friend."

The High King of Faerie nodded; it was all he could do while he watched his Chief King's Man fade, then stagger into a blur, then vanish completely. Emmel was gone forever. He had become, the King counted darkly, one more victim of Mazzin's lust for the Greencrystal.

SHE HAD CRIED and cried over Borril. She knew that there would be moments in her life when she would think of him with fondness. She would miss him sometimes. But even as she'd sobbed over her former lover and his tragic fate, she had never really stopped thinking about Thomas Lear and how much she loved him.

Lavender lay across her bed, tickling her nose with the tip of her beaded tail and considering the Court Singer. She imagined them dancing together at a costume ball in candlelight. He would be dressed handsomely, his beautiful brown eyes shining down at her with a smile he saved for her alone. She thought about walking through the castle's formal gardens with him in the sunshine, holding his hand and showing him the flowers and trees she loved best. She would learn to talk to him about poetry and music the way the Lady Terena did. In time he would find Lavender's mind as interesting as her body was irresistible. She would become important to him, and he would love her deeply all her days.

Yes, she had to make him see how much she loved and wanted him. If only she could think of a way to prove her love and devotion...

Lavender's stomach growled; it had been some time since she'd last eaten.

Still feeling solitary and a little sad as she got up from the bed, she reconsidered a walk through the castle to the Great Hall for her dinner. She did not feel like talking to anyone tonight. She would find something around here, and eat that instead...

...and eat that instead...

Inspiration struck. Lavender had a plan.

HE STAYED IN his private apartments for two days, seeing no one except his Men.

Fiall served him hot spiced wine in the hope of comforting some of His Majesty's ire and frustration. Distracted, the King nodded his thanks, but said nothing.

Annodin, a Brownie of ancient Irish descent, frowned at his King. "Sire, it pains me to say it again, but by tradition, you must soon appoint a successor, a worthy Elf, to take Emmel's position as Chief King's Man. The kingdoms of Faerie must be equally represented in service to the King. It has always been so."

"I remain aware of this, Annodin." The King had begun to scowl, but looking around at the five of his Men in the room and the concern and sadness on their faces, he softened his irritation for their sake. "It is a worthy reminder from the new Chief King's Man. I will rely upon your recommendations. I had, of course, already agreed to consider Borril in Emmel's stead..."

Two more of the Men, Dwindor the Dwarf, and Wyand, the lean, handsome Water Faerie entered the room, each carrying a cask filled with official-looking documents: scrolls with wax seals, envelopes stuffed to capacity with paper.

"Dwindor, what is that?" the King asked.

"Her Majesty suggested," reported the Dwarf tactfully, "that during this time of difficulty, perhaps you would assist in some of the Court business for a time?"

It was like her, the King thought. Until Mazzin could be located and dealt with, there was much work to be done. Every possible lead needed to be investigated, the Folk needed to be comforted and healed, and—based on the amount of documentation coming toward him in the two large casks—the rulers of the other seven kingdoms of Faerie were also offering aid or perhaps information. He knew she would work tirelessly; he also knew she had, despite their unresolved encounter at the end of the Rade, understood that with nothing to keep him busy, he would fall into his too-familiar bitter despair, when it was better for all if he were to remain useful.

Fiall was already clearing everything, pipes and plates and goblets and books and papers, from the long table as the King nodded.

"Gentlemen, it is time to get to work. Annodin: find us the next King's Man from the race of Elves. Fiall, arrange for food and drink. We are going to be here for a long while. And tell Her Grace's First Lady to inform Her Grace that we are prepared to take on as much Court business as she needs."

The King took a deep breath, rose from his chair and, with a long drink of his spiced wine, moved to the now-cleared dining table and reached into the larger of the two casks.

More than twelve hours later, no closer to discovering any information about Mazzin or his whereabouts, the King walked through the castle with Roydd, who moved several measured steps behind him. It was after moonrise as they passed the two guards that warded the short corridor that led to the long staircase to his Tower Room.

He was tired. He had worked hard but had nothing to show for it, which frustrated him. Even though the Folk from all over the Eight Kingdoms were hunting for the Goblin Mazzin and his Bogles, the King was certain that Mazzin would not be discovered until Mazzin chose to make his presence known. The King knew that when Mazzin surfaced, there would be more Mischief, made all the more terrible by his use of the Greencrystal.

It was too much to think about, but he would think about it anyway; there was no escaping that. He preferred to do his thinking and agonizing in the privacy of his Tower Room. Too many things were preying on his mind, too many more things were breaking his heart. He needed solitude, in a place that calmed and comforted him.

As he put his foot on the bottom step of the staircase that led up to his Tower, a voice he had not heard for several years startled him from behind. The King turned, and dismissed Roydd with a tilt of his head. The Goblin moved quickly down the corridor and out of sight.

"When you are in residence, I walk behind you perhaps half a dozen times a week. I do not force you to notice me—or the fact that I am still here and that I love you. I have never demanded, either publicly or in private, that you continue to acknowledge me," she told him, her soft voice both sad and kind. "I never touch your hand or your shoulder or your dear face."

The King froze, unable to speak.

"My time grows short, and I care less now about the way I behave. Unseemly, to be sure, but there it is."

Steady and calm, her voice wrapped itself as deliciously around him now as it had when they had first become lovers, once upon a time. His body recognized the sound of her. It automatically responded in ways he had not allowed for more than a dozen years. As he considered this, his heart nearly stopped in his chest, and then thudded with guilt at the truth of her words.

"It is not that I did not want to touch you, My Love," she admitted. "It takes all the strength I have in me, and all the love and honor I have for you, *not* to touch you. Living here at the castle, with you at once so close and so distant, watching you feel your way through all of your changes and your rages and your denials, and all of your many hurts, without being able to comfort you, knowing that I cannot have you for you will not have me...well, that has been something of a hardship on one who has loved you for a full, long lifetime.

"I still dream that you will come to me, even as I am now, and touch me, and fill my body and my soul with your own the way you did before I so cruelly lost what you once found beautiful in me. Do you not remember what we were to each other? Can you not forgive the ravages of age that I had no wish to know, and over which I had no control? I am not at fault in this, My Love! Oh, if you could but just close your eyes, and love me!"

He took his foot off the bottom step. He turned to face her voice as she continued speaking. It was the only thing to do.

"I do not blame you, My Heart. How could I? It was my fate to be born mortal, and to love only the King of Faerie...even when he could no longer bear the thought of looking at me!"

Tears spilled unnoticed down the King's face. His lips trembled as he whispered: "I was careless with you, reckless from the beginning. I have owned it throughout your life, and have taken much-deserved rebukes from some, and have borne vast, disapproving silence from others for it." His voice dropped to a painful whisper. "Terena, Sweeting..." and even the whisper broke at his effortless, natural use of the pet name he had once called her when they were alone. The name itself—and the sharp memories of both tender and passionate lovemaking the sound of her name conjured in his mind—left him struggling for control. He was drowning in guilt, despair, and bitterness, and could do nothing to save himself. He forced the words out loud enough for her to hear him. "I never considered what would happen. I did not realize that you would continue to age, that all I had done was delay the inevitable. I only knew that I loved you then, before, and paid the cost for it. I was so...so..."

"Disappointed," she supplied the word he couldn't find. "When my body lost its glow of dazzling youth, you did not mind that it moved through its glorious ripening into maturity. Those were such good years, My Love. But when my body began its fickle but natural—perhaps *unnatural*—decline and decay, I know you meant well,

171

and tried. Still, it was too much for you, my King who loves beauty in all things."

He felt her lift a tear from his face with her small, quivering hand. He did not flinch from her touch. He could not speak. His breath came in barely-restrained sobs.

"Do not suffer so, My Dearest One, for the choices you made in haste. Weeping over history is a pointless exercise. What we did, we did, and I am glad of it. Done was done, and there is nothing else to say. In truth, once I saw that my decline had begun in earnest, I was not certain that I wanted to have to see it, either," she teased lightly, with a distracted but clearly affectionate chuckle. She patted his hand. "You spared me that," she finished with a self-effacing but still somehow amused snort.

The King struggled for a moment, but found his voice and the ghost of a smile. "Are you well enough, then, Sweeting?"

"Well enough, Your Grace," Terena murmured, pleased that despite the other, more pressing things he had on his mind, he was focused on her. "Yet despite all else running amok in Elvenhome, I dearly wanted to hear your voice speak my name this night. I do not command you, of course. I do, however, most humbly request it."

It was little enough, he thought. *Far too little, much too late*. Tonight he had no energy for regret and self-recrimination; and there simply wasn't time. The irony of this trapped him between a tight laugh and an endless roar of mad frustration.

Terena cleared her throat delicately.

The King returned to the moment at hand, flashed a dazzling if slightly artificial smile. Then he teased her, as he often had when they had known each other well. "My apologies, My Lady. Thoughts related to matters of State, and other more personal notions, interrupted. I was wondering what boots I should wear tomorrow, and in

172

which garden I should prefer my breakfast. You were saying?"

"I was saying, Your Grace," the invisible mortal retorted, "that I believe I require the sound of your voice calling me by name. It has been far too long since I have heard you say it. Perhaps," she pressed slyly, with a smile he could not see but could positively feel, "perhaps it is that Your Grace has forgotten my name. Out of sight is, sometimes, out of mind."

They both gasped, shocked into a heavily-weighted silence by her words.

Suddenly she laughed, merrily. When he did not laugh with her, she gave his arm a playful shove. "Great gods, Garrhyn, will you not ever release yourself from ages of self-inflicted pain? You used to laugh often, and truly. Things are as they are. Laugh, my dear; it is the only way you will remember to breathe."

He nearly strangled in his attempt to force a sound out of his throat.

"Not your best effort, but I give you my thanks for the trying, in the circumstances." Somehow she found this endearing and funny as well, and giggled helplessly. Her laughter was a cloak he could almost wrap around his deepening distress. "Oh, My Dearest Majesty, how I do love you."

"Terena..." There; he'd said it, and it hadn't torn his heart into ragged pieces.

"Ah. You do recall my name." There was love, affection, gentle teasing, understanding and pleasure in her voice. He felt every nuance of it.

"Terena, I swear to you, if I could unmake—"

Her fingers pressed against his lips to save him from having to speak. "Shhhhhh."

His hand reached for hers. She allowed him to remove her fingers from his face, and she said nothing when he turned her invisible hand over, palm up, and kissed it softly.

"Terena, I am sorry."

"I am not certain that I am all that sorry, My Love."

"Can you forgive me?"

"You were forgiven many long years ago. You might consider leaving that particular sword-thrust behind you and allowing it to heal. It serves you not."

"I loved you," he whispered in misery. "I always have. I still do."

"I am glad of it."

"Terena?"

"Hush now, Your Grace, and revive yourself in your Tower. Give yourself time to rest and think, so that you can right the wrongs of that monster of a Goblin." Her voice moved away from him; she was walking back down the corridor. "Perhaps I will find myself following you again soon. Good night, my sweet Love."

IN HIS PRIVATE library, Guardian had been up all night, checking information against other, older references in the sea of documents he'd been reading and re-reading. He was sleepy, but determined to keep going. He needed to be sure.

A knock at the door jolted him wide awake.

He let Master Ocelot in. "Did you really find it, My Lord?" the wise and ancient Librarian and Apothecary asked, excitement dancing on his face.

Guardian didn't know whether to be pleased or depressed; he settled for being informative. "It appears to be so, but it is not necessarily happy news. It might be, though."

"What have you discovered?" Master Ocelot wanted to know.

"I believe I've found what I've been looking for. If this is the means by which I can stay Upworld, then it will be worth the small sacrifice."

At the word *sacrifice*, Master Ocelot's excitement turned to suspicion. He did not look happy. "Show me your sources. We shall see if we are on the right path."

Guardian led Master Ocelot to back to his library, and pointed to a book in which he had been taking detailed notes. "It is all there. I think I have taken it as far as I can."

"There is always another step to be taken, you only have to know that it is there so you can find it." It was quite late, and Master Ocelot was tired. He rubbed his eyes; when he moved his hands, Guardian saw that the old Elf's eyes were shining with determination. "Let us see what you have found, my friend."

A nervous Menace paced in front of Arrendel as the Water Faerie ate a light breakfast at his desk in his library.

"Oh, sit, *please*," Arrendel murmured as he ate a fresh apple and several slices of warm bread. "You are making my stomach clench with your stomping around."

Menace evaporated from the floor in front of Arrendel, and reappeared instantly, seated now on top of a tall pile of very large, very thick books on the desk.

"Very funny," remarked Arrendel.

"Are you certain that this is the way to stay Upworld safely?"

"It looks like it."

"It sounds wrong to me. Very nasty, too."

"I think you just don't want me to live Upworld permanently."

"There is something to that, My Lord, but that is not the point." A thought popped into Menace's head. "Have you discussed this with either of Their Majesties?" he challenged, jutting out his chin to punctuate the point.

Arrendel sighed. "Not yet." There were several things he should discuss with Callie and the King, separately of course, but he was not ready for those conversations. And if he had found the answer to his problem, if this was the charm, even that would take some thinking and conversation, too. He was sure his cousin would not be pleased. He was also sure his friend the King would not like it.

And if the truth were sitting on the desk in front of him, staring him down, Arrendel would have to admit to himself that he did not like the idea very much either. He was torn between his resolve to be with Maggie, and his uneasiness about the potential costs of staying with her.

Who had originally discovered this charm? Would it truly work? Who had proved that it was the right charm for his situation? How would he know, if he did not attempt it, test it, and live with it? What would Callie think? How would he talk about it with His Grace?

More importantly, how would Maggie react?

If Menace did not like the notion of this particular remedy—and Arrendel had to admit that there was not much that Menace did not like—then Arrendel needed to think about it some more.

At his desk in the Library, Master Ocelot was reading through ancient, sacred texts to find solid confirmation. Yesterday he had sent a messenger to a most learned Fey folklorist, a colleague who lived deep in a forest near the Western Islands just off the Faerie coastland.

He hoped they would learn something useful that would resolve Arrendel's problem but, he thought with a tired sigh, he wouldn't bet the Library on it.

"Master Ocelot told me that if Jareedle cannot confirm the efficacy of this charm, no one can," continued Arrendel.

Menace harrumphed and jumped down from the tower of books, landing delicately on the desk directly in front of Arrendel's face.

"I do not trust this charm, and you should not either, My Lord. Their Majesties will object but will not deny you what you desire. There is no question that Maggie will not like this. Neither will Abbey and Tristan."

The Spriggan stomped his foot hard on the desk, and vanished.

It isn't bad enough that the nightmares are eating me alive, he thought with a groan, *or that I'm resisting the idea of the charm, or that I miss Maggie, or that I have to talk with the King about all that transpired around the Mischief...I have Swiftaine aggravated with me, too.*

If he could have laughed, Arrendel would have. If he could have left his burdens behind for a time, and visited his friend Thomas Lear with a bottle or two of wine, he would have done that.

Instead, Arrendel sat in his study with his suffocating thoughts, and stared at the wall.

CALLIE STOOD ON the make-shift stage that had been erected near the main path to the forest. She held a goblet of Faerie wine in her hand as she surveyed the faces in the animated crowd gathered before her in the sunshine on this balmy February afternoon.

Although she still looked tired and a little sad, Callie beamed a confident smile for her beloved Fair Folk. "Misadventure and bad mischief have done us each and all harm. We have lost heart. We have laid aside our laughter and our music. It is time for us to move away from the harsh time we endured. We must find our hearts, remember our laughter, and make merry, for we are the Fey!"

There was wild applause and cheering from the Folk of Elvenhome, who, at their Queen's invitation, had come

177

to celebrate. This day they would eat, drink, dance and sing. Nearby, there were dozens of tables overflowing with food and wine.

She waited until the cheering quieted a bit, then continued. "First, the Court Singer will sing one of his new songs, followed through the day by others that we've come to know and love. All who wish to should come up on this stage, and sing or tell happy tales. And, if it pleases you, you might ask him to add his talents to your own."

The Folk were astonished, intrigued and excited at the thought of Thomas singing with them on the stage. This was something new, and they chattered and cheered their enthusiasm.

Callie continued. "As you will, my Fair Ones, eat and drink, laugh and play. Be merry —for the good of all!"

Sipping her wine, she nodded at Thomas, who carried his faerie-made guitar as he climbed the six wooden steps to mount the stage. As he reached Callie, he bowed. The crowd roared and stomped its approval.

Leaning in close to give him a kiss on the cheek, Callie whispered, "Thank you again. This was a wonderful idea." Thomas saw that there were tears welling in her sparkling brown eyes; she was still suffering, perhaps more than anyone except Guardian.

To make her laugh, he crossed his eyes, and slid into a crazed, exaggerated, sweepingly theatrical bow to her, and nearly fell on his face trying not to lose his grip on the guitar. Then he turned sloppily and repeated the strange cross between a bow and a curtsy to the assembled Folk, who howled with laughter and delight.

Thomas sneaked a glance at Callie. She was laughing, too. She blew him a kiss, leaving the stage to the man who had every eye on him. The gathered Fey grew quiet and waited for the music only Thomas Lear could give them.

They were not disappointed.

I'm sad and feeling numb and tired;
I can't move or even think.
I'm tense and wholly uninspired
As I pour another drink.

There's nothing wrong but nothing's right;
I can't see what to do.
I don't know what I need tonight,
But I think it might be you.

My soul is lost and it's so cold —
I'll find salvation on my own.
Filled with emptiness I can't hold,
I might be better off alone.

There's nothing dark but there's no light.
Will I survive? I wish I knew.
I don't know what I need tonight,
But I think it might be you.

They say a poet's moods and pain
Live in the tales he tells;
Oh, poets often are insane—
We write from self-made hells
...from our screaming, solitary hells...

You bring something steadying
To the chaos of my art
That makes me forget everything
But how to find my heart.

And if I find my heart and write,
The words will come out true.
Yes, I know what I need tonight—
To spend this night with you.

They say a poet's moods and pain
Live in the tales he tells;
Oh, poets often are insane—
We write from self-made hells.

There's something wrong, still something's
right,
Since you can guide me through
The madness of this poet's plight;
My escape from hell is you.

I know what I need tonight
You are what I need tonight...

From his Tower Room, where he had stayed alone for a full day and night, His Majesty the High King stood alone and unobserved as he watched from a window and listened to the Court Singer's song.

eleven

IN ARRENDEL'S DARKENED chamber, they sat together in misery-soaked silence.

The King would have opened the curtains and windows himself to allow some much-needed light to surround and comfort Arrendel, but he recognized his friend's dire need for the protection that the somber shadows pretended to offer him.

He cursed himself for not insisting on an immediate conversation. He had hoped that Arrendel would have sought him out instead, ready to talk about the unspeakable Mischief. This was not the case; the Water Faerie had spent too many hours alone, thinking himself into hopeless corners. As a result, Arrendel's usually warm, melodic voice sounded rough and brittle as he tried to talk. He seemed to have much on his mind, and was reticent to discuss it, in spite of the King's efforts to get him to say more than a few empty words.

The King sat very still, and waited.

In time, Arrendel's strained voice whispered through the gloom. "It is well that Alyria's child has come. By blood, the young princess is closer to the throne than I."

The King said nothing. He waited.

"Although I do not wish for her, not for anyone, to have to do the things royal obligation demanded of me," Arrendel added.

The King held his tongue, and waited.

"No one should have to do what I had to do," Arrendel muttered bitterly.

In the darkness, the King's single nod was barely perceptible. "Yet you behaved and comported yourself like a king. In all things, you did what was necessary and what was true. Nothing more, and nothing less."

Arrendel scowled, his disagreement coming out with a hiss. "I participated in a calamity."

"Untrue. You protected the Folk, which was your first duty. You were confronted with chaos and wrong, and you addressed it responsibly. You listened, you made the right judgment, and you did what had to be done—with justice. And you managed to do all of that with grace and mercy. You acted like a king, Arrendel, and a damned good king, at that."

The silence was heavy for a time.

"When," asked the King lightly, as if the thought were crossing his mind for the first time, "were you planning to go Upworld to your lady?"

"As soon as I can live with the horrors I have participated in, and move away from them. These are tales I would not want Maggie to ever know. She might..." Arrendel's voice trailed off into a dark and miserable place.

"You surely cannot believe that the lady would think ill of you if she knew what had transpired," prompted the King.

"I do not want to lose her. My love for her must not be one more casualty of this atrocity, this insanity."

The King's voice attempted to be gruff, but it was merely firm in its conviction. His words were matter-of-fact and irrefutable: "Despite your feelings in this moment, you were courageous, honorable, and just. This tale, these events, do not have the power to break you. In the end, only you can break you, and only if that is your choice.

"Kingship, Arrendel, is kingship. It is an internal, essential thing. You are either a king, or you are not, regardless of the circumstance in which you may find yourself."

"That is a noble sentiment, Your Grace. Does it also apply to you?" Arrendel's question was not unkind. It was asked from a vulnerable place in the Water Faerie's heart, and the King understood.

"In truth, I have not acted like a king for a long time. It has not served me, or my personal dragons. Nor has it served the Folk in any substantial way. I have stepped alone into the mire. The Queen has served the Folk with honor in my place.

"But mark this: the long years I spent living as something other than a king have been only on the exterior. Inside," and in the dark the King tapped his chest with a finger, "inside, very little has changed. My duty, my obligations, my love for and my need to protect the Folk and all things in our land—these things never truly faded. They have always been part of me, despite any unseemly situations I may have created for myself." The King cleared his throat. "Great gods, this is thirsty talk! Is there nothing to drink around here?"

"I don't know," Arrendel replied absently. "There may be. My Lord, if Her Grace had been unable or unwilling to serve the Folk after the death of your son..."

"Then at some point I would have had to find a way to continue to do what was required of me, and rule the land and the Folk as is my duty and my right. That is what kings do."

Arrendel considered this. He was grateful for the absence of light in the room; he knew that the King's cheeks were as wet as his own.

In the silence that followed, the mood shifted away from mutual loss and despair, and moved cautiously toward a relative balance that allowed both the King and Arrendel to breathe more easily.

When Arrendel could speak again, he grumbled good-naturedly. "I believe you are right. We need wine. I will find some at once."

He rose from his chair, and took a step before the King's voice chided him. "You have forgotten something, Lord Arrendel."

"I did? What did I forget?"

"Earlier, when you said you would go to your lady as soon as you could live with the Mischief and its consequences?"

"Yes, Your Grace?"

"You failed to point out that when you are ready to leave for a time, you will, of course, have requested so, and been granted permission by your sovereign Lord and Lady."

The King could feel Arrendel's smile flicker and slowly grow warm in the dimness.

"Forgive me, Sire. Upon my honor, I *meant* to say that. I have been, I suppose, somewhat distracted of late. My apologies."

"Indeed," conceded the King, with an invisible grin.

In the darkness, under the full moon on a night where the stars danced, a sky-clad Arrendel walked alone up the hill that led away from the castle, toward the loch. A soft breeze whispered into his ear as it lightly caressed his hair:

"Swiftaine is already planning to follow you," Callie's voice chuckled. "He believes he will be unnoticed. He is incorrect about that."

"I know," murmured Arrendel with amusement as he reached the top of the hill. "Can't you turn him into a wombat or something for a few weeks? I would like to have all of Maggie's attention for a while." The thought made him smile.

"Don't worry. I will keep him busy."

"Uh-oh...it's a good thing I'm getting out of your way, then. When you get down to business, you're a little scary, you know."

"Arrendel..." Callie sounded wistful.

"We've already said our goodbyes, Cousin. This is hardly our last parting, so don't sound so sad. We will sort everything out in its own time. And besides, there is no doubt that Swiftaine will drive Maggie crazy quite often, so there will be a lot of comings and goings between here and there for a certain stubborn Spriggan. Give me several weeks, and I'll send word regularly through one of the Glaistig families. I promise."

She sighed, and the breeze tickled his cheek. "Very well. I want you to be happy."

"I know." He smiled in spite of himself. "I am."

"Merry meet, Arrendel."

"Merry part, Your Grace."

"And merry meet again," they said together, sealing the timeless ritual blessing.

The moon watched as Arrendel approached the loch. He turned and looked back at the castle for a long moment. Then he stepped into the water, and effortlessly made his way, without a sound, to the center of Loch Elvenhome.

Seconds later, a loud splash mingled with a ray of moonlight and a flash of blue fire.

Arrendel was gone.

"DO YOU EVER write a song that is not beautiful?"

"On purpose?" Thomas glanced in the general direction of Terena's voice, and tried not to smile. "Of course not. Surely you know that every song I write is perfect in every way—by royal decree." He was playing the song he had written for Callie after the Battle of Bannockburn, "Beauty in Motion", as he sat on the bench in his garden with Terena.

"You think you are quite funny," Terena told him. "And sometimes, you are. No, I mean before you came here, when all that mattered to you was the music. Did every song you wrote then hold this much power?"

Abruptly Thomas stopped playing his guitar; her words had touched a place inside him he hadn't considered for a while. He remembered a time when it really *had* been all about the music. He had only wanted to write and play, to tell his stories and sing his gentle lovelorn dreams to anyone who would listen. When he had started making serious money, he had lost sight of that...

Terena chuckled amiably.

"Why are you laughing?"

"It seems that the men I like best can stop in the middle of a perfectly natural conversation and, without warning, travel so deeply down the private corridors in their minds that all else stops while they examine their situations or their choices, and resolve to be different or better...Oh, Thomas, your mouth has dropped open. Have a care, or you will inhale a butterfly."

Caught, he was amazed. "How could you possibly...I've never..." he sputtered.

Terena clapped her hands and laughed, but kindly. "Thomas Lear, I have been around artful, extraordinary men for a very long time. I have known many kinds of people. I find that the people who matter most in this world, and perhaps in other worlds, too, are those who—although they indirectly do much good for others—cannot manage to stray too far from the private dark and uneasy places they carry within them."

He grumbled good-naturedly at her, just so she would laugh some more.

"I think," she announced when she had stopped giggling, "that you should introduce yourself to the harp and the lute in your apartments. Everyone else seems to think so, too. Gifts from the High Queen of Faerie should not be ignored. That is rude, would you not agree?"

"They are beautiful instruments, Terena. I have 'introduced' myself to them both; I just haven't learned their secrets yet. No one should have to hear me try to play them. It's not good." He grinned in her general direction. "Not yet, anyway. But one of these days..."

"'One of these days'? What?" she prompted.

"One of these days, I'll write a song for you, and play it on the lute. Fair enough?"

"Yes, oh yes!" her delighted voice danced in the air.

A pretty young Elf Thomas had named "Vega" walked into the garden, and sat quietly beside the stone wall some distance away from the bench where Thomas and Terena sat. Thomas nodded a greeting at her, and Vega smiled back as he began playing another song. Vega was politely out of earshot of the conversation.

"Our dear Zodiac thinks I need watching these days," Terena said with only a touch of frustration. "That sweet child over there has been with me all week. She hovers without hovering. I cannot find fault with her presence, although I should like to. Everyone, it appears, wants to know approximately where I am, now. One fall, and such a fuss."

"Don't fall again, and there will be no fuss," Thomas told her. He had heard that she'd fallen, but didn't want her to know that. "Besides, if you were to fall and hurt yourself, no one would be able to see you, and they might trip and fall over you. Now *that* would create a fuss."

187

Laughing, he added, "It's not like Vega can see you anyway, so it's not the same as 'being watched,' if that's bothering you."

Terena sniffed indelicately. "I only fell down because I was not paying attention. Oh, Thomas, I must tell you! I approached His Grace, and he spoke! I followed him on his way to his Tower Room, and I finally addressed him directly. He stopped, and we talked together. It was brief, but it was wonderful. When I left him, I was thinking of all the anguish he is suffering over the Mischief and...well, you know all about that. At some point I may have been distracted, I think, and then I fell."

Thomas heard the joyful tears in her voice as she confided in him.

He wondered if she had really spoken with ScarF, or if she was off on one of her increasingly frequent imaginary side-trips. It didn't matter to him either way, as long as she was happy. He stopped playing, leaned the guitar against the side of the bench, and stretched.

"You don't believe me, but I don't mind." He could feel her rise, and walk around behind him. Her gown made subtle swishing sounds as she moved across the grass. "He was startled at first, but I pressed him to hear me. And hear me he did; I am afraid I had much to say.

"There was much on his mind, much grief and much anger. There was a sense of impotence about him that men of great power do not like. Yet he made a space of time for me, as he did in our past. He was kind, and he taunted me a little, the way he used to. Perhaps he loves me still, in his way. I believe that all is well with us at last; that is all my heart needs to know."

A flicker of a song lyric darted tantalizingly across Thomas' awareness. He grabbed it, named it in his mind, and tucked it away for later. He would write a song for—and about—Terena. She had become a close friend, and he enjoyed spending time with her, even in those moments when she slipped into her "happy place." He did not want to consider it dementia, although he thought it likely was.

"So you and ScarF are on speaking terms, then?" he asked.

"I wish you would not call him that, Thomas. It is unkind, and unworthy of you. Certainly it is unworthy of him."

He felt sure that Callie's feelings on the matter mirrored Terena's. He had never really apologized to Callie, although he remembered that it had stung her when he'd first renamed the man who'd turned out to be the King. He apologized to Terena for it now.

"You're right. It was reflex, maybe, but still unkind. I'm sorry, Terena. Her Grace says that the names I gave everyone must remain until my time here is over; they can't be changed. But I won't refer to him that way in front of you again. Okay?"

"Thank you, Thomas. You have a kind heart. And you know, in many ways you remind me of him."

Thomas let that one go right by him; clearly she was having a moment of dementia. He did not want to think about it. He changed the subject without missing a beat:

"The Friday poker game is just not going to be the same without Guardian. How would you feel about coming to the game and looking over the shoulders of the other players? It would not be cheating, it would sort of be—"

A startled gasp beside him was followed by a cry of pain and the sound of something stumbling against the side of the garden bench and the guitar resting against it.

Terena had fallen—hard. Thomas was on his feet in a fraction of a second. "Terena!"

Vega came running toward Thomas and the bench. "No!" he called to her as he hit his knees trying to find Terena without stepping on her. "No, Vega...go get help!" Vega turned and ran.

Thomas found Terena in seconds, first finding her tiny, cold hands. "I'm here. It'll be okay. I've got you." He sat on the ground, and very carefully slid the invisible old woman into his arms. He was astonished at how small and light she was. "Tell me where you're hurt, Terena," he pleaded.

"My chest," she whispered, sounding dazed. "It hurts so."

"Are you bleeding? Tell me where." Thomas ran his hands over her, and felt something wet on her face. "Did you hit your head? Terena? Talk to me!"

"I think I did. I do not know." She moaned and shuddered in his arms. "Why is it so very cold, Thomas?" Another gasp told him that she was in pain.

"Hold on, Terena—someone will be here to help soon. Stay with me."

"I believe I have finished," Terena murmured, almost too softly for Thomas to hear. Her breathing was quick and shallow.

"Wait...wait." Thomas was seized with an idea; he had to keep her with him until help arrived. "Wait, Terena! Look! I think I see the King coming!"

"My love is coming?"

"Yes...it's him. He's running over here toward you! Can you see him?"

She did not move her head; it stayed in the crook of Thomas' left arm. "I cannot see anything, Thomas," she noted quietly.

Tears filled his eyes.

"Is he nearly here, Thomas?"

"Yes. Terena, the King is coming. Wait for him." Looking up, as if he were seeing ScarF, he called loudly: "Your Majesty! Your sweet lady love has fallen and needs your strong arms!" Thomas bit his lip hard to keep from crying. Where the fuck was Vega? Why wasn't somebody here who could do something to help?

She knew he was lying about the King. He could tell by the clear focus he heard in her quavering voice. She had no time left for nonsense, and they both knew it. "You have been a good friend to me, Thomas Lear. I have loved you for it. You have made me laugh, and shared your songs, and treated me with great kindness. Now be kind to the King, my dear. He has much to do, and he is so very alone."

She took one last short breath, sighed heavily against him, and then she was gone.

It took less than a minute for her empty body to shimmer into view. She was thin, of medium height. Some of her hair, the color of moon-dappled snow, had slipped from the clasp at the back of her neck, and had fallen to her shoulders. When he smoothed it away from her face, he noticed how soft the hair was. He saw the deep gash in her forehead, probably from hitting the arm of the bench. It had bled quite a bit, but it was not bleeding now. He put one of his trembling fingers against it anyway.

She had the most delicate little hands. They were wrinkled and dry, marked with age, but their fingers were strong and straight. They had once been lovely.

Her gown was a bright shade of yellow, a touch too big for her shrinking frame. Her skin was deeply wrinkled, her face much too tight and thin, but she had high, elegant cheekbones, faint but still pretty arched eyebrows, and long, thick lashes. The lines beside her mouth and eyes swept upward rather than downward, a sure indicator that the woman who had lived in this body had, for the whole of her life, chosen laughter and love over anger and despair. Even with a body riddled with age and layers of infirmity he could only guess at, he could see that she had been an astonishingly beautiful woman, more than worthy of the love of a king.

She had the most intriguing, spectacularly gorgeous eyes he had ever seen. They were the deepest, richest shade of dark violet imaginable. Even in death, they were mesmerizing.

When Vega returned at a run, five minutes after Terena's fall, with Zodiac, Master Ocelot, Callie and three of her Ladies all rushing toward him, Thomas was still holding Terena's body protectively close to his chest.

"The King loves you, Terena, just as you said," he crooned to her as he wept, looking up at Callie helplessly. "He is on his way. He is coming, Terena, your King loves you. He will be sad that you have finally left Faerie. Remember what you said to me? The King loves you: that's all your heart needs to know."

THE BODY OF Lady Terena was lovingly laid to rest by the Folk in the ancient grove of hawthorn trees not far beyond the King's favorite flower garden. At the King's request, all Folk who attended the burial brought baskets and bouquets of red, purple, blue, yellow and white larkspur, for these had been Terena's favorites.

In his turn, Thomas placed several stalks of blue larkspur on top of the casket, and whispered, "I'm going to miss you..." before he forced a hard smile onto his face and moved away.

He glanced at Callie and the King, who stood together as they gave comfort to, and received comfort from, the mourners. Thomas was surprised to discover that the volume on the justifiable anger and disapproval he'd been holding against the King (for Terena's sake as well as for his own, and for Callie's too) had, surprisingly, perhaps moved down a notch.

Without warning, Terena's remark about how Thomas reminded her of the King flashed through his mind, and now, instead of flinching and instantly denying the allegation, Thomas found himself wondering in what way she had believed they might be similar.

After a moment, he forcibly slammed the door on this line of thinking, and turned to walk back to the castle alone.

He was afraid he already knew.

MUCH LATER THAT night, the High King of Faerie, the man Thomas Lear had named "ScarF," wept bitterly, inconsolable and alone, in the chilled darkness of his Tower Room. The last wisps of malevolent chaos in and around Elvenhome were still too much to bear. The actions and subsequent execution of the makers of the Mischief had stunned the Court to its core, and had all but destroyed Arrendel. How had this madness come to them and caused such great harm?

At present, Arrendel was safely away from all reminders of the pain and trouble, happily Upworld with the woman he loved. The King was relieved; Maggie's attentions would help Arrendel to come to terms with the Mischief and its aftermath. Still, the King was going to miss his friend. Tonight he felt the loss almost tangibly. Arrendel's expected three months away would seem much longer.

Mazzin and the Greencrystal Pendant were gone, beyond his reach. For now, anyway. He did not know how he would locate the Goblin and the Stone, but he had a bleak, sickening notion that he would not have to wait long for Mazzin's next move. He cast those worries aside as he considered a larger, deeper source of pain.

Emmel was gone, his choice to fade into death so much easier to bear than the loss of his son and the perceived shame on his name. The King had known Emmel for most of his life; he could not remember a time he had not had this friend close by. He would have to get used to the loss, but he did not think he knew how.

Terena was gone now, too, forever, her final moments made gentler in the compassionate arms of Thomas

193

Lear—instead of in his own, where, in truth, she would have longed to be. His soul burned as he accepted the fact that he had failed her as surely in death as he had failed her in life. He did not know what to make of the report that he had heard of Thomas' words of comfort at her end. *The King loves you. That's all your heart needs to know...*

Everywhere he looked, the King saw a disaster that he had unwittingly initiated. He could not understand how these things had gone wrong. He tried to make sense of it, but he had no words left.

There were only tears.

The King's emotions shrouded him in relentless agony as he stood alone in the Tower Room.

When, finally, his feelings and his problems could wound him no further, they blended then bled into the night sky, heralded by an angry blaze of golden lightning and a bellowing thunder that filled the space above the castle for several long seconds.

After that, all was quiet.

He had nothing more to weep about. He was strangely numb to all of it, and he didn't care why. As the realization struck him, he shrugged and continued to stare blindly out the western window into the vast and empty night.

It was over—done was done—and and he knew it.

The shattered, broken heart that the King had carried heavily in his chest for a time beyond measure had, at long last, been crushed beyond redemption.

twelve

Once upon a time, long ago, in a kingdom in the Midlands of Faerie, there lived a Dwarf of royal lineage called Dunnor. Dunnor was more than ordinarily gifted in the art of metalcraft, which has long been the passion and tradition of Dwarfs—sinnce shortly after the beginning of time. Unlike others of his kind, the Dwarf prince (for so he was) was not only interested in the mining and gathering of precious metals from the earth, but was rather more passionate about the craftsmanship of designing and creating swords and chain mail, crowns and helmets, torques, circlets, and rings.

Dunnor also made bells of all sizes and tones in gold, silver and iron. It was said that Dunnor's metalcraft was the finest and most beautiful in the Midlands, and quite possibly in all of Faerie.

One day, as Dunnor was walking through his uncle's castle (for his uncle was King of the Midlands), he caught a glimpse of the lady Lendia, an Elfin princess from Elvenstar, who was visiting the Midlands with her royal father. Dunnor had never beheld a more gracious lady; Lendia was sweet, gentle, kind, and lovely to look upon. She smiled shyly at him, and he found himself smiling shyly back. A heartbeat later, Dunnor fell in love with her, and a heartbeat after that, Lendia fell in love with him.

Lendia was the seventh daughter of a seventh daughter, and everyone knows that seventh daughters are blessed, whether they are Fair Folk or mortal. Lendia's particular blessing was the ability to recognize the essence of true love in the people around her. She could lightly hold a part of that love in her hands for a moment, the way a child will hold a butterfly before it sails skyward in summer.

In time, Dunnor and Lendia married and, as their love grew, they also married their gifts. Dunnor's metalcraft was infused with Lendia's ability to sense and translate the essence of true love into something tangible, giving the products of his art and craftsmanship an added magic unlike any that had been seen before in Faerie.

After their first child was born, Dunnor presented Lendia with a delicate silver necklace that he had made especially for her. Hanging from an intricately-woven chain was a bell, no larger than the first joint of a finger, with a sailing butterfly design cut into its filigree. The bell's tiny clapper had their intertwined initials carved into it. The sound the bell made as Dunnor placed the necklace in Lendia's hand was pure and sweet, and made them both smile.

"This is us," Dunnor told her with a merry grin.

"Not quite yet, my love," Lendia replied, her laugh gentle and warm.

Lendia put her left hand over her heart, and put her right hand and the tiny bell over Dunnor's heart. She closed her eyes, and listened for a moment. "Ah, there is the love," she whispered. "And it is true."

The bell came alive of its own accord, and began to chime happily in Lendia's hand.

The bell's beautiful sound made Dunnor's eyes widen in surprise and delight. Lendia's artistry had folded something most precious into the voice of Dunnor's bell: sweetness and strength from Lendia's own heart.

Her husband fastened the now-singing bell around Lendia's neck; she wore it proudly all of her days.

Their children were each born with a passion for metalcraft. One of them chose to make necklaces not unlike the one Dunnor had made for Lendia.

Eventually, Dunnor turned most of his attention to the making of swords. He made no more than three dozen other bell necklaces during his long lifetime. And so it was that the chiming necklaces, which, over time, came to be known as "Dunnor's Bells," were all the more valued for their rarity.

And it was said that throughout the generations, at least one of the heirs of the Dwarf prince and his Elfin princess held the secret of the creation of Dunnor's Bells, mastered the art of *breathing the essence of true love into the heart of each bell, and made necklaces in a secret workroom in the old castle of the Midlands Kingdom.*

It was also said that Dunnor's Bells came to life, chiming sweetly and softly, when the two people to whom they were attuned were near to each other, a gentle reminder of the sweetness and strength of true love.

HE ROSE FROM the loch as the mid-February afternoon moved toward a quiet, Highlands dusk.

He had enjoyed his long swim from Elvenhome. He'd been comfortably warm, and had visited friends, and passed familiar places along the way.

His time alone in the water had given him the opportunity to think, and to distance himself from the horrors of the Mischief. While he swam, he'd decided that his last talk with his friend the King—and then getting companionably drunk with him afterward—had done much to put things into a perspective he could begin to live with. He felt strong, relaxed, more like himself than he had in weeks.

And as he swam, the knowledge that he was moving closer and closer to Maggie made his journey all the sweeter.

The late afternoon was gray and chilly when he stood on solid ground. He smiled at the water, and then turned toward the path that would lead him to his lady. As he walked, wetness cascaded in shiny rivulets down his body.

In a few moments, both his skin and his long, blond hair were completely dry, leaving behind only the faint scent of jasmine and fresh water.

Sky-clad, Arrendel walked silently toward the cottage of the woman who held his heart. Excitement overruled his tired muscles, but he forced himself not to run, savoring the end of the longing he'd carried for months.

A cold breeze danced past him. He shivered and kept walking.

By the time he could see her front door, he was dressed in jeans, runners, and a blue sweatshirt.

He took a breath and stepped onto the porch. As he did so, from somewhere inside the cottage, a tiny but exuberant bell burst into a loud peal of surprised delight, then rang wildly.

He wished that he could see her face at the instant she realized why her necklace had begun to sing and shout.

She was in either the living room or the kitchen. From where he stood outside, he could hear the stunned recognition in her voice: "Oh my God!" It was a simultaneous gasp, laugh and cry—and it was entirely Maggie.

Seconds later, with the bell still ringing in its joy, the front door of the cottage flew open, and Maggie's pale blue eyes flashed at Arrendel's dark blue ones through the screen door.

She was laughing and trembling, still holding up the beautiful-but-noisy bell necklace. Her gaze glued itself to his, drinking him in, as she said almost—but not quite—matter-of-factly: "Hi. I certainly hope you've come alone. Otherwise, a Spriggan is about to die of embarrassment..."

The screen door opened.

Arrendel had come home.

If they spent most of the first two days after Arrendel's return in bed, no one was the wiser; they were blissfully alone, apart from Abbey and Tristan, who politely ignored them until mealtime.

On the third day, Maggie woke with the winter sunrise as the dawn's first light stretched in through the window.

She smiled. Arrendel was curled around her, still asleep. She resisted the urge to touch his face, or move closer into the warmth of him. She was content to look at him as streaks of morning slowly made their way across the bed.

Having him all to herself had been wonderful, she mused. They'd laughed, and talked, and kissed, all the while holding hands, reveling in physical contact.

It occurred to her that a good portion of the time Arrendel had spent with her before had usually been spent with Menace as well. While the annoying little Spriggan had almost always given them plenty of privacy, Maggie had been unpleasantly surprised on several occasions when Menace had spontaneously intruded on an intimate moment. The wee bastard had popped in, seemingly out of nowhere, and his timing had been terrible. Arrendel's grinning assurance that they were absolutely alone, and that Menace would not be visiting anytime soon, made everything that much lovelier.

Not too long ago she would have admitted that she had missed having Menace around. But lazily watching the new day's sunlight stretch gently across Arrendel's face, she was so glad to have only Arrendel with her that she almost laughed out loud.

"How can you tell when a Spriggan is up to no good?" Arrendel's drowsy voice whispered in her ear.

"I don't know," Maggie whispered back. "How *can* you tell when a Spriggan is up to no good?"

"He's all the way awake."

She laughed then, and moved closer into Arrendel's inviting embrace.

A week or so later, they drove to Inverness and went shopping for new clothes for Arrendel. Maggie bought herself a new hat, just because. Later they strolled through an art gallery. Walking together on the chilly streets, they ordered several cases of wine for delivery, looked in shop windows, and bought books, a new set of sheets, and a heavy wool blanket.

Eventually Arrendel casually mentioned how much the Faerie Queen had enjoyed Maggie's books.

"You're kidding!" Maggie gasped. "She saw them?" Surprise, and a little tension, widened her eyes. "She *read* them?"

"She read my copy of *The Faerie Queen's Mirror*. She got her own copy of that, and also *Dreams of the Fair Folk*. She commanded that they be placed in the Library at Elvenhome Castle.

"You, Maggie, are officially being read by the Fey."

She was speechless, and remained that way until they sat down for tea in a shop two blocks from where they had parked the car. Arrendel chuckled and ordered tea and cakes, watching with interest as the writer he loved tried to get her head around this astonishing information.

"Wow." Maggie said. "Wow."

"Spoken like a true professional writer," Arrendel smiled.

"Wow..."

"You said it," agreed Arrendel, with a grin.

It took Maggie another day or two to rationally approach the subject of Elvenhome with Arrendel. She was cleaning up in the kitchen after dinner, and he was pouring hot, spiced wine into stoneware goblets.

"About Elvenhome..." she began.

Arrendel looked up. "Yes?"

She hung up the damp dishtowel she'd used to dry the countertop, and followed him into the living room. He'd already laid and lit the fire, and the room was warm and bright.

"About Elvenhome," she said again, "we've never talked about it, at least, not in detail."

"No, we haven't, have we?" Sitting on the couch, he reached for her, and she sat close beside him. "We usually find other things to talk about. Is there something on your mind, Love?"

She shrugged, slightly embarrassed, but she showed him her heart. "It's a little convoluted, and I hate to say it out loud, but what the hell. I've always wanted to know all about your life, and all about Elvenhome, but my own stuff gets in the way. I recognize that I'm a little self-absorbed. It's the writer thing, I know. And I'm not exactly apologizing for it, but I kind of am, aren't I?"

"Not quite," he murmured helpfully. "Not yet."

"I've always been this way, even when I was young, and then when I was married to Sam. I don't mean to be, but I'm selfish. I'm self-involved. It's why I can live alone, mostly isolated. I write, I listen to music, I read, I watch TV, I mess around in the garden. Somehow my life is all about me, and I never actually questioned that.

"And then there's you, Arrendel. I love you. When you're with me, all I can think about and revel in is us, and how magical my world is when we're together. It's been that way since we met. And when I think of you, or of us, whether you're beside me or not, I think about us in the present, and I'm truly happy.

"And when you're gone, back to your other life, I think about you, and us, in terms of what I know here, in my life. I know I'm really subjective..." Her voice trailed off; she had nowhere else to go, and hoped that he could understand.

He did. "You come by it honestly enough, Margaret my Love," he teased her gently. "You're an artist. A serious one. As a writer you do spend a lot of time in your head, and that's not such a bad thing, especially when you create the wonderful things you do."

She frowned a little. "It's just that I have no sense of what your life is like when it's not overlapping mine. And

I've begun to wonder about the details, what you do all day, what you see. I don't know what Elvenhome is like, but I really want to. I never let myself indulge in the fantasy of sharing your other life. I know how different that world is from mine.

"I know by heart the stories you've told me, and I love them, Arrendel. I understand the fiction you filter the reality through. But I don't really have a sense of the place you go when you leave me. Sometimes I daydream about going back with you, although I know that wouldn't work. And since I recognize that Elvenhome is your *real* life, well..." She had run out of words, so she reached for the two goblets of wine, handed him one, and sipped from the other.

He waited until she turned to look at him. "What would you like to know, Sweetheart? Ask me anything, and I'll tell you."

"Well, I don't want a tale that I can re-imagine and retell. I want to know what your days and nights are really like in the castle of the Faerie Queen. I want to hear about people you know, what you care about when you're there. What you do when you're not with me."

"That's a tall order," he said quietly.

"Too much of one?" Maggie asked with an uneasy but hopeful smile.

"Wouldn't you rather watch some television? 'Casablanca' is on in half an hour."

She winced, unsure of her footing and wondering if she should have kept her mouth shut.

Teasing now, Arrendel took his time considering her request, slowly drinking his wine.

Finally he smiled, and put his arm around her. "Ask your questions, and we'll see where they take us."

"Really?"

"Really."

"Okay," she told him, settling against him. "Pick a day, and tell me everything that you did from the moment you got up in the morning until the moment you went to bed that night."

"You have that look on your face," he pointed out. "You're thinking like a writer."

An eager smile started to move across her face. "Actually, tonight I'm thinking like a writer in love. So pick a day, and tell me, Arrendel. Just tell me."

He could not refuse her so small a thing, especially such a wistful one.

Arrendel thought back to a busy day he'd had a few weeks before the Royal Progress left Elvenhome. As always when he told Maggie tales of Faerie, he protected all True Names but his own. He told her about when he'd gone riding with the Queen and some of her Ladies in the huge forest beyond the Castle. He referred to his new friend the Court Singer by title and laughed about the chess matches, and told her about a concert held in the Great Hall over a merry feast.

His curly-haired story-teller was thrilled and delighted.

When he explained to her how he'd won four goldfish, and also their large, glass soup tureen of a water kingdom, at a Friday Afternoon Poker Game, she laughed so hard she nearly fell off the couch.

Because she was under contract to get a new manuscript to her publisher by the end of April, Maggie worked on her current book project most days for five hours at a stretch.

While she communed with her typewriter, Arrendel read books from Maggie's extensive library, went for a swim in the February-cold loch several times a week, managed household repairs as needed, and began work on a canoe that he'd decided to build for them.

The evenings they spent together were warm and comfortable. When there was nothing particularly interesting on television, they took turns telling each other better stories. When it was her night, Maggie talked with Arrendel about the writing she'd done that day, or told him a tale that crossed her mind, one from her past or from the worlds of fiction that lived and breathed in her brain.

IT WAS THE middle of March in the Highlands. Arrendel had been back for almost three weeks when the Highlands saw its first heavy snowfall of the year. The flakes fell hard for a few days. On the third day, the electricity went out.

Well-prepared for the weather, and knowing that the power would be restored in due course, Maggie lit extra candles, and served ham sandwiches and hot soup that cooked in a cast-iron pot hanging from an iron rod built into the stone fireplace. They sat on the floor next to the coffee table, nearest the fire.

"It's your turn to tell tales true or imaginary. Which will you tell me tonight?" she asked cheerfully, handing him a plate.

"What would you like to hear?"

Maggie considered this. "Hmmmm. How about a true tale? Tell me, oh, what you were doing right before you left Elvenhome and came back to me this time," she decided.

The look on his face startled her.

"Arrendel...?"

He had not been prepared for the question. He had worked to put all thoughts associated with the Mischief behind a locked door in his mind, and keep them there. That door flew open now, and Arrendel found himself drowning in memories he'd struggled to suppress.

He saw Borril's unhappy but brave face, and remembered how the condemned Elf had bowed respectfully to him seconds before his execution. He saw Mazzin and the rogue Bogles galloping away on their fresh horses as other horses screamed and died. There was blood on the grass. There was so much noise in the air. Trees burned. The Folk were looking to him for help and direction. He passed judgment on the son of a King and saw him executed, too. The Greencrystal was in the hands of a scrying Goblin of the blood...

"Arrendel?"

He shook his head to clear some of the chaos, and tried to smile at Maggie. She did not attempt to conceal her concern, but she understood without being told that he could not talk to her about this. Not now, perhaps not ever.

She watched him, and bit her lip.

He stood up, and headed for the coat tree by the front door. He did not look back at her.

"We need more wood for the fire. I'll chop it." He grabbed his heavy jacket and a pair of fleece-filled leather gloves, and put them on as he walked out into the cold darkness.

Forcing herself to stay put and let him work out in his own way whatever was upsetting him, Maggie turned and stared into the blazing fireplace, pretending not to notice the two tall stacks of firewood standing ready beside the hearth.

He came back into the comfortable, warm cottage half an hour later, carrying an armful of firewood. This he stacked on the hearth with the rest of it. Then he took off his gloves and his coat.

Quietly Maggie came down the staircase into the living room, and moved to the kitchen. There she poured steaming cocoa into two cups. Arrendel joined her in the kitchen, and put his arms around her.

"I'm sorry," he began. "I had a bad moment, and I couldn't talk about it."

She put her finger on his lips. "You don't have to talk about it, unless you want to. I'm sorry if what I said triggered something unpleasant. Truly."

"I don't want to talk about it. It is not something I want to remember, and it's not anything you should have to know about. But it's nothing for you to worry about, either. It's over, it's not about a female or anything like that, Maggie. It had to do with something unmerry that happened at home. Okay?"

"Okay." Reassured that he would work it out and be all right, she hugged him, hard, then slid out of his embrace so she could sprinkle fresh cinnamon on top of the cocoa.

"It's really cold out there."

"I'd imagine. Did you chop lots of wood?" She handed him a cup, and he sipped it gratefully.

"I don't think we'll need any more kindling until *next* winter."

THE EXPECTED LETTER from King Horshog of the Northern Kingdom to the High King of Faerie was delivered by a messenger who did not wait for a response.

It was first read by Annodin, the King's Chief Man. Annodin took the document directly to Boston, who read it twice and frowned darkly. Annodin and Boston met with the King within the hour to discuss the situation.

Five minutes after they sat down with the King, Annodin was sent to the Lady Iris, so to inform Her Grace that her royal presence was respectfully requested in the King's Presence Chamber at once.

They rose when Callie walked quickly and alone into the chamber. As the guards closed the doors behind her, she reached the long table at which Boston and the King had been sitting, and sat herself down.

"Do we know where Mazzin is?" she asked.

The King frowned. "No. Not yet. But it appears that the game has begun."

Your Most Royal Majesty, and Brother King:

I am disquieted, desolate and destroyed by the death of my beloved son and sole heir, Prince Rierg Horsheel of the Northern Lands. That he would be used so foully, and then killed without diplomatic overtures or respect for his rank and bloodline, inspires nothing short of a father's rage and a king's vengeance.

I do not hold Your Most Royal Majesty personally accountable for the actual death of my son; I know that you and your Most Gracious Queen were not in residence in Elvenhome at the time of my son's death. Yet, because the perpetrator of the wrongful judgment against my heir held court in your absence by your own design, it is right that Your Royal Majesty should hear me, and know the depths of my fury.

Wrong has been done to me, and to the Folk of The Northern Lands. I request that your Royal Majesty, High King of Faerie, come to your grieving brother and vassal king to discuss recompense for this atrocity.

Should there be no reasonable recompense, there can only be retribution, the like of which our kingdoms have not tasted in well over five hundred years.

I do not threaten Your Royal Majesty; I do, however, ask for your presence, your wisdom, and a worthy discussion that will provide a viable resolution to the chaos your Heir Apparent has caused myself and, verily, all the Folk of The Northern Lands.

My messenger was ordered to depart upon delivery of this missive. I shall accept no response less than your presence as a Royal Guest in Elvenroad Castle in a week's time.
Conversation, or conflagration, Your Royal Majesty?
With all honor and respect,
Horshog REX

Callie let out a long breath when Boston had finished reading the document aloud. "Obnoxious," she said.

"'Obnoxious' is right, Your Grace," Boston said. "And he has made the first move, I would say."

The King was thinking. "Yes. And it was an interesting play. I suppose I would have been more concerned if he hadn't surfaced at all."

"He didn't mention Mazzin," observed Callie. "And he said nothing about the Greencrystal, or any potential use of it. But he was quite clear that he'd been wronged and that his son was executed unjustly."

"He wants you to repay him for his loss, Your Grace," Boston glowered as he spoke to the King, shaking his head. "And he wants you to do it in person, although there is no true compensation for what he has lost. He is treating the situation like a simple protocol problem that diplomacy can balance. That in itself is insane." He shot the King a steady look. "It is a trap, of course, Sire."

The King nodded. "It appears so, and knowing Horshog as we do, it has to be. He has set the table, and now invites me to the feast. He will call for 'justice,' knowing it is within my power to provide considerable remedy." Smiling at Boston, he added, "And it seems that Horshog has offended the shite out of you, Bann. Bad move on his part, I'd say."

Callie let the King's use of Boston's True Name go without comment.

Boston's eyes narrowed. "He is the least of your vassal kings, Your Grace, and yet is ever the most troublesome. That he would dare to send such a message, let alone possibly be a party to such Mischief...it is unseemly. It is also annoying."

The King waited until Boston looked up and met his gaze. Something silent passed between them, and Boston smiled and relaxed a bit.

Callie tapped her finger on the table in front of her, and squirmed in her chair. "He knows we suspect his involvement in the Mischief, so he says nothing about his cousin Mazzin. He will count on you to go and attempt to get information about that evil creature's whereabouts. He will either try to convince you of his innocence, or he will flaunt his complicity, depending on how the so-called 'conversation or conflagration' goes. The arrogance of that insufferable little Bogle!"

"We have had no word at all about Mazzin's location, nor has there been any activity that would indicate what he plans to do." Boston sounded as unhappy as he looked.

"It is unlikely that Mazzin is sitting quietly in a cave enjoying the beauty of the Greencrystal," the King replied. "The word here from Horshog is the opening gambit. It is possible that Horshog has the Greencrystal. I don't think he does, but I should find that out."

Agitated, Callie stood up and walked to the chair directly across from the King so she could see his face. She leaned against the top of the tall chair's back. "What is the next move, then, Your Grace? Will you ignore Mazzin, to see what he does next?"

The King smiled at his Queen; she knew him well. "That is tempting. Horshog was always somewhat entertaining when he lost control of the chessboard. In any other situation, I'd almost sit back and let him get angry if only to see what follows. But with the Greencrystal in the game, I have to stay actively involved." His gray eyes sparkled, more from exhaustion than excitement. "There is also the possibility that he is taking a high-handed position because he seeks my counsel but cannot afford to ask for it directly, so is demanding my presence so we can talk in private and he can maintain whatever appearance of sovereignty he chooses to show his people.

"There is only one way to find out. I will ride to The Northern Lands. I will meet with Horshog, and get things sorted."

"My Lord," Callie's voice was quiet but firm. "It is almost certainly a trap."

"Sire, it is a potentially *dangerous* trap, too," Boston advised.

"It is," the King agreed. "And a fairly clever one, if I know Horshog."

Discouraged, Callie sank into the chair she'd been leaning on, and looked her husband in the eyes. "I never especially liked the little stoat-faced bastard."

"Neither did I," he said.

At dawn the following morning, six of the King's Men sat on their eager horses outside the main entrance in front of Elvenhome Castle, ready for the long ride to the Northland Kingdom.

The King, astride WindRunner, towered over the High Queen, who stood beside the huge, handsome stallion as they spoke. Orchid and Juniper, wrapped in woolen, hooded capes against the cold, stood nearby in attendance.

"And you will refrain from provoking Horshog, until you can do it at your leisure?" Callie kept her voice low so as to not be overheard by her Ladies.

The King smiled faintly. "I shall attempt to control myself. This time."

"Is he likely to have the Greencrystal, do you think?"

"I doubt it. But that does not mean that Mazzin might not present him with it in due course. Horshog will hold Mazzin accountable in some part for his son's misadventure. Mazzin may need to drag himself back into favor, and he could use the Greencrystal to do it. That is the reason I will play this game with Horshog."

Callie looked troubled. "And if Horshog doesn't—and won't—have the Greencrystal? If Mazzin plans to use it himself? How much harm can he truly do? We do not know how strong he is. With strength and the Word, there is little he cannot do..."

He studied her. "What is at the heart of your concern, My Lady?"

The High Queen sighed. "I am worried, and that feels strange to me. If Mazzin uses the Stone here, and you are not here, what if I cannot protect the land and the Folk on my own?" She looked away before she met his eyes again. "What if I am not strong enough?"

The King laughed out loud, a generous, merry sound that brought unexpected warmth into the chilly air.

Stunned, the Queen stared up at him. "You laugh?"

"Of course I laugh," he said, and his eyes were kind. "The day will not dawn that you, Your Grace, will not be strong enough to master anything that dares raise its head to assail you. Alone, you are more than equal to any challenge. There is no question of that."

"I was not asking for reassurance," she frowned.

"Yes, you were," he countered in a whisper.

"You are right. I suppose I was." She shrugged. "I do not like it when I fret."

"Do not let exhaustion and despair blind you to your ability to rule and protect." He bowed his head at her, and she nodded back up at him. "Besides, Your Grace, if all goes well, I shall be back in Elvenhome soon, so you will not have to fret by yourself. We can fret together; it is the least we can do. Farewell."

When he turned and called to his Men, and they galloped away from the Castle, Callie didn't attempt to hide the ironic smirk that made her eyes glisten as the smirk grew into a private smile. It was a True thing: despite all, he knew her very well, and had made her feel a bit better.

She hoped she would not have anything serious to fret about, alone or otherwise.

thirteen

MAGGIE RUMMAGED THROUGH her dresser, looking for a specific notebook she knew she had stashed there eons ago. Seated in the cushioned rocking chair beneath the bedroom windows, he watched her with loving amusement as the April afternoon sun made her hair shine when she turned to look at him.

She talked as she hunted. "When I first started writing faerie tales, oh, easily twenty-five years ago, when I still lived in Boston, I thought that all my stories should be sort of in the style of Yeats."

The words came out before he'd thought about them. "Oh, you're much more fun than Yeats was, Maggie..."

"I got over it, though. The Yeats thing. What?" She hadn't exactly been listening.

"Nothing, my love." He smiled to himself, and watched her dig with frustration through the dresser's deep and very full bottom drawer.

She was muttering now. "It has to be here. I remember seeing it, dozens of times."

At the sound of his easy laughter, she looked over at him and chuckled, too, mostly at herself. "That notebook is full of stray information about faeries I'd been gathering over the years, things I hadn't heard before, and I want to check it with you to see if anything I'd read about is real."

He nodded, still smiling at her. She turned back to the crowded drawer. "It's stray subtext for the new stories, Arrendel. They have to be true, and right, too, or there's no point—ah, here it is!"

She lifted the small brown notebook and waved it triumphantly at him as she grabbed a pen from the drawer, then dropped herself onto the bed, facing him. Opening the notebook, she turned a handful of pages, skimming until she found what she was looking for.

"Here. A long while ago I made a list of things that are supposed to offer protection against faeries. Some of them are strange, and some sound really dumb, but anything's possible. You know all about that..." She glanced at him and he nodded.

"Let's have them, then, and we'll see if we can't get you some protection from faeries," he suggested, making no effort to keep the grin from his voice.

"It's too late for me," Maggie retorted in mock resignation. "I'm afraid I'm under complete enchantment. But if I can help some other poor mortal sod..." She laughed. She was glad to have him here with her. The misery of their last separation was all but forgotten when she looked at him now. She knew without saying the words that he felt the same way.

Lying on her side, she bit her lip and studied the list she'd compiled during one of her last frenetic bouts of research mania. "Listen to this one: 'The easiest way to protect yourself from faeries and to keep them out of your house, out of your bedroom'—and there's a lot of stuff about faeries and bedrooms, hmmmm I wonder why *that* is, and stop leering at me like that, Arrendel—'is to wear your clothes inside out, or just turn your clothes inside out and leave them beside the bed.' What do you think of that?"

Arrendel snorted. "I don't think it works."

She raised an eyebrow at him. "Oh no?"

"No. If it were true, I'd never be able to get into the bedroom. You have this charming habit of yanking your clothes off and tossing them on the floor by the bed. Most of the time, they're inside out by the time they land."

He smiled at her when she stuck her tongue out at him.

"Scratch that one," she conceded, drawing a line through the first entry. "Here's a great one: What about this...bells are supposed to be protection against faeries. Hmmm?" Maggie slid a finger under the thin silver chain around her neck, and pulled her Dunnor's Bell out from under her sweater, waving it at him. The bell, ringing quietly against her underclothes, now chimed happily. "That one's probably not right," she frowned.

He scratched his chin. "We like bells. Whoever came up with that never heard of 'faerie bells,' did they?"

"What about bells made from metals that are supposed to repel faeries? Like iron, maybe?" Maggie wondered helpfully.

"Dwarfs work in iron, Sweet One, and they're Fey. Where did you get this stuff?"

Maggie shrugged. "From all kinds of books on Celtic mythology and fairy folklore."

From his seat in the rocking chair, Arrendel grimaced playfully and shook his blond head.

"I'm thinking this is looking pretty bad for us mortals...no protection whatsoever from the Good Folk." Maggie snickered.

"None that I can see," he replied. "The only way an iron bell would protect a mortal from a faerie is if the iron bell weighed a ton or two and landed on the mortal—or the faerie," He laughed at the thought.

"All right, I get it," she snorted, and returned to the list. "Okay, how about running water?" Arrendel whooped with laughter. "The Water Faerie says no." Maggie ran down the list quickly. "Bread? Hot Cross Buns? Maybe because of the crosses, tying into Christian mythology?"

she looked up, saw him shaking his head, and looked back down at the page in front of her.

She brightened at the sight of the next entry, and asked hopefully, "How about salt?"

He shook his head and grinned. "We eat salt. It doesn't seem to protect us from each other."

"A bit of rowan wrapped with a piece of red wool, and carried in a pocket?"

Arrendel winced.

"All right, all right...there are still half a dozen possibilities on my list, but you'll just roll your eyes at them, so never mind. Hey, wait, here's an interesting one. What about prayer?" Surprised by this one herself, she ran two fingers through her curls and frowned. "Prayer?"

He pondered it for a moment. "Hmmmmm...much of Celtic mythology is built on a rigid form of early Christianity...but no. I don't think prayer enters into it." At this, she smiled softly to herself and mumbled something under her breath. He heard the sound but didn't hear the words. "What?" he prompted.

Caught, she blushed faintly but told him the truth. "I said, 'that's funny, I just spent almost five months praying rather fervently for you to come safely home to me.'"

In that instant, he found himself falling in love with her all over again; he kissed her with his eyes. The look on his face made her cheeks shine a deeper shade of pink, and she thought she might cry. She turned once more to the notebook in her hand to pull her focus from her welling emotions. "Okay, there's something here about horse shoes..."

He smiled at his beloved. "I'll be sure to have Her Grace mention that to Cassane."

Maggie smiled back, and scratched this off the list with the others. "Cassane's shoes don't seem to have had much protection for your friend The Court Singer, then?"

"Not that I can see."

She sighed and rolled her eyes. "I went through several very large piles of books to get this nonsense...and I don't even want to ask you about this last one, putting shoes beside the bed with the toes pointing straight out rather than pointing under the bed.

"You know what? I'm guessing that no one who contributed to the body of the folklore I've collected had ever actually *talked* with one of the Folk. And for some reason," she told him frankly, "I was more than prepared to believe that some ancient writers must have spoken to some of the Fey. Yeats said he did, but..." She groaned and tossed the notebook on the floor beside the bed. "It kind of makes you wonder, though..." she observed, meeting his eyes with a shining twinkle in her own. "If the folklore, however faulty, gives you some guidance about how you can be safe from Faeries, how to keep them out of your house, out of the kitchen, out of the closets—and God, if only it could work on Menace sometimes!"

They both snickered good-naturedly at this.

"If," Maggie continued, "the folklore specifies how to keep faeries *away* from your home, and especially out of the bedroom, how am I supposed to figure out what keeps a Faerie *in* the bedroom, Arrendel?"

"Keep looking at me just like that, Sweetness, and you'll always know," he said softly.

CALLIE CLOSED THE door to her bedchamber without a sound.

Before she'd walked ten steps down the hall to the top of the staircase, Iris was beside her. "Good morning, Your Grace."

Callie yawned as they moved down the stairs. "You let me sleep late, Iris. How kind of you."

"Your breakfast is ready. Will you be dining alone, or will Thomas...?"

"He is still asleep."

"Resting up, more like," clucked Iris. "You tend to wear him out, Your Grace."

Her Grace's businesslike demeanor was belied by the flash of merriment in her eyes. "What kind of a day do I have waiting for me? Is there a lot of 'Queen Stuff,' or can I go play?"

They had reached the dining table, which had been set for two. Carnation was setting a bowl of sliced goldenfruit next to a plate of warm bread and jam at Callie's place. Dahlia was pouring tea into a beautiful bone china cup.

Iris pulled the chair out for Callie, who seated herself and reached for the cup of tea, with a nod and a smile for Dahlia, who beamed with pride.

"My day?" Callie repeated to Iris.

"Your day, Your Grace, is lighter than usual."

Callie was reaching for the goldenfruit. "Wonderful! Once Thomas is on his feet, perhaps we'll go riding." She looked up at Iris. "How light is 'light'?"

"There are three petitions to read; one is quite long and you should probably give it to Boston to decipher in any event. You should find time to go into the Village to visit the tradesfolk at the Winter Faire—you always enjoy the time you spend there. You have not been to the Village since Thomas arrived. And there is a request for an audience with Your Grace, but I am certain it can wait."

"Who is seeking an audience?"

"Swiftaine." Iris' crisp disapproval was evident in her tone. She knew that this Spriggan managed to irritate the Queen more often than not.

The warm bread and jam were delicious; Her Grace was hungry. "I agree. He can wait."

AS HE DROVE back to the cottage from the village the next day, Arrendel thought about Elvenhome. As a general rule, he kept all serious considerations of his home, and what might be going on there right now, in the cottage's detached garage, where he was building the canoe. He'd gone to the village to pick up some new tools for the project, and that had given him ample solitary time.

If Mazzin had been located, or if he'd done something noteworthy, Arrendel would already know; he swam with the Glaistigs that lived in a neighboring loch twice a week. If there was news, they'd know to come and find him. Swimming with the Fey wasn't something he'd mentioned to Maggie. Still, he didn't feel as though he was withholding anything crucial from her. She understood that he needed to separate part of his world from hers.

And if Mazzin hadn't surfaced, then perhaps all was well enough and life in Elvenhome and thus all of Faerie could begin to return to normal. His relief came out in a hopeful sigh.

Although he'd been away only a little more than a month, he missed everyone, especially the Queen and King. It surprised him how much he missed spending time with his newest friend, Thomas Lear. He'd enjoyed listening to the Court Singer play his guitars and sing his songs and tell his stories. He had come to know the man fairly well, and Arrendel trusted him. The level and intensity of their conversations had forged a strong bond between them.

Arrendel wondered if he'd see Thomas again before his Year and a Day was over...

...which reminded the Water Faerie that he should talk with Maggie about the fact that he probably knew the charm that could keep him safe and well Upworld, and would allow them to be together from now on, without the unhappy forced separations they'd endured.

He wondered if he should simply perform the charm ritual alone, and then tell her he was here to stay. All things being equal, and not wanting to cause her distress, that might be best. On the other hand, he wasn't sure he wanted to have the *why didn't you tell me before you did this?* conversation with her, either. He would hate to have to own up to the idea that she very possibly would have been right about that.

He hadn't actually come to terms with the cost of the charm yet, but every day and night he spent with Maggie reinforced the rightness of staying, which meant he had to take care of it one of these days soon. He had the thing planned well, whenever he meant to go through with it. It could look accidental, if it came to that.

As he pulled the car into the long driveway and up to the house, Arrendel realized that he and Maggie hadn't broached the subject of when he would have to leave again for Elvenhome, to rest up after the effects of living out of his depth Upworld. That particular talk didn't usually come up until he had been with her a few months, and he'd started to weaken and fade.

He made a mental note to plan to talk with her about it as soon as he'd made up his mind about performing the charm's ritual. Satisfied, he reached for the box of tools and the bag of groceries he'd purchased in the village, and got out of the car.

He opened the front door and nearly dropped everything he was carrying.

Thomas Lear was singing "Dangerous Blue Eyes" quite loudly.

For a second or two, Arrendel was nearly toppled by confusion and context. By the time Maggie came out of the kitchen thirty seconds later, dancing around and singing along with Thomas, Arrendel had caught his breath, put the boxes and bag down on the table, and taken his coat and gloves off.

He strolled over to the stereo, lifted the album jacket for a look at his friend, and grinned happily.

Maggie, still singing, danced over to Arrendel and gave him a Welcome Home kiss. "Did you pick up the potatoes for dinner?" she asked, as "Dangerous Blue Eyes" ended and there was a few seconds' silence before the next song.

Nodding at her, Arrendel's grin broadened. "If there's nothing good on TV, whose turn is it to tell stories tonight?"

Acoustic guitar music, the beginning of the next song on the album, poured from the stereo speakers. Maggie tilted her head and smiled, not sure of what he was grinning about but enjoying the strangely happy look on his face. "It's yours, of course. You know that. Why?" She turned the volume down on the stereo and looked at him expectantly.

Spontaneously reversing a firm decision about which stories he'd tell of Elvenhome, Arrendel began to laugh, and put down the album jacket as Thomas Lear sang another song. "Oh, Maggie...I have a story to tell you."

WHEN THE SECOND message from Swiftaine arrived that day at the Queen's apartments, delivered by a liveried Guard, Callie was at her desk in her study, reading a petition from the elder Kelpies of Loch Alsh. They requested that Her Royal Highness come and mediate some minor territorial squabbles with their Naiad neighbors. Callie was considering a diplomatic way of telling them all to grow up when Lavender knocked on the door.

"Pardon the interruption, Your Grace..."

Still thinking about the petition, Callie looked up. "Yes, Lavender?"

"Another message has arrived from Swiftaine, Your Grace."

"Really?"

Lavender nodded. "He respectfully asks to speak with you privately, Iris said."

Paying attention now, Callie sat back in her chair and stared at the blonde Elf, who was fingering her tail beads nervously. "A *private* audience? Did he say what he wants to see me about?"

"No, Your Grace. But he seems to wish to speak with you very much."

Callie scrunched her face up in thought. "What could he possibly want? Clearly it has to do with Lord Guardian. I'd imagine he is itching to go Upworld to follow him."

"Perhaps he wishes to visit the Lady Maggie's cats?" Lavender suggested.

"That would not surprise me. But no; I told Guardian I would keep that Spriggan out of his way for a while, and I shall keep my word. Please ask Violete to find our friend Swiftaine, and inform him that the High Queen's pleasure is to speak to him next week about whatever might be on his mind." "Yes, Your Grace." Lavender turned to go.

"And Lavender...would you also have Iris ask the Court Singer if he will join me here for dinner this evening? Tell her venison, potatoes, and a hearty soup...with goldenfruit on the side as an extra treat for me."

A little while later, there was a distinctive humming near Callie's open bedroom door. The Queen, stretched out on a rose-colored chaise beside the large, sunny window, was reading Thomas' favorite novel. She put it down as the hum got louder, and raised her hand to signal permission for the humming's entry.

"What did he say, Violet?"

The small winged Lady fluttered in the air in front of Her Grace. "He did not say much, Your Majesty. Only that he must speak with you about a private matter of great urgency. He regrets, too, that he has compromised your good opinion of him." Violet saw the look of annoyed disbelief on Callie's face, and she shrugged as she hovered, her purple wings moving sensuously. "I know, Your Grace. But that is what he said."

"Well," Callie conceded, "he does know that I am as good as my word, and that he will be punished if he disobeys my order to leave Guardian and Maggie until Guardian indicates otherwise. I do not think he will ignore my wishes concerning this. Is it that I have not had enough Folk keep him occupied in Guardian's absence? You know, I could arrange to have him visit the Western Kingdoms for several months and..." The small Sprite's wings fluttered faster, and Callie caught the troubled look in her eyes. "What?"

"It is only that he looked so very unhappy, Your Grace."

Juniper had finished dressing the High Queen for her dinner with the Court Singer, and had begun to brush her dark hair. They were discussing which jewelry would be most attractive with the Queen's amber gown this evening when Iris walked into the bedroom and over to the Queen. She nodded at Juniper and said quietly, "Leave us."

Juniper immediately nodded back, and left.

Callie turned to face Iris, her question evident on her face.

"Your Grace, I have received word that Swiftaine is waiting in the corridor outside your Presence Chamber. He is quiet, causing no disruption. He is standing there, has been been waiting there, it seems, for several hours."

"Stubborn Spriggan," Callie wondered how far he was going to push her before she relented, and why. "I never considered him tenacious. I may have to revise my perception of him, when we talk next week."

"Your Grace, there is something else." Iris' frowned, uneasy. "He is not alone as he waits on your good pleasure. Master Snick...er...Ocelot, waits with him."

With no ceremony at all, Master Ocelot and Swiftaine were ushered into the Queen's Presence Chamber. The

High Queen of Faerie sat on her throne, and watched as they approached her. Four of the Queen's Ladies—Iris, Violet, Carnation and Rose—attended Her Grace.

"Master Ocelot. Swiftaine."

The ancient apothecary bowed deeply. The Spriggan bowed deeper still. Callie wondered if he was going to hit the floor.

"Swiftaine, you have brought reinforcement. Suppose you tell me what this is about."

The Spriggan squirmed uncomfortably, long fingers twitching. He gazed around the large room, at the guards at the doors, at the Queen's Ladies, and then at the Queen herself. "Your Grace..." he began, then stopped. He looked miserable.

Something was wrong. It made no sense for the Spriggan to have won an audience with her by allying with Master Ocelot, and then hesitating to speak. "Well?" she asked.

Swiftaine looked at Master Ocelot helplessly. The apothecary put his hand on the Spriggan's shoulder in a gesture of kind reassurance, and then addressed Callie.

"Your Grace, we may have a situation. If in fact we do, it might be well for all concerned if what Swiftaine must tell you is heard by your ears alone. He is honor-bound in two different directions. He needs your wisdom and wit to enable him to both speak and not speak." The Spriggan trembled slightly. "I am aware of enough of the matter to be able to assure you that, if I may be bold, Your Grace, he should speak with a few less Folk present."

Callie considered this. "Very well." She nodded at the Guards, who exited to keep watch on the other side of the doors. Then she glanced at Iris, who bowed, and began to usher the other Ladies out of the Presence Chamber. As the Ladies bowed and turned to go, Callie said quietly, "Rose, please remain and attend me."

The Pixie and her tall and pointed bright green hat turned back and moved to a position twenty feet from the Queen. She stood silent and unmoving, her dark eyes lowered in a considerate attempt to seem invisible in the circumstance.

The High Queen gestured. "Well, then? Swiftaine, Master Ocelot, what is this about?"

Master Ocelot and Swiftaine exchanged a heavy glance. The Master of the Library nodded gravely, and then turned his eyes to Callie and asked:

"How much does Your Grace know about Lord Guardian's research regarding finding a way to safely remain Upworld with his lady on a permanent basis?"

If Callie had been wary about whatever this strange conversation was going to be about, she relaxed now. "I know all. Guardian and I have spoken about it on several occasions. I have sometimes assisted in the gathering of the information that he seeks."

Master Ocelot looked grim. "We have reason to believe that you do not know all, Your Grace. We have grave concerns that we must share with you. Swiftaine here is caught between two sharp swords: his loyalty to Lord Guardian is at dangerous odds with the information he holds, that you should hold as well."

"Rose," Callie said, without taking her eyes from Swiftaine, whose unspoken tension seemed to fill the room, "we are going into the back chamber. Please arrange for refreshment for our friends and return at once to attend me. Gentlemen, follow."

As Rose and her hat hurried obediently out of the Presence Chamber, Callie stood up from her throne and walked behind it to the back wall, upon which hung a massive tapestry illustrating a huge Fey feast. Reaching the far end of the tapestry, Callie lifted the fabric aside, revealing a door. At her touch, the door opened, and the

High Queen went inside, with Master Ocelot and Swiftaine behind her.

There were two pitchers of fresh water and three goblets on the small round table in the tiny chamber. Rose stood by the door and resumed her stance of near-invisibility. Master Ocelot, Swiftaine, and Callie sat at the table. The Queen and the Master talked about Guardian and his quest. Swiftaine listened, his face pinched and anxious.

"What happened to the ritual charm you asked Jareedle of the West about? Guardian told me that you had asked for confirmation, Master."

"Lord Guardian had already gone Upworld by the time I received word from Jareedle and, sadly, that ritual charm would not have given the young Lord what he wants in any event."

Swiftaine was angry, frightened, frustrated, and agitated all at once. "That is not the point! He had already moved beyond that charm before he left."

Callie's eyebrows lifted. "What was he planning, Swiftaine?"

The miserable Spriggan met his Queen's eyes. "Your Grace, he found five references to one of the charms attributed to the Duke of Elvenstorm. He said it was consistent with other credible things he had studied about the Fey staying safely Upworld..."

Callie wasn't listening; she was thinking, fast. "The *first* Duke of Elvenstorm? The brother of the High King's great-grandsire?" Her eyes widened.

Swiftaine nodded unhappily.

"Great Gods, the first Duke was as mad as a hatless Pixie grandmother at a tea party—pardon me, Rose..."

Rose nodded, effectively hiding an inappropriate smirk as she touched her own tall hat. "Pardoned, Your Grace."

Callie stood up, and she started to pace. "I never bothered to read any of Elvenstorm's manuscripts, because apparently he was the member of the family who shifted himself into large birds and flew headfirst into trees. He was a kind man, by all accounts, and meant to be helpful, but he was out of his mind." She stopped, and stared at Swiftaine before she glanced at Master Ocelot's unhappy face. "This seems to be news to you, too, and that makes me nervous. If you did not know about Elvenstorm, then it's quite possible that Guardian didn't, either. What charm could Guardian possibly think was credible?"

With tears welling in his eyes, Swiftaine stood on the seat of his chair and muttered "I am in the right, still I have betrayed him. Unforgiveable...unforgiveable!"

The Spriggan nodded at the Master, who took a small scroll out of his vest pocket. This he handed to Callie, his fingers trembling.

She opened the scroll and read it quickly:

> To stay Upworld with Lady Love
> Affection you must prove;
> Forget the past it must be said
> Give your fingers to the blade.
>
> Webbed Water Sprites Fair water breathe,
> Fair light and food they need;
> But if Home for Love you do depart
> Be certain of who rules your heart
>
> To work this charm, repeat the rill
> "I do this for love, of my own free will."
> And with the blade does your world expand
> By cleaving off the two first fingers of your
> own left hand
>
> Once severed bury them by a loch

228

And over them a vow you make
To stay Above for all your days
And live in Love, in all love's ways.

Callie scoffed as she looked up. "He's far too intelligent and experienced to even consider this. He'd have laughed and ignored it."

Master Ocelot shook his head. "I agree with Your Grace, under most circumstances. Yet it must be said that the young Lord has not been himself since The Mischief. During your absence, he was all that the Folk could ask him to be, and he served well in his duties as Heir Apparent, but I saw myself that the toll on him was immense. I would suggest that he has been under heavy strain since that time. I have had some concerns that in his exhausted state of mind, perhaps he is not thinking as clearly as he normally does."

Callie listened, and bit her lip.

"His understandable choice to be with his beloved Upworld was likely deepened by his need to get away from the harsh memories of The Mischief. The last time I spoke with him, he appeared more than eager to go Upworld. Your Grace, he seemed *relieved*."

Sadly, Swiftaine raised his left hand in the air above his head as he lowered the two long fingers closest to his thumb. "The more he read, researched and studied, the more he needed to believe this to be the true answer he seeks. I tried to discourage him, for he has been too tired to think of anything else. This charm is a bad idea; even a Mountain Troll would think so. I told him that, too, Your Grace. "He does not wish to do this thing, but I know he will. He means to stay with her, no matter the cost."

Callie swore wildly and colorfully, enough to make Master Snick—who was two hundred fifty years her senior—blanch in surprise. She paced as she swore; no one else moved so much as a muscle. Rose stared at the floor, and wished that she were indeed invisible.

Before twenty seconds more had passed, the High Queen of Faerie made her decision. "How long will it take you to get to him?" she asked the Spriggan.

"Four stops, Your Grace," he whined, his misery shining in his eyes. "Four."

Callie mentally counted them, and sighed. "Swiftaine, I believe you're right. Not only will the ritual for Guardian's charm be horrid, it will be for nothing. The damned thing does not work, it cannot." The Queen moved to stand in front of him, and touched his shoulder lightly. "I will show you my gratitude later. Now, go to him. Stop him. Send word back to me. Go now!"

At the same instant that the Spriggan sprang into action and evaporated into the tension-filled air, Callie's spontaneous burst of verdant flame went with him, speeding him faster and farther on his way.

AS HE WORKED on the canoe in the quiet warmth of the heated garage, Arrendel wrestled with his problem. He hated the fact that he had to make a call and act on it either way. He knew he could find a way to deal with the finality of the thing, but actually making the decision? It was worth it in the long run, but was it the right thing to do? How would it affect the other people in his life? How would Maggie feel if...

It was the curse of his personality that he could see so many sides of a single issue, and then be haunted by the possibilities of a wrong move, the path overlooked, the best choice not chosen.

He felt trapped by fate, again, and swore irritably as he drove small nails into the wood. There were layers upon layers of repercussions, were there not? How could he do the right thing for everyone and still attain his goal?

He wondered what his cousin would do with his dilemma. She was always decisive. She acted swiftly once she'd chosen her path, and she never regretted her actions. Or did she? Arrendel didn't think so. She knew how to make a judgment call and stick with it. She made her choices instantly, didn't waste any time whining, then lived with the consequences of her actions.

Why wasn't he more like her? They shared blood, and he knew her better than he knew anyone else. He loved her as much as he loved Maggie; he had certainly loved her longer. Why hadn't he learned how to be spontaneously decisive, and how to live with the results?

He was tired. He'd noticed that even though his body had rested well, and he had physical energy again, his mind was still tired and restless as he tried to make sense out of things that should never have had to be considered. He did not believe he could face the decisions he'd had to make at home any more than he wanted to face the decisions that stood in front of him now. Thinking had never been a chore for him. Why did it seem so these days?

Of course Maggie had noticed his preoccupation, even from the depths of her own. He had assured her that he merely had much on his mind, and that it was nothing important enough to talk about while she was so focused on her work. Which was true, to a point: in his heart of hearts, Arrendel had not yet committed himself to the action of performing the ritual that would work the charm to keep him Upworld safely.

He could put off thinking about it all for another month and a half, perhaps two months. But then he'd find himself in this same intellectual space, with the added complication of the physical problems inherent in having stayed too long away from home.

No, he sighed and told himself, the anger in his frustration fading into a sad resignation in the face of his too-many choices. *No. Putting it off makes no sense.*

Prolonging the inevitable is not going to serve me, or anyone else.

He looked at the tools mounted on the garage wall and found the hatchet. It was in its place, hanging beside the axe and the other tools he used when he cut firewood. He shuddered involuntarily. Taking a deep breath, he put his hammer down on the work table, and walked over to the hatchet. He touched it. It was cold.

He was cold, now, too. He had begun to tremble slightly.

The decision was made. Had he made it, or had his fate made it for him?

Was it really that easy? He asked himself. *One minute I'm vacillating on every point, and the next, I'm clear and certain, and will do the deed. Or am I so tired of thinking about it that I simply can't think about it any longer?*

He shook his head to clear it. He did not want to gauge his courage or his strength, he simply needed to do this thing, and be done with it. He would deal with the resulting issues later.

Faeries do not lie, but they have been known, on occasion, to attempt to shield those they love with worthy distractions from a harsh truth. Arrendel would imply that the unpleasant injury was an accident caused by carelessness with the hatchet. Maggie would be upset by the event itself, and upset later when he eventually told her about the ritual that supported the charm. He would be able to help her see that this was the right—and only—thing to do. She would come to understand that he had made the best decision for them.

Still, he would miss the use of his hand. He wondered if there would be much blood, and how bad the pain would be.

With a resigned sigh, Arrendel raised the hatchet high above his head as he looked down at the delicately-webbed fingers of his left hand.

"Done is done," he said.

He raised the hatchet above his head and, gaining the necessary momentum, brought it down with all his might.

Arrendel screamed in blinding pain.

fourteen

ARRENDEL'S ANGUISHED SCREAM merged with a higher-pitched one, and the hatchet slammed to the floor behind him as Swiftaine, post-collision, made a hard crash-landing on the work table in front of him.

Water Faerie and Spriggan gaped at each other, each gasping for air, their eyes maddened and wild. They yelled at each other simultaneously.

"Don't do it!" Swiftaine demanded in a shriek.

"What are you doing?" Arrendel roared.

Out of breath, Arrendel slumped to the garage floor, and found himself sitting a foot and a half from the hatchet. He kicked it away, trembling as much from the adrenaline rush and the intensity of what he'd just attempted to do as from the emotional shock of having been thwarted.

Above him, Swiftaine was lying flat on top of the work table, all but passed out from exhaustion. The Spriggan's head hung weakly over the side so he could glare down at Arrendel.

"I told you it was a bad idea!" he barked hoarsely.

"I think you broke my wrist!" Arrendel scowled, rubbing it. "Are you insane?"

At that, Swiftaine rolled his head back onto the tabletop, and started to laugh. "No, I'm not insane...but apparently the Duke of Elvenstorm *was*..."

Inside the garage, they talked, stopping only for Swiftaine to pop unseen into the cottage to collect a much-needed bottle of whisky and two glasses. Arrendel was grateful for Maggie's preoccupation with her manuscript today. He was not ready to talk to her.

Seated on a short stepladder, he was still rubbing his injured wrist. Swiftaine had bounded into him out of nowhere and roughly forced the hatchet from his hand. "I suppose it makes sense, now, but I don't know how I missed discovering the fact of the Duke's insanity."

"Do not feel too badly about that, My Lord. Master Snick was shocked by it as well. But there was no doubt in Her Grace's mind. 'Mad as a hatless Pixie,' she said."

A smile tugged itself across Arrendel's lips; he couldn't help it. Sitting on top of the work table, his feet swinging below, Swiftaine poured more whisky into their glasses.

"It is good that I could be of service to Her Grace this day, My Lord. I have been perceived as something of a pest—"

"Oh, that's a stretch," Arrendel interrupted with a snort.

"—but she knew that I would be best at the task of reaching you quickly," Swiftaine continued without acknowledging the interruption or the sarcasm. "I would not doubt that she envies the Spriggan ability to move quickly from place to place. She shifts her shape magnificently, to be sure, but she is forced to journey in more traditional ways. She cannot travel like this!" He was gone.

Rolling his eyes, Arrendel turned his head and faced far to his left an instant before Swiftaine reappeared by the garage's door. Gesturing theatrically, Swiftaine popped out again, reappearing on top of the work table again. "It is good to be a Spriggan. Especially one who has earned the Queen's favor."

"For a short while, anyway. You will fall from grace soon enough. You always do."

Swiftaine tried to be offended, but he couldn't help himself; he laughed merrily, and Arrendel laughed with him. "You are right. I do."

"Her Grace will want word that you were able to avert the situation—for which, may I thank you again, Old Friend."

The Spriggan bowed his acknowledgment. "I have already given a message to one of the Glaistigs in Maggie's loch; she was waiting for me at the Queen's request. I spoke to her when I went after the whisky. Her Grace will know you are safe and well, apart from a sore wrist, before long."

The Water Faerie nodded. "Good. I do not wish her to be anxious on my account. I am certain she has other, more pressing things, on her mind."

"True enough," Swiftaine agreed. "There is much activity at the Castle, and I know more than Her Grace thinks I do. Do you wish to know of it, or would you rather not?"

Arrendel groaned as he braced himself. "Tell me," he said.

Tired but in a good mood after her long day at the typewriter, Maggie walked into the living room from her office, and was startled to discover Menace curled up asleep with Tristan and Abbey in Arrendel's favorite chair. She opened her mouth, but closed it again abruptly. The Spriggan was back.

A small sound behind her made her turn and smile at the man she loved as he walked to where she was standing.

He tilted his head in the direction of the sleeping piles of fur, his eyes questioning.

Maggie shrugged, smiled ruefully, and put her arms around him.

He held her close, and breathed another silent prayer filled with humble, if still somewhat shaky, gratitude. At Home, the King and Queen had everything as much in control as possible, and all was well here. Mazzin would be found, and stopped. For his part, Arrendel had Maggie to love. He promised himself that soon he would think of new ways to uncover the secret of staying Upworld with her.

All was indeed well.

And then he trembled, nearly overcome by the intensity of the realization that by the grace of the gods— to say nothing of the sheer force of Swiftaine's devotion, stubbornness, and speed—Arrendel still had his left hand.

THE HIGH KING of Faerie, and his royal vassal, the King of the Northern Lands, sprawled on long, facing couches in the center of a round, recreational suite and stared at each other, unspoken threats vivid in their eyes. Bright sunshine streamed in through tall windows, and made the golden oak leaves on the High King's royal circlet dazzle, spraying refracted light on the nearest walls.

Not a word had been exchanged for what seemed, to Horshog's attendants and also to the four High King's Men present, a long time. No one moved a fraction of an inch as the Kings silently measured each other. Everyone wondered who would speak first, and how this game would be played to their own master's benefit.

The stronger of the two rulers broke the silence.

"I believe the High Queen may be on to something, Horshog," said the High King casually, never moving his eyes from the Goblin King's. "She thinks you look alarmingly like a stoat."

Horshog didn't blink, but he gave his regal guest a bland smile. "Her Royal Highness is quite wrong, I regret to say."

"Truly?"

"It is my view that stoats aspire, Your Grace, to look like *me*."

The High King also smiled blandly, his eyes still on Horshog's. "I will be sure to re-educate Her Royal Majesty in this regard."

"I hope so—with my deepest respects, Your Grace."

"Most certainly, Horshog."

Neither King relaxed his stare even at some spontaneous but quickly muffled snickering from several of the attendants.

Horshog, still eyeing the High King, raised his hand in command. "Bring wine. Much wine. All shall attend me from the farthest point across the room."

Horshog's five servants scurried for wine and their new position, which appeared to be fully out of earshot.

The High King smiled a fraction more, gray eyes still holding the gaze of Horshog's black ones. He tilted his head very slightly, and immediately the King's Men strode to the area at the opposite position that several of Horshog's attendants occupied.

Wine was brought by one of Horshog's people, a shrunken Goblin who took his time pouring two large heavily-decorated cups, then ceremoniously sauntered around before he placed them on the small tables beside the long couches upon which royalty lay. The Goblin joined his fellows and waited for further instruction, while the Kings drank in silence.

When he had finished the last of the wine in his cup, the High King glanced lazily at his host while he scratched his ear. "Tell me, Horshog, is your great-uncle Riban still studying enchantment and practicing his thaumaturgical arts?"

"Here at the castle, do you mean, Your Grace?"

The High King shrugged. "Here, or anywhere at all."

Horshog shook his head. "No, not to my knowledge."

"Is he dead and gone, then?" asked the High King with a subtle raise of an eyebrow. "I had not heard."

"Oh, no, Your Grace. Uncle Riban is still among us, so to speak. He had something of a bad experience while recreating an ancient love charm for the heir of the Count of Discoll, quite an unpleasant-looking young man—looks as though he's related to the back end of a boar. Seems he wanted to attract a small multitude of young ladies simultaneously, to overpopulate his bed without expending too much energy getting their attention." Horshog giggled. "Anyway, Uncle Riban picked the wrong time to call on the ugly young heir...he was hosting a large gathering of his private guards, his military advisors, the leaders of his mercantile holdings, and his political council. Uncle Riban strode in, offered the charm as requested, and the ugly idiot demanded it be given to him at once, so that the expected adoring ladies would flock to him as soon as he finished with his meeting. But Uncle Riban did something wrong, missed a cue, forgot a word, who knows what. And suddenly every man within earshot fell immediately and somewhat violently in love with Boar-face. Including, it was said, Uncle Riban, until the charm eventually wore off. There was some bloodshed, some very soldierly thwacking, and more than a few dozen broken hearts before the episode concluded."

"How unfortunate," said the High King. "Or not, depending. So, Horshog, where is Riban now?"

"He has permanently retired to his manor at the eastern tip of my kingdom, where I'm told that he practices his strange art on his house pets, and has been documenting his ridiculous encyclopedia of historical magic. He is more or less harmless, but I am glad that he chooses to stay secluded from the world so I do not have to think about him. Why do you ask?"

Without taking his eyes from his host, the High King nodded acknowledgement at the servant who was pouring him more wine. "Small talk, perhaps. Simple curiosity, nothing more."

The two Kings continued to stare at each other for a long moment. Then the Goblin King sighed.

"So we come to it, Your Grace," Horshog began, looking away from the High King for a flicker of an instant, thus conceding the subtle stare-down. "We come to it. There is no recompense for the death of a son. How then will you satisfy the wrong done to me?"

The High King studied his wine cup, twirling it slowly in his hand to see the extravagant design work. "Your son, Horshog, was a monster."

"Yes, he was. But I had plans for him anyway."

The High King's eyes shot from the cup to Horshog's face in inquiry.

"I would never have let him rule, of course," Horshog continued with a shrug. "But I would have used him for a fascinating object lesson. Unfortunately, Your Grace, none of my wives like me very much, so it is improbable that I shall have any more sons." Horshog drank his wine petulantly. "Which puts me in an unenviable position in terms of succession."

"Let me guess: Your cousin Mazzin is next in line to rule after you."

Horshog nodded, frowning. "True. But at present he needs something of the magnitude of the Greencrystal to impress me. And also to keep me from killing him for all the unwieldy tangles his Mischief has caused the realm. One wonders if he plans to honor me with the Stone, or if he will attempt to use it to defend himself against my ire for his inconveniences. I can hardly wait to find out."

"So you do not possess the Greencrystal. I wondered if perhaps you had it here, and wanted to return it to me personally."

"Your Grace, if I had the Stone, my cousin would be no more, and I should be in a better position to bargain with you about many things, my next heir among them."

The High King knew Horshog was telling the truth. He was both relieved and discouraged about this. "Where is Mazzin now?" he asked.

"I do not know. I am only certain that he is not in the Northern Lands, or I would already have him."

The High King nodded. "So why did you send that stupid missive all but demanding my presence here? It was all I could do to keep Bann from coming with me so he could stomp on you himself."

"Ah," Horshog said, acknowledging the High Queen's Councilor's frustration with a wink. "Good. I wrote the message in the hopes of forcing the energy to move, so that Mazzin would be more inclined to come out of hiding and do something so we can find him, and *end* him."

We? thought the High King. *Maybe there is some small hope for Horshog yet.* He said aloud: "Does Mazzin have so many spies that he would be able to easily track my movements throughout the land? Or use them to hear conversations in my castles?"

"I doubt it." Horshog stopped speaking, considering whether he should admit to something or not. He decided to confess it: "He does not need spies or an army. Your Grace...he scries," he murmured.

"I know."

If Horshog was surprised by this, he did not let on. "It always seemed a useful tool, and Mazzin is quite good at it."

"You know the rules, Horshog. I did not write them, but I must uphold them. Can he scry and see us here?"

"Not as long as those bloodwine vines in the wall torches continue to burn." He pointed to the torches ensconced on all four walls of the room, and nodded at the dark gray smoke that protected them from being seen through scrying.

"Well done, Horshog." The High King frowned. "He will still have to be punished. He has much to answer for."

"He is of royal blood, Your Grace, and as such—"

"But he is badly bent toward the Unseelie way..."

"—True enough—" Horshog interrupted quietly.

"...and that is a problem," the High King finished, his eyes flashing at his vassal king as he smoothly rolled and rose from the couch. "Your cousin is going to cause a great deal of commotion if he is not found soon, and stopped. I agree with you that it is unlikely that he will come to you unless and until he feels he has need of something from you.

"Once he has been dealt with, come to see me at Elvenhome, and we will talk about your succession situation. In the meanwhile," the High King nodded at the still-prone Horshog as the King's Men moved to follow him toward the door, "in the meanwhile, stay out of trouble, so perhaps you will not *need* to worry about an heir for a while."

THE RAINY WINDSTORM that quickly darkened the early afternoon sky came without warning.

Maggie closed the windows in the living room. She loved storms, the wilder the better, and she found herself looking forward to the *Mother Nature Is Pissed* feel of this one. She smiled as she remembered the windy, rain-swirling night she'd encountered Arrendel for the first time. *And Menace, too*, she reminded herself.

The wind blew harder around the cottage, making trees bend a bit. The word "tornado" crossed her mind, but she discarded it as Arrendel hurried in the front door, closing it firmly behind him.

"Did you read or hear that we were getting a heavy storm today? Was it on the news?" he asked her as he removed his jacket.

"No," she replied. "This is strange for April, but it'll probably make for a lively evening."

The electricity went out a little while later, but Maggie had prepared for this inevitability. A dozen candles, a few well-placed torches, and a roaring fire lit up the living room, dining room and kitchen area.

Menace and the cats dozed in their usual pile in their usual place on one of the two couches near the fire. Maggie and Arrendel occupied the second couch, and listened to the wind howl and roar as the rain beat down hard on the roof and against the windows. Thunder bellowed irritably in the distance, over by the vast woodland a mile from the cottage.

"You haven't told me," Maggie began quietly, so as not to be overheard, "what brought him Upworld this time. Purposeful, or did he just miss you?"

Arrendel smiled, and wondered how to address the question without answering it. Inspiration struck: "Missing your privacy, are you?" he winked at her.

"Yes, a little," she said, eyeing him. "Avoiding the question, are you?"

"Yes, a little," he admitted, staring into the fireplace.

"Does it have something to do with whatever it was that upset you so badly at home that you don't really want to talk about it?"

He wanted to tell her; he knew he should tell her. But he had considered how much he'd have to explain and reveal: the layers of what had happened, why it had happened, the role he'd played in its aftermath and, finally what he'd nearly done in order to stay with her. There was as much sense in not telling her very much as there was in

243

telling her all. In truth, he could not decide which was the wiser course, the best choice. How long had he been this tired?

He belatedly realized that he had been silent for too long. Now she was studying him with concern. "My dear—"

At that moment, Maggie's cats, Tristan and Abbey, spontaneously woke from their nap. Their heads shot up, eyes wide, ears back and flat against their heads, and whiskers quivering. In a flash, they bolted from the couch, waking the Spriggan as they tore away from him and fled toward the back of the house.

"Hey!" Menace yelped. He had a few cat-scratches on his hairy arms. "Why did they—"

The sound of the wind grew louder and faster; Maggie thought she heard large tree branches cracking. The rain slammed against the house, as if in an attempt to break the windows. And behind it all, a series of heavy, rhythmic thuds shook the ground and seemed to be making their way toward the cottage.

Menace sniffed the air, and his eyes widened. He and Arrendel exchanged an alarmed glance that Maggie didn't see as she stood up and moved toward the windows to see what was going on. Menace nodded his head. Water Faerie and Spriggan were both on their feet, rigid with anticipation of something dangerous that they sensed as accurately as the cats had only seconds before.

The thudding came closer, louder now, competing with the noise of the storm around them.

"Maggie, come here, please," Arrendel had to yell to be heard over the chaos. She was beside him instantly. He reached for her, and for the Dunnor's Bell on the chain around her neck. He held her against him, and spoke directly to the Bell: "Please stay silent until she is safe."

The Bell made no sound, even when Arrendel shook it. "Good. Thank you," he said. Then he pulled Maggie even closer, and told her calmly, "Go to your office, my love. Hide in the supply closet, under a blanket or something. Be as still and quiet as you can. Stay there until I come for you."

Stunned, she pulled back a little, and gaped at him in growing alarm. He gave her a quick shove in the direction the cats had gone. "There is no time...go!"

Maggie looked into his eyes for a fraction of an instant longer, then turned, grabbed a quilt from the back of a couch, and ran toward her office at the far end of the cottage.

Now Menace was standing on top of the television, looking out of the windows to see what was happening. As Arrendel reached him, they understood the situation and identified it at the same time:

"Mazzin."

The rhythmic pounding and the shaking of the ground stopped. For a moment, the only sound they could hear was the angry wind hurling the wild rain around the outside of the cottage.

And then, as suddenly as it began, the wind and the rain stopped.

The quiet was overpowering.

Grimly, Menace glanced at Arrendel. "This is not going to be good," he whispered.

"I know."

Seconds later, the sounds of a great deal of wood shattering and metal crunching ripped through the heavy silence.

Arrendel and Menace ran out of the cottage to face whatever was out there in the wet, sunless afternoon.

The first thing they saw was the Cave Troll, methodically destroying Maggie's garage and everything in it—including Arrendel's canoe. Twenty feet tall, and about half as wide, the Troll had vaguely greenish, scaly skin. He wore a short vest and some material that passed for loose breeches. He roared incoherently and flailed his arms around as he smashed and stomped the small building into rubble.

Behind the Cave Troll, coming slowly into view, were a somewhat shabby band of Folk that were likely up to no good: four Gnomes, two Bogles, and five HobGoblins made their way toward the cottage, glaring at Arrendel and Menace.

Two taller figures walked behind the wave of Gnomes, Bogles and Hobs. One was a Phooka, a creature nearly seven feet tall with the body of a man, the bearded face and head of a bull, crowned with heavy, wild horns. He was naked, his skin a faint shade of blue-gray. He had a short tail, and the sharp and heavy claws at the ends of his fingers and the strong hooves of his feet punctuated the sense of danger he invoked.

Beside the Phooka walked a graceful, devilishly-attractive, and naked man-shaped creature. Something over six feet, he was a Bodach, born of shadows, mystery and lust. He was winged; his wings were the same dusky shades of gray, brown and blue as the rest of him. He was dark-eyed and smiling as he strode toward the cottage, the smile as dark, disturbing, and lecherous as the energy that flowed around him.

Menace was about to say something to Arrendel, but Arrendel raised his hand for silence as he caught sight of the person he'd been waiting for.

Mazzin strolled with deliberate ceremony at the end of the parade. He was enjoying the moment, and Arrendel could see why: around the Goblin's neck hung the Greencrystal Pendant.

Taking a deep breath, Arrendel muttered to Menace. "It's him. He's got the Greencrystal. It appears that he is going to use it."

"Oh dear," groaned Menace. "What do you want me to do?"

Arrendel's gaze never left the slowly-approaching group, even when the Cave Troll had finished destroying the garage and began stomping on Maggie's car. "Swiftaine, protect Maggie, and the cats. Her home, if you can." He swallowed hard, summoning up a small and subtle blue flickering of light around his hands. "Protect my love at all costs," he repeated. "It appears that I am going to be busy for a while."

"I hear and obey, my Lord—"

Menace was interrupted by a gravelly shout from the Phooka: "Surround the house! Do not allow the woman to escape!"

The Gnomes and the Bogles scurried to positions around the cottage. At the same moment, the HobGoblins rushed toward Arrendel, Menace evaporated into the air, the Cave Troll was eating the remains of Maggie's car, the Phooka roared as he raced directly at Arrendel, and the Bodach indolently slowed his pace to walk beside Mazzin, whose black eyes glowed with pleasure at the mounting chaos around him.

Arrendel's blue light was no longer subtle. It burned bright, hot, and potent as it grew from the space around his hands and began to fill the air. "Mazzin!" he yelled above the confusion, "Enough! You shall not cause harm this day, or any other! You are finished!"

The powerful Water Faerie lifted his hands in the air, pointed his fingers at the Goblin and his minions, and sent a burst of wild, blue fire blazing at them.

But Arrendel's fiery force didn't go very far. It took him a second to understand why.

Mazzin stood twenty feet from him, the Greencrystal raised high above his head. The Goblin had spoken the Word, and used the awakened Stone to diffuse Arrendel's blue fire. The bright blue light was dissolving in front of him.

Just as Arrendel realized that he could not lower his hands, or speak, the Phooka and four of the five HobGoblins crashed into him, knocking him to the ground. The fifth Hob dashed into the cottage, followed by a curious Bodach and an amused Goblin.

"Hurt him," Mazzin ordered over his shoulder before he went through the front door. "And when you have grown tired of hurting him, hurt him a bit more, then bring him inside."

"I have seen that she is in this house," said the Goblin from his position in the easy chair nearest the fireplace. "The scrying wine never lies. Find her." He ignored the beating going on outside as he smiled at the Bodach standing across the room, who was looking at Maggie's bookcases. "When we have what we came for, you may have the woman. It is the least I can do to reward you for your service."

The Bodach turned to face Mazzin, and inclined his head, a leering grin stretching his handsome face. Bodachs do not have vocal chords, but make up for it with extremely expressive facial and physical non-verbal communication.

The HobGoblin who had been sent into the cottage to find Maggie scurried down the staircase, shaking his head. He glanced around the living room, then scurried down the back hall to continue looking for her.

After several minutes had passed, the Phooka entered the house, sluicing blood off his hands, arms and chest. "Unpleasant, and *most* pleasant, business. I needed the exercise."

Mazzin stretched and yawned. "I do not want him dead. Not yet. Do not let them kill him out there."

"They will not. They will only come close." The Phooka looked around the room. "Much less than I expected for a mortal prized by Fey royalty."

"There is no accounting for taste, especially where mortals are concerned." Mazzin patted the Greencrystal protectively as, outside, Arrendel cried out in pain. "We will be on our way soon. Where is the woman? Why hasn't that idiot Hob found her yet?"

"Would you like me to take care of that for you?"

"Give him a moment. He is the nephew of one of Horshog's advisors; I might need him later." Mazzin closed his eyes and was still for a minute or two as he listened to the activity outside, and then heard it stop. When the quiet continued, he opened his eyes and noted to the Phooka, "It sounds as though our friend has either died or fainted. He is useful to me for a while yet, so I do hope he is still alive."

"Does it really matter, when all is as you command it to be?"

"Perhaps. Perhaps not. But I would prefer to keep all tools at hand until I am certain they are no longer needed." Mazzin considered something for a heartbeat, then smiled benignly. "Enough. We have work to do before this day ends. Deal with the Hob as you please. I will not need him after all. I do not care what Horshog thinks. I would wager that he is not going to easily reconcile with me, so I will consider that road closed." The Goblin's confidence was evident as his smile grew larger. "I no longer need Horshog, or anyone else. Get the woman; I want her to see her lover."

Mazzin winked at the Bodach, and laughed when the Bodach beamed at back at him, and licked his lips.

The Phooka strode through the room all but shimmering with power. "I will find her. And I will crush the useless Hob for keeping you waiting."

He moved through the downstairs swiftly, sniffing for the Hob and the woman.

He found the Hob opening and closing drawers in a half-bathroom, looking for Maggie as he lifted toothbrushes, toothpaste, nail clippers, emery boards, and other objects out of the drawers, examining each item carefully.

The Phooka entered the bathroom and asked the HobGoblin: "Why are you looking for a mortal woman in small drawers and cupboards?"

The Hob froze in place, startled by the Phooka's sudden presence, then he smiled. "I am being thorough. She is not easy to find. She may have shifted her shape. It would be a clever disguise."

"You are certain she is not hiding upstairs?"

Nodding, the Hob began examining a stack of washcloths in another drawer. "Yes. I thought she might be hiding under the bed, but she was not. She is in none of the rooms up there; therefore she must be down here."

The Phooka feigned satisfaction. "That is very direct thinking."

The Hob smiled proudly; HobGoblins do not often get praised for thinking of any kind. "Thank you."

The Phooka nodded and, raising his right leg, effortlessly stomped the HobGoblin to death before the startled Hob could even let out a scream.

Shaking off the blood, the Phooka went from room to room, sniffing for mortal.

He found himself standing in the center of Maggie's office. Nose twitching, he looked around, his eyes resting on the closet in the corner.

Without warning, Abbey darted from her hiding place under Maggie's desk, and desperately raced for the door.

The Phooka reached for the cat in mid-dash, grabbed her and held her roughly in the air by the scruff of her neck as he examined her. "I have not yet eaten. Cat does not usually appeal, but today, I am prepared for anything."

He raised the screaming, thrashing and squirming cat to his open mouth.

"Are you then prepared for *this*?" Menace popped into the room, and wrapped his arms and hands around the Phooka's leg, clawing and biting as hard as he could.

The Phooka roared in rage, surprise, and a considerable amount of pain. He dropped Abbey. The cat landed on her feet, sped past him, and disappeared.

So did Menace.

Angry now, the Phooka gave his bleeding leg a quick look and, checking around for the Spriggan and finding him truly gone, walked over to the small closet, opened the door, and sniffed.

He smiled when what looked like a pile of clothing on the far side of the closet floor trembled uncontrollably.

The Hobs that had done most of the beating dragged the unconscious Water Faerie into the cottage, and shoved him into one of the three cane-backed kitchen chairs. He was then tied securely to the chair with thick rope supplied by the Gnomes, who can always be relied upon to be carrying useful things in their packs.

A sudden shaking of the cottage coincided with the sound of demolition; the Cave Troll's huge hands crushed the far corner of Maggie's living room, taking down part of the roof, much of the outside wall, and some windows.

"Not while we're inside, Troll," Mazzin ordered, his voice raised to be heard over the din. "Go away and eat what you've got in your hand, and wait."

The disappointed Cave Troll muttered something incomprehensible, lifted the pieces of the house he'd crushed, and carried them away.

Satisfied, Mazzin surveyed the activity as he settled back into the comfortable chair by the fire, and waited. He did not bother to hide the expectant look in his eyes.

There was a frightened scream and then sounds of struggling at the back of the house. The Phooka had located Maggie.

The Bodach turned toward the noise, which blended with some swearing and the knocking over of some furniture as the Phooka half-carried, half-pushed Maggie toward the living room. As they moved down the hallway, Maggie gasped, and started to cry.

"She must have seen what was left of that idiot Hob," Mazzin told the Bodach. "An instructive sight. Perhaps she will take it to heart and behave."

The Bodach grinned hungrily, now sporting an erection that spoke for itself.

Mazzin smirked as the Phooka and the woman entered.

Maggie's eyes were wild with shock, fear, and incomprehension. She understood that she was in the presence of the Fey, but she had no context, and so could not put any of the pieces together. Confused and terrified, her eyes darted around the room, desperately looking for Arrendel.

She groaned when she saw him, and at the same time struggled harder in the Phooka's arms in a useless attempt to break free and run to the man she loved.

He had been badly beaten. Both of his eyes had begun to swell shut. Blood ran from his nose, his mouth, and his ears. Part of the delicately-pointed tip of his left ear, sticking out from his matted blond hair, was missing. His clothes were torn, and Maggie could see that he was bleeding under what was left of his sweater and his jeans. Arrendel's left foot was twisted the wrong way.

She was instantly grateful that he was unconscious. She also presumed that if he was tied to the chair, he wasn't dead. Not yet.

Twisting away from the Phooka, who only released her at a nod from Mazzin, Maggie forced herself to look away from Arrendel, and focused on the strange and unpleasant Folk in her living room. It took her no time to determine that Mazzin, whom she easily recognized as a Goblin, was the monster in charge.

"What do you want?" she asked, her voice weak and unsteady even as she glared at him. She had never truly considered that any of the Folk could cause this kind of harm. But then, Arrendel and Menace were the only Fey she actually knew. "Why are you here? Why did you hurt him?"

The Bodach took two steps toward Maggie. She saw his eyes, his lascivious grin, and his huge erection staring her down, and she froze. The dawning realization in her eyes made the Phooka laugh out loud as he stood beside her.

Maggie's mind was working slower than usual, but it was working. She realized that Menace was not here with these Folk, and a small hope flickered inside her. She knew that the Spriggan would never abandon Arrendel. She also knew that he had kept something from happening to one of the cats; she'd heard Menace in her office with the Phooka. She wasn't sure what Menace could do to help them, but she had to try and give him a chance to do something. Anything.

The Bodach walked toward Maggie, his erection pointing at her provocatively.

"Wait," she said, her eyes stuck on the creature's stiff member, "Wait. Stay away from me. I don't understand why you are here, or what you want..."

Mazzin rose from the chair, giggling merrily. "I think our friend here knows precisely what *he* wants."

Maggie took two steps backward, in a careful move toward Arrendel, but was stopped short when the Phooka grabbed the back of her neck and held tightly.

Menace! Maggie thought. *Menace, where are you? Help us! Please!*

"Leave her alone, Mazzin," Arrendel's hoarse voice whispered from behind her. "She knows nothing of this. Your business is with me."

With a regal strut toward Arrendel, Mazzin signaled for the Bodach to wait. The Bodach frowned and fluttered his wings impatiently, but stood still.

The Goblin stood before the Water Faerie, and examined the damage done. Despite his swelling eyes, Arrendel glared into Mazzin's, his voice growing a bit stronger as his anger grew. "Let her go. She cannot cause you harm."

"Neither can you, as you have seen," Mazzin replied, his tone almost amiable. He touched the Greencrystal, which hung safely around his neck. "The High King created a very strong magic when he made this Stone. I was not certain of the full measure of its power until I conjured the Cave Troll, and was able to overpower you. The Stone knows I am its new master. With it, I will recreate the world."

"The High King will come for you," Arrendel hissed. "He will find you, and take back the Stone."

Mazzin laughed again. "I will see him coming. The scrying wine never lies. I will watch for him, and I will be ready. Which is where you come in."

Arrendel coughed, and spat blood. Helpless, Maggie struggled against the Phooka.

"When the time is right, Arrendel, I will permit the High King to discover where we are. And when he comes to claim your body, I will end him, as I will end everyone who comes with him to fight me."

"No!" Maggie cried. "No!"

The irritation in Mazzin's voice gave the lie to the merry, care-free expression on his face. "You have caused me some unpleasantness. I have lost ground with my cousin the King of the Northern Lands, which I did not intend to lose. You killed my associates, one of whom was a prince I had plans for. You have hindered my game, and I dislike being hindered. I think it only reasonable, Arrendel, that before I kill you, I should cause you some inconvenience in return." He moved to a position directly beside Arrendel, and nodded at the Phooka. "Observe the consequences of what you have done."

The Phooka hit Maggie in the face, and knocked her down. He raised his leg to kick her, but Mazzin interfered. "Do not kick her, fool. Leave her mostly unharmed, so that our friend the Bodach can enjoy her. I did promise him, after all."

"By the gods, no!" Arrendel shouted.

Mazzin nodded at the Hobs, who had waited silently in the kitchen. At his nod, the Hobs began to hit and kick the defenseless Arrendel.

At that moment, Menace popped into the kitchen, holding two very large pots. These he slammed into the heads of three of the Hobs, knocking them down. The fourth Hob was felled by two of the others falling hard against him.

The Phooka charged toward Menace, his ferocious roar sounding like an angry bull fighting with a wild ram, combined with wild Fey howls of rage. Before the Phooka could get close enough to the Spriggan to grab him, Menace hurled the pots at the Phooka the instant before he vanished into the air.

Maggie, huddled on the floor, felt a small spark of hope. She looked at Arrendel, who was still conscious but in great pain. He met her eyes, and tried to communicate something to her, but there was no time.

Mazzin was roaring at the invisible Spriggan. "Each time you interfere, Swiftaine, I will hurt him more!" He raised the Greencrystal away from his chest, aimed it at Arrendel, whispered the Word, and said:

"*Pain.*"

Arrendel screamed in immeasurable agony. Blood poured from somewhere on the side of his head, and he jolted wildly against the rope that held him securely to the chair. His breaths came in sharp gasps.

Maggie forced herself up from the floor and made a dash for Arrendel, but Mazzin turned toward her, aimed the Stone, and repeated carelessly "Pain."

She hit the floor face first, engulfed in a physical torture that transcended anything she could have imagined. Lightning exploded in her muscles; she felt glass in her face and fire in her chest. She was nearly unconscious before she could draw a full breath to cry out. The evidence of her pain came out in wisps and gasps that were almost moans.

As Mazzin watched Maggie writhe on the floor, he staggered, dizzy now. The Phooka noticed and asked, "What is it, my Lord?"

Steadying himself, the Goblin nodded his head in understanding. "Ah. I see it. I am burning too much energy. It is challenging work to maintain a strong fist to hold Arrendel from striking back. I would not like to let go of him. He would attempt to retaliate."

"What can be done to assist you?" the Phooka wanted to know.

"I must conserve my strength. The storm took much power, and I grow tired. Holding all of the physical forms in order to do this work requires much concentration, despite the great power of the Stone." Mazzin closed his eyes and took a deep breath. "Where is the Troll?"

The Phooka moved to the open front door and looked out. "He is sitting by the small building he crushed, eating that bit of house he carried away."

Opening his eyes, Mazzin nodded his thanks to the Phooka. "We have no need of him at present. I can summon him later." He took a shaky breath, whispered the Word, and the Cave Troll slowly disintegrated.

"Handsomely done, my Lord," chuckled the Phooka as he watched.

The Goblin acknowledged the praise with a nod. "Royal breeding, and style." He took a deeper breath, and turned to face Arrendel. "Now, before we take you away from here, I want you to see what will become of your mortal lady."

Arrendel's eyes widened in sick horror as Mazzin motioned to the Bodach. "You have served me long, and well. Take your reward."

The handsome Bodach, no longer sulking, slid gracefully toward Maggie, who was still lying on the floor. He bent down, lifted her into his arms, and began to lick her face.

"Menace...Menace...Menace..." Maggie chanted in a desperate whisper as she tried to keep her face away from the Bodach's long tongue. "Menace, help us, please help..."

Struggling in the chair, Arrendel could not stop what was happening to Maggie. But he did manage to do the only thing left to do:

"Swiftaine!" he called as loudly as he could manage. "Swiftaine, help her!"

"Get the Spriggan!" Mazzin barked, irritable now. "You must catch him—kill him—I cannot hold him while I hold Arrendel also!"

Mazzin, the Phooka, and the one HobGoblin who was still conscious looked anxiously around to see where the wily Spriggan would materialize next. The Bodach was intent on experiencing the taste of Maggie's face.

Which, as it turned out, was a mistake.

Swiftaine's gleeful laughter arrived two seconds before he did, immediately behind the Bodach.

Normally just under three feet tall, Swiftaine now stood at nearly seven feet tall, all Spriggan, ready to defend Arrendel and Maggie.

Mazzin sputtered an order, but the Phooka didn't hear him. He was watching to see what the Spriggan was going to do.

Swiftaine tore Maggie from the arms of the Bodach, and shoved the winged creature hard with his left leg and sent him flying. He snarled at Mazzin as he gently set Maggie on her feet. "Can you stand?" he whispered, not taking his eyes off the others.

"Yes," she whispered back, her own eyes on the Bodach, who had landed on his arse on the floor, and seemed content to stay there, lazily observing the activity in front of him.

"Get behind me, Maggie. Let me know if that beast gets too near." Nodding, she stepped backward at once.

Swiftaine glowered at Mazzin and the Phooka as he took a step toward them, prepared to reach for both of them with his long arms. "You cannot be permitted to continue your Mischief. I will—"

The Goblin tightened his grip on the Greencrystal, and whispered the Word. Arrendel began to choke, as though he were being strangled. "Stop," Mazzin said archly, "or I will end Arrendel here and now."

"Swiftaine!" Maggie shouted, using the Spriggan's True Name for the first time.

Swiftaine froze, eyes wide with alarm.

"Better," Mazzin noted. "I see I have your attention." He let Arrendel continue to suffocate for several more eternal seconds, then released his hold. The Water Faerie coughed hard, but he breathed.

Momentarily ignoring everything else to focus on Swiftaine, Mazzin smiled a little ruefully. "You have the heart of a villain, I think, but you are tainted in the wrong direction. A pity. Perhaps I would have enjoyed your company in other circumstances. But we will never know, since I must end you."

Arrendel's hoarse voice interrupted Mazzin's. "You must not let him get you, my friend. You cannot hope to defeat him while he has the Stone. You are the only hope—go for help...go..."

The Phooka chuckled maliciously at the huge Spriggan. "Your blind, pointless loyalty will force you into cowardice. Run if you can, Fool. The tide is against you and yours."

His gaze moving quickly from Arrendel to Mazzin, then from the Phooka to Maggie to the Bodach and back at Arrendel, Swiftaine seemed uncertain about what he should do next.

"Take him," Mazzin told the Phooka, pointing. "Then break him."

The Phooka charged at Swiftaine, but he was too late. The large space Swiftaine had fully occupied a second before was suddenly empty.

A heartbeat later, he reappeared in his natural size, and speedily rammed into Mazzin with all his might. Mazzin hit the floor hard, reaching for a strong hold on the Greencrystal as he landed.

At the same time, Swiftaine grabbed for the Stone as well.

"Swiftaine!" Arrendel yelled above the insanity around him, "You must escape! It's her only chance! Do this for me!"

The Phooka had dashed across the room to help Mazzin and stop the Spriggan, but instead strode over to Arrendel and kicked him squarely in the chest. The Water Faerie fell forward in the chair.

Screaming in maddened rage, Maggie ran toward him, but was suddenly stopped short by the remaining conscious HobGoblin, who had been hiding under the kitchen table, waiting to be useful. He backed Maggie into the living room, where she stumbled as she reached the couch. She sank down without a word.

Arrendel was badly hurt and helpless; Maggie was injured and vulnerable. Swiftaine knew what he had to do. With frustrated tears streaming unheeded down his cheeks, he forced himself to look away from Arrendel and over at Maggie. He saw the sick panic in her eyes as he mouthed the words "Be brave"—and then he vanished into the air.

Alone and very frightened now, Maggie pretended that the Bodach wasn't staring at her, eagerly waiting for Mazzin to let him have her.

fifteen

NO ONE MOVED or spoke much; all was quiet for the better part of half an hour as everyone waited to see what Swiftaine would do next.

The Spriggan did not return to the cottage. Ever obedient to Arrendel, the Goblin's company realized that he had in fact gone for help instead. It was his only option.

After this, it took Mazzin less than five minutes more to steady himself, reassess his position, and act accordingly. The Gnomes were finally called in from outside, and along with the last HobGoblin standing, they dragged the unconscious Arrendel and the three groggy Hobs out of the cottage and back into the woodland where they had made camp the night before.

Maggie was seated alone on the couch farthest from the front door. She had wrapped herself in a blanket, but could not get warm. Her thoughts scattered aimlessly as she worked to stay calm and clear her head. She closed her eyes, made herself breathe deeply, tried not to think about how much her body hurt. She wanted to wake up from this particular nightmare, but she was running out of hope. She knew that she was not going to be able to outrun, outmaneuver or escape the monsters who studied her with rapt attention.

The Bodach, sitting on the couch opposite her, tasted her with his eyes, and pointed at her with more than just his fingers.

"My Lord, when," asked the Phooka, "will the High King receive your ransom demands? It seems to me that time is moving quickly—and we do not know how long we can keep Arrendel alive."

Mazzin smiled. "All is well, and as I will it. I sent the messenger to Elvenhome at dawn. I am surprised you did not notice. He should arrive at the castle in the next hour, if he is not there already."

"Do you imagine the High King will pay this ransom?"

"I have every confidence that he will. He will not have much choice, will he?"

The Phooka shook his head, and laughed. Then he rose from the floor, where he had been sitting across from Mazzin's chair, and made a lazy request. "I would like to remain in this form for a while longer, my lord, if it is not too taxing."

Mazzin frowned. "I need to rest, and I will do so for as long as the princeling is unable to rally his considerable power. You will see to it that he does not awaken for some time. It will be easier to regain my full strength if I am not also holding your..." and here, Mazzin smirked devilishly "...*taller* form for you, Slole."

The Phooka snorted. "What about the Bodach? Will he lose his form as well?"

The Goblin strode to the door. "Treln has also served me well. I promised him the woman, just as I promised you the King's dagger and the fun of beating Arrendel. I will allow Treln to keep his present form until he joins us at the camp...*after*."

Then Mazzin rubbed his finger along the surface of the Greencrystal and sighed, gratefully releasing the energy he had held around the Phooka. There was a colorless shimmering in the air, and the Phooka disappeared into it, leaving Slole (who was not very attractive, even for a Bogle) in its place, grumbling under his breath.

"Yes?" Mazzin asked casually, but with a hint of acid.

Startled, Slole hastily adjusted his attitude. "Nothing, my lord."

"I thought not."

Slole officially looked around the kitchen one last time to confirm that nothing they needed was still there, then slinked over to the front door. He stopped and turned to watch when Mazzin spoke again.

"Treln...?"

Somewhat grudgingly, the Bodach pulled his eyes from Maggie and glanced over to where Mazzin was watching him, amusement glittering in his dark eyes. "Treln, there is not time for you to...*take your time*, as it were. Return to camp within two hours, or I will send Slole back to collect you. Understood?"

Unfazed, the Bodach nodded, his gaze focused again on Maggie.

Laughing nastily, Mazzin followed Slole out the door, leaving Maggie entirely alone with the Bodach.

As soon as Mazzin's party was out of sight and sound, the Bodach did something besides stare at Maggie; he and his massive erection stood up, feasting his eyes on the mortal woman who was powerless to deny him.

She was numb. *Shock, probably*, she decided. As he took a step toward her, Maggie automatically slid further into the couch, but she met his eyes. "Don't do this," she began, lamely.

She wondered, in the abstract, if she could make a break for it and run...run *where*? She'd seen the Gnomes from the windows. She did not know how many were out there, how many might have stayed behind to keep her in the cottage. Her car was a large scrap of crushed metal, and the garage was gone. She could see that through the missing corner of the house. After this awful creature raped her, was he going to kill her, too?

The Bodach's smile was dazzling as he closed the space between them, and took her hand.

God, Arrendel, I should have learned more, Maggie thought, *I should have figured out how to protect myself from faeries. If I had, maybe...*

The Bodach pulled on Maggie's hand, forcing her to stand up.

...maybe I could make him disappear...

She vaguely noticed the heat of the Bodach's body as he pressed himself firmly against her.

And then he wasn't against her at all. He staggered about five feet from her, and then he opened his mouth to let out a wild scream that came out as only a long, ragged breath. He rolled onto his side, convulsed hideously for a minute, and then he faded into nothingness.

In that moment, Maggie got an education about one of the things that can protect vulnerable mortals from very bad faeries every time:

Heavy shears pulled from the wreckage of her garage, deftly wielded by a three-foot-tall Spriggan.

"Oh my God, my God, my God..." Maggie breathed, as she collapsed on the couch behind her. Swiftaine dropped the black-bloodied shears, and slid them under the couch. When he looked up again, Maggie was looking at him as though she'd never seen him before. "Menace—I mean, *Swiftaine*, if I may be honored to call you by your True Name—Swiftaine, thank you...thanks for...for..." Swiftaine nodded his permission, and Maggie's tears started, even as her thoughts and fears were gathering in her eyes as she tried to understand everything that was happening. Tears and words poured out of her in the same flood. She struggled to keep her brain working.

"That monster is gone...I get that. But Swiftaine..."

The Spriggan tilted his head.

"Swiftaine, when he doesn't show up, won't they come back for him? Won't they come back here and..."

The Spriggan took her hand into his. They had never actually touched before. Realizing this, she looked at his hand around hers and smiled, even though the corners of her mouth quivered in fear.

"Mazzin knows Treln is ended. He will have felt the energy fade." He patted her hand, and let it go as she wiped the tears from her face with the back of her other hand.

"And they will come back?" Maggie's eyes were wild with fear.

"I do not think they will." He narrowed his eyes in anger. "They have more important things to accomplish." Then he remembered something Arrendel had said. "Are you still wearing your Bell?"

Maggie reached under the neck of her sweater, and lifted the chain, exposing her Dunnor's Bell. "I rarely take it off..."

Her eyes widened as she arrived at the same conclusion Swiftaine had. She shook the bell lightly. It jingled, but stopped when she let it drop on its chain.

"The bell senses that you are indeed safe, Maggie, or it would not make a sound. That is a good thing to know."

"Arrendel..." Maggie put her face in her hands and wept. "We have to find him. We have to get him back...only I don't know what to do!" Sobbing, she suddenly sat straight up. "Arrendel told you to get help...are you going to leave me here alone? Swiftaine, you must go—and the cats and I..."

For the first time in a long while, Maggie thought about Abbey and Tristan. She went pale. Her cats, who lived exclusively indoors, were of course not in their normal, cozy places in the living room. Maggie's eyes flashed as she scanned for them. "Which of them did you save from that horrible creature?" Her voice trembled when she asked. She had not seen it, but she had heard— and felt—every second of it.

Swiftaine's glance darted around, too, looking for the cats. "Abbey," he told her. "Let's find them."

It was almost more than she could bear; her fear for her beloved cats added to her overflowing anxiety. It was too much; she could not help save the man she loved, so she had to do something to salvage some sanity and make something right. She had to find and protect her precious cats.

Although her body ached, Maggie ran up the stairs to look for them, calling their names as calmly as she could manage. Swiftaine scurried through the entire downstairs, making a clicking, purring sound that both cats would recognize.

When he emerged empty-handed from the back of the house, he found Maggie, also empty-handed, sitting on the stairs. She'd been crying again, and was beginning to panic. "They're not upstairs. And they're not down here, either...?"

Swiftaine walked over to the corner of the living room that had been destroyed by the Cave Troll earlier in the afternoon. He sniffed, then turned and faced Maggie.

"Please make a big pot of tea, and drink it. Turn on all the lights in the house, and build a fire. Go upstairs, bathe this day from your skin, and change your clothes. Make food and eat. I will find Tristan and Abbey for you." He would ward her with his life, for Arrendel's sake as well as her own. "No one will approach the cottage without my notice." She seemed unable to move from the stairs, although she was fighting her panic. "Go on, Maggie," he prompted almost gently, and she forced herself to her feet.

"Thank you," she whispered, and went upstairs. He knew she'd continue looking for the cats in unlikely places, but that would help her until she found her balance.

He turned back to the gaping space in the wall, and after a moment, walked through it into the darkness, replaying parts of this day in his mind.

Perhaps he should have told Maggie that during one of his spontaneous absences from the cottage earlier today, he had gone to Arrendel's Glaistig friends in the loch. He reported what was happening at the cottage, and asked for their help to get word to Elvenhome. They immediately sent messengers to the High King at Elvenhome Castle, and also to neighboring Folk in the forest, to keep eyes and ears on the malevolent group of Unseelies.

Neither had Swiftaine told Maggie that he had spied on the Goblin and the Phooka, and heard them discussing the messenger sent to Elvenhome with demands for the ransom for Arrendel. It annoyed him that he did not know what the ransom was. There had seemed to be no point in telling Maggie, since he did not have much information, and she could not help Arrendel in any event.

One thing was certain: the High King would learn of Arrendel's brutal beating and abduction one way or the other. The High King would deal with Mazzin; there was no question of that. It was simply a matter of time and, while this thought was potentially troubling, Swiftaine reminded himself that because Mazzin wanted something, presumably something important, he would have no choice but to keep Arrendel alive for the sake of the ransom. And that was all that mattered to the Spriggan at the moment. That, and finding his feline friends, who were lost in the night, and likely very frightened.

Swiftaine allowed himself a heavy sigh, felt a little better for it, and kept walking. His path was clear: he would find the cats, he would stay close to Maggie and keep her safe until Arrendel returned, and he would prepare for the coming of the High King.

First, Abbey and Tristan. The Spriggan darted toward the loch, sniffing. In mid-dash, he changed his mind, and instead headed for the path that led to the edge of the forest.

After he'd scurried half a mile, he stopped, listening sharply, ears twitching. Then, after studying the trees around him, he walked up to a sleepy oak. "Wake up, please," he barked. "I need your help."

LESS THAN AN hour later, Swiftaine returned to the cottage. He had planned to walk through the ragged hole left by the Cave Troll, but it had been shored up with floor pillows. He smiled; Maggie was setting things to rights.

He moved to the front of the house, walked in the front door, and closed it behind him.

She was in the kitchen, scrubbing. She had showered, changed, and lit a fire in the fireplace. She looked up at him; he could see that she'd been crying. "The cats—did you find—?" She had scrubbed the blood from the floor, the wall near where Arrendel had been bound to the cane-backed chair, and the chair itself. She was starting on the blood-splattered white kitchen drawers.

"Wait!" Swiftaine screeched, dashing to Maggie and all but tearing the soapy, wet rag from her hand.

She looked at him as if he were out of his small mind. "I couldn't bear to look at Arrendel's blood any longer. And when he comes home, he shouldn't have to see it, either." Her eyes filled, her voice quavered. "I have to clean it up, Swiftaine..."

"No, no you do not," he reassured her. "Do you not see? As long as his blood is here, it means he is still alive, Maggie!"

She did not have a point of reference, and so she did not understand.

The Spriggan grabbed for her hand, and dragged her across to the couch under which he'd kicked the shears that had finished the Bodach. There was no blood, where

268

there had been plenty before. Swiftaine reached under the couch, retrieved the shears, and showed them to Maggie.

They were clean.

"I thought you'd cleaned up all the blood when I was in the shower," she said, still confused.

"Have you seen the downstairs bathroom?"

"Yes. I was afraid to look in there again, but needed to get him...it...out of there." He remembered that she'd seen the dying remains of the HobGoblin that the Phooka had crushed when Slole had dragged her past it from her hiding place in her office. "When I finally made myself go deal with it, it was all gone. The drawers were still open, and some things had scattered to the floor, but..."

"And you thought I had cleaned that up, too?"

She nodded.

"When the Fey die, in Faerie or Upworld, something of us remains for a short time, but we entirely fade away, and all physical evidence of us having *been*," he told her gravely, "fades with us."

This was information Maggie had not heard before, but she knew he was telling her the truth. Her eyes lit up with a wistful hope. "So...so he's still alive, as long as the bloodstains are visible? Really?"

"I swear it," he promised her. "There is still time for the King to rescue him."

"The King?" Maggie gaped at him. "The King of *Faerie*?"

Before Swiftaine could answer, there was a brisk knock at the front door.

Startled, Maggie gasped, and looked at Swiftaine. Sudden fear darkened her eyes again.

"All is well," he assured her. "Sit there, take a deep breath, and be happy."

She sat down, mystified, as he strolled toward the front door.

As he opened it, he smiled broadly, and shot an affectionate look over his shoulder at Maggie. "Now you will experience one of the very few nice things that have happened today."

Swiftaine stepped aside, and two tall, nude, very beautiful Dryads, also known as Wood Elves, a male and a female, entered the cottage. After a nod from Swiftaine, they introduced themselves as Dendrion and Hazella. Each carried one of Maggie's cats; Tristan and Abbey appeared to be quite happy to be held by the Tree Folk.

Giddy with emotion, Maggie laughed weakly, ignored the tears streaming down her face, and hurried to stand before the Dryads.

Hazella, holding Tristan, spoke first. She bowed her head at Maggie, and gave her a friendly smile. "He attempted to climb my tree. He saw me and knew he would find shelter. He got a few scrapes when he ran from your trouble here, but he has been fed and given water and warmth, and all is well." Hazella gave Tristan a final scratch on top of his marmalade-colored head, followed by a soft kiss, and handed him to Maggie.

Maggie gave him a quick inspection, snuggled him close to her chest, and smiled her gratitude to the Dryad. "Thank you."

She acknowledged Maggie's thanks with a wide grin, and took a step back.

Dendrion stepped forward, his hand protectively on Abbey's gray back. "She has had a difficult day," he murmured, "but she feels safer now, and has eaten well, and slept a little. She ran far, and hid in the brush two miles from here. I heard her panting, and felt her fear. Her chest was bruised, from rough handling by evil Folk. I have helped her to heal."

From Maggie's arms, Tristan surveyed the living room, and noticed Swiftaine standing behind Maggie. Delighted to see his friend, Tristan squirmed, and Maggie set him down in front of the Spriggan, who threw his arms around the orange tabby as though they'd been separated for weeks.

Dendrion whispered something to the gray cat in his arms, met her green feline eyes, and nodded. Abbey looked at Maggie then, and pushed out of the Dryad's arms and into Maggie's. Once in the safety of Maggie's embrace, Abbey buried her face in the crook of Maggie's arm, and purred.

"Thank you," said Maggie. "Thank you both. I am more grateful than I can say." She searched the faces of the Dryads. "Is there anything that I can do to repay you for your kindness, for finding and returning my family to me? Anything at all?"

The Wood Elves glanced at each other, then at Swiftaine, and back at Maggie. "Anything?" they asked.

"If there is something that will serve to thank you, I will be glad to do it."

After a small hesitation, Hazella blushed as she asked: "When the King comes to end the Mischief, may we stand nearby to be of service, so to honor him?"

It took Maggie several long seconds to take in the request. This day had, beyond question, been the most surreal and blindly incomprehensible day of her life, and its many repercussions were racing in wild, desperate circles through her mind, keeping her uncomfortably off-balance. But once she thought she understood what she could do for the Dryads, it was easy enough to respond. She glanced down again at Swiftaine, who was sitting on the floor stroking Tristan contentedly, before she spoke. "Just as we are honored by your presence, I would imagine that the King will also be much pleased to have you near."

Dendrion and Hazella beamed bright smiles, said merry goodbyes to the cats, the Spriggan and the mortal woman, then turned and walked out the door, leaving behind only the fresh, earthy scent of the forest.

Well spoken, especially for someone who has never before spoken to the Dryads, Swiftaine's voice tickled her mind. It seemed natural, somehow, being able to hear him in her head, although this was the first time it had happened. Still holding Abbey close to her heart, watching Tristan and Swiftaine move together to a favorite spot on the floor in front of the fire for a nap, Maggie decided that nothing more could surprise her today.

She was wrong about that, though.

After a small, late dinner, a restless, exhausted but fidgety Maggie worked in her kitchen, finishing the washing up in a hazy, numb silence. Swiftaine (she did not think she could ever call him "Menace" again) was curled with Abbey and Tristan on the couch nearest the comforting fire; the pile of furry and hairy friends was asleep. Her cats were safe, and seemed no worse for the horrors of their day. Snuggled around them both, Swiftaine appeared to be sleeping soundly. She heard a gentle snoring, and almost smiled.

She couldn't help it; every couple of minutes, she caught herself stealthily monitoring the remaining smears of Arrendel's blood on the white kitchen drawers. On some level it was indeed macabre, but she ignored that thought in favor of allowing the reality of the blood to reinforce the notion that Arrendel was still alive.

The waiting was close to unbearable, but there was nothing for it. If Swiftaine had believed there was anything he could do to rescue Arrendel from Mazzin, he would have already done it. The Spriggan was obviously waiting for something else to happen, and that was that.

Maggie sat down at the kitchen table with a dish towel in her hand, and pondered the coming of the King of Faerie. She did not doubt his existence in the slightest; knowing and loving Arrendel took the crisp edge of disbelief out of the picture entirely. Nor did she doubt for a moment that he would come Upworld to the Highlands, free Arrendel from Mazzin, and deal with what the female Dryad, Hazella, had referred to as *The Mischief.*

Even in her rattled, emotionally-shredded state of mind, Maggie had noticed that Swiftaine had understood exactly what the Dryad was referring to, although nothing specific had been said about it. It seemed clear, though, that today's Mischief was not all there was.

Maggie's storyteller brain was putting pieces together that hinted at connections between Arrendel's return to her, his unspoken anxieties about something upsetting that had happened at home, and the insanity and violence of this day's events. Without specific details, it was nothing more than a mental exercise for a writer, clever at her craft; nevertheless, she saw connections, and that helped to dissipate the crippling clouds of random, helpless victimization that had suffocated her all day.

She considered this new view of the situation, and it gave her some breathing room.

There was a knock on the front door.

Jolted, Maggie looked at the clock on the kitchen stove. It was midnight, midnight of the longest day of her life.

The knock came again, this time a bit louder.

Recognizing that a bad faerie wouldn't knock on the door, and hoping like hell she was right, Maggie strode to the cottage's front door, and opened it.

The first thing that Maggie noticed about the woman standing on the other side of the screen door was that she had very beautiful deep brown eyes. Dressed in jeans, black boots, and a saddle-colored leather jacket unzipped enough to reveal a dark green cashmere sweater, she stared back at Maggie expectantly, but said nothing.

There was only one thing to do; Maggie opened the screen door and let the woman in, noticing her waist-length brown hair, the amber streaks in it that caught moonlight as she entered, and long, delicately-pointed ears.

From behind her, Swiftaine's respect-filled voice broke the silence:

"Welcome, Your Grace…"

Maggie blanched, frozen in place: Her Royal Majesty, The High Queen of Faerie, was standing in Maggie's living room.

It was a good thing, but it was one *more* thing, in a day where far too many things had happened; Maggie's mind finally hit maximum overload. As a result, she was spared having to come up with something respectful, helpful, or clever to say to the Queen of Faerie.

Maggie fainted.

They kept their voices low, so that the exhausted woman now sleeping on the couch by the fireplace would not be disturbed.

Callie sat at the kitchen table with Swiftaine, and listened without interruption as he told her in detail everything that had transpired that day, from the storm that Mazzin had created, until the arrival of the Queen. He left nothing out; he detailed Mazzin's company, Mazzin's use of the Greencrystal to render Arrendel powerless, the cruel beating, Maggie's interactions with the Phooka and the Bodach, the end of the Bodach, the return of the cats by the Dryads, and Maggie's collapse.

Callie sipped hot tea, and looked away from the Spriggan's face only to glance at Arrendel's bloodstains on the kitchen drawers.

When he had told her all that he had seen and heard, she asked him to tell her what he believed the next move should be.

"We have to go and get him, Your Grace," Swiftaine told her. "And then we have to destroy Mazzin and his band of monsters."

"I agree. But in order to do that, we must either secure or defeat the Greencrystal, Swiftaine, and that might not be so easily accomplished." She sighed, and poured another cup of tea, then stared into the cup. "Let me tell you what happened in Elvenhome today."

THE QUEEN HAD been alone in her Tower Room with her needlework when she was called away to the Queen's Presence Chamber. She presumed that the High King had returned from the Northern Lands, and she left her Tower at once; she was eager to hear about his encounter with King Horshog.

Boston had waited for her in the Presence Chamber, along with three other members of the High Queen's Council. Not one of them looked happy. Boston told her that a messenger had arrived from Mazzin, and that his message was for the King's ears alone.

"The King has not returned yet. We have not told the messenger that the King is not here," Boston added tersely. "We do not believe we should wait; there is a sense of danger and timing around this message, Your Grace. What will you do?"

"The King's ears alone, eh?"

Boston nodded.

"Very well," Callie said, bouncing a flicker of bright-blue light in her right hand as she made her decision. "Have one of the guards inform this messenger that His Grace, the High King, will see him presently, in the King's Presence Chamber. Make him wait precisely ten minutes, and then take him in, and leave him alone in there." She nodded at Boston, whose eyes held many questions. "Have guards outside every door, and I would like you at the door immediately behind the King's seat so you will hear everything."

Satisfied and still thinking, she had turned and walked away.

Swiftaine's eyes were wide and questioning, too. His fingers twitched with excitement, but he remained silent as Callie continued the story.

The messenger was escorted into the King's Presence Chamber by two liveried guards, who closed the doors behind him. He was a Bogle, no more than four and a half feet tall, dressed in dirty breeches and a stained shirt and vest, and brown shoes. He was tired and, had he not been about to deliver Mazzin's message to the High King of Faerie, he would have been surly and inclined to bark.

He kept his mood to himself, and walked toward the figure seated in the regal chair on the dais, three steps above the floor.

The Bogle reached the end of the carpet, which was six feet from the dais. He stopped, bowed, then addressed the King.

"Your Majesty, I come from His Grace Duke Mazzin of the Northern Kingdom. I have information for your ears alone, and then I am to await your reply, and carry it back to my master."

The King said nothing. He made a slight gesture with his hand, indicating that the Bogle should continue.

"Your Majesty: Duke Mazzin wishes you to know that he holds the Greencrystal Pendant, and that he means to keep it. He is, at this moment, Upworld in the Scottish Highlands. He has...*detained*...Lord Arrendel, your Heir Apparent, and holds him for a weighty ransom."

The King considered this before he spoke. "Has Arrendel been harmed?" asked the King. There was no emotion at all in his voice.

"Your Majesty might expect that to be so; Lord Arrendel caused my master no small amount of trouble, and my master may have felt the need to remind him of that."

"I see," the King replied, unimpressed. "Go on."

"My master wishes for you to journey Upworld with the ransom he requires, and lay it ceremonially at his feet. If you do this, my master will spare the life of Lord Arrendel, the Spriggan who serves him, and perhaps even the woman."

"Where is Mazzin now?"

"He is in the middle of a woodland near the home of Lord Arrendel's woman. I am certain that you will have intelligence on the location of the cottage."

The King's slight head movement implied that this was probably so.

"And the ransom for Arrendel, the Spriggan, and the woman?"

The Bogle began to grin; this was the fun part. He pointed at the King's head, and did not bother to cover his pleasure as he laughed. "*That*, Your Majesty. Mazzin wants *that*."

Standing on the kitchen chair and all but jumping up and down on it, his tension strained to the limit, Swiftaine could not stay quiet a second longer. "What?" he asked in as hushed a voice as he could manage. "What does Mazzin want?"

"He wants the King's oak leaf circlet."

Swiftaine nearly fell out of the chair as shock mingled with confusion. "The 'oak crown'? No! But the King wasn't in the Presence Chamber, Your Grace. You said he had not returned from the Northern Lands..."

Callie sighed. "Correct. The King had not yet returned."

"But the Bogle..."

"...the Bogle evaporated as soon as he specified the ransom."

"What?"

"Swiftaine, once the words were spoken, the Bogle dissolved. He was not real; he was a shade of a Bogle, presumably created by Mazzin with the power of the Greencrystal. Once he had accomplished his purpose, he disintegrated."

"What did the King say to this?"

Callie chuckled. "Hard to say. The King was not there, was he?"

The Spriggan frowned. "Did the Bogle know he was not addressing His Grace?"

"I don't believe so. It probably doesn't matter either way; it appears that his disintegration was triggered by specifying the ransom."

Swiftaine eyed Her Grace with a respectful approval. "You cheated!" he exclaimed. "You crafted a shade of the King! How did you—"

She smiled. "The mechanics don't matter. What the Bogle saw was the King, dressed and crowned appropriately. I am grateful that the Bogle was a shade; if he had been real, and had been ordered to return to Mazzin with the King's oak leaf circlet, we would have had a problem or two."

"Why?"

"It's not at the castle."

"Why not, Your Grace?"

"It's the King's crown of state."

The Spriggan still didn't understand, and said so.

"I believe he's wearing it at the moment," the Queen smiled.

Callie and Swiftaine grinned at each other, and then she said seriously, "I have set a few things into motion. When the King returns to Elvenhome, Boston will tell him about the ransom. Messengers between here and Elvenhome are ready to move when there is word; I arranged all of that when I traveled here, the same way you did when you came to help Arrendel." She took a sip of her tea. "I will deal with Mazzin in the King's stead, until and unless he has a different plan of action—and he well may, after talking with King Horshog.

"In the meanwhile, Zodiac is on his way here, with Thomas."

The Spriggan was surprised by this. "Thomas?"

"Yes. He wants to help. I, or *we*, may have need of Thomas' native mortal wisdom and experience while we do what must be done. I would like him to be close by."

Swiftaine nodded, agreeing with Callie's perspective.

"They should arrive soon; they used the Oak Portal, and then the road from Queensgate.

"Now, Swiftaine: there are a few things I must know before we go any further. First: what name does Arrendel use here? What does Maggie call him?"

Swiftaine opened his mouth, but another voice answered the question.

"He is 'Arrendel' to me, too, Your Majesty," Maggie said softly. "Whatever secrets he chooses to keep to himself, his True Name is not one of them."

Callie's eyebrows lifted as she looked from Maggie to Swiftaine. "You did not tell me this," she pointed out to him without a hint of accusation.

The Spriggan tried to shrug, but changed his mind half-way through the motion as he caught the Queen's disapproving eye. "Well...you did not ask me, Your Grace."

For an instant, Callie's face took on the shadow of a threat as she considered this new information, but immediately afterward, she made a noise that was almost a suppressed chuckle, and punctuated it with a smile of genuine amusement.

Walking into the kitchen, Maggie saw the pot of tea on the table. She stopped for a second, to take a mug from the cupboard, before she reached the Folk at the table.

Callie rose from her chair and extended her hand. "Maggie, I am—"

"The High Queen of Faerie," supplied Maggie, with far more confidence than she felt, politely shaking the Queen's hand. She bowed her head in genuine respect. "Welcome. And thank you for coming to help us, Your Majesty."

"Let's start again, shall we? Please call me 'Callie'; after all, I am, among other things, Arrendel's cousin." Both women sat down, and Callie poured Maggie a cup of tea from the steaming pot. "We have much to discuss, and very little time to do it."

Within ten minutes, Callie and Maggie were on the same page. Maggie had, upon waking on the sofa in the living room, heard much of the earlier kitchen conversation. Callie mentally blessed Arrendel for having chosen someone of Maggie's sharp intelligence, sparkling imagination, and unusual ability to accept and understand much of the unacceptable and incomprehensible things that had happened in the past eighteen hours.

Swiftaine remained silent and amazed as his Queen and his friend drank tea together and covered a fair amount of territory. Her Grace explained enough of the Mischief to put Maggie's experience with Mazzin, and her concerns over Arrendel's unspoken anxieties, into a perspective Maggie could handle. Maggie gave Callie a fast snapshot of her own history, and then her relationship with Arrendel, and with Swiftaine, too. (It was at this point that Maggie admitted that she had, until today, shamefully referred to Swiftaine as "Menace," which made Callie laugh so merrily and so long that a righteously indignant Swiftaine stomped out of the kitchen, looking for the comforting, non-judgmental companionship of his feline friends.)

Maggie defended the Spriggan without hesitation. "He was incredibly brave, and he protected me, Your Majesty."

"Callie," Her Majesty corrected.

"Callie," Maggie repeated. "He was wonderful. Arrendel will be proud of him."

"We are all proud of him, much of the time; although we enjoy the fact that we don't let him know it."

"I've learned that there is much more to him than I thought, and I'm grateful," Maggie told Callie, her eyes welling with tears. "He would have done anything to free Arrendel, or he'd have died trying."

"I know it well," Callie said with a kind smile, giving Maggie's hand a squeeze. "We all are indebted to our favorite Spriggan, it seems, whichever name he has been answering to.

"Before we talk about what may happen next, is there anything else you would like to ask me? I will tell you all that I can of what I know."

Maggie bit her lip in hesitation, but quickly pushed out the question that had been troubling her since she'd first heard about the Mischief and the role Arrendel had played in its immediate aftermath: "Arrendel never told me he was the Heir Apparent to the throne—your throne! Somehow he forgot to mention that he is important to a great many more people than just to me. Does this mean that his living here with me is not possible? Should I plan for us to continue as we have been, until the time he must stay in Faerie and rule?" She straightened, and sat up in her chair, then laughed faintly. "Sorry, Callie...I get it about heirs apparent and succession and accession, I wasn't thinking about you, I was thinking about me, as usual." Maggie frowned a little, then smiled in gentle self-deprecation. "I know this isn't the place or time to start worrying about tomorrows. I never thought about his royal responsibilities, even though I knew you were his cousin. Wow..." She took a deep breath, and mentally reshuffled her priorities.

I can see why he loves you, Callie thought as she watched Maggie lay her personal, wistful dreams aside

281

and focus on the here and now. *It is no longer an uneasy surprise to me that he would share his True Name with you.*

It was at that precise moment that the High Queen of Faerie determined that she would do all in her considerable power to help Arrendel and Maggie find a way to be safely and happily together. *But first things first*, she reminded herself. *We need to get him back.*

The sound of two car doors closing brought Swiftaine to the kitchen in seconds. "Your Grace..."

"I heard it, Swiftaine. Let them in."

The Spriggan hurried to the front door, and opened it before the two men could knock.

On her feet, Callie turned to Maggie, who was standing up and looking at the door. "Maggie, I meant to tell you: one of these men is my Lord High Chamberlain at Elvenhome—you may call him 'Zodiac,' as does everyone else. The other is my Court Singer. You might recognize him. He is a good friend of Arrendel's, and his name is—"

"His name is Thomas Lear. Arrendel told me."

Callie did not take the time to be shocked by this revelation; she could ponder it later. "Do not let his fame make you nervous."

Maggie smiled hopefully at Callie. "It won't. He's Arrendel's friend, and he's here to help. That's what matters."

They sat together in the living room in the small hours of the night.

"And there has been no word from the King?" Callie asked Zodiac, who was seated closest to the fire and gently petting Tristan; the large tabby was curled and sleeping in the Lord High Chamberlain's lap.

"None yet. We are certain he has left the Northern Kingdom, though. And we know he will come Upworld as soon as he knows about the ransom demand; that certainty, at present, is most comforting." Everyone responded to this side remark positively. Zodiac continued. "The King has not sent a message through any of the regular channels, which suggests that he is aware that he is being watched."

"Mazzin should not be permitted to scry, Your Grace," Swiftaine groaned miserably. "It complicates things."

Thomas and Zodiac had discussed the entire situation during their drive from Queensgate, so that Thomas would be of as much help as possible should any eventuality present itself. As a result, Thomas understood basically what scrying was, and now he had a question:

"What's to keep Mazzin from scrying to see what we're doing right now?"

Callie beamed at her Court Singer. "Good question. Before I came in the front door, I provided the house and the immediate area around it with a little added protection."

"Good answer," Thomas told her seriously. "So he can't see us here?"

Callie shook her head in the negative. "Mazzin cannot see us, nor can he hear us, and none of his minions can approach the house close enough to spy. As an added precaution, some of our friends in the forest are watching for the King's arrival as well.

"Ultimately, it doesn't matter. Mazzin will presume that the King is coming. Mazzin—with the Greencrystal— will be ready for the encounter, and he will not care what the King does, as long as that wretched, monstrous Goblin gets what he wants."

"Will the King really give Mazzin the circlet?" Maggie wanted to know. "How can he? It's one of the sacred symbols of his kingship, isn't it?" She looked around hesitantly. "He can't give it up, but it's the only thing that will induce Mazzin to release Arrendel…"

Sighing, Callie tried to look optimistic. "I haven't spoken with the King yet, so I don't know what he'll do. I am sure that he will know how to deal with Mazzin, get Arrendel back and hold on to his crown..." Her voice trailed into a silence that threatened to smother them all; in defiance she clenched her fists and told them: "In any case, we cannot wait long. We must have a rescue plan in place that is not wholly reliant on the presence of the King; we don't know when he'll get here to deal with Mazzin."

Finding themselves as determined as Callie was, the group talked strategy for the next hour. When all was said, despite some objections by Zodiac and some over-rulings by Callie, it was generally decided that:

1. Zodiac would return to Elvenhome by way of Queensgate, to await the return of the King and tell him of Callie's plans. At the very least, Zodiac and the King would cross paths going and coming.

2. Once in Elvenhome, Zodiac would make all of the arrangements for craftsmen from Elvenhome to return to Maggie's cottage and rebuild or repair all damage done to Maggie's home.

3. Zodiac would also arrange for Callie's treasury to finance a new car to replace the one the Cave Troll had stomped on and possibly eaten.

4. The pearl-gray Fiat would remain at the cottage for Callie's use, and to return Callie and Thomas to Queensgate and then Elvenhome when the situation was resolved.

5. Maggie would stay at the cottage and prepare for Arrendel's return. Everyone agreed that it was likely he would need some medical attention and Maggie would be best able to most quickly and efficiently gather what might be needed.

6. Swiftaine would have the responsibility of protecting Maggie and her home at all costs, and of protecting Arrendel when he was in the cottage, until the King arrived and all was accomplished.

7. Callie and Thomas would stealthily search for Arrendel's location in the woods, and they would spy on Mazzin, to be able to give accurate intelligence to the King, and hopefully buy Arrendel some more time.

And a last-resort effort: if the situation warranted it, Callie would confront Mazzin with the full force of her power, and while she was keeping Mazzin occupied, Thomas would collect Arrendel and get him to safety.

"I am not easy in my mind with the notion of Your Grace confronting Mazzin alone," Zodiac said, for the third time.

"Discomfort noted, my friend," said Callie. "And I'll try not to. The Goblin alone would not be a challenge, but the Goblin with his intention wrapped around the Greencrystal? Best to avoid it, if I may."

Swiftaine was not looking much happier than Zodiac did. "The King will not be pleased if anything unpleasant happens to you, Your Grace, and we did not make a move to either protect you, or stop you..."

"Which do you suppose you and Zodiac could do most effectively?" asked Callie with an eyebrow raised, suddenly ready to push back at them both.

Thomas put his hand on Callie's arm. "We're all tired, and that's not going to help anything." He nodded his head in Maggie's direction; they all saw how far beyond exhaustion she was.

Zodiac stood up suddenly, bowed to his Queen, mumbled something almost discernible about how difficult it was to protect so stubborn a monarch in spite of herself, and, moving to Maggie, set about helping her to stand up and getting her upstairs to bed for a few hours' sleep.

Going up the stairs with his arm secured around her, he looked back over his shoulder at Callie. "Get some sleep yourself," she whispered to him, and smiled lovingly when he nodded.

The Spriggan, who had been snuggling with Abbey on the floor by the fire, stood up and asked Callie if she wanted him to go outside and ward the house, or perhaps go talk to the Wood Sprites.

"You have had a busy day, Swiftaine. You should sleep, too. And perhaps dream of the ways that you should be rewarded by your King and Queen for your courage and loyal service to all this day."

If it were possible for a Spriggan to blush from head to toes, Swiftaine (to his horror) would have done so. Instead, he ducked his head as if looking for a fleck of lint on the floor, then made a feline sound in his throat, and darted toward the back of the house to the guest room, with both cats close behind him. A minute later, all three friends were falling asleep on the bed that Swiftaine normally slept in when he was at the cottage.

"That leaves us," Thomas said, pulling Callie closer to him as he stretched out on the leather sofa. "You need to sleep too."

"I'm too anxious to sleep, Thomas," she admitted. Still, she let him pull her to him, and curled up in his arms as they lay looking at the fire in silence.

After a while, she mumbled, "How strange. You are the first Court Singer to be temporarily away from Faerie. This has never been done before."

"Absent, with leave," Thomas teased.

"Something like that," she agreed, then frowned again. "If I think about this too much, I come close to being drowned by it. My mind refuses to comprehend the enormity of what has happened, and what could happen."

"Will the King make it here in time to save Arrendel?" Thomas asked in a worried whisper.

Callie lifted her head and met his gaze straight on. "Yes. He is the only one who can give Mazzin what he wants, and Mazzin knows that if he lets Arrendel...die...he will not only not get the oak leaf circlet, but the King will destroy him."

"Even with the Greencrystal in Mazzin's hands?"

"Even so," Callie answered, the certainty in her words conflicting with the tension in her voice. "I don't know how, but he will. He must, and he knows it."

They were quiet after that; perhaps they dozed as the darkness of the night softened toward morning.

When he opened his eyes right before dawn, he found himself looking directly into Callie's. "I like to watch you sleep," she said soothingly. "You were dreaming, I think."

He smiled. "You're right. I dreamt that I was playing chess with Guard—I mean Arrendel—and I was winning."

"That *must* have been a dream, Thomas." Callie giggled, and he swatted her gently.

"It's strange, knowing his True Name. He's 'Guardian' to me."

"He likes the name. But you will get used to calling him 'Arrendel.' I doubt he would have any objection to your use of his True Name, and all of us trying to remember to call him 'Guardian' around you would have been ridiculous."

Thomas shifted position a little, and pulled her with him. "When Zodiac and I were driving up the Highland Road, and he filled me in on a bunch of the things I didn't know—and there were a lot of them, Callie, you should have told me—the thing that struck me the most was the first time I'd ever heard Arrendel's name."

She made a non-committal sound.

"It was right after I woke you one night when you were having a bad dream. You'd said 'Arrendel' in your sleep, and when I asked you what an 'arrendel' was, you more or less told me not to worry about it. Do you remember that?"

She nodded.

"You were having a bad dream about Arrendel that night?"

She nodded again. He noticed that she was tense in his arms, when a moment before she had seemed calm and relaxed.

"*What* were you dreaming about Arrendel?" he pressed. Holding her now, he suddenly knew the answer an instant before she replied.

"This, Thomas," she said unhappily. "I was dreaming about *this*."

sixteen

THEY BREAKFASTED IN silence a few hours later.

Afterward, Maggie did the washing up, grateful to have some task to keep her hands busy, still secretly watching the bloodstains on the cabinet beside her. Swiftaine and Zodiac were outside, examining the damage done by the Cave Troll and Mazzin's other Folk; the Lord High Chamberlain took careful notes. Thomas and Callie were outside as well, sitting on the swing at the back of the house.

"What I don't understand," Thomas was telling Callie, "is how we're going to find him in the first place. He's somewhere in six hundred acres of woods, Callie. It could take us a full day, maybe two, to locate Mazzin or any of his gang, if we do at all. And it's not like we can drive around in there. We'll need to be pretty quiet."

Callie looked around at the flowers in Maggie's garden. "That's why Zodiac brought the 'Fiat.' Cassane can be quiet."

He felt her desperation, and admired her struggle to stay calm. "I know," he agreed. "But it's still a lot of ground to cover."

"I know," she groaned, and stood up, headed for the front door. "I know!"

Zodiac and the High Queen stood on the front porch, going over some final instructions. Thomas sat with Maggie in the living room, making general conversation designed to soothe the tension.

"Arrendel told me about your weekly poker games. He said you are very patient with him."

Thomas shrugged generously, and smiled. "He's won a hand or two."

"Not much of a poker face, I bet," Maggie said. "You can see everything he's thinking."

"True," Thomas agreed. "Still, it's really fun to see him win. He is so surprised...and so is everyone else at the table."

They laughed together, and Thomas took a good look at Arrendel's Lady.

"I have been itching to ask you, Maggie," he began, unsure of where he was going with his thought now that he'd started talking, "isn't this whole...'situation'...a little strange and, I don't know, hallucinogenic?"

She studied him. "Which situation do you mean? The whole 'Mischief' thing? Absolutely like something out of a Warhol-Kafka nightmare." She turned and focused on him. "Or do you mean the whole thing...the fact that you and I are in the company of faeries?" The strained look on his face answered the question, and she nodded. "Ah, I think I see."

"I'm only saying," Thomas blurted, backtracking a little, "that when I'm there, in Elvenhome, it seems normal enough, you know, natural. I've got friends there, and a life. I'm...happy. And I know that I'll head home to Los Angeles when it's time, and I'm good with that, too. I'm cool with the whole 'year and a day' thing.

"But now that I'm here, where life is more (or less?) real, Elvenhome feels more like a daydream and..."

"And you're losing your balance, maybe?" Maggie's question was gentle.

He nodded.

"Balance is overrated, I think, Thomas. At least, that's how it seems to me right now." She sighed. "Try this. Your 'normal' life is to be this famous musician, doing 'famous musician' stuff."

Thomas snorted in amusement; Maggie smiled and kept talking.

"So you're this famous guy, and here you are, sitting in the living room of a 'normal' lady who happens to have most of your albums. The balance of my 'normal' life has tipped; I have Thomas Lear in my house."

He started to speak, but she put her hand on his arm to silence him. "I think I'm learning that balance is always a nice thing to have—but maybe the reality of whatever is normal and balanced for you, once it touches the reality of what's normal and balanced for me, alters somebody's reality...hopefully for the good. Like with you and me, sitting here talking now. But sometimes, like with Mazzin and Arrendel, it's a different story."

Maggie was quiet as she considered this. Her hand on Thomas's arm trembled slightly. He touched it and gave it a squeeze.

"Which don't you have, Maggie?" His stray question pulled her focus from the emotional darkness she was approaching.

"What?"

"Which don't you have?" he repeated, a twinkle in his eyes.

She looked at him like he was speaking Cantonese, and rather badly at that.

Thomas couldn't help it; he grinned even though his tone was entirely nonchalant:

"You said you have most of my albums," he pointed out. "Which don't you have? I can get them for you. I know people."

His *non sequitur* did exactly what it was meant to do; startled, Maggie laughed out loud, and found herself effortlessly carried from one line of thought to another—far less serious—one.

Thomas Lear, Rock Star, Court Singer, and Companion of the Heir Apparent of the High Throne of Faerie, put his arms around his new friend, and gave her a hug. Then he whispered in her ear: "I haven't figured out how the hell we're going to do it, Maggie, but we're going to find him and bring him back."

Zodiac kissed Maggie's hand, and promised her that as soon as possible, the damage done to her house, garage and car would be repaired, rebuilt, and replaced. She hugged him, smiled, and went to make tea.

Zodiac then exchanged a few private words with Swiftaine.

Finally, he stood before Callie and Thomas. "My friend," he urged the Court Singer as if Callie were not right in front of him, "stay out of trouble. And do whatever you must to keep Her Grace out of trouble. She is an impetuous Elf, and would do well to remember to consider her actions *before* she moves through them rather than after she's finished with them."

"Very entertaining, Zodiac," Callie retorted wryly. "Fortunately for you, your perspective carries some weight with the Crown, and I daresay that you are right...to a point."

"Just so, Your Grace."

She turned serious. "Fare well. And tell the King all. And have him come to us quickly. We will wait for as long as we dare."

"Understood, Your Grace." He turned to Thomas. "Be careful. We will meet again soon."

With a nod, and a sharp last look at his Queen, Zodiac popped out of the room, and was gone.

They drank tea at the kitchen table and talked over their options for finding Arrendel.

"Callie," Maggie said sadly, "I don't know how you're going to be able to find him. Mazzin could be anywhere in the woods."

Faeries do not lie, even when they know it would make them, and others, feel better. Callie sighed. "I fear that, without the help of a little magic that has nothing to do with Mazzin, we will have to wait until he chooses to reveal himself. That would take away our ability to surprise him and get Arrendel away stealthily...which I was counting on."

Maggie understood. "If the meeting with Mazzin doesn't go well."

Callie nodded. Thomas' head whipped around, and his eyes met Callie's; she silenced him with a look.

Swiftaine wanted to know something. "Is it the King's consideration, as well, that he would have to wait for Mazzin to make his presence known before the King could approach him?"

Callie nodded in the affirmative.

"Well, then," Swiftaine said with certainty, "Mazzin's not likely to harm Lord Arrendel in the meantime." He looked at the faces around the table. "Right?"

"I hope so," Callie said grimly. She rubbed her neck and sighed. "We need some magic that Mazzin can't anticipate."

Swiftaine frowned. "Apart from Your Grace, we have nothing."

Maggie stood up and stretched. "I'll make more tea. And then maybe I'll scrub a floor or two..."

Callie, who had been looking in Maggie's general direction when she stood, gasped, her eyes wide, her mind working fast.

Thomas saw Callie's expression, and looked around the kitchen. "What?"

Callie rose, and moved around the table to where Maggie was standing, staring at her. "What is it, Callie?" Thomas asked again.

The High Queen of Faerie stopped in front of Maggie, her eyes wide, the beginning of a smile making the corners of her mouth twitch.

Callie was almost afraid to ask, but she managed it. "Maggie? What's that around your neck?"

As she had stretched, the silver chain that she always wore had moved slightly, revealing a portion of the small, silent bell that hung from it. Maggie slid her hand to the chain, and showed Callie the Dunnor's Bell that Arrendel had given her for her last birthday.

Callie's eyes were on the beautiful charm, and they filled with tears.

"What's wrong, Callie?" Maggie asked. "Arrendel gave this to me."

Thomas did not understand what was going on any more than Maggie did. Both mortals watched as Callie's mood moved from exhausted despair to delight.

"Oh, Swiftaine...?" Callie's tone was clipped, but the look on her face as she stared at Maggie's necklace was beaming brightly.

"Your Grace?"

"Swiftaine, it appears that you did not tell me that Arrendel has given Maggie a Dunnor's Bell." She smiled sweetly, the soul of innocent inquiry. "Whyever not?"

Puzzled for a second, the Spriggan watched his Queen with unmasked suspicion, hands twitching. Then, in a flash of realization, he began to grin, too, his growing delight matching hers.

There was only one answer to her question, and Swiftaine gave it as blandly as possible despite his excitement. "Well, Your Grace, you didn't ask me..."

The High Queen and the Spriggan burst into merry laughter, leaving Thomas and Maggie entirely bewildered by the exchange in front them.

Dancing now, Callie flung her arms around Maggie and cried, "He gave you a Dunnor's Bell! Great Gods, Maggie—you have a Dunnor's Bell!"

Callie stood in the living room, and finished her hushed conversation with Swiftaine, who stood on the coffee table in front of her.

"I know that she will remain safe in your care. If for some reason things do not go well on my end, if any of Mazzin's Folk return here, defend her at all costs. Do whatever it takes to protect her, Swiftaine. And when it is truly over, offer to take her to Elvenhome where, by my invitation and gratitude, she may remain as long as she chooses, according to our rules of law. The King and the Council will honor my invitation. It is far less than she deserves, but it is all I can think of to offer her, if I fail..."

"Then perhaps Your Grace should not fail," he squeaked gravely, as the front door opened and Thomas and Maggie walked in.

"I'll get the sandwiches ready," Maggie was saying, and she hurried into the kitchen.

Thomas had four large canteens, each covered with a cloth bag and filled with loch water, slung over his shoulders.

"As my Queen commanded," Thomas said, laying the canteens on the table.

Beside the filled canteens sat a blanket and a six-foot length of strong rope rescued from the remains of the garage. There was also a first-aid kit and a large, sharp butcher knife from Maggie's kitchen, wrapped in a dish towel.

"Except for the canteens, this all needs to go into your pack," Callie told Thomas. He nodded and filled the backpack.

Another thought occurred to her, and she chuckled. "Thomas, we're leaving in ten minutes."

He took another minute to finish packing, then, without a word, Thomas headed for the bathroom.

"Swiftaine," Callie asked, "please fill the last canteen with fresh drinking water, and add a small amount of sugar to it." The Spriggan nodded and moved into the kitchen at once, passing Maggie, who carried four sandwiches wrapped for the trip. She placed them in the bulky backpack, and zipped it up.

The two women looked at each other and took deep breaths. "Maggie, let's get this done."

Together, they walked up the stairs and into Maggie's bedroom.

Once there, Maggie sat on the bed, reached into her night stand for a pair of scissors, and handed them to Callie. She reached for the clasp of her necklace.

"Wait!" Callie reminded her, and Maggie froze in place, then dropped her hands. "You must say the words we talked about, or the Bell can't help us. We need the charm."

"Right. Sorry..."

Taking a deep breath, Maggie began again, and touched the bell that hung quietly from the chain around her neck. "Bell, hear me, and help me to find Arrendel."

She looked at Callie, who nodded encouragement.

"Bell," continued Maggie, "You must find him, and quickly." She then reached for the clasp of the chain, which was at the base of her neck, and released it. "You are tied to me, as you are tied to him who gave you to me as a token of what we share. Hear me: I yield your magic to one who knows how best to use it, but I will surround you, too, so that you will be able to sense him. Sense him quietly, sing only to the one who carries you toward him, so that you will not betray the presence of those who work to save him." She looked at the Bell, which she held in her open hand. "Do you understand?" she asked it.

An unacknowledged tear trickled down Maggie's cheek. It landed on the Bell.

The Bell (which had been silent except when on the outside of Maggie's clothing and physically moved) chimed actively, but quietly.

Maggie looked up at Callie, who nodded.

"Bell," whispered Maggie, "I will be with you, in a way. Find Arrendel."

Callie leaned down in front of her and, scissors poised, snipped off two of Maggie's dark curls. Together they tied and knotted the curls firmly to the silver chain on either side of the Bell. They looked at each other, and Maggie spoke to the Bell again as she placed it almost reverently in Callie's hand.

"Bell, I put Arrendel and myself in the hands of the High Queen of Faerie. She will carry you, and will hear you when you search for him." Maggie touched the Bell as it rested on Callie's hand, then sat back and watched.

A soft blue glittering of light danced like falling snowflakes around Callie's outstretched hand as she addressed the Bell. "Bell," asked the High Queen, "You see who I am. Will you trust me to carry you to Arrendel?"

The Bell waited until the glitter gently settled around it, then chimed in her hand.

"Will you speak only to me until all is accomplished?"

The Bell chimed again, a bit more determined this time.

"Thank you," Callie said.

Maggie was crying now. She looked at the Bell, and closed the loose ritual the way Callie had asked her to: *"Merry Meet, Bell. Merry Part, and Merry Meet Again."*

The Bell chimed a sad goodbye to Maggie, and then was purposefully silent.

"Time to go," Callie said as she slipped Maggie's Dunnor's Bell deep into the pocket of her jeans.

WHEN THE WOMEN returned to the living room, Thomas was already at the front door. He was loaded down with the four canteens of water from the loch, and a full backpack, several sandwiches, plus one full canteen of drinking water.

Callie was looking around for something. Thomas noticed, and pointed to the hiking boots beside the coffee table. She sat down, put the boots on, slipped a jacket on, and looked around.

"We've got everything," Thomas told her.

"All is as you asked, Your Grace," added Swiftaine, who sat on the couch petting Abbey nervously, his fingers twitching in their anxiety.

"Well done, Swiftaine." *Remember what I have commanded about Maggie*, she whispered in his mind. His nearly imperceptible nod was sufficient response.

Maggie and Callie exchanged a hug. Words passed between them that Thomas could not hear. Callie then moved to the Spriggan, and put her hand on his arm for a fraction of a second, removed it, and turned to Maggie.

"Keep an eye on him, will you, Maggie? He is resourceful, and strong, too—but he has a tendency to get worked up. Don't let him collapse the cottage on you, all right?"

The Queen's offhand grin, coupled with the withering look on Swiftaine's face, made Maggie laugh in spite her tension.

Only Swiftaine saw Callie wink at him.

Callie patted the pocket of her jeans, and joined Thomas at the door. "Let's go find Arrendel."

ALONE IN THE woodland's late-morning sunlight, Mazzin sat with his back against a huge tree. He held his wooden scrying bowl in both hands, and gazed into murky, burgundy-colored liquid. Beside him was a corked bottle that held the last of the dark wine that aided him in his divination.

"Excellent..." he muttered. "The High King prepares to leave Elvenhome and bring me the ransom. See how he thunders at the King's Men and the Lord Chamberlain." The Goblin smiled at the King, whom he could see clearly in the bowl. "How dangerous you look, Your Majesty. But you are no challenge for my Stone, and very soon, I shall be High King."

He watched for a few minutes more, chuckling as the King, wearing the prized oak leaf circlet in his long, dark hair, paced angrily then hurled a golden flash of fiery light against the wall of a large chamber, doing minor damage and clearly making his attendants uncomfortable. "You are King for a short while yet, Your Majesty. I will be King here...and as it is written, 'As above, so below; as within, so without.'" Mazzin laughed out loud. "My kingdom grows and grows, and I need only sit and observe."

He took one hand off the bowl, and lovingly patted the Greencrystal, which hung from the doubled-up chain around his neck. "But that will change once the King provides me with his circlet. I know great power lives in that as well. You, my Stone, will help me to unlock that mystery, if the King will not readily share his knowledge."

"Good plan," said a ragged, pain-filled voice from twenty feet away. "I wish you luck. You'll need it."

Alarmed, Mazzin looked up. Once he identified the speaker, he relaxed again.

"The Princeling is awake for a moment," he announced with a snort, to no one in particular. Slole was gone, commanding the Gnomes and Bogles as they patrolled the area a mile around where Mazzin sat. The

Goblin knew, of course, that Treln would not be returning. For the present, the single focus of Mazzin's attention, apart from the scrying bowl and the Greencrystal, was the Water Faerie seated against and tied to a tree. "Go back to sleep on your own, Arrendel, or I will have Slole's fists help you to sleep again when he returns." He laughed at his own joke.

Nearly fully conscious for the first time since he had been tied to the kitchen chair in the cottage, Arrendel sighed as he watched Mazzin return his gaze to his scrying bowl.

The Water Faerie looked at the forest around him, and wondered in a daze if he could rely on help from the trees or their Sprites. He listened with care, trying to sense presence, and realized with a shock just how very alone he was.

Taking stock of his immediate situation, he reckoned that everything was somewhere on the other side of grim. His left eye was swollen shut; if he worked at it, he could almost see a thread of light through it. He could see nominally out of his right eye. *That* was something, he thought. His head ached miserably. There was a cut somewhere on his scalp that burned below the ache, and there was something wrong with the tip of his left ear. He was sharply aware that his ankle was broken; he worked hard not to look at or think about it. He assumed he had at least one broken rib, maybe more. He frowned as he acknowledged to himself that he would have to ignore the cuts, bruises, scrapes and other assorted pains from the body blows if he was going to be able to think clearly.

His throat was dry. He realized that he was dry all over, and that added a silent layer of anguish to his physical misery.

After a furtive glance at Mazzin, Arrendel experimentally strained against the ropes that bound him to the tree. The ropes were strong; he was not.

This was not good.

He struggled to clear his mind enough to begin to think about what to do next. Then, in a frenzied flash, he remembered what had happened at the cottage. His heart all but stopped, then hammered against his chest, as he thought of the last time he'd seen Maggie and Swiftaine.

And the Bodach.

Great gods: he had left Maggie alone with a hungry and vile monster, and had all but commanded Swiftaine to leave her to get help. *Oh, Sweet Maggie...forgive me for...his hurting you...* His apology was as anguished as it was silent. For a long moment, he felt as though he were lost in pain beyond his capacity to endure and survive it. His breath caught in his throat. This insanity was too much for his battered body and heart to deal with. Desperate for release from any part of it, he struggled to stifle a sob.

Strategy, his aching head roared suddenly as it harshly demanded his focus. *Strategy is required! Think, damn you! How can you help the King? How can you help Maggie? What will you do? Your only choice is to do something useful.*

A heartbeat later, Arrendel's head slumped forward, and his breathing slowed.

Mazzin looked up from his scrying, and over at Arrendel, then he settled back and smiled into the bowl as he saw the High King get on a huge stallion and ride alone toward the Oak Portal, as fast and furious as an ill-tempered wind.

It took desperate, painful thirst to ultimately push Arrendel into the mental space to confront his captors. Upon opening his eyes and committing himself to action, his throat seemed full of sandpaper, but he cleared it anyway, and looked over at Mazzin with as much ambivalence as he could muster as he croaked:

"Mazzin, I would appreciate a cup of water."

Mazzin's head turned. He was standing near where he'd been sitting earlier, talking with Slole. Arrendel counted four Gnomes spread out beyond where the Goblin and the Bogle stood.

"It has been a long time since I've had anything to drink," Arrendel continued lightly, despite the gravel in his dry throat. "May I have water?"

"Silence yourself, WaterFowl," Slole barked icily, annoyed at the interruption.

Arrendel said nothing, and calmly waited for what he hoped would happen next.

It occurred to Mazzin that if Arrendel died of thirst— or of his wounds, for that matter—his own bargaining power with the High King could be sorely minimized. As he preferred to have all decks stacked in his favor, less work being required of him that way, it made sense to allow the Water Faerie a small cup of water.

He nodded at Slole, indicating that the Bogle should get water to Arrendel.

"What if he tries something?" Slole grumbled under his breath.

"Fool, he can't try anything. He's powerless, as long as I stay his power and hold my Stone. The Water Faerie...drained dry." He ordered Slole to give Arrendel something to drink.

Slole whispered something to Mazzin that he didn't like; in sudden rage, Mazzin hit Slole on the head with the heel of his hand and yelled, "Of course he can't hold the cup himself, he's tied to the tree! Do it! Give him water! Hold the cup for him while he drinks. He can have as much as he wants. Then go check on the Gnomes and stay out of my sight!" Mazzin strode off in a huff, and sat down on a tree stump thirty feet away, on Arrendel's right. He soothed his temper by stroking the Greencrystal, and he whispered his plans to to the Stone as he relaxed.

302

As Arrendel slowly sipped water out of a metal cup, held by the tight-lipped and irritable Bogle, he played his next move in his head with as many variations as he could think of.

He had painfully but gratefully swallowed four cups of water before he nodded to Slole that he'd drunk his fill. Slole threw the empty cup hard against the tree, above Arrendel's head, and stalked off to obey Mazzin.

When the Bogle was out of earshot, Arrendel sent a silent prayer for courage into the afternoon sky, and the game was on.

"Mazzin, I thank you," Arrendel said, humility and gratitude in his voice.

Still focused on perfecting his plans, Mazzin waved a dismissive hand in the air.

Arrendel waited.

Mazzin seemed to be humming to himself.

Arrendel waited a little while longer.

Then he said, "I know you still have the Greencrystal. Speaking as one who has experienced the result of your talent with it," and here he laughed in self-deprecation, "it appears that you know how to use the Stone quite well."

Distracted from his thoughts, Mazzin looked at Arrendel, studying him to see where this line of conversation was going.

The Water Faerie was nonchalant, his comments delivered as gentle throwaways. "I am only saying, Mazzin, that you appear to have learned a great deal about the Greencrystal in a very short time...which, I confess, is as impressive as it is alarming.

"And yet one wonders if you have learned all there is to know, before you need to know it."

If Mazzin had considered this, his face did not reveal it. He tilted his head toward Arrendel, who casually leaned back against the tree to which he was still tightly bound.

Arrendel waited, and considered taking a nap. He yawned, stretched where he could even though it hurt, and closed his eyes.

"I know all there is to know," Mazzin's voice hissed directly in front of Arrendel a moment later. "I know my Stone."

Although he'd been startled, Arrendel was not surprised. He opened his right eye slowly, and peered at the Goblin, who stood before him with a light sheen of exasperation on his unattractive face.

"That is well," Arrendel replied cautiously. "I have known of the Greencrystal since its creation, and there are many things about it that I do not know." He gave these words to Mazzin without rancor or judgment. "But then," he added, "I have never been destined to wield it. You have."

The Goblin pushed his face very close to Arrendel's, hunting for clues to where this talk was taking him. "What is it that you are trying to discover, then, Princeling? There is nothing you can do to change what Fate has decreed—"

Arrendel's unexpected interruption stopped Mazzin in mid-sentence. "I was wondering: What will you do if you ask the Stone to do something that it does not wish to do?"

"What?"

"As I said," Arrendel replied, not unkindly. "If you ask the Stone to do something it does not wish to do, what will happen, and what will you do then?"

This did not appear to have occurred to Mazzin before.

"The Stone did not object when you created the powerful wind and rain storm, or when you recreated the Cave Troll, the Phooka and the Bodach." Arrendel's voice did not catch in his throat as he spoke, although his heart sank in his chest. "The Stone did not object when you froze my ability to stop you at first, or when you used it to cause pain to my lady. Nor does it object to you holding my power fast, even now, so I cannot move against you."

304

Mazzin stepped back, and smiled as he remembered this. "What is your point, Princeling? My Stone and I act as one."

"Perhaps," Arrendel admitted. "Still, the Greencrystal was created by union of the powers of the High King and his Queen, who perhaps infused the Stone with their joined essences, and what they believed to be right and true."

"That may be," Mazzin said, with a flicker of uncertainty in his voice.

"What I mean is, nothing you have done thus far has presented the Stone with an action it may disagree with. The Stone is a gift of earth, of air, of fire, and water, bound by the magic of the High King and Queen. It is most powerful, and I would not be surprised to learn that it has a mind of its own."

Uneasiness showed in Mazzin's eyes for a fast second before he covered it with a narrowed scowl, but Arrendel saw it, and pressed on as if the notion were merely academic.

"If you ask the Greencrystal to do something that it does not like, I wonder what will happen. Don't you?" Arrendel coughed, and spat a little blood. "Could I have some more water, please?"

Mazzin looked around to see if Slole was available nearby, then sighed resignedly as he himself bent down to retrieve the cup the Bogle had hurled at the tree. Arrendel was certain he saw the unmistakable shade of growing doubt in the Goblin's dark eyes.

THE EARLY AFTERNOON was cool and bright as Cassane carried Callie and Thomas into the woodland. Nestled behind the High Queen, Thomas watched and listened as he tried to make sense of things around them.

"Callie, I can't hear Cassane's bells, but I can see them. What's up with that?"

Focusing on other issues, she didn't look over her shoulder at him when she responded. "He can hear them, and so can I."

"But I can't," he repeated.

"Neither can Mazzin or his accomplices." Callie patted his leg. "Let it go, Thomas. Accept that the explanation is less interesting than the notion of it."

He groaned good-naturedly. "You make it all so easy."

They didn't speak for a while as Cassane moved them through the trees. Varying degrees of stress and anxiety tugged at both the High Queen and her Court Singer as each silently considered the potential danger ahead of them.

The quiet was good for Thomas, and gave him time to regroup a little. He'd been tense and on his guard from the moment Zodiac had come to him yesterday with the news that Callie needed them Upworld. *Funny to think of it that way, "Upworld,"* Thomas thought, *since it's the only world I'd known.*

He'd been listening and learning new things and helping to plan Guardian/Arrendel's rescue, and he'd been watching everyone around him, and trying to be helpful. There hadn't been time to stop and think about himself. Now there was time for that, and all he could really consider was how different Callie looked to him, without the designs on her face and body. He'd become so accustomed to the beautiful markings as part of her that it had been almost shocking when he'd seen Callie coming out of Maggie's kitchen toward him. Her smile had been genuine, her dark eyes had flashed with pleasure and relief, and her kiss had been most welcoming. Still, he'd had to do a double-take because something was missing.

He understood, of course. She'd explained it the first time he'd seen the markings, when they'd first arrived in Elvenhome together, nearly six months before. It made sense, but (and this he found ironic and amusing about

306

himself) yesterday it had taken him a little while to get used to seeing her *without* them, when at the beginning he didn't think he could bear to look at her face *with* them.

Thomas Lear, Rock Star, Court Singer, Lover of the High Queen of Faerie, and Rescue Team Member, smiled. He was changing in more ways than he could have dreamed possible. He wasn't sure he liked it, and he worried a little about where the changes might lead him, but, on the other hand, somehow he was getting to be a little philosophical about it all.

And that made him grin in spite of himself.

Callie dug into her the pocket of her jeans, and pulled out Maggie's Bell. After a thought, she wrapped its chain around her right wrist several times to form a bracelet of sorts. This done, she shook the Bell tentatively; when there was no sound, she smiled with gratitude.

"I can't hear that, either," Thomas pointed out testily.

"And neither can Mazzin," they said together, dissipating some of the tension when they laughed.

Thomas peered over Callie's shoulder at the Bell. "Does it have any idea where Arrendel might be?"

She sighed. "Not yet."

"Do we know if we're going in the right direction?"

"We're going 'in,' and that's all we know so far." Callie clicked her tongue at Cassane. The stallion picked up speed.

Something nagging and nervous had occurred to Thomas. "Hey...do you think Mazzin can see us coming? Maybe he's scrying and watching us?" He frowned. "Should we be *worried*, Callie?"

She responded immediately, which diffused some of his growing tension. He realized she'd already thought about it and had it covered, at least for the sake of conversation. "It's possible that he's watching us, Thomas, but it doesn't really matter. He may be scrying specifically for the King, in which case he wouldn't necessarily see us. If he's watching the woodland around wherever he is, he might see us. He knows that someone's coming for Arrendel. And he'll be ready."

Thomas attempted to stifle a groan, and Callie chuckled. "Don't worry," she assured him. "We're ready, too."

He did not want to admit to himself that he had no real idea what that meant.

For the next twenty minutes of the trip through the dense woodland, both Callie and Thomas were silent again, each looking around for subtle movement anywhere in the greenery. They rode, glancing at trees, noticing thickets and shrubs, checking out anything suspicious among the flowers, the grasses or along stray paths.

All seemed still and peaceful in the sunlit, chilly afternoon.

Thomas also watched Callie, from his vantage point immediately behind, a little above, and around her, as she toyed with Maggie's necklace, still braceleted around her wrist. Callie was absently rocking that wrist, shaking the Bell, anchored in place with Maggie's dark curls. Momentarily, Thomas entertained himself with the idea of the necklace as a silent totem rattled for protection from unseen evil spirits, but the more he thought about it, the less he liked the idea, so he killed the thought in haste, and focused on other things.

As Cassane moved through the forest, Thomas could see that the stallion's bells were shaking, too, as he galloped nearly noiselessly toward the center of the woodland. To Thomas' ears, Cassane's bells were as silent as Maggie's was.

It was just a little too weird, even though he thought he understood. He groaned, mostly in self-defense.

"What is it?" Callie asked, still studying the woodland as they rode through it.

"Nothing. I just shouldn't watch the bells not making noise. It's doing a number on my head." He laughed, unconvincingly. "I know you can hear them, and that's...anyway, are you getting anything from Maggie's Bell?"

"It doesn't sense Arrendel yet. I'm hoping that as we get deeper into the trees, it will sense him and chime for me." She looked around, frowning. "It's so quiet here, and all seems as it should be. Which is good. Also not good." She sighed. "We need to lighten the mood." Straightening herself, she patted Thomas' thigh, and asked, with an enthusiasm she did not necessarily feel, "Do you know the story of Dunnor's Bells?"

"No. And I thought there was too much going on at Maggie's to ask about it earlier."

"Well, then...I shall tell you the tale. It deserves far more merriment in the telling than I have in me just now, but it's still one that brightens the heart." She gave his hand a little squeeze, and while they watched the forest around them, Callie began.

"Once upon a time, long ago, there was a Prince...he was a Dwarf, by the name of Dunnor..."

seventeen

CALLIE WAS RIGHT. By the time she had finished telling Thomas the entire story of Dunnor's Bells, another hour had passed, and they were both in a better frame of mind.

"It's that kind of a tale," Callie added.

The question was out of his mouth and into the air before he could stop it:

"Do you have one?"

Unaccountably, she froze, although his question was a logical one and she had half-expected it. She understood that her issue was not with the question at all, but with her personal reaction to the only answer that she could give. Fair Folk do not lie; however, this does not mean that there are not times that they would prefer to fabricate a thing rather than speak the truth, and thus avoid feeling pain.

And there was pain here.

Behind her, he was already back-pedaling, attempting to cover his thoughtlessness with anything that came into his mind. Unfortunately, nothing did.

Callie took instant pity on his discomfort, turned a little so she could meet his eyes.

"Of course you have one," he sputtered in embarrassment. "Stupid question. Sorry."

"Do not fret, Thomas," she said lightly enough. "Of course I have one. Only I have not worn it for a very long time."

He considered this as she turned around again to look out into the forest in front of them. A ray of sunshine lit up Callie's arm and hand, and for a moment, Maggie's Bell sparkled in the dazzling light. Looking over Callie's shoulder at the tiny thing, Thomas found himself wondering about the story of Dunnor and the Bells he and his queen created together, and about the active and, all right, *living* love they proclaimed. Thinking about Callie's own Bell made him curious about seeing it, and also made him sad to think that her Bell had to be...lonely?

Her voice came calmly and quietly. She was reading his thoughts again. "It's a Bell made for a Queen, and it is altogether beautiful. It is comfortable, and at rest in a very small box, which sits in a larger box that can be found on a shelf in one of the closets in my Tower Room. I have not had occasion to look at that Bell for a long time.

"There's nothing more to say about it just now, is there, Thomas?"

He sighed. "No. No. It just came out, I don't know why I asked. It was stupid—"

Her gasp of surprise cut him short.

"What—?" he asked, looking around for movement, or danger, or both.

Callie stretched her right arm out to her side, hand open so that Thomas could see it: Maggie's Bell was dancing on her palm, bouncing as it soundlessly heralded the news.

Her words came breathlessly. "Wherever he is, he's close enough for the Bell to sense his presence. Thomas, I think we've got Arrendel."

The bell was a perfect compass. Watching it in her hand, and moving in a circle as the Bell indicated

311

Arrendel's position, Callie was certain of the direction she needed to go in order to find him.

They stopped in a quiet and shady thicket, and dismounted. Callie thanked Cassane and whispered in his ear; he nickered softly. Thomas wondered what she was planning.

Maybe he wasn't nervous now, maybe it was only the intensity of the thing, the revving up for something he'd never done before and still didn't truly understand. All he knew for sure was that Callie needed him, and that Arrendel might need him. He was not convinced that he would be useful, but he would do whatever she asked of him.

At least he would try.

She turned to him now, her eyes bright. "I am going to follow the Bell farther into the greenwood, and find him."

Thomas started to say something. She cut him off with a smile and a touch on his arm. "I am only going to look, and assess the situation. I will come back to you when I've seen him, and then we will go and get him."

"It's going to be that simple?" he asked.

"No. Probably not." She patted his hand. "I need you to stay here with Cassane. Once I find Arrendel, I will come back here, and you and I will collect him. Then Cassane will take you both back to Maggie's cottage, and I shall wait for the King."

"That's how it's going to happen?"

Callie laughed, her merriment almost infectious. She was laughing at herself. "No. Probably not. But it's the best idea we've got.

"We may have no control over events, and we rarely have control over timing, but we can absolutely set right action into motion and add our energy to the task as The Wheel turns—and harsh, wrong things are made good and new again."

"So I just wait here?" Thomas asked, unsure whether he was relieved or insulted.

"Just so," she replied. "You can stop carrying the water and the backpack now."

As Thomas divested himself of the things he had slung over his neck and shoulders, Callie took two of the four canteens filled with loch water and slipped them over her own shoulder. "Cassane knows what to do if anyone approaches. Stay close to him until I return."

With a loving stroke to Cassane's long face, and a kiss on Thomas', Callie turned and moved quickly into the woods. The stallion and the man watched her until she was out of sight.

Maggie's Bell was hanging on its chain around Callie's neck, Maggie's hair still tied to the chain on either side of the Bell. It rang loudly in Callie's ears, but did not disturb the trees or the other denizens of the forest.

"All right, all right, I hear you. We know he's that way," Callie muttered to the Bell as she stepped around a large stump. "It's all right. We're going to get him."

Comforted, the Bell quieted a bit. Callie patted the Bell, whispered reassurance, and kept moving.

Sixty feet later, she stopped abruptly, as if she had slammed into a wall.

There was pain.

Blinded by the sheer force of the pain's intensity, it took a moment for the fact to register that the immense ocean of physical discomfort did not belong to her.

It was Arrendel's.

Callie closed her eyes against the misery, but the momentary darkness did not help very much. It was all she could do to stay on her feet; her body felt distress and injury that her mind could not sort through quickly enough.

She forced herself to breathe. Then she opened her eyes. With her right hand, she made three fast clasping gestures and whispered something urgent into the air.

Bright blue light cascaded around her, and wrapped her in a sparkling, sapphire embrace. She breathed the light in, and exhaled the pain until it was gone.

It did not matter if what powered her immediate surge through the trees was sudden fear or unbridled rage. With the Bell guiding her, Callie sped deeper into the forest.

I am here, and I am coming for you. Where are you? She sent the words to his mind, and hoped he could hear her.

The woods were silent when she stopped running and listened for anything out of the ordinary. There was nothing but the sound of her own ragged breathing.

Angry and frustrated, and perhaps a little frightened, Callie slammed her hand against the trunk of an oak tree and swore vehemently.

A small red fox, perhaps frightened by her noise, darted past her and fled deeper into the wood.

It occurred to her to follow it, but in the same instant, she looked in the opposite direction, the way from which the fox had come.

Maggie's Bell jumped and sang in silence, but at the top of its voice.

Callie ran, hard and fast, for half a minute, then froze in her tracks. Her heart all but stopped when she found what she was looking for.

If it was a trap, she didn't care. She would deal with that later. All she could see was Arrendel.

Callie glanced around to see if anyone or anything was near. It appeared not, but that did not matter. She moved quickly to him, and tried not to cry.

Slumped forward, sitting on the ground, he was secured to the tree by cords of heavy, ragged rope. Blood and dirt were matted together in his long blond hair, which hid his face from immediate view. His clothes were torn, some of the blood on them still wet.

She knelt beside him and gently settled him back against the tree, moving his hair away from his face. He was unconscious. He'd been beaten, far more badly than she had allowed herself to think about before. His skin was pale, and much too dry, beneath the blue and purple bruises that covered much of his face.

Callie slid the two canteens of loch water from her shoulder, opened them, and poured their contents liberally over Arrendel's head, face, and body. She watched, waiting for an immediate response. But he didn't rouse when the water drenched him and was absorbed.

It was then that she saw his broken ankle and the displaced foot attached to it. She groaned; she was out of loch water.

"Oh, Arrendel," she whispered. "What have they done to you?" She couldn't help it; she was so relieved to have found him alive, but so alarmed by the condition she'd found him in, that she began to sob. "Forgive me, Cousin..."

As Callie fought for control, a Gnome stepped from behind a huge oak tree. His confusion was evident, but he shook it off and said in a gruff voice, "Come with me, Your Majesty. Lord Mazzin was expecting the High King, but he will want to see you."

As the Gnome approached, Callie kissed Arrendel's forehead and whispered "I'll be right back," before she stood up, her tears forgotten.

The Gnome attempted to sound authoritative, but he was out of his depth when she gave him an imperious glare. "I must take you to Mazzin, Your Majesty," he insisted.

"No. Not yet." With a graceful shrug, the High Queen of Faerie disappeared in a brilliant flash of azure-blue light, which hovered protectively around Arrendel after she was gone.

Callie reappeared beside Thomas, who was sitting quietly on a felled tree in the thicket, playing with words in his head.

"Holy shit!" Thomas yelped, startled.

"Sorry."

On his feet now, Thomas looked at her. "Did you find him?"

She nodded. "He's hurt. Very badly."

"Is the King there?"

"I don't think so. The Gnome who was watching for someone to show up was expecting the King. I had to leave Arrendel there so I could come back and get you both." Callie nodded at Thomas, her mind already moving into rescue mode. She walked over to Cassane, who was smelling pretty yellow flowers in the grass, and put her face against his.

Thomas couldn't hear what she said, but it seemed to him that Cassane understood whatever it was. The huge stallion tilted his head, looked into Callie's eyes, then over at Thomas. Thomas could have sworn that Cassane nodded.

Callie returned to Thomas, and they frowned at each other.

"You're not waiting for the King," he said.

"Can't," she said.

"You're going to deal with Mazzin on your own."

"Looks like it. Although I hope the King's on his way."

"Me, too." Thomas took a deep breath. "Okay. Tell me what you want me to do."

She told him. It was simple, and also very complicated. He did not want to think about it too much.

To comfort him, she pointed out: "It's easy, Thomas. All you have to do is to stay on Cassane's back until you get to Arrendel, give him a little first aid, then get him onto Cassane's back, make sure both of you stay on Cassane's back, and direct Cassane to get you to Maggie's. And then *really* make sure you both stay on Cassane's back."

Oh Goddddddd... Thomas thought.

"Do only what I ask, but do it. And ignore everything else you might see or hear around you. I need you to do that—and to not have to worry about you—while I'm dealing with Mazzin."

And with that, Callie vanished from sight.

Startled again, and not startled at all, Thomas shot an appeal in Cassane's general direction. "No dress rehearsal. We're live. In concert. On stage. Like...now..."

WHEN CALLIE POPPED back into the space beside Arrendel, she was surrounded by half a dozen Gnomes.

Gnomes are moderately bright as a general rule. They take a little longer than other Folk to understand things, but once they do, they get the job done.

It took these Gnomes about fifteen seconds to realize that they were in the presence of the High Queen of Faerie.

"Great Caps on Pixies!" one of the older Gnomes gasped. "I think that's the High Queen!" His comment was commendable, since Callie was not dressed in her usual regal garb, and she did not bear the subltly-moving royal markings on her skin that would have instantly identified her to her people, regardless of their mental acuity. "The Queen!"

There was some shuffling and bowing, and a bit of mumbled confusion about what the Gnomes should do next, since they had instructions from Mazzin to guard Arrendel and await the arrival of the High King.

Callie took a step forward, and met the eyes of each of the Gnomes. "Hello," she said in a blithe tone, although the lightness in her voice did not move to her face, which was looking more than queenly. It was also looking angry.

And powerful.

The group of Gnomes stepped back a few paces.

"Better," Callie said.

From behind the huge oak that had hidden the single Gnome before, Slole came forward, and gave her a careless, mock bow. "Your Royal Majesty," he acknowledged. "We are happy to see you."

Callie said nothing, and appeared not to notice when the protective blue light that she had left around Arrendel slowly faded away.

"Dare I ask...is the High King with you?" The nasty Bogle's eyes darted around the area as he moved toward Callie and Arrendel. "Surely he is not in hiding, waiting to see what happens before he reveals himself?"

Callie bit back a retort, and eyed the Bogle.

Slole had reached them. He stood for a moment beside Arrendel and, without warning, kicked him hard.

The next instant, a fiery blue lightning bolt tore into the space around them, and Slole was hanging, upside down, thirty feet in mid-air. The Gnomes stared up in horror at the screeching Bogle (Bogles do not like heights), then over at Her Royal Highness, who had bent down to look at Arrendel.

"Where is Mazzin?" she asked them with irrefutable irritation, leaving no room for discussion.

Two of the Gnomes pointed north. "He awaits the King over there. On the other side of the copse. Five minutes' walk from here."

"Let's go see Mazzin, then," Callie said, glaring up at Slole. "Before it begins to snow." (Bogles do not like cold weather and they detest snow.)

Three Gnomes stayed with Arrendel, and three moved with Callie to where Mazzin sat, gazing into his wooden scrying bowl.

"The King is coming..." Mazzin declared, his voice dreamy. "The King is coming..."

The Gnomes waited for the Goblin to acknowledge them. When after some minutes he did not, one of the Gnomes cleared his throat loudly enough to be heard.

After a few more moments, Mazzin looked up and over at the Gnomes and the High Queen.

"The King is coming, Madam, and I have my hostage. Your presence is unnecessary."

Callie gave him a sweet smile. "Is this true?"

"Certainly," the Goblin smiled back. "Unless he has given you the ransom."

Callie's smile grew larger. The game was on.

"If he has not, Mazzin, are you going to let me take Arrendel out of here while you wait for the High King to arrive?"

Mazzin seemed to consider this. His smile shifted. "I do not think that would be wise, do you, Your Majesty?" He rose, and slipped his hand into his shirt, tugging the Greencrystal into the light.

Callie looked at the Stone dismissively. "It has been a long time since I have seen that. You're certain it's the original, then?"

"Yes." Mazzin raised the Stone into the air above his head, whispered The Word, and mumbled "Birds."

Birds began to scream and shriek and wail in the trees around them. Dozens began to fall, dead, from the sky and the greenery.

Callie's eyes grew wide. "Stop it, Mazzin. Your show of force is unnecessary."

He gazed at her, his look daring her to cross him; she did not. "Very well. You understand what my Stone and I can do. No lesson is required."

The birds stopped their wild noise. The ones who had not fallen to the forest floor flew away, a mass exodus of terrified wings scurrying through the uneasy air.

"Where is the King?" Mazzin asked. "I know he is coming. I have seen it."

"I have not seen the King. I do not know where he is. But if you know he is coming, I am glad of it." She took a step toward the Goblin. "I wish to take Arrendel to safety and tend to his injuries. Are you going to allow that?"

"Sadly, Your Majesty, I cannot release Arrendel until I have the ransom. Else, what would be the point?"

"I was hoping you were not going to look at it that way. His injuries worry me, and I would prefer he got some attention."

"In due course, Your Majesty," Mazzin said almost politely.

"Ah," Callie replied. "Due course, indeed."

The Goblin gave her a self-satisfied grin. "You will forgive me if I point out that you have made an error?"

Callie nodded, although her puzzlement was evident in her eyes. "Error? What error?"

His grin turned into a smirk. "When you left Arrendel just now, you surrounded him with a small but protective blue magic. You have revealed your signature, Your Majesty. I can identify your power. Somehow, I almost regret having to take it away from you. But of course I must take it, for my own protection."

As Callie watched, Mazzin mumbled the Word, raised the Greencrystal, pointed it directly at her, and ordered, "Stone, silence the blue power at once."

From some distance away, they could hear faint sounds of Gnomish surprise peppered with terrified rage as Slole dropped without ceremony from his position thirty feet in the air, and landed with a disgusting thud on one of the Gnomes. There was much shouting, shrieking and barking.

"Oops," Callie said without sympathy. "Poor Bogle."

"What was that?" Mazzin asked with only mild curiosity. He nodded at one of the Gnomes, but signaled for him to wait as Callie responded with a shrug.

"All that was holding your friend in the air was a little bit of that blue light. You smashed a Bogle."

"Ah," said the Goblin, stroking the Greencrystal tenderly and tilting his head to study the Queen. "I hope you will not object overmuch, Your Majesty, but I think it a wise course to have you wait with us for the King's arrival. Secured, of course."

Two of the three Gnomes approached Callie with caution. One of them was carrying a thick length of rope like the one that bound Arrendel. Mazzin stepped out of their way.

Callie looked at the Gnomes, the rope, and back at Mazzin. "Oh very well," she sighed. "Have it your own way."

Encouraged, the Gnomes moved toward Callie.

Just then, a bright, golden light charged the air, stopping everyone in their tracks.

"Or not," Callie said with a smile.

The sound of slowly-flapping wings moved toward them from a place somewhere above the trees. Callie looked up, but saw nothing. The Gnomes looked at each other, nervous.

A moment later, there it was. Outlined in shimmering, radiant light, a dark avian creature with a wingspan of about fifty inches appeared above the forest. It let out a loud, predatory caw and aimed itself downward, its empty eyes focused on Mazzin, Callie and the Gnomes.

Mazzin paid no attention to the Gnomes as they ran for their lives. With the Greencrystal in hand, he studied the huge bird as it flew closer. "The light is golden," he said to the Stone, or perhaps to Callie. "All the Folk know that golden light is the signature of the High King. He is coming, I have seen it."

Callie was watching the winged predator approach. "If it's not the King, we might both be in trouble."

"I do not think so." Mazzin lifted the Greencrystal into the space above his head as the huge bird sailed into the air above the surrounding trees, screeching as it flexed and stretched its talons.

Mazzin whispered the Word to the Greencrystal, then cried in a loud voice: "Stone, stop the bird."

Gold and green light shot from the Stone, and flew into the air hot and fast to meet the creature. Upon collision, the huge bird's golden outline got brighter, and the Stone's fiery brilliance faded into the late afternoon sunlight.

The bird did not even slow down. It got bigger. And perhaps angry, as it flapped its massive wings and aimed itself toward Callie and Mazzin.

"Mazzin..." Callie said, stepping back against a wide-trunked tree. "Mazzin, you'd better do—"

"Stone!" Mazzin shouted. "Confound the creature's vision with clouds! Make thunder! Make lightning brighter than the light that surrounds the creature! Ignite the sky to destroy the evil thing!"

The Greencrystal was instantly obedient. The sky clouded around them, and it began to rain. A fraction of a second later, wild thunder roared and boomed, punctuated with lightning flashes that tore through the air above their heads, exploding when they touched rock, tree, or ground.

Unable to see them now, but still looking, the huge avian screamed in frustration somewhere close by.

"Stone! End the great bird! I command it!"

It took only a minute or two before one of the howls of preternatural thunder met with a perfectly-timed shard of wholly-unnatural lightning and struck the bird. There was a sickening crackle of broken wings; an angry whimper sounded seconds before a heavy thud rattled the forest floor.

With a crow of delight, Mazzin kissed the Greencrystal and dashed to his scrying bowl.

The entire avian event had taken just under five minutes. It had been all the time that Callie had needed.

It was at the precise moment when Slole fell from the sky that Cassane, bathed in glittering green light, the silver bells in his mane jingling, and with Thomas Lear securely on his back, had leaped from seemingly nowhere into the middle of the post-fall confusion.

The stallion landed as Slole picked himself up off the Gnome he'd all but crushed in his landing. The Bogle ignored the all-but-flattened Gnome, and shoved the others out of his way in a wave of fury that threatened violence.

"That royal slut will pay for this!" Slole screamed. "I will slice her and make her bleed while she dances for her life! I will have her, and then I will kill her! I will crush her with—"

The raging Bogle never saw the huge hooves that silenced him. With a powerful rearing of his back legs, Cassane kicked Slole so hard that the ranting Bogle went flying high across the thicket, his quick journey suddenly interrupted when he connected head-first with a tall tree. Then Slole hit the ground, trying to figure out what had happened.

Cassane's neigh sounded dangerous as he took two steps toward Slole, his intent unmistakable.

Afraid now, and screeching, the Bogle fled into the woods, running in the opposite direction, away from the Gnomes, and away from the strange cawing noise that was coming from near the area where Mazzin and Callie were.

Thomas jumped down from Cassane's back and approached the Gnomes, who were in a panic as they tried to decide whether to follow Slole into the woods or hurry back to Mazzin. Towering over them, Thomas made their decision simple.

"Run!" he commanded, jumping up and down, his eyes wide with easy-to-read terror. "I don't know what's going on back there with Mazzin, but this big horse hasn't eaten yet, and he really likes Gnomes! I've seen him eat three at a time, and it's just awful! Run! *Run!*"

Thomas waited as the Gnomes took a few seconds to fully comprehend the nuances of the situation. Gnomes are a little slow on the uptake.

Ten long seconds after that, after some inaudible discussion, they got it.

Wailing in fear, the Gnomes scurried in the same direction that Slole had gone, disappearing into the trees.

Thomas turned and ran to Arrendel.

He'd never been good with sick or injured people, mostly because he was almost never in a situation where he'd had to deal with them. He knew little about first aid apart from the obvious, and he wasn't too sure about that, either. He did not know what to do with an unconscious person who was not merely drunk and passed out. But in this moment, if Thomas hesitated at all, the hesitation was only in his mind. He dropped to his knees beside his friend, threw the canteens and the backpack down, opened the pack wide, and dumped it out on the ground beside him. He picked up the butcher knife wrapped in the kitchen towel.

The ropes that held Arrendel to the tree were cut away. Thomas caught the Water Faerie when he fell forward.

"Oh shit," Thomas muttered as his anxiety and uncertainty tag-teamed him and made him feel a little nauseous. He had never seen anyone this badly beaten. He wanted to look away, but he couldn't afford to. "Not good, Buddy. This is bad."

The small first-aid kit was not going to be much help.

He gently pressed Arrendel back against the tree trunk, and looked at his face. His friend was nearly unrecognizable under all the bruising and swelling. Thomas tried not to get too caught up at the sight of all the blood and the scary, unnatural-position of Arrendel's foot.

Forcing himself to focus, he took a deep breath and remembered what Callie had told him about dealing with Arrendel's damaged ankle.

There was a chill in the air now, and a lot of racket coming from a short distance away, but Thomas, recalling Callie's further admonition, allowed himself to ignore it. Glancing around to make sure that Cassane was still close by, and confirming that no one else was there, Thomas opened one of the canteens, and slowly poured its contents over Arrendel's left foot and ankle.

She had not told him what to expect, so he was startled when he saw what happened. As the loch water touched it, Arrendel's foot seemed to almost dissolve. Thomas noticed that it appeared to change shape as the water poured over it, as if Arrendel's foot were a liquid mass rather than a solid one.

By the time he had emptied the second canteen over the foot and ankle, Arrendel's foot was somehow back in place, and the horrible swelling of the ankle had reduced considerably.

"Holy shit..." Thomas breathed. *Don't think about it, Thomas, just do it*, Callie had said. "Holy shit," he said again.

Digging into the pocket of his jeans, Thomas pulled out Maggie's Bell necklace. Callie had given it to him when she was explaining what he needed to do for Arrendel. As requested, the Bell remained silent as Thomas removed Maggie's curls from the chain, and fastened the necklace around Arrendel's neck, tucking the Bell under his torn, bloody shirt.

Then Thomas shot a quick look at Cassane, who was watching, nickering his support. "Almost there," Thomas told the horse nervously. For a crazy second, Thomas thought he saw the stallion nod his approval.

He returned the butcher knife to the backpack, and picked up the blanket, deciding how best to do the next thing.

Cassane whinnied as thunder crackled and rogue, malevolent lightning taunted from too close. Thomas nodded. "I know...I *know*!"

Thomas managed to more or less wrap Arrendel in the blanket, then grabbed the rope from the canvas bag, and slipped it over his shoulder, stuffed the empty canteens in the pack, and closed it up before sliding it onto his back. Opening the remaining canteen, he was gentle as he opened Arrendel's mouth and poured some of the sugared water into it. He waited a moment, then poured more in, and tried not to worry when there was no response from his friend. He took a long drink himself, then slipped the canteen over his shoulder.

Finally, as carefully as he could, Thomas lifted Arrendel's blanketed, broken body, and stood up. He turned and walked toward Cassane.

"What do I do now?" he asked the stallion. "All I know is that I've got to get him up on your back, and hang on to him and not fall off, and you have to get us out of here." He was not sure now how this was going to work, and he couldn't think straight. "What do I do?" he asked again. "How do I..."

By the time Thomas reached Cassane, the graceful horse had settled on the ground. Lying down on his front legs, back legs in a kneeling position, Cassane looked up expectantly at Thomas.

In a flash of hope, Thomas understood.

He deposited Arrendel in the saddle on Cassane's back, then, after a nod at Cassane, slid into place behind

Arrendel. With the rope, he secured Arrendel's shoulders and chest tightly against his own.

Thomas Lear took a deep breath. "Okay, Cassane," he said to the stallion, sounding not much more brave than he felt. "We're ready."

Cassane moved from his lowered position, rose smoothly, and stood up. Thomas and Arrendel did not fall.

"Oh, boy," Thomas exhaled the words. "All right. Here goes nothing: Cassane, the High Queen wants you to get us to Maggie's. Quick. Safely. Uh...please."

Thomas tightened his grip on Arrendel, closed his eyes and stifled a yell as the huge stallion turned around and sped out of the greenwood as a huge clap of thunder met with a sharp slice of lightning and a loud, strange, bird-like scream.

WITH A GLARE of distain, Mazzin looked up from his scrying bowl, and fixed his eyes on Callie, who stood motionless among a loose ring of tall trees. Although she looked nonchalant as she examined the flora around her, her mind was racing. When was the King coming? Why wasn't he here? Should she herself challenge Mazzin, and get it over and done with so there would be no more Mischief and no danger to either Faerie or all the people, mortal and Fair alike, who lived Upworld?

She knew she was not as powerful as the King, and that she had little if any experience in this sort of battle. She also knew that her abilities were strong, and many. She was courageous, clever, resourceful, and powerful enough to do what might be required of her, and she knew it. Mazzin would find her a formidable opponent, if it should come to that.

She hoped it wouldn't.

It took her a moment to step away from her thoughts. She noticed that things were too quiet. She turned, and saw Mazzin watching her as he placed his half-empty wooden bowl on the ground. He cringed as a slosh of the wine soaked his fingers.

"You are going to run out of wine for your spying," Callie said, her face calm.

"Perhaps," Mazzin replied, standing up and taking a few steps toward her. "But there is still enough for me to see what I need to know."

Callie tilted her head and watched him approach. "Oh?"

"I see and feel that Arrendel is no longer my hostage."

"Sorry about that."

"I hope you understand, Majesty, that I need to hold you hostage against the ransom in Arrendel's place. This would not be my first choice, but it seems to be the only option available to me at the moment. If you would be so kind as to—"

The Goblin had reached Callie, and was about to make a grab for her, which she knew would be a mistake. Mazzin would be far more powerful with the Greencrystal in one hand and the High Queen's hand or arm in the other.

A spontaneous shield of bright orange light appeared between Mazzin and Callie, as strong as if it were made of iron. The force of the shield made Mazzin fall back several yards.

He studied her for a moment, then laughed as he raised the Greencrystal at her. "Stone, quiet the orange power."

The blaze of orange light faded at once. There was nothing between Callie and Mazzin now.

She waited to see what he would do next.

She didn't have to wait more than a few seconds. "Stone: surround the Queen with an army of Gnomes, Bogies and Brownies obedient to me alone."

He's learning fast, she thought ruefully.

A second later, she was in fact surrounded by Mazzin's shadow army. The Folk Mazzin had conjured were a bit of a surprise to her, though. A distant part of her brain marveled at how simple and literal-minded the Stone seemed to be. All of the newly-made individuals she glanced at were not Gnomes and Brownies and Bogies, they were incredibly unattractive composites of the three, each bearing differing degrees of sometimes disparate physical attributes.

These hybrids of Mazzin's clearly overtaxed imagination numbered in the hundreds, and they closed in on Callie.

There was only one thing to do, and Callie did it.

In less than a heartbeat, she surrounded herself with a shining purple glow and shifted her shape. With strong purple and gold wings that pushed the closest of the shadow soldiers out of her way, she darted straight up into the air and out of harm's way.

"Stone," she heard Mazzin command, "Make the trees reach out for her. And quiet the purple light."

Soaring upward, Callie was distracted by the collective wail of a group of Sprites who lived in the trees that were suddenly turning and stretching their boughs toward her. Mazzin took hold of the purple light she had played with, but her wings were her own, not truly contingent on the purple magic she'd used to distract him.

Without warning, she collided with the top bough of a tall, tired oak tree who had been compelled to turn his heavy branches toward her and had caught her in the face as she flew. Momentarily blinded and dizzy, she kept her balance, and moved out of the way, hovering at a safe distance from all of the trees as she rubbed her head where she'd hit it, and touched her chin, which had a long, deep cut that hurt and was bleeding. Clear vision restored, she ignored the dizziness, knowing it would pass, and wiped the blood from her chin on the sleeve of her jacket.

The tree and its ancient Sprite cried out in horror at the sight. "Majesty! Blood! Royal blood!"

She reassured them at once, her tone both regal and maternal. "It is nothing. You are not to blame. Rest now, and be at peace." She looked around at all of the trees that had been forced to extend their branches to catch her. "All of you, rest. I shall deal with this insanity. Do not worry, Precious Ones."

And with that, Callie lowered herself to a space ten feet above the head of the tallest of the shadow soldiers, and fluttered there as she considered what to do next.

Suspicious, Mazzin watched her from a position behind the warped Fey army.

Pink light danced with a pearlescent shimmering in Callie's right hand. "Butterflies," she suggested.

Ten thousand butterflies of every shape, size, description, color and wing speed filled the air below her. They fluttered in the faces of each of the shadow soldiers. They surrounded Mazzin so that he could not speak, and could not move enough to point the Greencrystal at Callie, who had begun to chuckle. There were more butterflies around the army than there was air to breathe, which forced the soldiers to move away, out of their tight formation, and spread out.

"Stone: quiet the Queen's pink light. Set the butterflies on fire and burn them out of the way!"

Enough was enough. Callie was getting bored with the game, but she still needed to buy time for the coming of the King. And she needed to protect the butterflies who, unlike Mazzin's army, were not shades. They were real, and she had called them.

"Stone! Hear me!" Callie called from the air, wondering if it would remember her. "Stone, I know the Word too." She wondered what the Stone would do, if it would answer to both Mazzin and herself, or if she had to be touching it in order for it to hear her.

It was time to find out. In a hurry.

She hesitated for only a fraction of a fast second; it had been too many hundreds of years since she had spoken the name of the child—her long-dead child—that would awaken the Greencrystal's power. She did it now, with a silent prayer that the pain she was about to be wrapped in would not be suffered in vain.

"Stone: the Word is...*Garrhydan.*"

She did not take the time to consider if a piece of her heart tore. She did not acknowledge that she wanted to hold the taste of the long-unspoken name in her mouth. She took a deep breath and addressed the Greencrystal, silently reminding it that it had once belonged only to her. "Stone! Do not harm the butterflies, please! Let them sail away on their own, in safety."

"No!" Mazzin roared, a little worried that the Word was no longer a secret from his army. He clenched the Greencrystal harder. "Stone! Hear me!"

The butterflies began to fly away in all directions, in their own time.

Take your time, Callie's voice whispered around them. *Move quickly enough to escape harm, but slowly enough to anger Mazzin and buy the King more time. I give you thanks for your aid.*

"Stone: Wind!"

A strong wind rose and rushed the butterflies out of the immediate area.

Callie moved toward the ground, wondering how close she could actually get to the Greencrystal. Mazzin and his army watched as the High Queen touched down lightly on the grass. Her wings vanished.

Her voice was soft and low. She knew she didn't have to shout for the Greencrystal to hear her. "Stone...bees and midges, please, a bit of distraction for the army, and for Mazzin, too."

Amid much yelling, crying, screaming and swearing as the insects descended on the Gnome/Bogie/Brownie army in a massive wall of stings and bites, Mazzin bellowed: "Stone! Snow!"

The air became frigid. Snow began to fall, and the buzzing and whining of bee and midge quieted, finally ceasing as the cold, wet air quickly put them to sleep.

Observing this, Callie frowned. She was tired. Her head ached and her chin hurt.

With a flick of her wrist, she made all the sleeping insects vanish for their own safety.

Agitated, she wondered why the King had not arrived. Had something else gone wrong? She acknowledged to herself that she had trusted that he would appear and take on the full responsibility of dealing with Mazzin. The protection of the Folk, and making right the wrongs of Folk, too, fell under his authority. He had stepped outside the realm of his duty before, of course, many times. But this time, she had been certain that as soon as he had been made aware of this latest Mischief, he would come Upworld at once to Arrendel's aid and...

...and there was no help for it. She was going to have to deal with Mazzin herself, alone.

Decision accepted, she frowned as she considered her options again. She was not as naturally diplomatic and disarming as the King was when he chose to be. He was the effective, persuasive charmer who had always used his wits rather than his energy to accomplish his purpose. Callie, on the other hand, has always been swift in her judgments, and direct in her actions. *Sometimes*, she reflected, *perhaps a little too swift and direct...*

She admitted it to herself: she was sure the King would manage the current situation far more deftly than she would.

But he was not here. She was.

And it was time to act.

Her face must have changed; Mazzin was staring at her, trying to read her mind. Was there now a determined look on her face where a more playful one had been only moments ago?

The Goblin lifted the Greencrystal high in the air over his head, and pointed it at her, prepared to speak.

Callie spoke first. Her voice, dripping with infinite patience, was firm. A copper-colored light danced around her as she pointed at him. "Mazzin, you are getting tired. I believe your arm is too heavy to hold the Greencrystal while it does your childish work."

To his amazement, Mazzin's arm wobbled a bit as he instructed the Greencrystal to quiet the diffused coppery glaze.

She was nearly out of tricks, and tried to think strategically for a fast second. She understood that she could not let Mazzin's strange soldiers capture her. She also knew she had to protect her signature green light as a last resort. With the Greencrystal in his control, if Mazzin saw her green energy working he could quiet it, and she would be powerless.

She needed some time to figure out how to get the Greencrystal away from Mazzin. Only then could she end this.

She had an idea, and stifled a giggle. Fiery red light burst spontaneously from the palms of Callie's hands, which she pointed at Mazzin's army. "Backward feet!"

Every one of Mazzin's shades, the soldiers he had created in bulk, fell over as their feet instantly moved from the front of their ankles to the back of them, or from the back of their ankles to the front, depending on where they'd started. In any case, their balance gone, the Gnome/Bogie/Brownies would be shocked and helpless for a short while. Most of them would not be able to stand up and figure out how to move around anytime soon.

Did Mazzin understand that the making of a thing was quite a different matter than the unmaking of it? She supposed she'd find that out soon enough.

While the horrified hybrid Folk struggled with their feet, Callie turned, jumped over and around Mazzin's army, and bolted as fast as she could, deeper into the forest, away from Mazzin and the Greencrystal.

Pushing hard, she ran for several minutes. As she slowed down a little, she glanced over her shoulder to make sure that nothing and no one was following.

Satisfied, she breathed a sigh of relief, and sped up as she turned her head to focus on the forest in front of her.

It was at that moment that she collided with The High King of Faerie.

eighteen

FOR MAYBE TWENTY-FIVE minutes after he'd positioned himself and Arrendel on Cassane's back, Thomas was still afraid to open his eyes, and with good reason. The duty-focused white and gray stallion was almost literally flying through the forest. The very few times Thomas had gathered the courage to peek out from under his clenched eyelids, he was so frightened by what he could *kind of* see hurling past him that he nearly screamed. He had no idea how he had not fallen from the jet-propelled stallion's back yet. He couldn't afford to think about that.

He did not fail to notice, though, how steady and strong Cassane's hooves felt and sounded as he raced through the trees, and how smooth the ride seemed when Thomas kept his eyes more or less closed. He tried to ignore the wildly-jingling bells in Cassane's mane; they told him how fast the horse was moving. The sound was anything but comforting right now, no matter what Callie thought...

Trying to breathe normally, Thomas held on to Arrendel with one arm, and gripped the saddle with his other hand. His thighs and calves were in an involuntary fight-to-the-death grip with the horse as he kept himself snug up against the back of the saddle behind Arrendel.

He had no idea how the hell he was going to be able to walk once he got to Maggie's, assuming, please God, that he did get back to Maggie's.

Eventually he moved himself toward an uneasy sense of calm by remembering his first ride on Cassane's back, and how Callie had reassured him that he couldn't fall even if he'd wanted to. Cassane, she had pointed out then, would never have allowed for such nonsense. Thomas hoped that the same idea applied here, and that Cassane was keeping that in mind as he darted around shrubbery and raced between large rocks and trees.

A random thought tickled him. Here he was, physically tied to a badly-injured Arrendel, riding a horse that was all but soaring through the biggest forest he'd ever seen, he wasn't positive that everything was going to work out according to plans he wasn't even sure about...and, without warning, he got a quick mental image of himself and Arrendel.

"Oh my God! We're Butch and Sundance!" He couldn't help it; he laughed out loud.

"We are?" came a strained, faint voice from in front of him. Arrendel was conscious.

"We are," Thomas laughed.

"Good," Arrendel conceded, his voice weak. "But...who are Butch and Sundance? No, wait. Tell me later, when I can enjoy the tale."

The forest flying past them, Thomas felt Arrendel test the rope that held them tied to each other.

"Am I still tied up?"

"Yeah, but you're tied to me. Only so you can't fall off and I can't drop you while Cassane gets us back to Maggie's."

Arrendel appeared to be more accepting of his circumstance than Thomas could ever have been. "I seem to have missed a bit of the action," he murmured, then he coughed.

"We should be home soon, I guess," Thomas informed his friend. "I don't know where we are, exactly, since I can't make myself look."

The Water Faerie quivered with suppressed laughter. "Ouch...but that's funny."

"You going to be okay for a little while longer?"

"I hope so," Arrendel said.

Me, too, Thomas grimaced to himself. His friend seemed very frail, and had to be in a great deal of pain.

They were both silent for a moment, listening to the pounding of Cassane's hooves against the ground, then Arrendel asked "Thomas...about Maggie..."

"I've met her, she's wonderful. Wait, sorry, I mean, she's fine, she's safe. Swiftaine is with her."

Arrendel's eyes filled as he said a grateful, silent prayer. If an unchecked gasp or perhaps a sob escaped from the Water Faerie's throat, Thomas manfully ignored it.

"I promise you, she is fine," repeated Thomas. "Your pal Swiftaine will kick the ass of anyone who gets too close to her, so you'd better watch yourself. He's a little freaky when provoked, I had no idea how tough that little guy is. Damn!"

"I see," Arrendel said, trying not to laugh because it hurt rather a lot to do so. Even with his eyes closed, the world was spinning a little more than he could handle. "One last question, my friend, before I sleep again. Where is Callie?"

"I don't know for sure...but I think she's dealing with Mazzin."

"No..." Arrendel groaned.

Thomas did not bother to mask his anxiety. "Yes."

To be continued in *Done is Done, Part Three of A Year and a Day*

Done is Done: A Year and a Day, Part Three

Coming soon.

Even Spriggans know that it's not over until Done is Done.

Find more by Lisa Courtney
Web: http://www.courtneyink.com
twitter: @courtney_ink

Acknowledgements

It's my habit to write personal thank-you notes by hand (my grandmother insisted upon it, and I'm still a little neurotic about that).

That said, here is another thank-you note, sort of. Less personal than usual, and not by hand, but honest and heart-felt nevertheless.

Thank you, **Ellen Kushner**, for writing *Thomas the Rhymer*, and for the cover artwork by **Tom Canty**. The cover caught my eye at first glance, and The Rhymer took up residence in my head and never went on vacation. He simply waited for me to catch up with the magic.

Thank you, **Gordon Lightfoot**, for the lyrics and music that have been and continue to be part of the soundtrack that is my life. My love for your work fed my need to make Thomas Lear's songs worthy of you, and of me as well.

Quieter but sincere thanks to **Frey** and **Henley**, too, who taught me a little bit about composition and performance that I would never have grasped on my own.

Special thanks to **Paul Camelia**, my own Arrendel, for giving me plenty of room to do what I do.

Most of all, thank you, **Ladies of the Book**, who listened and read and watched me pace and fret, waited while I put the project down for a couple of years, and were the best emotional and creative support imaginable when I picked the thing back up and got serious about it again. And you **Ladies** who handled the production to get Thomas Lear and his friends (and, uh-oh, *me*) out there— there aren't words, not really. I love you all, and thank you so very much: especially **Jane Mackinnon, Stacey Eck, Kristie Lundberg, Sally Sloley, Brenda Potts, Nancy Monson, Shari Wetherby, Rebecca Stevenson**, and my beloved godmother **Betty** (even though she never took to Thomas, and suggested about two dozen times over the years that I kill him off because she did *not* like his attitude; I got even with her by giving her surname to Susannah, with the desired effect of annoying Betty ever so slightly, and potentially forever).

www.ingramcontent.com/pod-product-compliance
Lightning Source LLC
Chambersburg PA
CBHW060355260626
47160CB00006B/2324